Discovery . . .

Justin carried her across the cabin and gently laid her down on his bed. "There'll be no stopping us this time, Cara," he told her thickly. "I want you more than I've ever wanted another." Urgently, he crushed his mouth to hers for a brief kiss. "Let me love you," he murmured against her lips.

Cara gazed at him knowing she wouldn't, couldn't put a stop to this, but where it led, she had no idea. They'd come as far as this before and always she'd been left wanting, of what was a mystery to her. Her voice low with desire and hesitant with uncertainty, she said, "I . . . I don't know what to do."

Justin felt his loins tighten at her answer and the last of his restraint broke. "I'll show you," he promised and kissed her with scorching intensity. With knowing fingers, he guided her garments off her shoulders and down to her waist.

"Justin," she gasped.

"Easy, love," he whispered. "Don't be frightened. . . ."

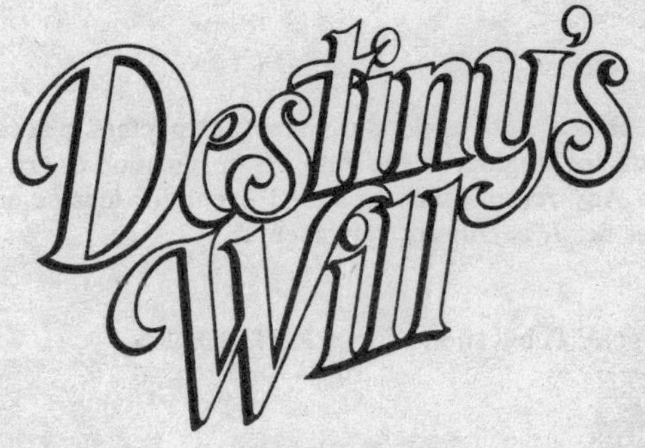

Elizabeth Ann Michaels

POCKET BOOKS
New York London Toronto Sydney Tokyo Singapore

This book is a work of fiction. Names, characters, places and incidents are the product of the author's imagination or are used fictitiously. Any resemblance to actual events or locales or persons, living or dead, is entirely coincidental.

An *Original* Publication of POCKET BOOKS

POCKET BOOKS, a division of Simon & Schuster Inc.
1230 Avenue of the Americas, New York, NY 10020

ISBN: 1-4165-0725-6

This Pocket Books paperback printing September 2004

10 9 8 7 6 5 4 3 2 1

POCKET and colophon are registered trademarks of Simon & Schuster Inc.

Printed in the U.S.A.

For Michael

A very special note of thanks to

The Librarians and Interpreters of the
Colonial Williamsburg Foundation

And also to
My Agent, Joyce A. Flaherty
and
My Editor, Caroline Tolley

Destiny's Will

Prologue

August 1811

Edward Justin Reynolds, the sixth Earl of Ellsworth, sat at his mahogany desk engrossed in a stack of papers. Across from him, waiting in respectful, watchful silence stood Mr. Huggins of the legal firm Huggins, Huggins and Barrows. The thin, owlish solicitor peered over his metal-rimmed glasses at the earl waiting for a sign, however small a look, a nod, a raised finger, that would indicate he was to continue. Mr. Huggins prided himelf on his ability to read the earl's silent dictates and to interpret them correctly. This ability had taken a considerable amount of practice to achieve, months of frustration, and not an undue amount of consternation. But the end result had been a continuing association between his firm and the Earl of Ellsworth.

The silence in the room was disturbed only by the sounds of the rain beating against the windows in a broken staccato, and the rustle of papers as the earl read through the legal documents Mr. Huggins had just presented to him.

The contents of those documents, Mr. Huggins was sure, would prove to be a pleasant surprise to his lordship. He couldn't imagine that anyone would not be pleased to find he had just inherited an estate. Not that the earl was in need of any more wealth. Lord knew the man was wealthy beyond reason. In addition to his town house in London's most fashionable quarter, he owned five other homes throughout England and a plantation in America. With the exception of the land in Virginia, which he had won on the turn of a card, all properties had been handed down to the earl upon his father's death seven years earlier. But the majority of the man's wealth; the priceless Greco-Roman art treasures, the fabulous jewels, the fleet of ships that sailed worldwide, had all been acquired through his extraordinary business acumen.

The earl scanned the last page before him. One dark brow quirked upward slightly and Mr. Huggins continued.

"As you can see, my lord, while Henry Fairchild left no debts, he did die an impoverished man. The estate, Fairfield, is still intact, but in a desperate state of disrepair." Mr. Huggins paused briefly to glance over his spectacles at the earl before continuing. "The man's association with your father and Lord Grenville is the only evidence I could find as to why the inheritance has been passed to you."

At the mention of the former foreign minister the earl glanced up, but said nothing.

"The man left behind several relatives who could stand to gain considerably from such an acquisition." To emphasize his point, the solicitor handed the earl a list of names of Henry Fairchild's relatives. Adjusting his glasses on the bridge of his nose he proceeded.

"There is one item, my lord, that needs immediate and further consideration." Again he looked over the metal rims. "Henry Fairchild left behind a daughter."

A slight frown creased the earl's face. Leaning back, he rested his elbows on the chair's arms and placed his fingertips together to form a tent.

"The girl is an only child and still residing in the house. She and her father lived in moderate comfort until several years ago, when Fairchild began investing too frequently and very unwisely."

Mr. Huggins's voice went on briefing the earl about the Fairchilds. "Henry's business ventures had kept him traveling to America and France for the past two years. The managing of the estate had been left to the daughter, and it is to her credit alone that the estate was kept from going to auction."

The earl raised a hand to halt the intrepid Mr. Huggins. He rose from his chair and strode to one of the long French windows, unaccountably annoyed with the entire matter. His cobalt blue eyes scanned the elegant garden situated behind the house and he appeared to Mr. Huggins to be momentarily distracted.

Quite the opposite was true. The earl was intensely examining the situation. The girl could not remain where she was. The property was legally his, and the implications of her residing in one of his houses would only cause the kind of social stir he would not tolerate. She would have to leave immediately, perhaps go to one of her relatives. He recalled the list of names. A clergy in Wales, an elderly spinster aunt in Scotland, a distant cousin in America. Not an optimistic choice in the lot.

Justin Reynolds, as the earl chose to be called, could not be considered by anyone to be a sympathetic man. He had little tolerance for overstatement of any emotion. Any softening of his nature was limited to his dealings with his sister, Lenore, and his grandmother, the Lady Lydia Gray. As a shrewd and powerful businessman he was considered by some to be cold and unyielding. His association with his friends was casual. Affairs with his mistresses were physical dalliances at best, with no emotional ties whatsoever. He was infamous for coldly leaving behind a string of broken hearts and wounded prides.

But now, for some reason unknown even to Justin himself, an uncomfortable twinge of regret rose up in him for evicting a girl who had no reason to be left homeless. He wondered at his very uncharacteristic reaction to the situation. It left him feeling unsettled. He did not like the feeling one damn bit, and irrationally anger welled up within him. The last thing he wanted was to be morally responsible for some chit he had never laid eyes on. Damn Henry Fairchild and damn his daughter!

Turning back to Mr. Huggins, he said darkly, "I am not in any way legally responsible for the girl."

"Most definitely not, my lord," Mr. Huggins agreed quickly, then hesitantly added, "However, you are her landlord of a sudden."

At the subtle reminder, Justin threw his solicitor a steel-edged look of displeasure and crossed back to his desk.

Mr. Huggins swallowed nervously. "How would you like me to handle this, my lord?"

Justin's hand cut through the air in a curt, impatient gesture. "With your customary efficiency I would hope," he snapped. "Damn, I don't care where she goes, just get her the hell out of there. Send whatever her name is to one of her relatives, send her to my grandmother for all I care!"

Mr. Huggins hesitated in indecision, unsure of exactly how seriously he was suppose to consider the earl's off-handed suggestion. "Lady Gray, my lord?"

"Why not? She's always taking in stray cats. Being the sentimentalist that she is, this should appeal to her sense of romance."

Mr. Huggins hoped with all his heart that his face displayed none of the awe he felt. His instinctive reaction was to sink into the nearest chair and relieve his knees which suddenly felt incapable of supporting him. Never, no never had he expected Justin Reynolds to concern himself with Cara Fairchild's plight.

"As you wish, my lord," Mr. Huggins said as steadily as possible, looking through his glasses for once.

The earl stacked the papers on his desk into a neat pile, but his snapping blue gaze lingered on the man before him. "Steady, Huggins," he said, noting the little man's slip of composure and correctly assuming the reasons for it. "Just settle this matter and be done with it."

"Very good, my lord."

"Yes, I'm sure you think it is," he replied dryly, glancing

at the clock impatiently. He was expected at his ship within the hour. By morning he would be sailing to Spain as Captain Justin Reynolds, temporarily leaving behind his title of earl. The business of acquiring a new stallion for his magnificent stable lured him south. The fact that Spain was no place for any Englishman to be at the moment was of minor importance.

A restlessness that he had long ago recognized as part of his nature urged him toward the fringes of danger, providing him with an excitement he found very satisfying. Slipping in and out of Spain for the sake of purchasing a horse and enjoying the sexual favors of a certain dark-eyed, dark-haired Castilian beauty was the type of risky venture he thrived on.

Quickly he concluded his business with Mr. Huggins, the matter of Miss Fairchild already fading in significance and soon to be forgotten.

Chapter One

November 1811

"The Earl of Ellsworth can take his high-handed, dictatorial, overstuffed arrogance and throw it to the wind! He may own my home, but he most definitely does not own me!"

Finishing her heated tirade with a glare in her eyes and a defiant tilt to her chin, Cara Fairchild turned and entered the coach that stood waiting at the steps of Fairfield.

In the past two months Nigel Bennett had heard these words more times than he cared to count. Not spoken exactly and precisely as Cara had voiced them at the moment, but they always carried the same sentiment: Cara Fairchild did not like the Earl of Ellsworth. Not surprising under the circumstances. The events that had led to their association were very unusual.

Nigel pulled his redingote about him and entered the comfortable coach in which he and Cara would be riding and decided to drop the subject of the earl. Having firsthand experience with Cara's determined nature, he knew it would be pointless for him to say anything more.

Cara lifted turbulent green eyes to the facade of the once-grand Fairfield, her heart aching as the coach lurched forward, drawing her farther and farther from the only home she had ever known. She was unaware of the confused and painful expression playing across her face, and of the watchful gaze of her solicitor.

"Cara?" Nigel's voice interrupted carefully.

She looked at Nigel Bennett, all the hurt she was feeling shining in the clear depths of her eyes. A poignantly sad silence filled the space between them, joining the muted gray light of early morning. She continued to gaze at Nigel for a thoughtful moment, then let her eyes shift out the window to the fog-shrouded Fairfield. The house seemed to recede, then was hidden from view completely by a line of trees. Her eyes dropped to her lap briefly before lifting to Nigel again.

"Why?" she asked quietly.

Nigel did not pretend to misunderstand. He knew exactly what she wanted to know. But he was no closer to an answer now than he had been in September.

"I don't know, Cara," he replied kindly. "It is something we may likely never have an answer for."

She sighed. She supposed she ought to accept the fact that her father had left her homeless and practically penniless. However, that wasn't an easy task. She could understand if she and her father hadn't cared for each other or if he had been mean and spiteful. Then it would have made more sense that he will his belongings to someone other than herself. But that had never been the case. Henry Fairchild had always been a caring, doting father and she had loved him dearly.

"Do you think the earl will take care of Fairfield?" she asked, a slight edge in her voice.

Nigel answered easily. "Yes, most certainly, if his other estates are anything to judge by. He is a man who takes great pride in his possessions, and he has the means to insure he has the very best."

His words were meant to offer comfort, but they had the opposite effect. Cara ground her teeth together and focused her eyes out the window. "A man of great pride and unlimited means. Is that why he's so arrogant, thinking he can just order me about like he most probably does everyone else? Because he has all the money necessary to have everything his way?"

Seeing the stubborn tilt to Cara's chin, Nigel was careful to keep his words as neutral as possible. "As I've stated before, Cara, the earl's offer was very generous. He wasn't obliged to be concerned about you."

"Offer?" she scoffed. "It was an order, a command, a dictate!"

"Call it whatever you wish. The fact remains, the earl did make provisions for your welfare." Try as he may, Nigel could not disguise the note of censure in his words.

Cara turned her head to squarely face Nigel. "I don't need the earl to make 'provisions' for me. And I resent his thinking he has the right to do so."

Nigel Bennett was never at a loss for words, but he also knew when discretion was needed. Wisely he kept his thoughts to himself.

Alice Bennett was gazing out her front parlor window when the coach that carried her husband and Cara Fairchild rumbled past.

With a sigh she turned back to her lifelong friend, Miriam Hedgepeth. "Well, they're off to London."

Miriam Hedgepeth reached for another sweet tart, but stopped and looked inquiringly at her friend. "Who?"

"Nigel, and Cara Fairchild."

Miriam's hand resumed its path to the plate of morning pastries. "A shame, a shame, that's what it is, Alice. Nothing but a shame."

"Yes, you're quite right about that," Alice agreed, setting her round figure onto the needlepoint-covered settee.

"How long has it been now since Henry Fairchild died?" Miriam asked, more for the sake of dredging up tiny town gossip than for any genuine concern.

"Almost three months."

Miriam swallowed a heavily sugared sip of tea, her lined lips pursing primly. "The poor dear, I don't know how she's managed all this time. I just don't know. First with her mother dying when she was just a little thing, and then that *father* of hers leaving her by herself for months and months. And now this."

"She hasn't had an easy time of it, has she?" Alice shook her head slowly.

"It's all her father's doing, yes, it is. Instead of wandering from one provincial country to another, he should have been here seeing to his daughter's future." Miriam snapped her cup on its saucer with a decisive click as she worked herself into a mild stew. "He ignored his responsibilities, is what he did. Just ignored them as blithely as you please. And now look what's happened."

"Cara is without a home."

Miriam cast Alice a quick, exasperated look. "Well, there is that, but I was referring to her unmarried state."

This was a topic the two cronies had discussed often in the past two years since Cara had turned a marriageable age. As far as they were concerned, at nineteen, Cara was fast approaching spinsterhood.

"I've told Nigel more than once that she was just wasting away in that run-down old house of hers," Alice said.

"If you ask me, she was lucky she even had that house to live in for as long as she did. What, with the way she had to sell off one possession right after another, the place must be a veritable shell."

Alice poured herself another cup of tea before she remarked in a whisper that was almost conspiritorial. "I haven't set foot in the hall in too many years, but Nigel tells me that it really is quite pitiful. Entire rooms empty, cold drafty leaks in the third-story ceilings, paint peeling from the walls."

"See, I told you. Not a bountiful lot for his lordship, no, no, indeed not." Miriam gave a ladylike sniff as she took an almond pastry from the sweet tray. "What on earth could Henry have been thinking when he wrote out his will?"

"I don't know, Miriam. No one knows, not even Nigel."

"My dear, surely he must have some idea. After all, Nigel was his solicitor."

Alice's light brown eyes widened in acute innocence. "No, I assure you, Nigel was just as befuddled as everyone else. As far as he knew, Henry didn't even know the Earl of Ellsworth." She dropped her eyes to the cup and saucer resting lightly on her sparse lap, and her teeth nibbled anxiously at her lower lip. "Nigel didn't even know that Henry had changed his will," she murmured.

"What!"

The near shout snapped Alice's eyes up to Miriam's astonished face.

"I said, Nigel didn't . . ."

"I heard that," Miriam croaked, waving her teaspoon excitedly. "But what did you mean by it?"

Alice's face was a picture of anxious doubt, but the riveted look on Miriam's face prompted her to continue. "I really shouldn't be telling you this, but it's just all so strange. Nigel was Henry's solicitor for the last twenty years. He knew everything there was to know about the man, except this will. Henry had it drawn up a year ago in London, all quite legally leaving everything to the earl."

"Alice Bennett, you never told me this before," Miriam chided dramatically.

There were a great many things Alice knew about Cara Fairchild's unusual affairs that she hadn't been at liberty to tell. But as Nigel's wife she couldn't afford to be totally indiscreet, even though she was dying to tell it all. As much as she wanted to, she wasn't able to confide to her best friend that the Earl of Ellsworth had offered Cara a place to live with his grandmother, but the girl had actually turned him down. As far as the locals knew, Cara was leaving for America because she had no other choice, but Alice knew otherwise. What she didn't know was why Cara had decided as she had.

It made little sense to Alice, but then the entire matter

was quite beyond her. From Henry's awful drowning at sea, to Cara's leaving for America, of all places, it was just too, too strange.

Alice Bennett may have been perplexed by Cara's actions, but Cara knew exactly what she was doing. As the coach rocked and swayed its way through drizzly England by way of mud-choked, wheel-rutted roads, she had an abundance of time to reflect on her life.

Three months ago, she had been eagerly awaiting the return of her father from America. She had yearned for their reunion with an intensity that bespoke their close relationship. That his ship had been overdue by several weeks had caused only mild concern. After all, even in these modern times of the nineteenth century, ships were rarely on time. But two weeks became a month and Cara's concern had escalated with every passing day. Each night she had retired with a prayer for her father's safety and each morning she rose with renewed hope that that day she would hear the sound of her father's coach driving up the crushed gravel drive.

The coach that wound its way up the path to Fairfield seven weeks after Henry should have returned had not contained her father. It bore, instead, Nigel Bennett, and the news he had brought Cara had been devastating. The ship on which her father had been sailing home had sunk.

Grief had ravaged her heart. Not since the death of her mother had she experienced such soul-rending pain.

In thinking back, Cara wondered how she had coped with what had followed. Betrayal. The thought was as bitter now as it had been when she had been informed of the contents of her father's will. With her gaze focused unseeing out the coach window, she admitted it was a terrible way to feel about one's own father, but she did, and no amount of soul-searching alleviated the response she felt to his taking her home away from her. Her heart was torn between a lifetime of love she had felt for him and the hurt and doubt she lived with now.

And then the Earl of Ellsworth had entered her life. Snuggling deeper into the folds of her worn blue cloak, she simmered with righteous ire, once again, at his treatment of her. With no regard to her sorrow, with what she considered a total lack of consideration for her feelings, he had ordered her out of her home and into his grandmother's. Just like that, she mentally snapped her fingers. She'd barely come to terms with her father's death, hadn't even begun to fully comprehend the loss of her home, and he had issued his dictates as though she were a mindless idiot.

Sitting across from Cara, Nigel saw the tight expression of her face and knew instantly what thoughts were running through her mind. Only one person created that glint-eyed gaze and thin-lipped tightening of her jaw. The Earl of Ellsworth.

"Having seconds thoughts?" Nigel offered, hoping against hope that she was. He had tried his utmost to convince her to stay with the earl's grandmother, but all of his attempts had been in vain.

Cara came out of her silent musings with a start. "No, I am still determined to do this." At the disapproving shake of his head, Cara sighed. "Please, Nigel, I do not want to debate this again. You know how I feel about the matter."

Oh, Nigel did indeed know, but that wouldn't deter him from trying to change her mind. "I think you are being hasty, Cara."

"I know you do," she said softly.

"I wish you would give some consideration to the idea of living with the Lady Gray on a temporary basis." He saw her about to retort and quickly continued. "Just for a short while. Then if you found the situation not to your liking, you could make the journey to America."

"The situation is already not to my liking." Her green-eyed gaze was unwavering. "I will be no one's charity case."

They reached this same impasse every time they discussed the issue. Realizing futility when he saw it, Nigel changed his tactics. "Then at least remain in England, for Heaven's sake."

Cara thought Nigel a perfect dear and she knew he acted

out of his sense of duty and a concern for her, so she did not take offense at his gentle badgering. But she wasn't about to change her mind.

"Let me see," she stated matter-of-factly, humoring him with an ill-concealed smile. "I believe we have discussed the possibility of my being a governess. I'm certainly qualified, if formal education counts for anything. True, I have no experience, but I dearly love children."

"You know I could arrange a suitable situation for you," he pushed, taking the conversation seriously while he knew she did not.

"And you know that I find the idea of endless days closeted in the nursery, regimented to someone else's schedule intolerable." She was weary of the talk and sighed. "Please, Nigel, no more." She knew what was next. He would suggest a companion and she shuddered at the thought. She knew she was far too independent to be tied to the side of an aging matron, her life reduced to little more than fetch and carry. Marriage? To whom? As isolated as Fairfield was, she had had little opportunity to meet many men. And, she admitted with a wistful ache in her heart, she simply couldn't marry for the sake of a roof over her head. If she was ever fortunate enough to marry, she would do so for love.

It seemed there were few alternatives for a young woman in England. *In England*. But not so in America. Every letter she'd ever received from her cousin Beatrice in Virginia had been filled with glowing accounts of a fresh, courageous way of thinking that appealed to Cara. America, her instincts cheered. It was the glimmer of hope that had sparked her soul two months ago, and it had grown into a small but steady blaze of purpose that had carried her to this very day.

The trip to London was uneventful, but as the coach reached the city the weather seem to take a turn for the worse. The smoke from the chimneys never had a chance to rise. The icy wind which blew off the Thames whisked the smoky mist away into the night, as it rushed over docks and into alleys, screaming its way around house corners, in between floorboards and up under patched quilts.

Few people braved the frigid night with its sky of ebony ice. Those who were unfortunate enough to be about on such an evening scurried to their destinations, but were reprimanded with numb hands and feet for so foolishly trying to cheat the elements.

Cara glanced across the cramped space separating Nigel and herself, and a soft smile pulled at her lips. Through everything that had happened he had stood beside her, offering comfort as well as legal advice. And even though he was adamantly opposed to her decision, he had, in the end, aided her in her quest to start a new life in America and had made all the arrangements for her passage. He had been a dear friend and she was going to miss him.

The coach came to a halt and Cara peered closely out the window, straining to catch her first glimpse of the ship that would take her to her new life.

"You don't have to do this," Nigel said, carefully taking hold of one of her cold hands.

The gentle urging in his voice, as well as the comforting assurance of his hand on hers, brought a lump to her throat. She gazed back and saw the silent plea on his face, the look in his eyes that clearly hoped she had changed her mind. She hadn't.

Her eyes pooled with tears as she laid her other hand upon his, and her lips trembled into another smile.

Nigel watched her pale face and waited. Neither spoke and finally he accepted her silence as answer.

"All right, Cara." He patted her knee. "If you'll just remain here a moment, I'll see that everything on board is in order."

Nigel left the coach quickly and Cara used the time to blink back the tears and collect herself. She fumbled in her reticule for a hankie, and not being able to find it, resorted to dabbing at her eyes with shaking fingertips. Muttering to herself about such foolishness, she drew her cloak up around her chin and set the hood more firmly around her head. Moments later when Nigel returned, he found a dry-eyed and composed Cara.

Nigel and a frigid wind escorted Cara on board the *Wind Dancer*. The ship's first mate, Mr. Collinsworth, came forward, hands tucked into the pockets of his heavy jacket, and Nigel made the introductions.

"Good evening, ma'am," he said, touching a hand briefly to the brim of his hat. "Is this all you have?" he questioned, indicating Cara's worn luggage.

"Yes," Cara replied, thinking Mr. Collinsworth had come closer to the truth than he could imagine. "Yes, that's all." Everything she owned was within that one bag and that, Cara reflected, did not amount to much. Three dresses, in addition to the one she wore, a small assortment of underclothing, one nightgown, a light shawl, and several toilet articles.

"Well, that's it then. I'll show you to your cabin."

Cara hung back momentarily and Mr. Collinsworth, sensing that the young woman desired a moment of privacy, stepped aside.

The enormity of what Cara was about to do gripped her, wrenching her stomach painfully. Turning to Nigel, she put forth a brave face.

"Thank you," she said with only a slight tremor in her voice. "You have been as invaluable to me as you were to my father."

Nigel smiled proudly. "It has always been my pleasure to serve the Fairchilds to the best of my abilities. I only hope I have not failed you in this instance."

"The decision was mine to make," she reassured him quickly. "Please do not worry. All will be well."

Nigel hoped that she would feel the same way when she discovered what he had done. Well, it was useless to worry now.

"Good-bye, Nigel." The two clasped hands in farewell. For a moment Nigel looked as though he were about to say something, but the look evaporated and he left the ship.

Cara followed Mr. Collinsworth through a door leading off deck. Four doors lined the wooden walls of the lantern-lit companionway and they stopped before the only door on the right.

"Here you are." He proceeded Cara into the room and set about lighting a lantern. The flickering light revealed a tiny cabin, sparsely furnished. A small washstand stood against the far wall and beside it was a black, boxlike stove. A floor-to-ceiling cupboard was built into the wall to her left, and Cara thought that a wise conservation of space because she had never seen such a compact room. Against the wall to her right was a bunk.

Phillip Collinsworth turned in time to see Cara lower her hood and smooth a wayward curl from her face. His breath came up short and had he been walking he would have stopped dead in his tracks. The beauty of the woman stunned him. Luminous emerald eyes were fringed with incredibly long lashes and accented with delicately curved brows. High cheekbones gave way to the soft curves of her oval face. Her hair, a deep shade of rich auburn, was swept away from her face to the crown of her head and left to swirl to her shoulders where the tresses disappeared inside her cloak. Her creamy skin was without flaw and almost glowed in the lantern's soft light.

Cara stepped before the stove and raised her hands to catch the warmth. With a backward look over her shoulder she smiled her gratitude.

"It's going to be a cold night," Phillip Collinsworth explained absently and he wasn't sure how the words came out or if they even made sense.

She turned from the stove to face him, and the poor man felt the full force of her beauty.

"Is it terribly late?" she asked, totally oblivious to the havoc she was reeking on Phillip's senses.

Giving himself a mental shake, Phillip glanced around as though to get his bearings. "Just before ten o'clock. I know you must be tired so I'll say good evening."

He stepped to the doorway. "This door has a lock. Even though the crew is restricted from this companionway unless they have particular business with the captain, it would be wise if you kept it locked.

"The captain?"

"Yes," he nodded to the door at the end of the short hall. "Captain Justin Reynolds's cabin is there. Also, Mr. and Mrs. Taylor will be sailing with us. They're across the hall. And that door next to their cabin opens to a dining salon for passengers' use."

She gave each door a careful look before turning back to the first mate.

"Is there anything else I can do for you?" he asked hopefully, absolutely loath to part company so soon.

"No, I'm sure I'll find everything I need," she answered, giving the cabin a cursory glance. "Thank you."

"Yes . . . well, if there's anything I can do for you, anything at all, call upon me at anytime." He took a halting step back into the companionway, stretching his departure to the limit. "I will see you in the morning then."

"Good night and thank you."

"Well . . . that's it then. Good night."

Closing the door, Cara gave a sigh of relief. Fatigue had settled upon her in the last few minutes, and the nervous anticipation she had kept at bay all day threatened her now. She prayed one last time that she was doing the right thing. Maybe she should have followed Nigel's advice and gone to live with the earl's grandmother. The earl. Just the thought of that man's officious orders stiffened her spine. It made her blood boil every time she thought of the way he had assumed he could tell her how to live her life. How dare he!

With renewed resolve, she unpacked.

Cara lay in bed with eyes closed, listening to the sounds of the ship. Still half-asleep, her mind struggled to put a name to the unfamiliar creaking. The sound grew more faint, then ceased altogether, only to return and resume the pattern.

She turned her head to one side and scanned the cabin. Sunlight streamed in through the window, creating a small, bright square on the wooden floor. Groggily Cara watched the sun-square slide across the floor, up the wall, then back down onto the planks.

With a start she sat straight up. The ship was sailing. In a flurry of flannel nightgown and bed covers she scrambled to the window, mindless of the cold floor on her bare feet.

The window's limited view showed nothing but ocean. They had left England and she was actually on her way to Virginia. Her sweet laughter bubbled over with the sheer thrill of the moment. Craning her head from one side of the window to the other, she tried to get a better look, but all she managed to see was the same restricted scene.

A quiet tapping at the door interrupted her. Wrapped in a blanket and careful to keep everything but her head behind the wooden portal, she opened the door to find Mr. Collinsworth.

"Good morning, Miss Fairchild." His brown eyes gazed longingly at her beautifully rumpled appearance, and a huge smile creased his face.

"Good morning, sir." Cara smiled delightfully, still caught up in her gay spirit.

"Captain's compliments, ma'am. He would like to see you in his cabin as soon as you can . . . that is, when you're . . ."

Cara looked down at her bare toes peeping out below the blanket and laughed. "If you'll give me a few moments, I'll be right with you."

Standing outside Cara's closed door, Phillip Collinsworth wondered how he was going to endure a month of her smiles.

Cara set about dressing, determined to start the first day of what she thought of as her new life looking her best. Quickly she splashed cold water on her face, then donned a long-sleeved, dove gray gown of light wool. A high cream-colored collar and matching cuffs softened the severity of dress. She brushed her hair, making the strands crackle, then swept the front of the shining mass to the crown of her head and let it cascade down the length of her back. A simple cream ribbon and two combs secured the rich tresses. Having no mirror to judge by, she could only hope her appearance was suitable.

Collinsworth practically jumped when Cara opened the door. Still fussing with one of her cuffs, she missed his rapt expression.

"I hope I haven't kept the captain waiting." She lifted worried eyes to the first mate. "Mr. Bennett, my solicitor, made it very clear that on board a ship, a captain is law unto himself. I don't want to do anything to alienate the man."

"Not to worry. You've made ready in record time." His eyes swept over Cara's trim figure, lingering on the swell of her breasts. Perspiration beaded his upper lip and he forcibly dragged his eyes away.

He rapped twice on the captain's door, then held it open. "He's expecting you," he whispered as Cara entered the cabin. She was surprised when he didn't follow her in, but closed the door behind her.

"I'll be right with you."

Cara turned toward the sound of the rich, masculine voice. She found Captain Reynolds seated behind a large, intricately carved mahogany desk, the majority of his head and upper body hidden behind a wide map he held before him. "Please, be seated."

A little taken aback by the brusqueness of the order, Cara nonetheless sat in a wine-colored leather chair opposite his desk. Silent moments passed and when the captain still hadn't so much as glanced her way, Cara turned her attention to the cabin.

The room was spacious, being well lit by two windows behind the desk. Just enough furniture filled the space to be functional and comfortable, and Cara found the burgundy and deep wood tones tasteful and masculine. A side table was set in the far corner to her right. Along the same wall was a large bunk and a tall Chippendale armoire of the finest cherry woods. On the opposite side of the room stood a sturdy table and chairs, and Cara wondered if Captain Reynolds took his meals there. But most interesting, and what truly captured Cara's attention, was the floor-to-ceiling bookshelf along the wall behind the table and chairs. She had never imagined a ship would have such a collection of books.

The library at Fairfield had been the very first of the possessions to be sold in order to pay the debts. It had been several years since she had last read and she sorely missed the pastime. Her emerald eyes scanned the leather-bound volumes and her expression became wistful as she hoped she might be able to borrow a book or two.

With a sigh she glanced back to Captain Reynolds, fully expecting him to still be engrossed in his reading. Instead, she found him sitting back in his chair watching her.

Her eyes opened wide at the sight of the man before her. For several heart-stopping seconds she could only stare, her mind absorbed in aesthetic wonder. Never had she seen a man as handsome as Captain Reynolds. His lean, tanned face was ruggedly sculpted with a straight nose, firm mouth, and strong jaw. Eyes so blue they shone like crystal cobalt held a trace of cynicism that somehow only managed to add to the man's attractiveness. Hair, the deepest shade of brown, caught each ray of sunlight and gleamed in an absolute harmony of umbers.

For a moment Cara lost all train of thought, until she saw his lips curve upward into an amused smile. Immediately her eyes flew to his and a startled gasp froze in her throat. His gaze held hers with a sensual look, devouring in its intensity, that seared straight through to her nerves. Her heart began to race and she could feel a deep blush rise up, washing her face with evidence of the effect he was having on her. Embarrassed and confused, she jerked her eyes to her lap.

Justin Reynolds watched the vivid blush stain Cara's cheeks. When she had first entered the cabin, he hadn't even looked at her. But when he had, the picture she presented made him put aside his work and focus his full attention on her.

With frank, masculine appraisal, he let his eyes roam at will, touching on her straight, pert nose and sensuously shaped lips. His gaze descended along the long line of her neck to the swell of her breasts before dipping lower to the trim line from waist to thigh.

Cara could feel the weight of his stare and it unnerved her. His bold look made her senses spin with the realization of her own femininity. The silence between them became charged, and frantically she searched for something to say to break the tension.

"Mr. Collinsworth said you wished to see me." She seized the first rational thought that came to mind and managed to get the words out through stiff lips.

Her averted gaze missed the thoroughly appreciative look Justin swept along her figure, and his very wicked grin.

"Yes, I do," he replied smoothly, waiting for her reaction to his double-edged words. None came and he continued politely. "I'm sorry I was not on board last night to welcome you. I trust your first night went well."

Cara took a deep, steadying breath and forced herself to meet his eyes. Oh, the man was far too handsome.

"Yes, I slept very well, thank you." Her steady voice gave no indication of her fluttering insides. "I was surprised, though, to find we had already left England."

Justin rolled his map and set it aside. "We left before first light." Coming around to the front of the desk, he propped a hip against the shiny surface and folded his arms across his wide chest.

Cara marveled at the smooth grace with which he moved, especially for such a tall man.

"Did Mr. Collinsworth explain our routine on board?"

Cara shook her head, explaining she had arrived quite late and had retired almost immediately.

Justin outlined the expected voyage, touching briefly on their intended course. The ship was manned by a crew whose ranks included a first officer, a cook who doubled as the ship's doctor, a helmsman, and too many others for Cara to remember. Meals were served three times a day unless they should encounter a storm and then the galley was all but shut down. Cooking food while the ship was being tossed about the ocean was almost impossible; meals would be quick and cold.

Listening to the rich timber of Justin's voice, Cara was distracted by its smooth quality. His words flowed easily and she wondered how many times he had given this same speech. He was relaxed, and by watching his face it was clearly evident that he thoroughly enjoyed being at sea. She fancied that he looked like a sailor, with his darkly tanned face. She watched his body shift ever so slightly with the roll of the ship, bracing his weight effortlessly with his long legs. Without meaning for them to, her eyes followed the long line of muscular thighs upward along the snugly fitting black pants to his lean waist. Her gaze roamed across the white shirt that covered his wide chest and broad shoulders. It wasn't until her eyes were resting on his finely chiseled lips that she caught herself, realizing that she had let herself become distracted by his devastating good looks. Immediately she forced her attention back to Justin's words and listened to what he was saying.

"This ship is at your disposal. You are free to come and go as you please, as long as you do not interfere with the smooth operation of this vessel. If you should ever need anything, do not hesitate to call upon me."

Justin paused briefly before continuing, but in that instant Cara sensed a subtle change in mood.

"There are, however, areas that are off-limits to all passengers. The hold and the crew's quarters. It would be unwise for any passenger . . . especially you, to venture into either place." The blue in his eyes intensified. "Especially the latter."

Cara's innocent mind was several steps behind in understanding why Justin's words should single her out. She searched his face, waiting for him to elaborate. Their eyes met and suddenly she stumbled head over heels into comprehension.

"Yes, I quite understand, Captain," she said, a vivid blush coloring her cheeks again.

Justin watched her intently, a slight frown creasing his brow. "You would also do well to remain in your cabin after dark unless you are accompanied by me or an assigned crewman. My men are a good lot, but they are men and I would hate for any unpleasantness to occur."

Cara couldn't quite manage to meet his eyes, and her gaze fastened on her fingers, nervously plucking at the fabric of her dress. His bluntness was disconcerting and she was certain her face was scarlet.

"Now, do you have any questions?"

She was grateful for the change of subject and breathed a sigh of relief. "How long will it take to reach Virginia?"

"With luck, four weeks, possibly five. We should make Hampton Roads port by the first of December." Justin stood and returned to his seat behind the desk. "The trip will pass quickly. There are other passengers for you to share your time with. Should you not meet them today, you will have the opportunity to do so tonight." He gave Cara a disarmingly charming smile as he informed her, "It is customary on the *Wind Dancer* for all passengers to dine with me on our first night at sea."

Cara's face lit with expectation, her green eyes sparkled. "Thank you, Captain. I would be honored." A dimple appeared hesitantly in her cheek, irresistibly drawing Justin's eyes to the creamy surface.

Moments later, when she stepped into the companionway, Cara's spirits were soaring. Her pulse beat as though she had run a hard course and she found herself smiling for no accountable reason. She chided herself for being silly and assured herself that her joy was due to the successful beginning of her journey and the unexpected, welcomed invitation to dinner. But her heart laughed at her and laid the full cause on Justin Reynolds.

The remainder of her afternoon whisked by, and by early evening her anticipation of the night ahead was like a glowing tingle, fluttering in her stomach. It was a rare occasion for her to dine formally. She didn't count those times when she had had dinner with Parson Fletcher and his wife and their brood of children. And an infrequent tea with Alice Bennett couldn't be categorized as a formal dinner. She dressed with special care. Teeth nibbling at her lower lip, she surveyed her gowns. She knew the choices by heart, one blue, one gray, one black, and one burgundy. All were several years old and definitely showing signs of wear. Wistfully she thought how nice it would be if she were able to go to dinner dressed in lacy pink or velvet white. A new, utterly feminine creation that hadn't been mended repeatedly or faded from too numerous washings. Scanning the dresses again, she sighed and ran her fingers along the folds as they hung together in the closet and wondered which of the dresses Captain Reynolds would find most attractive on her. Just as quickly, she shook her head, blushing at her thoughts, and chose the black, deciding it would suit the formality of the occasion.

Despite its shortcomings, the dress was elegantly simple and most becoming to her figure and coloring. A delicate ruffle edged the modestly cut V of the neckline. The waist was fitted just below her breasts, accenting their fullness. Long sleeves belled slightly before narrowing to points which just covered the backs of her hands.

She swept her hair up into loose twists and secured the shining mass with her combs. A few wispy curls teased the nape of her neck, adding to her guileless look of innocence.

Dinner was a sumptuous affair. Pea soup was followed by roast mutton, hogs pudding, corned round beef, duck, pork pies, and vegetables. Cara couldn't ever remember seeing so much food, let alone at one meal, and she enjoyed the tasty offerings. But after years of enduring pitifully inadequate amounts of food, her stomach was unprepared for the sheer quantity before her. By the third course, she was forced to only sample small bites.

She immersed herself in the witty conversation, laughing gaily and bantering lightheartedly. Charles Taylor proved to be a most entertaining gentleman. He was a great admirer of Benjamin Franklin and Cara thoroughly enjoyed his charming company. At age sixty, he had seen most of what life had to offer and regaled the others with his humorous outlook.

"'Blessed is he that expects nothing, for he shall never be disappointed' as my Ben would say," Charles quoted, raising his crystal wine goblet in a toast. "My grandfather's philosophy, to be sure, much to the chagrin of my father."

"Why so, sir?" Phillip asked.

Charles leaned back in his chair like a thin, wizened sage and regarded Phillip. "Upon my grandfather's death, there came into my father's possession a trunk heavily laden and securely locked. The speculation as to the contents of that trunk far surpassed what the trunk actually contained." He paused to run a gnarled hand over his sparse white hair, effectively building the suspense of his tale. When his silence lengthened, Phillip eagerly prompted him to continue.

"My grandfather's legacy was a trunkload of Mr. Franklin's *Poor Richard's Almanack.* My father was never very impressed, but I have always been most appreciative."

Regina Taylor looked to her husband, thirty years her senior, and mentally sneered. The old fool had told that same story more times than she could remember. She wanted to pull her hair out in frustration. Instead, she carefully sipped her wine and let her gaze slip discreetly to Justin. He was an impressive man. Handsome, virile, and if her very womanly instincts were correct, a man who indulged his passions. She smiled inwardly, thinking the passage home had suddenly become very promising.

"Isn't that right, dear?" Charles asked.

"I'm sorry, Charles, my mind was on something else," Regina replied smoothly.

Charles laughed good-naturedly, regarding his wife with faded blue eyes. "Ah, I forgive a beautiful woman anything."

Regina was indeed a beautiful woman. Hair and eyes as black as night set up a startling contrast to her milky white skin. The upward tilt of her eyes, her smooth, high cheekbones, her generous, carefully painted lips, all combined with her dramatic coloring to give her an exotic look.

"I was saying that once we are home and settled, we should entertain our present company with a ball, perhaps."

"A marvelous idea, husband," she remarked, then added in a sugar-coated, teasing voice, "It would give me a chance to show off my latest purchases." Her long fingers waved across her décolletage in a languid gesture that drew everyone's attention.

"Is your necklace one of them?" Justin asked, his eyes resting on the gems.

Regina looked at Justin with a practiced smile, allowing her eyes to drop to his firm lips for the briefest moment before lifting her gaze to his again. "Why, yes it is, Captain. Isn't it just beautiful?"

"Most dramatic," Justin replied with a knowing one-sided smile.

Cara regarded the dazzling jewels. The piece draped Regina's neck, dipping low to the deep cleavage revealed by her sapphire blue dress. She watched the precious stones rise and fall with the woman's breathing, creating a sparkling glitter that helplessly drew one's eyes to the lush roundness on which the gems rested. The display was disconcerting and Cara wondered innocently if Mrs. Taylor was aware of the necklace's effect.

The group was lingering over after-dinner drinks, wine for the women, brandy for the men. Cara listened intently to Justin, finding his presence electrifying. There was a powerful energy about him that made even the simple act of sitting near him exciting. She enjoyed his satirical sense of humor and marveled at the ease with which he conversed. Looking at him now, her heart fluttered at the sight he presented. He was formally dressed in unrelieved black, from crisp cravat to shining boots. His superbly tailored jacket fit perfectly over his broad shoulders and firm chest. The light from the candles cast his face into dynamic masculine relief, sharpening the strong lines of his jaw and adding a mellow glow to his blue eyes.

Justin looked up to find Cara's inquisitive green gaze on him. Their eyes met and she quickly looked away, unable to control the blush that heated her cheeks.

Collecting her thoughts, she concentrated on what Phillip was saying.

The topic of conversation had come around to the latest trade routes to the Far East, a topic Regina found infinitely boring. She gritted her teeth and sighed inwardly, silently wishing that she could be spending this time alone with Captain Reynolds. She glanced at Justin and saw his glittering blue eyes on Cara's face, and the green claws of jealousy raked her pride. Her black eyes narrowed maliciously over the rim of the fragile glass and she abruptly listened to the conversation for the first time.

"My father traveled between Madagascar and Plymouth quite often," Cara was saying, "and he never had a great deal of hope about the Cape."

Her quip drew chuckles.

"If it weren't for the island of Madeira," Phillip said, "the journey would be quite abominable."

"And there is a great deal to be said about the native wine, dangerous as it has been known to be," Charles chuckled, referring to Richard III drowning his brother in a vat of Malmsey Madeira.

"Ah yes, the infamous Malmsey," Justin added, lifting his goblet for a drink. "Although I do not relish the idea of an imminent death, its prospects would be softened somewhat by the notion of departing as did the Duke of Clarence."

"It would make passing away more tolerable," Cara commented with a rueful grin.

The entire conversation was beyond Regina and it vexed her extremely that everyone, including that chit of a girl, Cara, understood the exchange.

"I do prefer port," Charles added, "but if I had no choice in how I was to meet my end, I think I could put aside my preference and tolerate drowning in a Malmsey-butt."

Justin leaned back in his chair, his long fingers toying with the stem of his glass. "My preference is also port, however, I have found several wines, one in particular from Canton, that I find unusual."

The mention of China was especially intriguing to Cara and she turned eager eyes to Justin. "Have you actually been to Canton?"

He regarded Cara's enthusiastic smile, thinking it made

her look like a guileless child. "Yes, several years ago. I found the experience interesting."

Cara was about to ask Justin to elaborate when Regina interrupted. "I've always thought of the East as barbaric. Surely those people can't possibly be as civilized as we are."

"Quite the contrary, Mrs. Taylor. While the cultures are dissimilar, there does exist a great deal of civility."

"Well, I have absolutely no desire to sail halfway round the world. I find the entire matter of months and months on a ship revolting. Even the one month it will take to reach home is taxing to my system." Regina finished with a slight pout on her lips as she sent Justin a pitiful look.

"My wife is not the best of sailors," Charles explained. "On the journey over she was not well."

"I was at death's door, I was so sick. How anyone can stand the constant rolling is beyond me." Regina lifted a languid hand to casually touch the nape of her neck. "But then some women are just more sensitive than others, I suppose. Wouldn't you agree, Miss Fairchild?"

Cara turned to Regina, genuinely surprised. This was the first time throughout the entire meal that Regina had spoken directly to her. "Yes."

Regina gave her a bland smile. "You're not the least bit affected by the movement, are you?"

Cara wasn't certain if Regina had meant an insult or not. She looked at the sweetly smiling Mrs. Taylor, and although she saw no outward signs of animosity, Cara's intuition warned her to caution. "No, I don't seem to suffer from the ship's motion."

"You must have a great deal of experience at sea then. Are you a world traveler also?"

"No, as a matter of fact, this is my first trip."

Regina turned with a dismissing shrug. "Charles and I have traveled throughout all of Europe. I do so enjoy the excitement, especially the shopping." She pursed her lips at Charles. "Although he wouldn't let me buy the most fabulous gown from Madame Courbet's."

"You'd make a poor man of me, Regina," Charles replied laughingly.

"I know. As it is you do spoil me so," Regina said, then turned to Cara again. "Are you familiar with Madame Courbet's of London, Cara dear?"

Something about Regina's too sickly sweet tone left Cara feeling uneasy. "No, I've never been to London."

"Never been to London?" Regina trilled, as though she found the idea absurdly quaint. "And here you are, sailing all the way to America, and by yourself. Whatever did your parents say? They couldn't have been in favor of it. I mean, I thought all English ladies never went anywhere without a chaperone."

Cara felt as though she had been slapped in the face. This time there was no mistaking the insult, as subtle as it was. The implication that she was less than a lady seemed to hang in the air. Surprised and uncomfortable expressions registered on everyone's faces, except Regina's, who sat casually sipping her wine, a look of pure innocence plastered on her face.

Hot emotion singed its way through Cara, making her eyes glitter like the most sparkling emeralds, and her delicate fingers clenched the folds of her skirt. As far as she could tell she had done nothing to antagonize Regina, yet the woman seemed intent upon making Cara the target for her spite. Well, she wasn't going to let the woman ruin her evening, or the entire voyage for that matter. She'd see to that right now.

With admirable self-control, Cara reined in her temper and turned to Regina with a lethal load of graciousness. Despite the vivid blush that stained her cheeks, she smiled at Regina, raised her chin, and spoke with firm determination.

"My parents did not say anything about this, Mrs. Taylor, because they are dead." Cara's voice quivered ever so slightly, but she continued with quiet dignity. "I am traveling without a companion only because I could not afford to hire one."

Regina looked away from the solemn green eyes, unable

to withstand the proud righteousness on Cara's face, and fumed silently. So the little miss wasn't as spineless as she appeared. She had badly misjudged Cara's strength of character, and her blunder had made her appear rude and vindictive. Hiding behind a sham of sympathy, she tried to cover her reckless behavior.

"Cara, dear, I am so sorry. I did not mean to pry. I was merely concerned about your welfare."

Although the words were spoken in earnest, Cara was not convinced of Regina's sincerity. "I appreciate your concern, but Captain Reynolds has advised me of the possible pitfalls on board this ship." She glanced at Justin, finding him watching her closely. Quickly she looked back to Regina. "I feel assured of my welfare."

An hour later, Justin sat alone before his desk. He had removed his jacket, waistcoat, and cravat and, in a casual air, had turned back the shirt's cuffs and loosened several buttons. A thin cigar lay burning in a pewter dish, the smoke curling almost lovingly around his dark head as he made an entry into his log. His bold writing recorded the day's events from dawn to dinner. With a frown he laid aside his pen and reached for the cigar.

The whole evening had come to a stilted conclusion in the wake of Regina Taylor's comments. He clamped the cigar between even, white teeth, squinting through the lazy smoke and leaned back in the chair. What a sultry bitch. He knew her type. Had even bedded one or two upon occasion, but had made sure never to get more involved than that. Regina's type leaned toward viperish ways and aggressive temperaments that could make for an unusual time between the sheets, but once out of bed, required too much finesse in handling to be worthwhile. He found her behavior tonight to be rude, but not surprising.

Cara Fairchild, on the other hand, was most definitely full of welcomed surprises. She had handled Regina most efficiently. Most women he knew would have reacted to the situation with shocked indignation or a suitably scathing retort, possibly followed by a tearful retreat out of the room. But Cara had maintained her composure and without so much as a raised eyebrow or a harsh word, dispatched Regina with a delicate brutality that was truly admirable. Smiling lazily through the wreath of smoke, Justin tried to remember the last time he had actually admired a woman.

He took a long draw on the cigar and gave Cara his full attention. She had occupied his thoughts during the day more often than he cared to admit. She was a stunningly beautiful woman and for a moment he immersed himself in the mental picture he had of her. Her face was exquisitely sculpted with high cheekbones and a delicately rounded chin. Almond-shaped eyes of the most remarkable green were fringed with long, dark lashes. Her lips were sweetly molded and he could easily imagine his own lips passionately capturing hers. All of this was framed by the lush mass of auburn hair that curved around her shoulders to her trim back.

Her slender body was voluptuously curved and the thought of its allure made Justin clench his teeth as he felt a tightening in the pit of his belly. She was a tempting little thing and it was, he admitted, more than her face and body that made her so appealing. At dinner tonight she had conversed with a witty charm. He found her unpretentiously intellectual and extremely well-read. He had been genuinely surprised by her scope of knowledge and even more surprised that he actually enjoyed listening to her.

As a rule Justin's relationships with women were primarily physical. If any of his mistresses had an opinion that mattered, he didn't care. Now, he suddenly found himself intrigued by more than a delicious form and a lovely face. But there was something else, something he couldn't quite put his finger on. A strange feeling of recognition, as though he knew her, but couldn't quite place her. He had been plagued by the feeling all evening.

It came as no surprise to Justin when he found he desired Cara. She wasn't the usual type of woman he dallied with. For one thing, his instincts told him she was a virgin. Normally he would avoid them as he didn't have the patience to tolerate their girlish notions of romance nor their mothers' schemes for matrimony. But there was a refreshing quality about Cara, a natural unaffected femininity that only enhanced her beauty and made her all the more desirable.

Justin gave in to an almost predatory sensation. It had been years since he had played the game of pursuit. With his sensual good looks and enormous wealth, women actively sought him out. After years of being chased, the idea of reversing the habitual role he had fallen into appealed to his basic masculine strength. He would enjoy seducing Cara Fairchilds, and of his success he had no doubt.

Chapter Two

Cara stood at the rail of the *Wind Dancer,* braving the chilled gusts that filled the sails and pressed her ever closer to Virginia. The clear cerulean sky forecasted smooth sailing and seemed to echo Cara's state of mind. She had settled in to the ship's routine with no problem. Most of her time was spent on deck and she marveled at her sense of anticipation. England was forever away and America beckoned with timely promise.

She looked down the length of the quarterdeck and a frown puckered her smooth brow at the sight of Regina Taylor. If there was one drawback to her journey at all, it was to be found in Mrs. Taylor. Cara saw the American couple during meals and intermittently throughout the days. Charles had been his usual charming self, and while he was present, Cara was spared the bite of Regina's spiteful nature. But an air of dislike existed between the two women, and Cara was continuously on her guard.

The wind sliced through Cara and she pulled her worn cloak more snugly about her. She supposed she ought to return to her cabin as she was becoming too cold to remain on deck much longer. But the thought wasn't that appealing. The cabin was confining and she had nothing with which to occupy herself. Years of managing Fairfield had kept her days busy and she was unaccustomed to inactivity. Sitting idly in the tiny cabin left her feeling restless and at loose ends.

She gave a sigh and let her gaze scan the waves one last time.

"Is there something amiss?" a deep voice asked from right behind her.

She turned with a startled gasp. Justin had come upon her without a sound and stood smiling down at her most handsomely.

In the two days that had passed, Cara had been at constant odds with herself to keep her emotions in check. Whenever she had chanced to speak with Justin Reynolds, she hadn't been able to stop the rush that swept through her. She reacted the same way now and hoped that she could keep the silly look of elation from her face. She managed to form her lips into dignified lines and stop her hands from convulsively grasping the wooden rail. Now, if she could only get her wobbly knees to cooperate.

"No, quite the opposite in fact." She sounded disappointed.

One of Justin's dark eyebrows rose in question.

She gave a gentle, musical laugh. "I would like to stay here on deck, but I can't tolerate the cold for too much longer. However, the idea of returning to the boredom I find in my cabin is very displeasing."

"Well, if it's something to keep you busy that you're looking for, I'm sure I can find something for you." He grinned devilishly, his eyes sparkled teasingly. "We have several hundred yards of jute that need splicing. I'm sure Mr. Barnes would be most grateful for the assistance. Or if that doesn't suit you and it's something more adventurous you're after, the rigging on the mainsail needs to be checked before the day's out."

Looking skyward, he rubbed his chin thoughtfully. "Of course your skirts could pose a problem of sorts."

Cara's laughter bubbled over. "You're quite impossible, Captain. I thank you all the same, but no thank you." She smiled engagingly, leaving Justin with a picture he'd remember warmly and repeatedly. "I'm afraid I'll leave all of that to your seamen."

"In watching you these few days, Miss Fairchild, I'd say you'd make an excellent sailor. You seem to have been born with your sea legs."

Cara blinked at the comment, shocked that he would be so forward as to want to discuss her anatomy. "I beg your pardon, Captain."

Justin threw his head back and laughed at her indignation, while Cara watched with wide eyes, not having the slightest idea why he found the situation so humorous.

Seeing her bemused expression, Justin brought his laughter under control and explained. "Miss Fairchild, I have just paid you the highest compliment any seaman can give to someone. I simply meant that you seem to be a natural sailor since you handle the ship's motion with ease."

Absurdly pleased with the unexpected praise, Cara gave her legs a quick glance before looking up at Justin. His face still bore traces of his mirth, softening the hard planes in a devastating manner.

For several pleasurable moments he considered her face beaming up at him. A delicate blush stained the velvet contours of her cheeks, her pink lips were sensuously molded, and he was acutely conscious of her subtle fragrance, reminding him of lush summer roses.

Carefully lifting a silky auburn curl that swayed teasingly in the breeze, he painstakingly draped it over her shoulder, his knuckles grazing her chilled cheek like the subtlest kiss of a gentle mist. Sweet, rippling shivers ran across her face and down her neck and suddenly Justin's simple gesture became one of surprising intimacy. Their gazes met and

Cara let herself be drawn into the depths of the fathomless blue. It was happening again, her mind signaled in warning: this uncontrollable urge to let her eyes drink in the sight of him, this incredible need to completely fill her mind with his image and surround herself with his masculine vitality. The sensation was frighteningly exhilarating.

With a supreme effort, she yanked herself back to reality, the heated blush on her cheeks mute evidence of her inner turmoil. "Well, I suppose I should go now," she said somewhat lamely, her mind searching for a dignified retreat from the battle she was having with her own will.

Justin watched her nervously twist her fingers, and while she made a valiant effort to keep her features composed, her face was bathed in rosy complement to the effect he was having on her.

"Perhaps I can save you from your boredom, Miss Fairchild," he said, unwilling to let her escape just yet and deny himself the pleasure afforded him by her beauty. "If you care to choose a book or two from my shelves, your hours may pass more enjoyably and quickly."

Surprised pleasure parted Cara's lips. She didn't think she'd ever have gotten up enough nerve to actually ask him if she could borrow one of his books. But here he was making the offer himself.

"Oh, Captain, I would so enjoy that." Happiness welled up within her. She could hardly believe her good fortune or his kindness.

"I'll be in my cabin after luncheon," he said. "Come by then if you wish."

With a beguiling smile wreathing her face, Cara agreed, then went to her cabin feeling absurdly happy.

Shortly after two o'clock Cara knocked on the door to Justin's cabin. Only a moment passed before he swung the door open and invited her in.

"I hope I've come at a convenient time."

With a grand sweep of his arm at the rows of leather-bound volumes, Justin put her mind at ease. "Have at it," he said.

Cara stood before the books. Milton, Chaucer, Molière,

Shakespeare greeted her like long-lost friends, bringing with them poignant memories of her happiest days at Fairfield. She gave Justin a quick, grateful look over her shoulder.

"I don't know how to thank you, Captain."

A flash of dubious humor crossed Justin's face. Just off the top of his head, he could name at least a dozen ways.

Nearly a half hour passed in total silence in the cabin. Cara studied the books, giving careful consideration to which she would choose. Justin sat at his desk catching up on paperwork, something Cara was mildly aware of, and openly watching Cara, something she was totally oblivious to.

Her back was half-turned to Justin, giving him an excellent view of her trim figure. The deep burgundy dress she wore was not in the best condition, he noted, but it did display her enticing curves to advantage. The square neckline was cut to just above the first swell of her breasts. Definitely attractive in a modest sort of way, but not nearly enough skin was exposed to suit his tastes. Her hair hung in one long, thick braid down the length of her back. It pleased him that she hadn't cut her hair short as was the current vogue. He liked the way it swayed sinuously whenever she turned her head, and he could easily picture the loose auburn mass veiling their faces as they made love. With the dark leather of the books and the deep tones of the wood as backdrop, her skin shone white, and just as he imagined her hair flowing around them as they arched together in passion, he had a clear mental picture of the pearllike skin of her naked breasts and thighs contrasted against the rich wine of the bed covering.

When Justin looked again to his log, a sensuously dark smile pulled at his firm lips.

Cara finally made up her mind and only when she went to pull the desired books from their places did she realize that she couldn't remove them. A narrow strip of wood extended upward from each shelf, creating a lip that kept the bottoms of the books from sliding forward. An identical strip extended downward from the shelf above over the tops of the volumes. Very effective in making sure the library didn't go flying around the room in rough seas, Cara mused, but how did one go about getting something to read? She wiggled a thick collection of folk ballads, trying to tilt it sideways just enough to clear the miniature overhangs. The book wouldn't budge. She tried a slender volume, hoping it might tilt more easily than the first. Still no luck. She pursed her lips in confusion. The books had to come out. After all, they had gone in. But how? Setting her arms akimbo, she glared at the shelves as though they had just become curious animals.

Justin's laughter jerked her around. "I was wondering when you were going to try to take a book down," he said, rising from his chair and coming around his desk.

"I know this is going to sound silly, Captain, but I can't seem to remove the books." She lifted her hand in a vague wave at the shelves.

Justin walked to the end of the shelving and snapped a series of hidden latches that released each wooden strip. "I had these designed for the sole purpose of saving myself some time," he explained, as he lifted one of the narrow pieces. "I enjoy reading and I spend enough time on board that I don't deny myself that pleasure. I also have no intention of picking books up off the deck every time we hit a swell."

Cara watched him take down a red-bound novel and wondered if he ever denied himself anything in life. He was so self-assured in everything he did. Even while standing idly thumbing through the pages, he exuded a powerful aura of a man who is always in control. His lean rugged jaw and piercing eyes attested to his determined masculine pride.

"What have you decided on?" he asked, not missing Cara's unintentional stare.

Pulling her eyes away, Cara collected her thoughts. She selected Shakespeare's *Macbeth* and a collection of short stories by Cervantes.

Justin's dark brows quirked upward. "Interesting

choices," he remarked dryly, taking *Novelas Exemplares* from her. "You intend reading this?" His words were liberally laced with doubt as he flipped through the Spanish text.

Seeing Justin's dubious expression, Cara slanted a sideways look at him with merriment in her eyes. Carefully keeping the smile that threatened from her lips, she replied, *"Si, pienso leer este libro."* Justin's eyes narrowed and Cara laughed. "Why do I get the impression, Captain, that you think I'm rather stupid?"

Justin was genuinely surprised. "I wasn't aware that I did."

Cara looked pointedly at the book he still held, then raised laughing green eyes to his.

"Point well taken," he remarked dryly. He plunked the book in her outstretched hand and leveled his gaze on her enchanting face. She was a woman of many facets, perhaps more than he had realized. Leaning his shoulder against the shelf, he openly studied her. "You surprise me, Miss Fairchild."

Cara's face pinkened under his lengthy perusal. It made her uncomfortable when he looked at her so intently. She sensed the humor of the moment fade away and she felt a growing nervous excitement. Instinct made her want to look away from the shining light in his eyes, but she screwed up her resolve and faced him squarely.

"Because I speak Spanish?"

"Because you speak Spanish," he admitted with a casual shrug of a broad shoulder. "Because you would rather spend your time reading than lazing your time away. Because you don't allow Mrs. Taylor to get under your skin." A wicked grin creased his tanned face for a second then disappeared. When he spoke again, his tone filled with serious intent. "Because you're courageous enough to sail to America by yourself."

No power on Earth could have forced Cara to look at Justin a moment longer. She blushed furiously and, hugging her books to her chest, lowered her gaze from the scalding flame in his eyes. The change in mood between them was unsettling and suddenly she was unsure of what to say or do. She never imagined that he had ever given her a second thought and was totally unprepared for his words that proved her wrong.

"And because you blush so beautifully whenever you're embarrassed," Justin murmured softly.

Cara's breath caught in her throat. He was no longer leaning against the shelves, but stood directly in front of her, only a few inches separating them.

He lifted a hand and lightly cupped her heated cheek, drawing her face upward toward his. Cara felt exquisite shivers run down her spine and she let go the breath she had unknowingly been holding. Chancing a quick look into his eyes, she found his gaze lingering on her lips and unconsciously she licked the pink surfaces in sheer, uncomfortable self-consciousness.

Tension grew within Cara and robbed her of her will. The touch of his hand, the mysterious look in his eyes seemed to melt her bones. She had never experienced anything even remotely like these sensations, and part of her mind told her to run. But before she could react and as though he had read her very thoughts, Justin laid a gentle finger on her lips, silencing anything she had intended to say and, at the same time, keeping her rooted to where she was.

The tanned finger traced her full lower lip, teasingly, ever so lightly. A warm languid pleasure stole over her, dispelling the fleeting panic of moments earlier. Who would have thought such a simple gesture could be so exquisite? The touch was blissful, beautiful in its simplicity, a lover's touch.

Cara's eyes grew wide. Where had that thought come from? She didn't have any idea of what a lover's touch felt like, so why had she thought such a thing?

The thought shocked her back to reality. She had been too caught up in the headiness of new sensations to be aware of the current that existed between them. But she noticed it now and she felt both confused and frightened.

She took a step backward, the books she held suddenly becoming of major interest to her.

"I should be going now," she murmured, turning to leave. "I'm sure I've kept you from your duties long enough, Captain." She stopped before the door and watched Justin stride purposefully toward her, his face set in hard planes. She had no idea of his intent and no desire to find out.

"Thank you again for the books," she blurted out quickly.

Justin watched her emotional retreat. Anger flared briefly within him until he saw her pulse beating frantically along the slim column of her neck. In careful study he noted her fingers plucking nervously at the leather bindings. She was trying to keep her face blank, save for an overly polite smile, but she couldn't hide her heightened color. He admitted she was putting up a good front, but he had seen the passion in her eyes and an eager anticipation that was full of promise. Sardonic amusement softened his brittle look.

"My pleasure, madam. Let me know when you finish those and you can choose more."

"Thank you," she said, looking away.

Justin held the door open for her, but his deep-voiced words stopped her just outside his cabin.

"Just for the record, Miss Fairchild, I think you are anything but 'rather stupid.' "

Uncertain of the meaning of his words, Cara turned back. She scanned his face, but his expression gave no evidence of his thoughts. Feeling a loss of composure once again, she smiled weakly, then quickly left for her cabin.

The next morning she was standing at what was rapidly becoming *her* spot at the rail before seven o'clock. She hadn't seen Justin since she had left his cabin the previous afternoon. But that hadn't kept him from invading her thoughts. Time and again as she had been reading, her mind had replayed the scene in his cabin. With remarkable ease the image of his chiseled features and heart-stopping smile had distracted her, making *Macbeth* seem mundane. The simple act of holding the leather-bound volume had played havoc with her senses, as her mind had contemplated his hands holding the very same book. With little effort she had been able to visualize his warm fingers skimming the fine parchment and, just as easily, she had remembered the touch of those fingers on her cheek. Even now, with the wind whipping at her hair, she could still see him striding toward her with a powerful grace that exuded authority and tightly leashed strength. Just the thought of his handsome face caused her stomach to grip and her face to blush.

Her reaction puzzled her. She didn't understand how he could unnerve her so effortlessly, as he had from their very first meeting. And no matter how she viewed the situation, she couldn't find a logical explanation for the fact that even though he made her feel nervous, he also made her feel alive and surprisingly happy. She smiled as her thoughts lingered on the moment when his fingers had caressed her lips. Some small, prudish corner of her mind told her that at his very first touch she should have delivered a stinging reprimand and left his cabin immediately. At least, that is what Miss Peele, her old governess, would probably have done. But, Cara mused, it was doubtful Miss Peele had ever met a man quite like Justin Reynolds.

Cara looked to the eastern sky, heavy with violet clouds, just barely tinged at their edges with yellow. The soft glow of early morning bathed her face in a most flattering light and accentuated the beauty that drew admiring glances from every man on deck. Even Charles was affected by the sight she presented. Emerging from the companionway, his eyes caught sight of Cara and he paused for a moment. With an artistic eye, he appreciated the splendor she afforded him in the truest aesthetic sense.

Out of the corner of her eye, Cara spotted him and flashed him a smile that originated in her heart. In the four days they had been at sea, Cara's opinion of Charles had not changed. In fact, she found she liked him more with each passing day. He was the epitome of gentlemanly conduct combined with just enough devilry to keep her entertained, yet very much at ease.

"You are certainly looking lovely this morning, my dear," Charles said, joining her.

She didn't feel particularly noteworthy, but she thanked him prettily. "It must be the sea air."

Cocking his head to one side, Charles studied her features. "No, I doubt the air has anything to do with your beauty."

"Charles, you'll be turning my head with your flattery," she teased back, not taking him seriously for a moment.

"You doubt my words?"

"Entirely."

"You wound me, Cara." And to prove his point, he laid a blue-veined hand over his heart.

"And you still flatter me." Cara shook her head ruefully.

"And if there was ever a woman more deserving of flattery than you, I have not met her."

"Well, I wouldn't know."

"Oh, come now. Certainly scores of suitors have presented their testimonies to your loveliness."

Cara laughed helplessly, but shook her head.

"What? You mean young men these days have dispensed with the pleasures of wooing a young lady?" He sounded so affronted that Cara laughed outright.

"No, I mean there have been no suitors."

Charles's jaw dropped open. "No suitors?"

"Well, none to speak of." Cara shrugged.

"I don't believe it."

"Fairfield was somewhat isolated," she explained. "We didn't have many visitors."

"But what of the young men from nearby?"

Cara's smile turned a bit wistful. "There were a couple who wanted to marry me."

"But your father wouldn't have any of them for a son-in-law," he concluded, thinking that if Cara were his daughter, he'd have a devil of a time letting her go.

"No. I wouldn't have any of them."

Charles's white brows rose in question.

"I didn't love any of them," she said simply.

Turning his white head to one side, he gave her a discerning look. "What do you know about love?"

Cara hesitated a second or two before answering. "I'm not sure I know anything about it. But I believe it's essential when two people marry." She thought back to the good times at Fairfield. "My parents loved each other. They laughed together, and cried, too. They were content with each other's company and I don't think they had any secrets between them. They were the very best of friends. I saw what my parents shared with each other and with me and I'd like to have that if I ever marry."

Charles was silent and she continued.

"When my mother died, I think the heart went out of my father. Things were never the same after that. I don't mean with the lack of money, the debts, but with his spirit. He tried his best to support Fairfield, but we slowly lost it all and that didn't seem to bother him, because when my mother died, he lost everything that ever meant anything to him."

It had been a long time since Charles had heard anyone speak so honestly about love, without jest or a trace of embarrassment. A long time ago he had spoken that way, felt that way. Before he had met Regina.

He had still been an idealistic man then, believing in the beauty of the heart and the soul. One look at Regina and he had thought he had captured it all. Oh, how he had loved her then, wanting to make her life a paradise as he had thought she would make his. Unfortunately, he had learned quickly that her beauty did not reach her heart, but rather was only a lovely covering for a selfish nature.

His marriage had been a far cry from what he would have wanted, but it hadn't been without its bright moments, either. He and Regina did suit in most ways, she was passable company for him, and he was the provider she needed. And, he could honestly admit that they shared a friendship of sorts. But not love, no, never that.

Charles mentally shook his head. He had thought himself immuned to the yearnings of the heart. Yet here he was, listening to Cara, and he suddenly found himself longing for what was lost to him forever.

"Well, those young men were probably penniless rascals." Charles's voice was slightly gruff. "Out to take advantage of you. Weren't worth a damned, pardon me, shilling, the whole lot of them."

"Charles," Cara exclaimed, her expression one of incredulous humor. "I'm the one without a shilling. I am one of the most penniless people I know."

He looked at Cara's lovely, smiling face and shook his head. "Cara, my dear, you are very much mistaken." His eyes roved her face and for a moment Cara thought they looked moist. When he spoke again, his voice was full of emotion. "You are one of the richest women I know."

The two shared breakfast, enjoying each other's company over beef and biscuits, coffee for Charles, tea for Cara. Regina was absent, still in bed and not due to rise until well into the morning. As if by mutual consent, neither mentioned her. Instead the conversation centered around Charles's plantation, the James River, and Virginia in general. It became obvious to Cara immediately that Charles loved his home, his work, and his country. With pride lighting his faded blue eyes, he described the acres of fields and his plans for the next season. He was so genuinely enthused about his topic, that he spent close to an hour in almost nonstop monologue.

He was in the process of explaining crop rotation when he was seized by a horrible fit of coughing. His thin shoulders shook with each spasm that shuddered his entire frame. The coughing was fierce, almost too harsh for him to bear.

"Charles, are you all right?" Cara asked in frightened concern.

With a shaking hand, Charles held his white kerchief to his lips, waiting for the next seizure to grip him. Over the white linen, he smiled tiredly into Cara's troubled green eyes. He didn't wish to burden her, and tried to speak the words to reassure her, but again his chest heaved. Bent forward, he gripped the arm of his chair, helpless to stop the coughing that scraped his lungs and shortened his life.

Alarm sent Cara out of her chair. Torn between wanting to wrap her arms around Charles in comfort and support, and running to Captain Reynolds for help, she knelt beside him and laid a gentle hand over his trembling one that gripped the chair with white knuckles.

The fit finally ceased and he slowly sat back, his face white and drawn. Too exhausted to open his eyes, he leaned his head against the back of his chair, the handkerchief he still held pressed to his mouth, liberally spotted with blood.

Cara gasped at the sight. Without opening his eyes, Charles knew what caused Cara's fright. He had seen the same thing all too often.

"Charles?" Cara asked in a hesitant whisper. He didn't answer. Had he even heard her? "Charles," she repeated more soundly, "should I get someone? Regina? Captain Reynolds?"

A rasping laugh came from behind the handkerchief and Charles opened his eyes. He found a certain humor in what Cara said. "No, dear. There isn't anything the first would do to help, and there is nothing the latter can do."

Seeing Cara's confused look, he tried to ease her mind. "I appreciate your concern, but I'm better already."

Cara wanted to dispute that, but something about his feeble attempt to minimize the episode cautioned her to discretion. Instead she asked, "Can I get you anything?"

"Perhaps a glass of water."

She did as he asked and the cool sips seemed to help.

"Can you tell me what's wrong?" she asked kindly.

Charles sighed. He wouldn't mind telling Cara if he thought it might serve some useful purpose. But the truth of the matter was that he was a dying old man, who was slowly coughing his life away. There was no help for him and the best he could hope for would be to live out the next year or so as happily as he could. Telling Cara any of this would only cause her sorrow and still change nothing in the end.

"Now calm yourself, my dear," he said, sounding almost convincing. "I'm fine, just not a young man anymore."

Cara's troubled gaze dropped to the stained kerchief Charles was stuffing in his coat pocket. "But the blood."

"Damned, pardon me, nuisance." He waved his hand dismissively and gave a casual shrug. "All pretty dramatic, but nothing to fuss about, I tell you." He drew his shoulders back and added, "Now, stop this worrying and get on with you."

Cara didn't know what to make of the situation. He seemed so ill, his coughing wasn't ordinary, and her instincts told her he was glossing over the entire episode for her benefit. Still, with eyes that were now clear and hands that no longer shook, he did appear better.

"Well, if you're certain you're all right." Her voice was doubtful.

"So all right that I'm going to have myself another cup of coffee and maybe even help myself to more beef. Now, off with you. I won't have you witness my gluttony."

Rising, Cara smiled weakly, not yet convinced of Charles's welfare. She didn't believe for an instant that he wasn't terribly ill, but he was well enough for her to leave him.

Charles determinedly kept the smile on his face until Cara was gone, and then he slumped, exhausted, in his chair.

Cara took her stroll on deck under a thickness of clouds and increased winds that threatened bad weather. Disquieting thoughts of Charles robbed her of the peaceful pleasure she would have derived from her solitary time on deck. She remembered Mr. Simpson, the gardener at Fairfield, coughing as Charles had, and that poor man had died from such attacks. Her worry for her new friend grew.

Walking the length of the quarterdeck, she pondered Charles's words, wondering what he'd meant when he said Regina wouldn't do anything to help him. It was such an odd statement for a husband to make about his wife and sad that it was probably true. Her heart was heavy for

Charles, not only for the physical pain he was so stoically suffering, but also for the lack of compassion from his wife.

By late afternoon the sky was blanketed in heavy ocher-gray clouds and the wind was forceful enough to cause the *Wind Dancer* to pitch at stomach-churning angles. Captain Reynolds's cabin boy, Willie, knocked at Cara's door and informed her that the captain wanted all passengers to remain in their cabins. All lanterns were to be extinguished and stoves were left to grow cold.

As the storm grew worse, Cara gave up trying to move about her cabin. She found the safest place was the corner of her bunk. Braced against the wooden wall, she kept her mind off the dangers of the storm by concentrating on the second act of *Macbeth*.

By the last traces of light coming from her one window, she read through the first two scenes quickly, her mind's eye picturing Banquo and Macbeth and the castle at Inverness. But by the time she reached the third scene, the ship's movements made reading increasingly difficult.

A sudden lurch tilted her across her bunk, nearly sending her to the floor. Straightening her skirts, she resettled herself then found her place in the book.

The drunken porter's monologue brought a smile to her face, even as the double meaning of his bawdy words sailed over her innocent head. His intoxicated fumblings were comical, but Cara's laugh became a frightened gasp as the ship rolled violently. Her world turned on its side, wooden walls and floors creaking against the strain, before it shook itself into a swaying, undulating, upright position again.

Pressed against the side wall, Cara's head swirled with the opposing motions, making her stomach ache with queasiness. She had no time to right her spinning senses when the ship was thrust upward and she slipped backward, thumping her head against the other wall.

Wedged into her corner, rubbing the bruised spot on her head, she realized just how much worse the storm had become. Dusk had been snuffed out prematurely, leaving Cara surrounded by matte black, and for the first time she felt truly afraid.

With each passing minute, as the storm's intensity increased, battering the *Wind Dancer* with raging winds and water, Cara's fear grew. The ship plunged and crested and it seemed that at any moment it would crash over and sink.

Terrifying images of her father's death filled her mind. Was this how he had died, as he had sailed home? Had he sat alone in a wildly rocking cabin, waiting for dark, cold walls of water to engulf him?

"Oh, Papa," she whispered, the words escaping through stiff lips as she steadied herself against a sudden nauseating lurch.

Closing her eyes, she pressed cold fingers against her mouth, fighting down the sickening feeling in her stomach. At that moment she would have given anything to be back on the safe, solid ground of Fairfield. But it was forever lost to her, and the bewilderment and hurt she still felt at her father's choice to give it to the earl intensified with the fear she felt now.

The room tipped precariously, nearly pulling Cara from the bunk once again. As she pushed herself back into her corner, she yanked herself away from her panicked thoughts, telling herself not to become hysterical.

"I'm going to stay calm," she told the room. "Just because Papa drowned doesn't mean I shall do the same."

The sound of her own voice, shaky though it was, soothed her raw nerves somewhat, until the bottom of the ocean seemed to open up and the ship dropped straight down. Her stomach was suddenly lodged in her throat and she cried out in fear.

Trembling, she waited for the next crazy shift, but the ship's movements calmed momentarily. Almost afraid to hope that the storm was over, she leaned back against the wall, drawing her knees up to her chest. With wide green eyes, she stared into the dark cabin trying to find anything to focus her gaze on and give some stability to her spinning head.

But the storm was far from over, and in the next instant a violent pitch toppled Cara out of the corner and across the foot of the bed. Sprawled on her stomach, she moved about, trying to right herself, only to have the ship dip back in a sharp reeling motion that threw her to the wooden floor.

Her shaking hands groped around, trying to find something to cling to. Trembling, she rose to her knees, her eyes huge and straining against the black void, but once again she lost her balance and fell sideways. She slammed against the bunk with a jarring impact that snatched her breath away.

Alone, engulfed by total darkness, the walls and floor moving riotously, Cara was filled with terror. Horrible images of her father, bloated with brackish water, combined with soul-rending thoughts of that same water filling her nose and lungs, and she lost her hold on her panic.

Forgotten was the captain's order to remain in the cabin. She had to get out . . . could not remain there to die. She had to find Captain Reynolds . . . he would save her.

Half-crouching, half-sliding to her right, she finally bumped into the black stove. It took her a moment to recognize the shape, and then instinct took over. She turned around and scrambled across the room, heading in a straight line for the door she knew was opposite the stove. When she was almost to the door, the ship heaved, sending her forward with a force that slammed her against the same wall she sought.

Pain erupted in her shoulder. Gasping, she rose to her knees, bracing herself against the door, and fumbled for the latch with shaking hands. Her fingers found the cold metal and she hauled herself upward, holding on with all her might as the floor slipped out from under her. Within seconds the ship righted and she seized that moment to yank the door open and stumble into the companionway.

For one terrible moment, the ship seemed to hang suspended in motion. The walls screamed in oaken strain, briny green water forced itself under the companionway door. And then the *Wind Dancer* finally crashed downward in a collision with the ocean. Cara's scream, as she was thrown against the far wall, pierced the night. Her head struck the door and pain burst behind her eyes. Blackness engulfed her and she dropped limply to the wooden floor.

Chapter Three

Cara woke by small degrees. She knew she was conscious, but beyond that she had no thoughts. She lay with her eyes shut, aware only of the darkness behind her closed lids. In the remnants of unconsciousness, the idea of opening her eyes never occurred to her.

She was crying suddenly. The tears slipped out from beneath her long lashes, running across her cheeks and into her hair.

What was wrong?

She hurt.

Where?

Her sluggish mind couldn't make sense of her random thoughts and with equal ignorance didn't register her shaking hand lifting to her head. Here was the pain.

"Easy, love." A voice was there beside her, and a firm hand taking hold of hers. She held on, reluctant to relinquish the comforting touch.

"Cara."

Her mind was still absorbed with the feel of the hand.

"Cara."

What did that voice want?

"Can you hear me?"

Her wayward brain stubbornly refused to answer. It wanted to sleep and it did.

The roaring sound of water crashed in Cara's ears, reverberating in and over, through and off her skull, thumping on every nerve until her head felt near to bursting with throbbing pressure. The tidal rush pounded, then withdrew like the ebbing tide. It was back within seconds, more gently this time, but still fierce enough to bring a moan to Cara's lips. Captain Reynolds's voice called to her from a distance and instinctively she turned her head toward the sound. The deep tones triggered a natural response in her and suddenly it was imperative that she go to him.

She concentrated all her energy on reaching him, and struggled through the waves of senselessness that threatened to engulf her. Drawing on the strength each of his words provided, she came awake and cautiously opened her eyes.

Captain Reynolds's face swayed and dipped momentarily before settling into place, with the rest of him sitting on the bed beside her.

"Welcome back."

"What happened?" she whispered.

"You hit your head." He smiled slightly, his eyes probing hers, and held up three fingers. "How many?"

Cara focused in on his hand, saw the raised fingers, yet somehow couldn't find the answer.

"It's all right." His blue eyes sliced to the purple bruise that began over her right brow and ran across her temple and into the hairline. "You have a nasty bump, but you should be fine in a few days. How's your arm?"

"My arm?"

"Yes," he answered patiently, "your arm."

She blinked in momentary confusion. Her right shoulder

and arm ached painfully. Why hadn't she noticed that? She didn't question how he knew, but said simply, "It hurts."

"I don't doubt it," he remarked as he left her. He was back in seconds with a glass of water. Carefully slipping an arm below her head, he lifted her from the pillow and held the glass to her lips. When she'd had her fill, he eased her back.

"Three," she stated tiredly.

"What?"

Her eyes closed wearily, struggling to reopen. "You held up three fingers."

"Good girl," he said, watching her eyes futilely flicker open several times.

"Cara?" he tried, but she had already slipped into sleep.

Dim sunshine greeted Cara when she next opened her eyes several hours later. She was instantly aware of two things: One, she could think clearly, and two, not only did her head and arm hurt, but her entire body felt as though Lord Wellington's army had marched across Spain by way of every one of her muscles.

Significant details her mind had failed to recognize hours earlier were abundantly clear now. She remembered the storm and that last terrifying moment when she was certain the ship was about to sink. She had been helpless to save herself from being thrown against the wall. After that, nothing, until now.

But that wasn't quite right. She had been awake earlier and Captain Reynolds had given her some water. How many hours ago had that been? she wondered with a frown. Instantly she was sorry as the slight downward movement of her brows pulled at her throbbing temple. Carefully, she probed her swollen head, wincing at the pain.

Glancing around the room, she took stock of her whereabouts. She was in Captain Reynolds's cabin, lying in his bed. . . .

Her eyes widened in shock as her thoughts came to a skidding halt. A crimson blush started at her toes and coursed its way clear to her forehead, even as she prayed her suspicion wasn't true. Gingerly she lifted the covers. Oh God, not a stitch!

"I had to remove them," Justin said from the doorway.

With round eyes, Cara snatched the blankets to her neck as she watched Justin advance into the cabin.

"Your clothes were soaked. I had no idea how long you lay out there," he tipped his head back toward the companionway, "but by the time I found you, you were chilled to the bone. You're lucky you didn't get pneumonia."

Cara's face flamed. No one other than her mother and her nanny had ever seen her completely naked, and she had only been a child then. She was a full-grown woman now and this man, this magnetic, ruggedly handsome, thrilling man had removed every bit of her clothing. Almost choking on her embarrassment, she shut her eyes.

Justin's hand cupped her chin and raised her face, but she still wouldn't lift her eyes.

"Look at me, Cara," he commanded quietly, as he sat beside her.

Hesitantly she did so.

"Be realistic. I couldn't very well have left you in wet clothes. And I didn't know how seriously you were hurt." He glanced to the bluish bruise on her shoulder peeking above the blanket. "Either way, the clothes had to come off."

She couldn't deny the logic of his words. She latched on to them as she would a lifeline, setting aside her instinctive modesty. It was that or drown in her own mortification.

"You're quite right, of course, Captain. I . . . umm . . . thank you."

Justin grinned, shaking his head in wry amusement. "If you're trying to sound unaffected, you're failing miserably."

As intended, his sting distracted her out of her modest misery. She glared at him in surprised indignation. "You're laughing at me, Captain Reynolds."

With Cara lying in his bed, beautifully naked and so close he could feel the heat of her through the bedclothes, laughter was the last thing on Justin's mind.

"I assure you, I am not laughing at you." He lifted a long curl and idly toyed with the end.

"It sounded like it."

He smiled warmly into her eyes. "It must be the knock on your head."

That earned him a shaming glance. "I am quite clear-headed."

"You weren't a few hours ago."

Cara forgot her pique. "How long have I been asleep?"

He glanced to the clock attached to the top of his desk. "Twelve hours, on and off, since I found you. You had a rough night."

He looked as though he had had a rough night, too. In growing concern, she noticed the dark stubble of a night's growth of beard that tinted his lower face, accentuating the sharp planes. The blue of his eyes was made all the more brilliant by the traces of red strain that surrounded them, while subtle lines of fatigue were dented around his mouth. Gone was the normally well-tended styling of his umber hair; in its place, a windswept swirl of spray-darkened strands. Cara mentally squirmed. While she had been asleep or unconscious, he had been fighting the horrors of the storm to save his ship. And when it was over, instead of being able to come back to his cabin to rest, he had been taking care of her. He was tired and the least she could do, she decided, was give him back his bed as quickly as possible.

"You look as though you haven't slept," she said kindly.

"I haven't."

"Don't you think you should?" she offered in gentle innocence.

The lazy play of his fingers on her curls stopped and he looked at her with serious intent. "Yes, I would like to be in this bed."

"Perhaps if you would help me then. I'm quite sore and I'm not sure of exactly the easiest way to go about this."

He gazed down at her, hunger lurking behind the sensuously lazy drop of his lids. "My fondest wish, madam, but are you in any condition?"

"Well, with your help, I think I'll manage," she said looking directly at him. "Do you mind?"

A startled speculative look joined the wolfish grin on his face. "No would be an understatement," he drawled.

"Could I have my nightgown then?" she asked awkwardly, the blush back in her face again.

Justin laid a hand against her flushed cheek. "I can understand why you might feel more comfortable with it on, but trust me, you won't need it."

A jumble of conflicting thoughts assailed her at once. Did he mean to help her back to her cabin in her present state? Not if she had anything to say about it. Perhaps he meant to wrap her in the blankets. It really would be much simpler if she had her nightgown, and much more reassuring, too.

"If you don't mind, Captain, I really would like to have my . . . I mean I would prefer it. And then I'll leave you to your own cabin."

"What?"

"I've imposed on your time and your room long enough. You need to sleep and I need to return to my own cabin."

Justin shot to his feet, glaring down at her with dangerously narrowed eyes. Abruptly he turned on his heel and stalked to the armoire. Returning, he flung one of his white shirts into her lap. "This should make you feel better," he snapped.

Caught off guard by his sudden change in mood, Cara could only stare openmouthed at Justin's retreating back. He stood rigidly before the windows, rubbing the back of his neck in a gesture Cara thought looked tired and annoyed.

Swallowing nervously, she slowly levered herself up against the brace of pillows, fighting the pain that shot out from her arm. In worried haste her hands fumbled with the shirt as she tried to put it on, but her aching body made her movements stiff and clumsy. With her lower lip caught between her teeth, she darted an anxious look at Justin's back and tried again. Her efforts were only marginally better as she managed to slip the sleeve up her arm, but without being able to shrug the garment around her, she was only half-clothed.

As much as she needed to ask Justin for help, she couldn't bring herself to do so. It was obvious she had burdened him enough already, and her pride refused to allow her to bother him further. She'd have to put the shirt on by herself and quickly.

She shut her eyes, mentally bracing herself against the pain and quickly sat up and pulled the shirt around her. Her whole body screamed in protest, robbing her of her reserve of strength. She curled into the pain with a silent moan, unable to stop herself from tipping over the edge of the bed.

Strong arms were there to catch her before she even had a chance to think about hitting the floor. She welcomed the sure, solid strength and relaxed gratefully within the comforting circle.

"You little fool," Justin's voice snarled just above her ear. With a gentleness that belied his angry words, he laid her back. "What were you trying to do, knock yourself out again?"

Had Cara not been so physically weak, had the events of the last twenty-four hours not taken their emotional toll, she could have withstood the brunt of Justin's temper. But at the moment she didn't have the stamina of mind or body to tolerate his condemnation.

Yanking her dignity, as well as his shirt, close to her breast, she gritted back the throbbing in her head and regarded him with an injured show of haughtiness that bordered on disdain.

"You have made your displeasure very apparent, Captain. I was merely trying to relieve you of your obviously unwanted duties as nursemaid."

"You don't know the extent of my displeasure," he bit out.

Unfair, Cara's mind protested. "I didn't ask you to bring me in here," she reminded him heatedly, "but you did. Now you want me to leave and when I do my best to accommodate you, you yell at me."

Frustration and fatigue riding him hard, he planted a hand on either side of her head and leaned down, bringing his face close to hers. "Would you like a lesson in how you can 'accommodate' me?"

Cara shrank back from the fierce gleam in his eyes, but glared right back from a safer distance. "I would like to go back to my cabin."

"You should have never left it in the first place! I gave you an order to remain in your cabin. What were you doing in the companionway?"

Being treated like a child did not sit well with Cara, and her chin came up indignantly. "I thought we were going to sink," she stated through set teeth.

Justin jerked upright. "If this ship were going to sink, the entire thing would have done so, including the companionway." He ground his words out in a sneering insult that made Cara gasp. "If you were one of my crew . . ."

"Well, I'm not," she blurted out, exhausted and upset enough not to be cautious with her words. "I'm one of your passengers and I've never been in the middle of the ocean, in the middle of a storm." She saw Justin's startled expression, but chose to ignore it. "There's no need to continue taking me to task, I know I made a mistake and I've paid for it."

The dark frown creasing Justin's face only fueled her anger. "Go ahead and scowl at me," she snapped, glaring right back. "I don't know why you're making me feel so awful about this. I feel badly enough as it is." Her anger was giving way to a horrible clog of emotion in her throat. "I'm sorry I left my cabin, I'm sorry I hit my head, and I'm sorry you had to bring me in here."

The pain in her head was getting worse and unconsciously her fingers kneaded her temple. She knew in a remote corner of her mind that she was losing control, but she didn't seem able to stop herself.

"I'm sorry I was frightened." Her words came out on choking sobs she fought to restrain. "I . . . I'm sorry . . . I thought I was going . . . to . . ." she gasped to get the words out through the tears and pain, ". . . to drown like my father!"

And then the dam broke. Wrenching sobs tore through her as she covered her face with both hands in abject misery.

Justin watched Cara's slim figure shake with the force of her weeping, and his scowl darkened. Angry tension chiseled into every line of his powerful body, he stalked across the cabin and without a backward glance slammed the door behind him.

The loud bang of the door only magnified Cara's distress and despair. Crying all the harder, she pressed the trailing cuff of Justin's shirt to her face, soaking the fabric, all the while heaping verbal assaults on Justin's head. He was the most insensitive, brutish barbarian she had ever met! All she had done was ask for her nightgown and he had gotten angry with her. Tears spilled unchecked. Who did he think he was, insulting her the way he had? He might be the captain, but that didn't give him the right to treat her so rudely.

When her tears were nothing more than trembling sighs, she lay with the shirt cuff pressed to her lips and stared at the closed door with red swollen eyes. Her own temper had dissolved with her crying, reduced now to a righteous miff. She wasn't ready to forgive Justin for his unkind behavior, but she did magnanimously concede that he may have had reason for being short-tempered. After all, he had suffered an exhausting, sleepless night and her presence was just aggravating him. She had no idea when he was going to return, but she knew that when he did, she was not going to be there as a target for his foul temper.

Pushing back the covers, she eased her legs over the side of the bunk, but the motion proved too much for her. She moaned and gripped her head between both hands, sitting motionless as she waited for the pain to subside. On a steadying breath she rose and made her way across the room, vowing with every step that the captain would find no more fault with her.

By the time she entered her own cabin, her face was

drawn and colorless. Slumped against the door, the room seemed the size of a ballroom, the bunk miles and miles away. With a supreme effort, she pushed away from the door and, through the force of willpower alone, walked the last few steps to her bed.

Whatever Justin expected to find when he returned an hour later, it sure as hell was not an empty cabin. Having worked off his anger on deck, he was now ready to deal calmly with Miss Fairchild. However, awaiting him were only rumpled covers and dented pillows.

Cursing, he swung around to the side table, poured himself a liberal dose of bourbon, then nursed it distractedly from the chair behind his desk.

Damn, but he was tired. He had sailed the *Wind Dancer* through countless storms, but he couldn't remember one that had matched this one. Though short in duration, it made up in sheer strength what it lacked in length. Luckily, the ship had held up under the strain with only a few damages to be repaired. Sipping his drink, he smiled, feeling a satisfaction he felt only when he bested a dangerous situation.

His gaze sliced to his bed and he turned his thoughts to Cara. So, she had a temper, did she? It was of little consequence, as long as she didn't vent it with any frequency. He never could abide shrewish behavior in his women, no matter how beautiful or desirable they were, and he wasn't about to put up with it from Cara. It was annoying enough that she behaved like a damned virgin.

He wasn't accustomed to dealing with innocents. The women in his life knew their way around the intricacies of seduction. He supposed that was why, to his experienced ear, Cara's suggestion to sleep had meant an invitation to make love. With a rueful grin he decided he was going to have to get used to her naivete. But it would be worth it. The perfection of the sweetly seductive curves he had found beneath her clothing, when he had undressed her, was astonishing.

His mind skimmed back over the heated words she had hurled at him. She had been frightened by the storm. He took a good, long swallow of his drink as he admitted she had had every right to be. He knew seasoned sailors who had fallen apart under such stress. But that didn't explain why she had left her cabin.

The tightening in his stomach reminded him of the surge of apprehension he had felt when he had discovered her still body slumped against his door. Judging by her injuries, she had been lucky she hadn't broken her neck. As it was, she was going to have a headache that would keep her immobile for the next few days.

He looked to the door. How in the hell had she walked out of this room when she could barely sit up? Surging to his feet, he left his cabin.

Cara answered the knock on her door with a call from her bunk. Nervous shivers ran down her spine at the sight of Justin's unreadable face. She knew they were going to have to face each other sooner or later, but in her heart she wished it could be some other time. She felt at a distinct disadvantage, lying in bed, still wearing his shirt, with a headache that made thinking difficult. Defensively, her chin came up and she met his serious gaze with one of her own, one that was neither reticent nor aggressive, but simply watchful.

"Captain," she said levelly.

Justin saw the unshakable resolve in her green eyes, and a smile twitched at his lips at her spirit. "You have no business galavanting all over this ship."

"I was not 'galavanting' about this ship. I just walked down the hall."

"And barely made it," he said dryly, coming to stand beside her. "You're as white as the sheets."

"Have you come in here to take up where you left off?"

"And where was that?"

"With your yelling at me."

He sat next to her, knees spread, and leaned a forearm on one long thigh. "If I recall, you did your share of yelling," he reminded her with an I-told-you-so smile. "And most effectively."

She looked askance, unbending a touch at his smile. "I didn't like being compared to your sailors."

"Words spoken in the heat of the moment." He shrugged casually. "The comparison was unjust."

"Thank you."

"To my men."

At Cara's indignant expression, he laughed richly. "They're less of a problem. But cheer up, Cara, if all my problems were as delightful as you, I wouldn't have a care in the world."

Cara didn't know whether to be outraged or flattered, but either way, she couldn't keep from smiling. It was obvious he had come to make amends for his earlier behavior, although he had yet to come right out and apologize. Somehow she doubted he would, and she sensed that this was as close to 'I'm sorry' as he was going to get.

"Well, I forgive you," she declared with capricious smugness, 'delightful' still singing through her veins.

For what! Justin's startled expression asked as eloquently as any words could have.

"For losing your temper with me," she answered his look. "I know you really didn't mean to, as you were very tired. And I apologize for railing at you." She spoke the words lightly, but she truly meant them. She did not want to be at odds with this man. Her expression softened, and the look she turned to Justin pulled at his conscience.

Unflinching, she returned his probing gaze, steadfastly watching each flicker of emotion that crossed his face. Her heart thumped in anxious expectancy, waiting for him to meet her halfway in their contest of wills.

His hand reached out, and with infinite tenderness, Justin traced a finger along her delicate jaw. "You really are delightful," he murmured without a trace of teasing.

The space between them became charged, as sweet joy filled Cara's heart, replacing the hurt that had been there earlier.

"Get some rest," he ordered gently. "I don't want you up again for at least two days."

She nodded against his fingers that lingered at her cheek.

He left without another word or look. For long moments afterward, Cara lay awake, unable to shake the feeling that something had changed between them.

She slept peacefully for the remainder of the afternoon. When she woke, dusk was neutralizing the colors of her cabin into shades of gray. The rest had worked wonders. While it hurt to touch her head, the grogginess that had plagued her all day was gone. Her arm and shoulder were still sore, but she expected only time would heal that.

Without warning, her door swung open, admitting a soft yellow light from the companionway and a burly man she had never seen before.

"So, you're our damsel in distress," his loud voice boomed around the room.

Cara's eyes were huge with wonder as the stocky figure came forward. He stopped by her feet, tray in hand, and openly returned her regard with discerning eyes. Without giving her a chance to speak, he placed the heavily laden tray on her lap, then turned to light the lantern.

Cara had no idea who this bear of a man was, but oddly, she didn't feel at all threatened by his presence. He stood tall and barrel-chested, with legs slightly bowed. His large face was rugged, tiny lines radiating from the corners of his big, round eyes, and his skin had the look of old, worn leather.

As she studied him, it seemed that everything about the man was overly large. Even his bizarre clothing looked huge. A wide-paned plaid of green, white, and black hung around his legs to form loose-fitting trousers of emormous proportions. His shirt, made up of a different plaid, colored in yellow and red, was covered by a too-long leather waistcoat whose edges along front plackets and sleeve holes were rubbed free of any color.

The stranger dragged the room's only chair to Cara's bedside and thumped the piece down. With the back facing him, he straddled the seat, setting his great fists on his wide-spread legs.

"Now, captain says you took a knock on the head." His deep brown eyes scanned the side of her forehead.

"Yes, that's right," she replied in bewildered amusement.

"He says you got the dizzies."

"Well, yes." She was trying to keep the laughter from her voice. Somehow she couldn't imagine Captain Reynolds using that phrase to describe her condition. "I do get dizzy when I move too quickly."

The animated face screwed itself up, drawing the bushy strawberry blond brows together into one continuous line. "Know your name?" The voice retained all of its original volume.

"Yes, Cara Fairchild."

"How 'bout your mum's name?"

Cara could only surmise that he was a doctor, of what caliber she wouldn't guess, but that would explain the questions. "Elizabeth Lacey."

The man scrubbed a hand across his mouth and chin, giving a satisfied nod. "Know where you are?"

"Yes," she answered politely, and then because she just couldn't resist, asked, "Do you?"

He sat back, squinting out of the corners of his eyes at Cara's teasing grin. There was silence for several seconds, then he threw back his head and roared with laughter.

"You're a cute one, you are." He chuckled.

"Thank you, sir," she acknowledged graciously.

"Ach, none of that 'sir' business for me. You save that for the captain or for Mr. Collinsworth. No, you call me Percy, just like everyone else. Percy Pettingill."

"How do you do, Percy? Are you a doctor?" she felt compelled to ask.

"Not a learned one, but I know what there is to know." His tone turned serious as his chest puffed up proudly. "I took a look at you while you was out. No broken bones, but it's going to feel like it." Giving Cara no time for any embarrassment, his chin jutted out in the direction of her head. "And this bump to your head scrambled your brains, it did. Doctor would have a word for it, but it all washes down to the same thing, a mighty sore head. Best thing is to stay right where you are."

"I don't seem to have much choice," she informed him. "Captain Reynolds has ordered me to stay in bed for two days."

"Listen to the man, knows what he's talking about, he does." A throaty, rumbling laugh erupted. "He's taken a good whack or two. Three years ago in Barbados, why . . ." Percy caught himself, realizing in midsentence that he was about to relate a tale unsuitable for a lady's ears. He covered his slip with a cough and chose another course. "Well, you do like the captain says." He slapped a hand against a thick thigh and stood. "Now, eat up if you can, I made that special for you."

Cara looked to the delicious food before her. "You cooked this?"

"That and everything else you been eating since you come aboard. I'll take it real personal if you don't do justice." He sounded gruff, but at the door he turned and winked broadly. "Be back for the tray later," he said and then closed the door with a bang.

The meal was wonderful, but there was little chance that Cara could finish it. Percy Pettingill had served up portions that were better suited to himself. The doctor-cook came by as promised to collect the dishes and reissue his medical advice about staying in bed. Cara agreed to do as she was told and tried to settle in for the night. But try as she may, sleep eluded her. She turned from side to side in an effort to get comfortable, but nothing worked. By eleven o'clock she gave up, telling herself that she had slept most of the day away and she simply wasn't tired.

What she needed was a change of scenery. Being confined to the tiny cabin was boring, but she wasn't about to disobey Captain Reynolds's order. And she really didn't think she could go far. But she could make it as far as the door, just for a quick look down the companionway.

Carefully, she rose and opened the door enough to peek her head into the hall. It was empty and silent. No lights slipped out from underneath any of the doors. She was just about to resign herself to the fact that she was going to be the only one awake, when Captain Reynolds entered the companionway from the deck.

Inwardly, Cara groaned. Was she forever going to be caught defying his orders? In her own mind she had good reason to be up, but she didn't think he'd see it her way. She sighed and cast a guilty look at him.

"What are you doing?" he asked.

She chose not to answer his question without asking one of her own first. "What kind of a mood are you in?"

Justin leaned against the doorjamb with a knowing look. "Why?" he asked suspiciously.

"Because if you're in a good mood, I can tell you the truth. If you're not, I'll have to be very diplomatic with my answer."

Justin growled low in his throat and opened the door. "Get back into that bed," he commanded as he followed her back to the bunk.

"This is getting to be a habit," he said once she was all tucked in.

"What? My disobeying your orders or my lying in bed with you sitting next to me again?"

"Both," he said aloud then amended silently, *but I could get used to the last one.*

She looked at him shyly. "Are you going to yell at me?"

"Would it make a difference?" he questioned exasperatedly.

"Yes, I don't want you to be angry with me," she answered, gazing at him cautiously. In the subdued lantern light, the hard planes of his tanned face appeared softened, the blue of his eyes mellow. Cara's eyes traveled the strong, lean edge of his jaw to his firm lips, and she was helpless to keep her pulse from racing. The fine white linen shirt he wore enhanced the powerful lines of his chest and arms, complimenting the long, muscular length of his legs. Once again, she was struck by the sheer male potency of the man and his innate ability to make her acutely aware of him.

Her response brought a smile to his face. "I'm in a very good mood."

A relieved sigh preceded Cara's words. "I was tired of lying in bed. I couldn't sleep, though not for lack of trying, I assure you. Just don't tell Percy."

Leaning up on her elbows, she stiffly tried to push herself up into a sitting position. Instantly, Justin slipped his arms around her and gently eased her higher against the pillows.

"Better?" he asked.

The warm, embracing ride, with her hands lightly resting on the breadth of his shoulders, was disappointingly short. It was, however, long enough to shuffle her thoughts about.

"Better?" he repeated, giving her a discerning look.

"Yes, much." She forced herself to concentrate, but it wasn't easy with his leg pressed so disturbingly close to her hip. His ability to frazzle her nerves was disconcerting and his nearness only intensified the effect. The traitorous blush that colored her face gave away her flustered wits.

"So you've met Percy," he said, not missing her heightened color. He could feel the first pulse of desire tighten his insides and he let his gaze drift from one fine feature to another.

"Yes, he was here earlier."

"What did the old tyrant have to say?"

She repeated Percy's diagnosis.

Justin chuckled in private remembrance. "Ah yes, 'scrambled brains.' "

Cara eyed him saucily. "I see you're familiar with that malady. Percy did mention that."

"Did he?" His eyes dropped to her sensuously smiling lips.

"Mmm." She rolled her eyes in merriment. "That and something about Barbados, but he didn't elaborate."

"A good thing," he murmured distractedly.

Something about his tone and the look in his eyes brought Cara up short. Unnamed, it nevertheless sobered her with its intensity and she nervously looked away.

"Do you still have the dizzies?" he whispered, his words a velvet caress.

"No," she said weakly.

"That's a good sign." The seductive drawl of his voice melted her nerves.

"I wish you wouldn't do this," she said hastily.

"I haven't done anything."

But you're going to, her mind screamed.

You're right, his answered.

Cupping her chin, he raised her face and gazed into her wide emerald eyes. She was a rare combination of strong-willed determination and artless seduction, all enticingly packaged in sensuous curves and vivid beauty.

The whisper touch of his fingers along her jaw, the hooded, smoldering look in his eyes held Cara captive. She felt a languid warmth spread out from her stomach and flow through her veins. She sat motionless, barely breathing, any thought of protest blown away like ashes.

Closing the space between them, Justin lowered his head, and his lips took hers in a tender assault. His mouth slanted insistently over hers with hungry thoroughness as his hand slid back through her lustrous mane of hair, and his other arm circled her back, pulling her tightly to his chest. With devastating expertise, he kissed her, drawing Cara into their heady exchange until she was a willing participant. His tongue ran along her lips, teasing, persuading, demanding entrance, until she instinctively understood his need and parted her lips beneath his. Mindless with drugging sensations, her hands slipped up to his chest, unconsciously molding her pliant softness to his unyielding strength. Craving passion ripped through Justin's body at Cara's response, and he tightened his arms around her. His tongue plunged into the warm recesses of her mouth while her hand clung to his shirt for support. He could feel the hardened buds of her nipples boring into his chest, and his kiss deepened, wringing from Cara a soft moan of desire. The sound filled his mouth, and his hand traveled around her ribs, upward to her breasts.

Cara jumped and weakly pushed against the very chest she had been holding on to, tearing her mouth free. Shocked by the much-too-intimate touch of his hand, she pulled back in his arms.

Justin sat back, encircling her waist with his hands and gazed at her exquisitely flushed face, stunned by the force of the desire she so effortlessly aroused in him. For a moment he watched the rapid rise and fall of her breasts before lifting his eyes to see the lingering traces of passion combined with innocent confusion written all over her face. In agonizing regret he realized he had pushed her too far in what was obviously her first sensual encounter. Methodically breathing to slow his racing pulse, he fought down the demands of his body, cautioning himself to pursue her in gentle stages.

Cara pressed trembling fingers to lips that still felt pleasantly bruised. Never in her wildest dreams did she ever imagine that men and women kissed in such a manner. Her stomach wrenched just thinking about how his tongue had caressed hers and she lifted awe-filled eyes to his.

"Are you all right?" he asked, seeing her bewildered look.

Was she all right? Would she ever be the same? "I don't know," she whispered.

Unable to keep from touching her in some way, he lifted a long reddish curl, twirling the end around his thumb. When he spoke, his voice was a lazy, seductive drawl. "Haven't you ever been kissed before?"

"No," she said shakily, thinking that the kiss Tommie Driscoll had smeared over her lips and chin when they were both twelve couldn't possibly qualify.

A week ago her answer would have been a nuisance to Justin, but now, surprisingly, it filled him with a strange possessiveness. "Did you like it?" He knew from the spontaneous ardor with which she had reacted that she had, but the elemental maleness in him wanted to hear her admit it.

The rosy blush on Cara's face bloomed flaming scarlet, but she saw the wicked gleam in his eyes and refused to admit her embarrassment in front of his blatancy. "Yes, I enjoyed . . . I mean, it was quite . . . nice . . ." Her bravado was short-lived, and her words dwindled to a sigh. She raised a pathetic face to his. "It was most improper."

Justin's expression turned pained. "Who told you such

a thing?" he asked derisively. "Some dried-up old prune of an aunt?"

Cara burst out laughing. He had just described Miss Peele, her former governess, who had lectured her long and hard on correct behavior. The humor of the moment eased her tension, and some of her easy charm returned. "No, wrinkled, shriveled Agnes Peele. She was my governess until I was thirteen and she was very succinct on such matters."

"Oh, was she," he said mockingly, liking the dimple in Cara's cheek.

"Yes, she was."

"What else did Miss Peele have to say?"

Her chin tilted upward in imitation of Agnes's no-nonsense attitude. "She said that proper young ladies were kissed only by their husbands."

Justin mentally strangled Agnes Peele. He did not want Cara harboring such inconvenient notions, and his hand caught her chin, drawing her face toward his.

"It is obvious that your Miss Peele was never alone with a man, much less truly kissed by one." His face was so close, Cara could feel the breath of his words caress her lips, while his blue eyes drilled into hers. "Men and women, regardless of their marital status, have been kissing, and a great deal more, since the beginning of time."

Wide-eyed, holding her breath, Cara thought for one frightening moment that she was going to discover exactly what 'a great deal more' was all about. But Justin dropped his hand and stood back, towering over her.

"I will see you tomorrow. Now, get some sleep." At the door he turned back for one final look, then left.

Without moving, sitting perfectly still, Cara watched Justin leave, then continued to stare at the door. Almost afraid to move for fear of breaking the spell he had cast on her, she basked in the glorious happiness she felt. His kisses had been like nothing else she had ever experienced, or was ever likely to. The tingling sensations were still with her, filling her with a joyously luscious warmth.

The stern visage of Agnes Peele elbowed its way into

Cara's conscience, repeating the same words its owner had preached nearly seven years earlier. The behavior of women of sound upbringing must always be beyond reproach. No woman of good breeding would allow a man to take liberties.

But Captain Reynolds said men and women have always kissed, her conscience explained.

You should have stopped him.

I wasn't able to.

Then you shouldn't have enjoyed it.

No! her heart interceded. The feelings he aroused in her were too wondrous to be wrong. They made her happy. He made her happy, happier than she had ever been in her entire life.

Chapter Four

"You shouldn't be up!"

"I will not eat another meal lying in that bed."

"You are a stubborn little monkey, Miss Cara!"

"And you are a bullying tyrant, Percy Pettingill."

The two stood nose to chest in their spirited discussion. Cara, wrapped in nightgown and blanket, glared up at Percy, who looked down at her in superb annoyance.

"I ate dinner there last night, breakfast there this morning, and I don't like to sleep in crumbs."

"What are you two arguing about?"

Percy and Cara turned to see Justin standing casually in the open doorway.

Before Percy had a chance to say anything, Cara tugged at the blanket and explained. "I wish to eat here at my table," she said with a regal lift of her chin, and glanced at the small table in her cabin.

Percy gave her an accusing glare, but pleaded his case to Justin. "It's too soon for her to be up."

"I am feeling much better," she stated emphatically.

Jamming his huge fists on his hips, Percy turned back to Cara. "Which is why you shouldn't overdo."

"Enough you two," Justin ordered on a laugh.

Percy glanced from Justin's grinning face to Cara's set features. With a sigh he realized he had just met a stone wall in Cara's determination, and that he could expect no help from the captain. "Make your crumbs at the table then, but it's back to the bunk as soon as you're done."

Justin strolled into Cara's cabin with long-legged grace. "I'll watch over her."

Percy contemplated this for a moment and seemed mollified by this compromise. He grunted his approval, then added, "Just make sure she eats."

Cara smiled up with angelic sweetness. "Percy, your cooking is so delicious, how could I not help but eat up every morsel?"

Percy's silence and a shrewd squint told Cara what he thought of her nonsense and she had to laugh.

"I promise to eat and I promise not to tax myself," she said, sincerely touched by his concern.

"See that you do," he warned with a wag of a finger beneath her pert nose. Feeling his reign of supremacy as doctor hadn't been too badly jeopardized, he left Cara and Justin, slamming the door on his way out.

There was silence for a moment, then Cara turned to Justin. He was standing close, dressed in clothes meant obviously for work. His charcoal gray pants ran the distance between lean waist and black calf-length boots. The bulky cream-colored shirt he wore seemed to exaggerate the contours of wide shoulders and muscled chest. Without meaning to, she let her eyes capture and savor the long length that defined his body and the crystalline blue and warm tans that fashioned his face.

Suddenly, she felt awkward, standing there beneath his intense gaze, and self-consciously, she pulled the blanket more snugly about her. "Thank you for rescuing me." Her words sounded strained.

"I seem to be doing that lately," he remarked smoothly.

Swathed in her cocoon of wool, she appeared more fragile than ever. Somehow that morning she had managed to tame her fall of hair into a single, sedate braid. With only errant wisps of auburn curls framing her face, the purple-and-yellow bruise across her forehead stood out starkly against the white of her skin. He had thought about that skin, and a great deal more, last night as he had lain in bed, his body taut. He was unaccustomed to denial, and in the aftermath of Cara's short-lived passion, his senses had been keenly honed with expectancy. Lying on his bunk, he had absorbed the rush of desire she had powerlessly evoked, had clamped down on it, molded it until it was a mellow glow that left him incredibly stimulated. Now, in the brilliance of day, he gazed down on her bent head and appreciated the subtle, if not frustrating, nuances of anticipation.

"Are you well enough to be up?" His sensual musings deepened the timbre of his voice.

"Yes. I was just so tired of lying there," she explained, then added with a slight grin, "and Percy can be very stubborn."

Justin's brows arched in dubious humor. "What does that make you?"

She met his look. "Determined."

Grinning at her adorable insolence, he gave her no warning, scooped her up in his arms, and strode over to the table where her meal was set on a tray.

"Captain Reynolds, what are you doing?" she asked incredulously. Riding snugly against the firm wall of his chest brought a tightening to her stomach. She took a quick glance at his face, so close to hers, and swallowed hard.

"I would have thought that was obvious," he said, standing by the chair. "If you have to ask, then maybe Percy was right and you do belong back in bed." He turned toward the bunk.

"Don't be obtuse, Captain," she chided, trying unsuccessfully to sound stern. She had no defense against the feel of his arms about her or the warmth in his eyes, and her words came out as a gentle admonishment. "You know perfectly well what I mean. I am capable of walking."

The line of his lips stretched in wry amusement as he placed her carefully in the chair. "You must be making some progress if you can stand your own against Percy."

She settled herself, trying to rearrange the blanket in a more modest drape. With stiff muscles she tugged and pulled and, within a matter of moments, had drained the reserve of her strength.

Justin watched her work with her woolen cover and saw the wince that tightened her features. "Still sore?"

She sent a tired glance heavenward, her exasperation clearly evident. Closing her eyes, she heaved a sigh and pulled in the loose strands of her frayed nerves. What was the matter with her? One minute she was fine and the next, she was on the verge of tears. She hurt, but somehow she knew that the cause of her lack of composure went beyond that.

"I seem to be short on patience, Captain," she apologized, opening her eyes to the real source of her disquietude.

"It's to be expected," he reassured her. "You more than likely won't be your charming self for several more days." He came around behind her and lifted her heavy braid over her left shoulder. "Perhaps I can help."

The warm touch of his fingers on the nape of her neck sent Cara's back into a straight, vertical line. "Relax, Cara," he coaxed quietly, "this will ease some of the stiffness."

Cara's instinct was to panic, as fragments of ingrained conventional proprieties assailed her. "I . . . I don't think I'll be able to eat with you doing that."

"Yes, you can. Trust me."

The shivers that curled up her scalp and down her spine were delicious. With gentle pressure, he worked the ache from her muscles and soothed her tension. His fingers never strayed from her neck or shoulders, and soon Cara gave herself over to his tender ministrations.

"Where did you learn to do this?" she asked languorously, carefully lifting her fork for a bite of lamb.

Justin carefully massaged the delicate curve behind an ear. "From an old Indian in Virginia."

"An Indian?"

"Yes, a pilot of sorts, long dead now. He'd help guide us through the shoals whenever we made port in Norfolk."

Cara paused in her eating. She'd read ghastly accounts about the natives of America. "Are there still Indians there?"

Justin shrugged casually. "None to worry about. Most have gone south or west. The local watermen are about the only nuisance there these days."

She turned her head to glance up over her shoulder. "Who are the watermen?"

He cupped her chin with long fingers and eased her head back around. "The local fishermen. They rake their clams, harvest their crabs, pull in their fish, and hold a grudge forever."

Cara tipped her head to the left as his fingers concentrated on her neck. "I sense a story here, Captain."

"Not a particularly entertaining one. A few years back, the people in Virginia were upset because a British ship, the *Leopard,* attacked an American ship, the *Chesapeake*. Finish the beans," he reminded her when she'd stopped eating to listen. "It was a minor incident actually, but some of the watermen won't let it rest." Not wishing to interrupt their cozy sojourn with worrisome matters, he didn't tell her that most Americans, particularly those in Virginia, had been in a fury over the British attack. He refrained from mentioning that the *Chesapeake* affair was just one of many serious issues that threatened trouble between the two countries.

"Why did our ship attack theirs?" she asked tranquilly, becoming more and more relaxed with each passing minute.

Justin peered at her pleasantly languid face and matched the tone of his voice to her expression. "The *Chesapeake* was carrying some of our own sailors and we needed them back in order to fight that little French mongrel of illegitimate parentage. Tip your head down."

Smiling at his description of Napoléon, Cara closed her

eyes and tucked, her chin. "Was an attack necessary? Couldn't we have just asked that our men be returned?"

"Our consul in Norfolk did just that, but the commander of the navy yard there, a Captain Decatur, flatly refused the request. The man even went so far as to declare that the four men were actually Americans we had impressed into our service."

"What happened?"

"When the *Chesapeake* put to sea, the *Leopard* objected by way of several broadsides. The *Chesapeake* lowered her colors, and we retrieved our men. Unfortunately in the process, several Americans were killed."

The loss of lives, regardless of the persons' nationalities, pulled at Cara's heart. "And that's why these watermen in Virginia are still angry?" she asked with just enough sympathy to prick Justin's very British sensibilities.

"Cara," he remarked smoothly, careful to temper his words. "You needn't feel sorry. The Americans had their revenge several months ago when they attacked one of our ships, the *Little Belt*. We lost eleven men."

Cara reflected on the situation for a few moments. "Do Americans dislike all the British?"

"We're not thought of very kindly by a great many, but we're tolerated, primarily for commerce reasons."

"That would include these watermen, wouldn't it? Don't they need the trade of goods like everyone else?"

Justin grinned ruefully. "If you ever have the dubious pleasure of meeting any of these tradesmen, you will realize immediately that they are a very secluded, self-sufficient group."

"What do they do that is so bothersome?"

Shaking his head, Justin berated himself for having even mentioned the damn fishermen in the first place. But who would have thought she would be such an inquisitive little thing? Again he censured his answer. "They remind everyone that they're Americans."

"And that makes them a nuisance?"

"Sometimes." The watermen's activities of instigating unrest and fueling the Virginians' anger with Britain was the last thing Justin wanted to discuss. The pulse beating at the base of Cara's neck was the important issue and he studied the sweet flesh with extreme interest.

"Have they ever bothered you?"

"No."

Before Cara could question why not, she took a sharp breath and beneath his fingers, Justin felt the reflexive jerk of her muscles when he applied too much pressure. "That sore?" His hand came to rest on the curve of her shoulder where it sloped to her arm. Through the worn fabric of her nightgown, Cara could feel the heat of his hand, and it shocked her. Somewhere during the course of the soothing massage, the blanket had slipped down to the small of her back. With one hand, a hand that had been mesmerized into negligence, she held the cover loosely over her breasts. She had been too lulled by the feel of his fingers and the sound of his voice to take notice. But now she was excruciatingly aware of her state of undress and the heat of not only his hands, but also his body close behind her, penetrating the thin flannel of her nightgown.

She was instantly, overwhelmingly aware of him. In that moment, her mind recalled his lips on hers the night before, his hand against her breast, and her pulse began a mad dash through her veins.

"I'll . . ." She had to swallow past the sudden tightness in her throat. "I'll be fine."

He watched her draw the blanket higher. "How does this feel here?" he asked, letting his fingers slowly curve around the nape of her neck and rest on the delicate line of her collarbone.

"Fine."

"And here?" His other hand skimmed like the barest whisper down her other arm, stopping at her waist.

"Fine," was all she could manage. But she wasn't, not at all. Her skin felt sensitized and every nerve in the path of his questing fingers was quivering.

"And this?" he murmured thickly, just before he pressed his lips to the base of her neck.

Her insides melted. Fluid heat emanated from that spot

below her ear, where his lips were gently pressed, and liquified her entire body. The luscious sensation was drugging, and closing her eyes, she whispered a throaty sigh. Unconsciously, her head arched back and Justin took full advantage of the irresistible offering.

His lips and tongue tasted the column of her neck, moving upward to catch the lobe of her ear between his teeth. The jolt of pleasure Cara felt shot through her heart, making it pound in a rapid beat, raced down to her stomach, twisting it in a wrenching squeeze, then arrived at the pit of her belly, leaving her with a near painful throb.

For the briefest moment, his lips left her and she felt an unexplainable loss. Opening her eyes in search of him, she found his face directly in front of hers. Their breaths met, mingled, then became one as Justin kissed her in demanding, searing passion. She tasted like honey-laced tea, and eagerly his tongue plunged into her mouth. Cara returned his kiss, timidly at first, but with his mouth covering hers to create a riot of sensations, she gave into her desire and ardently returned the sensual play.

Justin gloried in her unabashed response. The feel of her lips, the pleasure she created, took him to the edge of his control. It wasn't his intent to frighten her as he had the night before, but he was loath to stop. His lips slanted across hers, drinking of their sweetness and building a yearning fire within them both. Cautiously, his hand slipped up to the topmost bow in a series that held the front of the gown closed. One sure tug and the fabric parted. His tongue teased its way along her jaw to her neck, while his fingers unerringly found the second bow. The loops and knot fell free.

Cool air touching her heated, bare skin intruded on Cara's bliss. And as unwanted as the intrusion was, she couldn't ignore the wave of uncertainty that accompanied it. Her eyes flew open a fraction of a second before her body tensed.

Justin felt her reaction instantly and lowered himself to his haunches in front of her. One hand at her waist, the other raised to her lips, a finger caressingly silenced her shy protest.

"Ssshhh, love." His voice was a ragged whisper. "Don't be frightened."

Cara swallowed convulsively as she felt herself drawn into the blue depths of his eyes.

"Do you know how beautiful you are? I ache to hold you, to kiss you, to touch you as no man ever has." He matched his actions to his words and brought his lips to hers in a quick, but very thorough kiss.

"Captain? . . ."

"We are beyond that," he cut her off. "Say my name."

Absurdly, the word stuck in her throat. To use his given name was to cross over into a private realm.

"Say it."

Her eyes searching his, the name came out on a sigh and a gentle smile. "Justin."

The smile he returned was darkly sensuous and devastating in its male potency. "That wasn't so hard, was it?" His gaze dropped to her cheek. "I like this." A long finger caressed the dimple that edged her mouth. "And this." The finger traced the contours of her lower lip. But when his eyes raised to her forehead, his expression turned serious.

The nightgown's third bow slipped apart at his touch. Heart thumping wildly, Cara helplessly watched as he parted the front and painstakingly eased the fabric aside, baring the swollen bruise on her right shoulder. She could only wait, his very intensity immobilizing her. The silence lengthened, and then he leaned forward and it was all Cara could do to keep the tears from her eyes. With infinite care he kissed the bluish mark marring the perfection of her skin.

Tenderness, lovely and profound, filled Cara's heart and she sat speechless, dazed by the emotions within her. Even when Justin drew the front of her gown closed, she could only sit in mute wonder.

Slipping an arm behind her back and the other beneath her knees, he gently lifted her from the chair, the absence of the blanket quite intentional. He made no move to either set her down or carry her back to the bunk, but stood silently, gazing intently down at her. His eyes roved her face, sliding over her forehead to her nose, running along her heated cheek to linger on her parted lips, then upward to fix on her wide green eyes.

Cara felt the touch of his gaze like the butterfly's caress it was meant to be and she was powerless to look away. In her heart she had no desire to do so. Timidly her hand slid up his chest, her fingers coming to rest on the edge of his jaw.

Slowly, ever so slowly, Justin lowered his head and pressed his lips to hers for one last kiss, the gentlest of kisses. The contact was the barest hint of lips touching lip and then it was gone.

"Come," he whispered, "let me put you back to bed."

Cara recovered with remarkable speed. She remained in bed for the full three days as ordered, rising only for brief spells to look out her window or to take a meal at the table. Restlessness tempted her, but she didn't even consider trying to leave her cabin. Percy Pettingill proved to be the tyrant she had called him. He showed up routinely with her meals and then shamelessly took advantage of the situation by issuing doses of medical dictates that brooked no argument. But despite his gruff words and overbearing attitude, Cara found she liked Percy. It was easy to see that the man had a tender heart that was as large in its capacity for compassion as the man himself.

In the quiet solitude of her cabin she had hours in which to think about Justin. In fact, she could think of little else. Her mind replayed their moments of shared intimacy, recalling all the swirling rush of emotions she had felt while in his arms. Just the thought of his lips on hers, his warm tongue caressing hers, brought the heat to her face. When her thoughts strayed to that moment when he had kissed her bare shoulder, she closed her eyes, moaning in a mixture of confusion and excitement.

Justin did not return to her cabin again and Cara was both relieved and disappointed. In his arms she had experienced new and wondrous, but overwhelming feelings. She was glad to have time to try and sort through her bewildered emotions, but she couldn't deny the empty yearning she felt at his absence.

On Percy's approval, Cara was allowed visitors. Phillip was most solicitous, practically falling over himself in his concern. He called several times during her confinement and for his company, Cara was most grateful.

Charles stopped by each afternoon for tea. Cara truly looked forward to their quiet afternoons together. She sensed a loneliness within her newfound friend and was glad that she could bring him a degree of happiness, especially since she suspected he received little from his wife.

Regina remained something of a mystery to Cara. She admitted to herself that she did not like the woman. From the few things Charles had actually mentioned about her, and from what little experience Cara had had with her, it was apparent that Regina was not an easy person to get along with.

Unfortunately, during Cara's third afternoon of recuperation, she realized just how unpleasant Regina could be when the latter decided to pay a visit. Fully expecting Charles for tea, Cara was taken aback when Regina entered the cabin instead of her husband.

"Regina," Cara said, silently wishing she hadn't been so quick to call out an answer to the knock at her door.

Leaning against the closed portal, Regina let her gaze wander over the tiny compartment in an obvious inspection. Only after she had seen her fill did she actually look to Cara. With ill-concealed humor, her dark eyes widened.

"You certainly are a pitiful sight."

Cara hadn't expected condolences, but Regina's remark fell short of even polite conversation. Self-consciously, Cara started to draw the covers up to her shoulders, but caught herself and determinedly raised her chin.

"I'm afraid I had a little accident."

"So I heard," Regina replied offhandedly, gazing about again. "How do you manage in this closet?" she asked, her voice a condescending purr.

The tone was enough to prick Cara's ire. Nonetheless, she answered in a civil manner. "I survive."

Wandering casually to the window, Regina replied over her shoulder, "Well, I imagine it's all a matter of what one is used to."

Cara took the brunt of the insult and gritted her teeth. From her position propped against the pillows, she had to glance back over her shoulder in order to see Regina. Somehow, Cara figured the woman wanted it that way. "I am glad, for Charles's sake, that he could afford better accommodations."

Regina flicked a cool glance at Cara, before turning back to the window's view. "Yes, my husband is quite wealthy. It's just one of the benefits of being married to him, I suppose." Turning abruptly, she sauntered across the cabin, trailing a finger along the small table. "Oh, I'd forgotten. You wouldn't know about either wealth or marriage, would you?"

There was no doubt in Cara's mind that Regina was here for the sole purpose of antagonizing her. Irritated, she pushed herself into an upright sitting position, ignoring the slight wave of dizziness that assailed her.

"No, Regina, I don't," she stated emphatically, not even trying to hide her annoyance.

Regina's brows quirked upward at Cara's tone. "My, my, but your little bump on the head seems to have put you in a snit."

"Percy says it is to be expected."

"Ah, yes, that big cook." Regina smiled. "He does fancy himself a doctor." Without warning, the smile dropped off her face and her look became nasty. "He's been dancing attendance on you, as has every other man on board this ship."

Cara was shocked by the resentment that pulled Regina's face into tight, unforgiving lines. Warily, she regarded the other woman. "That isn't so," she said carefully.

"Oh, isn't it? I've seen them coming and going, my husband included." She scoffed and dragged her gaze over Cara's nightgowned figure. "What they see, I'll never know. But it doesn't really matter. There isn't much of any real significance that you can accomplish in your condition, especially with Captain Reynolds."

At the mention of Justin, Cara's eyes rounded and Regina was quick to jump on the unspoken disclosure. "Have I struck a nerve there?" she laughed coldly. "What a pity you're confined here while he goes about his business. But don't worry. He isn't lacking for company."

Any response Cara might have made was forestalled by a tapping at her door. Grateful for the interruption of the galling discussion, Cara called for the visitor to enter.

Charles stepped into the cabin and immediately stopped short at the sight of his wife. Smiling, he said, "I didn't know you were planning on paying a call, Regina. Had I known, I could have made arrangements for us all to have tea together."

With an angelic smile fixed on her lips, Regina turned to her husband. "That's quite all right, Charles. Cara and I were just having a chat. I was telling her that she doesn't look at all the thing, yet. She shouldn't try and get up too soon."

Peering at Cara in concern, Charles searched for signs of a relapse. She did appear pale and there was a certain tension about her lips. Knowingly, he turned back to Regina, his gaze assessing. "Perhaps your chat tired Cara out."

"I'm sure you're right," Regina agreed, wanting only to be gone now that Charles had arrived. "And I don't think she needs a room full of people, either." Stepping to the door, she gave her husband a sweet smile. "Why don't you stay and keep her company and I'll be on my way. Take care, Cara."

Before either Charles or Cara could offer a comment, Regina took her leave. In the wake of her abrupt departure, a heavy silence lingered.

"Did she upset you?" Charles asked quietly.

Cara's eyes snapped to Charles. His face was etched with worry and regret. "No, Charles. We merely talked." For his sake, she would lie.

Knowing his wife well, Charles shook his head. "I can

just imagine what you talked about." He scrutinized Cara's face again, then sighed. "You don't need to spare my feelings, Cara. I am well aware of Regina's temperament."

Not knowing what to say, Cara nibbled on her lower lip, silently watching as Charles pulled the chair to the bedside and took a seat.

For a moment, he simply returned Cara's gaze before reaching out and taking one of her hands in his own. "I am sorry you had to be subjected to Regina's company. Had I known she intended to see you, I would have been here."

Broken dreams and shattered hopes reflected in Charles's eyes, making him suddenly appear vulnerable and frail. The sight broke Cara's heart and instinctively she wanted to offer what help she could. Yet she knew Charles would reject pity or sympathy. "You are here, Charles," she murmured with an encouraging smile.

Giving a wry laugh, Charles looked to his lap. Sorrow and self-contempt threatened to overwhelm him, but he shook off what he considered to be a pathetic weakness and put forth a brave front. After all, he had made his bed, he would have to lie in it.

Clearing his throat, he announced, "I think I am ready for tea."

Squeezing his hand in silent support, Cara agreed.

It was with definite relish that Cara emerged from her cabin on the fourth day. Not even Percy's dire warnings of a relapse and his growling threats not to tire herself could deter her.

Still pale and stiff, she made her way on deck, stopping at the quarterdeck rail. She looked about her, searching for signs of damage to the ship caused by the storm. As far as she could tell, nothing looked out of the ordinary and she concluded that the *Wind Dancer* had weathered the storm far better than she.

Her eyes made a thorough search of the main deck, then back to the quarterdeck. It was as she lifted her gaze to the poop deck that Cara realized she was looking for Justin.

She chided herself for behaving like a silly schoolgirl. Spinning around, she yanked her eyes away, only to have them land on Justin himself, and her breath froze in her throat. He stood atop the forward deck, openly watching her with serious concentration, booted feet braced apart and hands set on lean hips.

She couldn't contain the surge of joy she felt at seeing him again. A dazzling smile lit her face as he made his way toward her. His long legs made short work of the distance between them and she admired the easy grace with which he moved.

"I didn't expect to see you for at least another day. Does Percy know you're up and about?" His perceptive gaze scanned her features.

"Yes, he knows," she said in a tone that clearly said Percy knew, but didn't approve.

"Oh, it's that way, is it?" He smiled like a conspirator.

"I'm afraid so." She laughed, feeling wonderfully alive in his presence and loving every minute of it.

"How did you manage it?"

Her smile turned impish. "I threatened him with dire circumstances."

Justin let his eyes rake down the slender length of her, then return along the same course. "Considering your size, it couldn't have been anything physical."

"No, it wasn't," she answered coyly, feeling breathless from his perusal.

"Knowing Percy, it had to be something devious."

"No, actually it was quite simple." She beamed rather smugly.

Justin chuckled ruefully. "Simple? Where Percy is concerned, nothing is simple."

"Oh, I beg to differ, Captain. Why, Percy is the picture of affability, as long as you know how to get around him."

"You forget, Cara, I am captain here and I don't have to, as you put it, 'get around' anyone."

"Yes, well, rank does have its privileges," she demurred sweetly, unaware of the innocently seductive way her lips pouted, irresistibly drawing Justin's eyes to her tempting mouth. She missed his penetrating look and continued with an air of mock seriousness. "But since I am without rank or even position, I had to resort to other means."

"Out with it, Miss Fairchild."

Cara raised her chin jauntily, managing to keep the smile from her lips, but not her eyes. They sparkled with the glowing effects of their shared humor and her tingling awareness of Justin.

"I told him that he dresses like a walking nightmare and that if he did not let me out, I was going to report him to the nearest port authority for frightening women and young children."

Justin's rich laugh sounded around the ship. He slowly shook his head in amazement, picturing this tiny slip of a woman standing up to a giant the size of Percy. "You are merciless," he chuckled.

"Me?" She couldn't believe her ears. "It's Percy, you mean, as you well know. That man was born giving orders." She tilted her head to one side, her expression one of capricious doubt. "Are you sure he isn't captain of this ship?"

Justin's eyes narrowed slightly, but his smile still lingered. Instead of answering her question, he asked one of his own. "Have you lunched yet?"

Cara hesitated, hoping he wasn't about to order her back to her cabin to rest. They had talked for only a few minutes and she had hoped they could have more time together. "No, I haven't."

"I was on my way to my cabin to eat. Join me."

For a fraction of a second, Agnes Peele loomed in Cara's conscience, scolding her about the impropriety of dining alone with him. Stubbornly, Cara pushed the mental image of her prudish governess away, reasoning that everything she had done since her father's death had been unorthodox. What was the harm in having lunch? Besides, she admitted, she truly wanted to be with Justin.

Not waiting for her reply, he took her elbow and steered her across the deck. At the companionway door, Cara drew back and leveled a mildly accusing look on him.

"I didn't say yes," she said with a lopsided grin.

The teasing glow left Justin's eyes, leaving in its place a penetrating light that seared right through her. The space between them became charged and Cara felt a trembling inside her at the quicksilver shift in mood.

"Were you going to?" he challenged slowly, his face now set in hard, cynical lines.

She considered refusing, something within her balking at his self-assured assumption that she would agree. But just as quickly, she squelched the notion. "Yes," she answered softly.

The brittle look on Justin's face ebbed away and he led her off deck.

The conversation at lunch flowed easily, covering a wide range of topics from favorite authors to plant life indigenous to America. Cara was consumed with curiosity about her soon-to-be new home and plied Justin with a steady stream of questions. She listened to his every word, loving the sound of his voice. She decided it was the most masculine voice she had ever heard, deep in tone and clear in resonance. He was never at a loss for words, speaking articulately and always with an unmistakable air of command.

When the meal was cleared, they sat with only wineglasses before them, Justin's almost empty, Cara's nearly full.

"You barely touched your wine," he observed. "Was it not to your liking?"

"Oh, no," she was quick to assure him. "It's just that I'm not accustomed to drinking wine. I'm afraid my tolerance is minimal at best."

"I would be careful of who I informed of that interesting fact," he advised, watching her closely. The sunlight from the windows shimmered on the silken length of auburn hair cascading down her back, framing her face in a golden red glow. "You could get yourself in a great deal of trouble."

Cara didn't understand and a delicate frown puckered her brow.

Seeing the naively bemused look, Justin shook his head

disbelievingly. "Whatever could your parents have been thinking of when they had you educated?"

In the face of what sounded like criticism of her dear parents, she regarded Justin with an injured air. "I assure you, Captain, I had the most extensive study. It was my mother's desire that I be schooled beyond what is thought adequate for a female. In addition to having been trained in what I would call the drawing room necessities—piano, painting, and pouring tea—I speak four languages fluently and can read six, including Greek. I have been tutored in history, a subject I found stimulating, and mathematics, one I found indispensable."

Justin smiled to himself. She had completely misunderstood his statement, a fact that only illustrated her naivete. He considered the dark glitter in her eyes and the lofty tilt of her chin. Believing the Fairchild honor was at stake, she had defended it with a very ladylike manner. Quite the same way she had set Regina Taylor in her place at dinner, he mused. She may look fragile, a delicate young thing, but it was becoming more and more apparent that Cara Fairchild possessed a strong streak of righteous dignity. She had a strength of character that made her stand her ground against anyone, first Regina, then Percy, and now himself.

"You mistook my words," he explained. "I meant no insult to your parents, but you are so ingenuous that at times it amazes me. What I meant was, should someone with less than desirable scruples know of your susceptibility to spirits, particularly a man, he could very easily ply you with enough drink to besot your normally very clever mind."

Surprised because she would never have thought of such a thing, Cara's mouth fell into a silent O. She considered the matter for a moment, then smiled broadly, knowing she would never allow herself to become that intoxicated. "Oh, I hardly think that likely."

"Are you so sure?" he challenged lazily, leaning back in his chair.

"I'd lay odds on it," she quipped, resting her elbow on the table and her chin in her hand.

"Are you daring me?" he asked with a very wolfish grin on his lips.

"No."

Justin laughed and she clarified quickly. "Not because I know you would win, but because I don't have any money with which to bet."

"I could make you a loan," he offered easily.

She laughed and shot him a shaming glance across the table. "And I'm sure your interest rates would be so exorbitant that no matter how much I won, I wouldn't have enough to pay back the loan and the interest and I'd end up owing you for a bet I won. No, thank you."

Surprise joined the humor in Justin's eyes. "You did study mathematics, didn't you?"

"Yes."

"And you found it stimulating."

"No, I said I found it indispensable."

"How so?" he asked, wondering how she had become as knowledgeable as she had.

"I acted as my father's steward," she remarked easily. "I kept all the accounts for our estate, credits, expenditures, records of salaries."

The last bit of information caught Justin's attention. "Salaries?"

"Yes, those we employed had to be paid. The grounds keepers, stable hands, household staff. I took care of all the finances from paying creditors to accounting for investment incomes."

Justin's surprise escalated. She spoke of a lifestyle that was comfortable if not wealthy. His narrowed gaze slipped to the shabby-looking dress she wore. The garment, sewn simply, with long, tight-fitting sleeves and a scooped neck, was devoid of any costly frills. Constructed of an inexpensive fabric, the gown at one time might have been a bright royal blue, but was now blue gray in color. The rest of her limited wardrobe was in much the same condition. And he had never seen her wear any jewelry, not even the simplest ring or brooch.

"Why did you leave England?"

The sudden change in conversation caught Cara by surprise. Unprepared for his too-blunt question, she took a deep sigh and slowly released it. "It's a rather long story. I don't want to bore you."

Justin would not be put off. "I'll let you know if that happens."

Uncertain of where to start, she shifted her eyes to her lap. She hadn't spoken of this situation to anyone other than Nigel Bennett and it was difficult for her to explain the matter now. "I didn't leave home," she remarked with a slight shrug. "It was more a case of my home leaving me."

Her unease and dejection were obvious. "I assume the cause was your parents' death."

"My father's."

"What happened?"

Cara's head tilted to one side in a poignantly sad gesture. He watched her eyes briefly scan the cabin before meeting his.

"My father was returning home from America, when the ship he was on sank." She paused and took a steadying breath. "It was all quite unreal, actually, just my solicitor informing me, no funeral service, no grave to mourn over."

"You were alone? No brothers or sisters?"

"No, I'm an only child."

Creditors, Justin reasoned, thinking that was the only logical explanation for her to have lost her home. "Your father was indebted?"

"Yes, for many years, but not to the point of being destitute. We still had the house and the land, although there was very little else. The servants had to be dismissed years ago, which is why I gradually assumed the role of steward."

"The necessity of mathematics."

She smiled briefly.

"If the creditors didn't take everything, then why did you decide to leave?"

Her composure slipped, and she took a sip of wine.

"Because I didn't inherit. My father willed everything to someone else."

Justin's dark brows pulled into a frown. An odd thing for a father to do to his only child, leave her without a place to live.

The girl is an only child . . . she had been managing the estate for several years. . . . Snatches of a months-old conversation with his solicitor returned to Justin and the most incredible suspicion took hold in his mind. Fairchild. Henry Fairchild, but what was the daughter's name? He couldn't recall; it had been insignificant at the time.

Justin rose from the table and went to stand before the windows. "What was your father's name?"

"Henry Fairchild."

"And the person who inherited your home? What is his name?"

"The Earl of Ellsworth."

A wave of pure, raging anger swept through him and he slammed a hand against a beam. Damn it all to hell! No wonder she had seemed so familiar to him. He had been haunted by the feeling of familiarity for days, an elusive teasing that had kept him speculating about her. He should have recognized the name, but Fairchild was common enough and she was *supposed* to be in London. His anger sizzled; she had defied him and he wasn't accustomed to anyone doing that.

He mentally cursed again. What in the bloody hell was she doing here? He had ordered her to his grandmother's and that, dammit, was where he assumed she was.

What a brazen little fool she was to disobey him and then glibly inform him of his own identity. He couldn't accept her presence as sheer coincidence, so what game was she playing at? If she expected to entice him into relinquishing Fairfield to her, he would disabuse her of that notion right now.

He swung around, his blue eyes blazing, his mouth drawn into a hard, grim line. Scathing remarks were about to be issued in a deadly voice when he paused at the look on Cara's face. He saw only an innocent curiosity without any trace of deceit, and a wide-eyed look of surprise. The recognition that should have been in her eyes was absent. She didn't know, his instincts told him. She didn't know he was the Earl of Ellsworth. It was true, his mind confirmed. As high-principled as she was, if she had even the smallest notion of who he was, she wouldn't be sitting there calmly returning his look.

True, few people were privy to the fact that Captain Reynolds and the Earl of Ellsworth were one and the same. With the exception of Percy, Phillip Collinsworth, and Willie, no one associated with this aspect of his life knew him as anything other than a sea captain. And the reverse was true of his associates in England. Only his secretary and England's foreign minister were aware of the dual nature of his lifestyle.

But he found it difficult to believe that she had gone through the legalities involved with her father's will, and had not made the connection between the two names. Surely Captain Justin Reynolds and Edward Justin Reynolds were similar enough for even her artless mind to recognize.

"Captain, is something wrong?" The tension Cara felt emanating from Justin was like a tangible thing. She lifted worried eyes to his fiercely implacable face, wondering what had caused the sudden and frightening strain between them.

Justin's reply was slow in coming. Leaving the window, he came around in front of his desk and leaned back, his long legs stretched out before him and crossed at the ankle. It was his iron self-control that kept a rein on his temper, but a muscle defiantly ticked along his firm jaw.

"No, there is nothing wrong. I was just wondering how it is that you came to be here."

The unyielding set of his features contradicted his words and Cara answered cautiously. "With my home given to another, I had nowhere to go. I wrote to my cousin, informed her of my coming, and bade my solicitor to arrange for my passage to America."

"On this ship specifically?"

"No, not this one in particular. Any ship carrying passengers would have sufficed."

"It was your solicitor who chose mine?"

The intensity of his gaze on her was unnerving. Despite his assurance that all was right, Cara was becoming increasingly uncomfortable. "I . . . that is yes, Nigel handled the entire matter." She frowned at the shrewd look on his face.

"What do you mean you had nowhere to go? I'm sure you must have had options less drastic than America."

It wasn't in Cara to lie. "Well, there was actually. The earl wanted me to live with his grandmother."

"That was generous of him."

"Possibly," she replied with a dismissing shrug.

In a very controlled motion, Justin crossed his arms over his chest. "As I see it, he wasn't obliged to be concerned about your welfare."

"True," she admitted, "but no matter how good his intentions were, the situation would have been intolerable."

"How so?" He was genuinely surprised.

"Captain, I may be a pauper, but I am not without some pride."

His dark brows snapped downward in two straight vertical slashes. "You are not a pauper," he said, irritated by her self-slander.

Cara laughed ruefully at his reaction. "It is unfortunate, but it is also quite true. I have no home, only the clothes I brought with me, and no money to speak of. Five pounds to be exact."

He was shocked to realize she was so impoverished. While he hadn't given the matter a great deal of thought, he'd assumed she'd been allowed some finances, or had been adequately dowered at the very least. Coming back to the issue at hand, he demanded, "What does that have to do with your living with the man's grandmother?"

"Everything." She lifted a hand in an imploring gesture, wishing he could understand without her having to explain. With a sigh she rose and stepped to the bookcase. She trailed a finger distractedly along the leather bindings before turning to face him.

"In what capacity would I have lived with her? Guest? Companion? Homeless, penniless orphan? And for how long? Would I have awakened one morning only to have the fine lady or her grandson finally tire of me and put me out? Or marry me off to the first man magnanimous enough to take me without a dowry?" A ragged, weary sigh escaped her. "My whole life would have been completely dependent upon strangers. I could not tolerate being indebted to someone for my very existence."

He shot her a derisive look. "As it is now, you barely have an existence. And unless this cousin of yours is landed, you'll find your life in America more than you bargained for."

Cara's chin came up and she gave him a measured look. "I am not afraid to work, Captain. I have done so most of my life."

Justin scoffed. "You gave up a cushioned life for one of questionable comfort and privilege because you're too proud and stubborn to accept what's been offered."

Her spine stiffened and she hung on to her composure. "Offered?" She was incredulous. "The man is arrogant beyond measure! He didn't offer, he dictated. He didn't even have enough decency to discuss the matter with me personally."

He pushed away from the desk with deceptive calm. What a little ingrate she was. "The man was generous."

"The man is a cad! He just ordered me about, as though he had the right to do so." Her patience was nearly exhausted, and she was trying her level best not to lose her temper, but his goading and the issue itself were straining her to her limit. "He just snapped his fingers and his solicitor came running. Just a wave of his pen and my solicitor was ready to help me pack my bag."

Justin strode to the rows of books, and if Cara hadn't been so absorbed with her irate feelings, she would have seen the dangerous glint in Justin's eyes. As it was, she missed the awful calm of his words. "You know nothing about the man. You've never even met him."

Her arm swept out toward the door. "I wouldn't know him if he walked into the room this very minute. But his actions have been eloquent enough. And"—she paused to purse her lips tightly while she wrestled with her annoyance—"I am not stubborn."

Justin's blue gaze sliced through the space separating them. "Madam, beneath that porcelain facade of yours is the most willful streak of determination I've ever seen."

Her eyes widened in shock. How dare he accuse her of being willful and stubborn! Of all the insufferable . . . why this entire matter didn't even concern him and she had been a fool to discuss it with him. "I don't know why you're being so irate about this, but with all due respect, this is none of your business."

In two long strides he stood before her. "I'm making it my business," he ground out with a nasty smile.

Before Cara had time to react, his hands snaked out and hauled her up against him. A protest formed on her lips, but it was smothered as Justin's mouth crushed down on hers with punishing force.

She twisted within his arms, straining to turn her head away, but his arms only tightened more painfully about her. "Please," she gasped against his lips, her hands pushing against the wall of his chest. "You're hurting me."

Justin's head came up and she gazed up at his taut features. "Why are you so angry with me?" she demanded to know.

When he gave no answer, her confusion quickly turned to indignation. "I don't want you to kiss me this way. Let me go!"

Her command brought him up short. No woman had ever asked, begged, or requested to be released from his embrace. The lure of his wealth and title, combined with the promise of unlimited passion at his experienced hands, brought scores of hopeful women his way. Yet here was this proud, angry innocent demanding he let her go, and for the life of him, he couldn't. The feel of her lush body pressed against his lured him with its enticing curves until anger was dashed away and replaced by a sensual hunger he admitted no other woman could evoke so easily within him.

Seeing the look of outrage on her face, he relaxed his hold, determined to change her expression to one of exquisite rapture and make her feel the same burning passion he felt.

Carefully, he stroked his hand over her satin cheek. Cara watched the anger drain from his face, felt the tension leave his arms, but she was still wary. He lowered his head a fraction; instinctively she drew back. Pausing, his fingers captured her chin, his liquid, seductive gaze never leaving her, and Cara stood rooted to where she was. The warm touch of his hand, the compelling look in his eyes had a strangely calming effect on her and she felt her ire subside. A curious sensation of anticipation pervaded her and she held her breath, waiting.

Blood rushed through Justin's veins at the expectant appeal on Cara's face. His arms gathered her close and he kissed her, his lips slanting over hers insistently. Her own lips parted beneath his, and at the thrust of his tongue into her mouth, her body melted against his solid frame.

For a frantic moment she questioned her sanity, but she couldn't deny the yearning she felt to be right where she was, held securely in his arms, returning his kisses. She entwined her arms around his broad shoulders, her hands caressing the taut muscles. Giving herself over to the sensations she knew he would create within her, she pressed eagerly against the lean strength of his body. A groan of pure pleasure emanated from deep within Justin's chest and he tightened his hold around her, flattening her lush breasts against his chest.

His mouth left hers, taking a path along the satin of her heated cheek, to the fine line of her jaw, and then upward to her ear. Waves of pure pleasure ran down Cara's spine to her stomach and lower to the intimate core of her being. While his lips lingered on the madly racing pulse of her neck, his hands skimmed across her ribs to the trim hollow of her waist, then lower, pulling her thighs against the intimate proof of his arousal. His hips moved in an exotic rhythm, crushing his hardened length against the softness of her belly. Instinctively, Cara answered his movements and Justin was inflamed. He crushed his mouth on hers again, his tongue delving into the sweet recesses of her mouth. His other hand came up to caress her breast, molding the ripe fullness to fit his palm. The fabric of her bodice was pulled aside by his impatient fingers, and his lips lowered to plunder the sweet flesh of her breast.

Cara's breath caught in her throat at the moist, greedy touch of his mouth. Her tenuous grasp on sanity fled and she gave herself up to the hungry yearning that engulfed her. Her whole body trembling, she arched against him, glorying in a newly discovered passion.

A distant thumping sounded in her ears. Was it the blood pounding through her veins? It came again, only louder this time, distracting her and finally jerking her back to reality. Her dazed eyes flew to the door as the knocking sounded again.

Justin's head snapped up, his blue eyes almost black with fury. Frustration such as he had never known before exploded within him. His hunger for this woman was beyond physical bearing, and his body demanded he assuage the devouring passion that raged through him. His mind was drugged with the effect she had on him and he was loath to let her go. The knocking came again.

With teeth clenched, he drew a ragged breath and released her. "In a moment," he called in a voice cracked with suppressed violence.

Realization set in too rapidly for Cara to handle. Never having experienced the depths of all-consuming passion before, she was unprepared for the riot of emotions that flooded her and the physical reaction that left her senseless. She whirled away from Justin, fumbling with her bodice. What had happened to her? How could she have lost control of herself like that? Sick with doubt, she covered her scarlet cheeks with trembling hands.

Not willing to let the moment die, determined to salvage

the remnant coals of desire and keep them burning until they could be fully ignited later, Justin reached out to draw her back. To his surprise, she jerked away. Spinning around, she faced him with huge eyes, shaking fingers pressed to lips still red and swollen from his kisses.

His brows drew into a frown. "Cara?" he questioned cautiously.

She couldn't answer, couldn't find the words, any words.

"What is it?" he asked, and made a move to take her in his arms.

She quickly stepped back, holding up a slender hand as though to ward him off. Shaking her head in jerking movements, she finally managed to speak. "No, no . . . don't."

Justin's frown became a scowl. "I'll ask again, what is it?"

"I shouldn't have . . . I . . ."

Before she could make a move, he reached out and caught her by the shoulders. "You shouldn't have let me kiss you?" he snapped. "You shouldn't have let me touch you and make you feel things you think are wicked?" He gave her a rough shake and snarled. "Because of some absurd social dictate, you're going to deny what you feel in my arms." He yanked her against him, and his mouth crushed down on hers in a kiss that left Cara shaken to her very soul.

"Deny it," he demanded in a fierce whisper against her lips. "Deny you want me."

Afraid to acknowledge anything, she pushed against him. Swearing a vicious oath, he let her go. Blindly, she ran out of the cabin, not even looking at Percy who stood waiting in the companionway.

Percy looked to Cara's closed door then turned to peer at Justin with a queer squint.

Justin planted his tightly clenched fists on his hips, faced Percy, and dared him to say one word, just one word that was out of line. "Well, what is it?" he growled.

Percy had known Justin long enough to realize that now was not the time to overstep his bounds. "Mr. Collinsworth needs you on deck, Captain," he replied wisely.

Justin glared at the man as though mentally picturing his early demise. He swallowed the string of curses he had been about to hurl, and stalked from the cabin.

Percy followed at a slower pace, shutting the cabin door behind him. The companionway door slamming shut drew his puzzled frown. His eyes moved to Cara's cabin, then back to the companionway door. He scrubbed a hand across his chin, his eyes squinting speculatively. For a moment he paused, then gave a low whistle. The voyage to Virginia had suddenly taken on some very interesting aspects.

Chapter Five

Williamsburg, Virginia

Demented screams emanated from deep within the Williamsburg Lunatic Asylum. Sitting in the concealing shadows outside the building's massive brick structure, Olan Wright swilled down another gulp of the cheapest of whiskeys, then let his laughter join the chorus of ghastly human voices echoing in the night.

With his one good eye, he peered down Nassau Street, hoping to catch sight of some unsuspecting fool who was stupid enough to be walking the streets of Williamsburg after midnight. Most people remained in their homes after dark, but every now and then, a stranger passing through or a cocksure student from the college ventured out and Olan would use those opportunities to pad his pockets.

It had been nearly two weeks since his last run of good luck. He had been sitting in this very place, when he had spotted Martha Trent weaving her drunken way down France Street. Robbing the little sot had been as easy as pissing in the stream. Of course he hadn't meant to snap her neck. That had just happened when she had begun to make a fuss. At the thought, he cackled a gleeful laugh and took another drink in a silent toast. Damn, who would have thought that a drunken woman would put up such a fight. She had clawed and kicked and howled. He had had no choice but to shut her up. It really was a shame, too, because she was the only whore who hadn't minded spreading her legs for him, for a few extra coins, of course.

Suddenly angry, he threw his empty jug aside and cursed every woman he had ever known, every slut who had ever turned away from the sight of his scarred face or laughed at the awkward gait of his limp. But mostly, he damned to the agonizing fires of eternal Hells, the British soldiers that had turned him into what he was.

It was those scum from England who were responsible for leaving him with only one eye. It was their fault that his body was so twisted and ugly that even the cheapest doxy would have nothing to do with him.

He slumped back against the cold bricks and let his mind dwell on the past. Olan knew he had been a fine-looking lad once, with enough between his legs to keep the women and himself happy. That had been before October of 1781, when he had been unlucky enough to find himself in Yorktown. The memory was enough to make him shudder.

On a lark, he and his cronies had followed the scores of soldiers down the peninsula. It had been a game, an adventure, until the bloody battle that was to lead to the end of America's war for independence erupted around him. Then the game had turned sour. He had found nothing amusing about being shot at and, alone, had fled to the dense woods surrounding the tiny port town.

When the siege finally ended, Olan had congratulated himself on managing to stay alive. He had crept from his hiding place and headed for home, pausing only long enough to pick the pockets of British soldiers lying dead in the isolated woods.

He had laughed at his own clever scheme. Too late he realized that he wasn't alone with those corpses. Three

British soldiers, very much alive, had witnessed his thievery. It had taken only a matter of minutes before they left him for dead.

The sounds of hideous human moans jerked Olan back to the present. He shoved the memories away, but basked in the hatred that had kept him alive all these years. He reveled in the maddened hunger for revenge that was the focus of his life. Silently, he vowed, as he had every night since that time in Yorktown, that every Englander who crossed his path would pay for what they had done to him. He would kill each and every one.

From the poop deck where he stood, Justin looked forward and scrutinized the workings of his entire ship. He could see Christopher Astor atop the mizzen mast, checking the manila rigging. Across to the forecastle deck, Billy Fuller and Noah White sat cross-legged, repairing lengths of canvas sail, while Joshua Jenkins agilely slipped over the starboard rail to tighten the backstrap wires running upward to the masts. Justin passed his critical eyes over every man before him, watching for signs of weakness, assessing the quality of workmanship, evaluating the efficiency of time and energy. For long moments his sharp look cut to each of the fifteen or so men that were presently topside, until he was satisfied that the operation met his standards. Then he turned his gaze on Cara.

He gave her as thorough an inventory as he had given his men and ship. He watched her stroll the quarterdeck at a leisurely pace and his thoughts turned dark. What a little termagant she was, proud and willful. He had been right yesterday in calling her stubborn. She didn't yield easily, but when she did, the effect she had on him acted like a potent aphrodisiac.

Lighting a thin, dark cigar, he drew deeply and savored the aroma, just as he savored the thought of the passion she had displayed the day before. Having expected the same reticent responses she had afforded him thus far, he had been surprised by her eagerness. She had boldly returned his kisses and relished his intimate caresses with such ardent innocence that he had been helpless to think of anything other than possessing her.

He openly studied her, his gaze drawn to the grace of her movements as she sidestepped a barrel of pitch, then stopped to talk with Phillip Collinsworth. Seeing the smile she sent the man, Justin's teeth clamped down hard on the end of the cigar. He knew Collinsworth would be all but useless in a matter of moments. All she had to do was turn those sweet lips of hers up into a smile and every man on board stumbled in his tracks. As though to verify this fact, his gaze raked the men and found too many distracted by the sight of her.

"Damn," he swore softly.

"You say something?" Percy stood behind Justin, casually leaning back against the taffrail, and had been, in the past moments, completely ignored by his captain.

Justin swung around and leaned both forearms against the same rail. "No," was all he offered with a scowl.

"Ah, thought you did," Percy remarked, sending Justin an innocent look of feigned nonchalance. "Thought you said something 'bout Miss Cara." He ignored the shrewd, knowing look he received and shoved his way into the issue. "She was sorely upset leaving your cabin yesterday."

The inquiry beneath the statement was impossible for Justin to miss. He had half a mind to tell the big ox to curb his curiosity, but he also knew Percy wouldn't have instigated the discussion if he didn't have something on his mind that would eventually be said, one way or another. Besides, the two of them had been through too much together for him to be keeping secrets now.

"We were discussing the Earl of Ellsworth," he stated flatly.

Percy's bushy brows snapped straight up in startled question.

"Mmm . . . she thinks he's a 'cad.' "

"She knows? . . ."

"No," Justin interrupted. "She doesn't know that I'm one and the same."

Percy was evidently confused. "How does she come to know you and the earl and *not* know?"

Justin exhaled deeply and flicked the last of his tobacco out to sea. "I inherited her father's estate. She couldn't very well go on living there, so I had her packed up and moved in with Lydia."

"Your grandmother? Why?"

"It seemed a good idea at the time," Justin replied with a casual shrug.

"And?"

"And we never actually met. If you remember, back in August you and I were somewhat occupied with that business in Spain. I assumed she was in London. However, it seems Miss Fairchild has a strong aversion to being told what to do."

Having firsthand experience with Cara's strong-willed nature, Percy smiled broadly, but when another thought struck, the smile faded. "I'm surprised you agreed to take her aboard."

Justin's reply was a long, silent sideways glance and a faint pull at the corner of his lips.

"You didn't know?" Percy concluded accurately.

Shaking his head in disgust, Justin clamped his lower lip between his teeth and slowly released it in a gesture Percy knew declared total annoyance. "It was a paltry affair and I was anxious to leave the boredom of London. I let Huggins handle it. And Collinsworth booked the passengers. Her name didn't register when I saw his list."

"Care to explain how she came to be on *this* ship then?"

"As far as I can tell, her solicitor put her here. She said he made all the arrangements for her passage."

"Think he made the connection?"

"I'd say so." Justin wasn't pleased about that. Distractedly, he ran a hand across the back of his neck. "He more than likely saw the wisdom of my plan, and since she wouldn't agree, he did the next best thing and set her here."

Percy's booming laugh jerked Justin's head around. "Must 'o been a bit of a shock," he choked out between rich chuckles, "you finding her here. There's not many that goes their own way against you, but she did, I'll give her that." The admiration in his voice was obvious. "So, what 'cha planning to do 'bout it?"

"Nothing."

That sobered Percy immediately. "Nothing?" Justin Reynolds was not a man to be crossed. Those foolhardy enough to do so ultimately saw the folly of their mistake. The fury of his retribution, in whatever form it took, was known to reduce a person to a mass of quaking nerves. Not that Percy wanted that fate for Cara, but she had dared a great deal, unknowingly, but had done so nonetheless. He found it remarkable that, in response, the man known throughout more than one country for his ofttimes dangerous temperament was going to do "nothing."

"She doesn't need to know." And for personal reasons, Justin wanted it that way. Cara may despise the earl but she most definitely liked the captain.

By all rights, he should still be furious with her, but oddly enough he wasn't. He didn't want to examine his feelings too closely, but he had to admit that she did have the strangest effect on him. Maybe it was her courage against all odds that intrigued him. He'd never met a woman with such strength of character. Perhaps it was her ridiculous lack of coyness. Damn, but she could be brutally honest. That trait was exceedingly rare in the women he knew.

He was suddenly annoyed and uncomfortable with his thoughts. In self-disgust he reminded himself that she was a beautiful woman and his reaction to her was prompted by desire.

Percy pushed away from the rail. "It's your matter," he said, heading for the ladder descending to the quarterdeck. "Just go easy on the lass."

Coming to stand beside the burly cook, Justin gave him a pained look. "Don't tell me you're soft on her, too."

Percy looked Justin right in the eye. "She's a sweetheart, she is," he stated emphatically, daring Justin to contradict him. With that last word, he made his way to the lower decks.

Justin turned his attention to Cara once again and in that moment she lifted her head and their eyes met. The space separating them crackled with an electrifying current, making each vitally aware of the other. For endless moments, time was vanquished, surroundings disappeared and the two were enveloped in their own silent world of sensations. Cara's hand unconsciously rose to her throat and at the contact of her chilled fingers against the heated, flushed skin, she blinked. Whirling, she rushed from the deck to her cabin.

He watched her hasty retreat. He would let her run away for now. He'd be patient and give her time to adjust to her own sensuality. A certain headiness flooded him at the thought of his being responsible for her awakening, and his desire for her grew. Yes, he'd give her a few days and then he'd see to it that they continued where they'd left off.

Out of the corner of his eye, a flash of red caught Justin's attention and he turned to find the source of the distraction. Regina, dressed as though she were taking a Sunday walk in the park, stood openly watching him. He acknowledged her with a brief nod of his head and in return received a sultry smile laden with promise.

Dispassionately, he watched her approach then stop before the ladder and gaze evocatively up at him. He had seen that look far too often, on scores of women, and knew exactly what lay beneath her one-sided grin.

"Mrs. Taylor," he drawled, gazing down at her from his elevated height atop the poop deck.

"Captain Reynolds," she returned. "I hope I haven't caught you in the middle of your duties."

"My duties are never ending, madam."

A look of feigned distress crossed her face. "What a pity. I thought you might be persuaded to show me your ship. It is a fascinating vessel, much like its captain."

Crossing his arms over his chest, Justin ignored her quip. Dallying with another man's wife was a practice he had never engaged in, no matter how desirable the woman in question was. He was not about to sacrifice his principles for someone like Regina Taylor. "I can arrange to have Mr. Collinsworth give you a tour, if you desire."

Pausing for a potent moment, Regina quirked one brow upward. "What I desire would best be discussed between the two of us, in private."

With brutal indifference, he flicked his gaze over her exotic features and down the length of her figure cloaked in red velvet.

"Perhaps you had best look to your husband for such private dialogues."

Regina gasped. Unaccustomed to being refused by any man, she opened her mouth to lay a blistering tirade on his head, but suddenly stopped short. Justin Reynolds was unlike any man she had ever encountered. He was going to require special care if she wanted to reap the benefits he could give her.

She tipped her head to one side, giving him a knowing look. "Perhaps you will change your mind, Captain. I know I won't." With a final smile she turned and strolled away.

For the next two days, rain poured down on the *Wind Dancer* and Cara was secluded to her cabin or the dining salon. Dampness permeated the walls, the floor, and even the bedding. An occasional down draft sent the cloying odor of smoke back into the stove, then into the close confines of the cabin to join the mustiness generated by the foul weather.

Normally, Cara would have tolerated the conditions, but ever since she had fled from Justin's cabin three days earlier, her mind had been in a distracted turmoil that shortened her patience. Now she chafed at her inactivity and was irritated by the dank chill.

Sitting on her bunk with her back pressed against the wall, she snapped her book shut and set it aside. For the umpteenth time she glanced out the small porthole and wished she could be out on deck. At least there she would find enough distractions to keep from being haunted by the one thought that threatened to consume her. She had fallen in love with Justin.

She gave a soft groan and, drawing her knees up, wrapped her arms about them and laid her head against her arm. She didn't know how it happened or even when, but his impassioned kisses and heart-warming charm had captured her heart. It had hit her like a lightning bolt three days ago when they had stood looking at each other across the space of the deck. She had been so unnerved by the revelation that she had run to her cabin.

Rolling her eyes, Cara imagined Agnes Peele in the throes of apoplexy at her behavior. Hadn't her governess spent years lecturing her on the finer points of decorum? Hadn't she sternly preached that young ladies of any worth did not go about engaging in amorous rendezvous? And they certainly did not brazenly fall into a state of love. But there was no help for it, Cara reasoned. The strict woman may have told her what was considered to be unseemly behavior, but she had never given advice on how to prevent any of those very things from occurring.

Justin had been right. Agnes Peele had never been properly kissed. If she had, Cara knew the spinster's lectures would have been far different.

For a few blissful moments, Cara allowed herself to bask in the lovely feelings generated by her thoughts. Years of loneliness fell away and she felt a contentment of spirit she never dreamed possible. The pain she'd endured as a child over the loss of her mother was eased by the memory of Justin's gentle ministrations. His singular attention to her welfare assuaged the ache of those endless months she'd spent without companionship, waiting for her father to return from yet another of his journeys. She gloried in Justin's masculine strength and pride and power, and when he kissed her, her heart felt near to bursting with all her love.

Part of her wanted to throw her arms up to the sky and twirl in abandoned glee, to laugh and spin and proclaim her love for all to hear. But another part of her compelled her to be silent and restrained and thankful that the weather had kept her isolated for the past few days. She had needed the time to adjust to the realization of her feelings, but she was still overwhelmed by the enormity of it all.

Sitting up, she shook off her thoughts and rose from the bed. Having no intentions of spending another afternoon in fruitless self-examination, she gave a quick swipe of her hand over the wrinkles in her dress and went to the dining salon in search of Charles and a cup of tea. The steaming brew was waiting in a pewter service set on the table, however, it was Regina who occupied the room instead of her husband.

For a moment Cara hesitated in entering the salon. The sight of Regina was not encouraging, especially in light of their conversation of several days before. Cara mentally groaned. She had no desire to take the brunt of Regina's waspish ways. But neither was she about to let the other woman intimidate her into leaving, especially when she had her heart set on a cup of tea. With a polite smile, she shut the door and entered the salon.

"Hello, Regina," she offered pleasantly.

Coolly composed, sitting regally at the head of the dark pine table, Regina silently watched Cara take a seat. Behind the sparkling black eyes lay a wealth of malicious intent and she relished the chance to vent some of her animosity.

Mentally she sneered. She suspected that the good captain had cast his eye in Cara's direction. It was the only plausible reason for his cool attitude regarding Regina herself. The thought was too bitter to endure and she sought to assuage her pride. Charles had given her a warning to behave and leave Cara be, but as with most things her husband said, she had just tolerated his edicts and then discreetly did as she pleased.

"My, my, my, don't tell me that you've had another jaunt about the ship. I don't know how you stand it."

Careful to keep her face expressionless, Cara regarded Regina. "No, I haven't been out."

"I didn't think the rain would deter you. You seem to have such a penchant for all that wind and cold."

"It doesn't bother me. It's all a matter of personal preference, though."

"Yes, I imagine so," Regina replied, shrugging indolently. Her gaze swept over Cara's casually arranged hair and naturally tinted cheeks in search of fault. Her close scrutiny, however, only revealed Cara's natural, youthful beauty. Spitefully, she gritted her teeth and focused her attention on a much more discernible deficiency. "I must say, Cara, this journey is playing havoc with your wardrobe." She paused to take a delicate sip of tea and smother a nasty smile. "Your dress isn't quite the thing."

Cara didn't need to be told that her dress, the gray with cream cuffs and collar, was in sad shape. She had been wearing this same dress the night of the storm and it had become soaked with the salty ocean water while she had lain unconscious in the companionway. Percy himself had seen to its cleaning, but despite his best efforts, the light wool fabric had warped and shriveled in places, giving the garment an oddly wrinkled appearance.

Helpless to keep from doing so, Cara looked to Regina's dress. A clinging, vivid pink silk gown shot through with silver threads. The empire style exaggerated her generous curves, the small capped sleeves baring her arms and the exceedingly low scooped neckline revealing a great deal more.

"I'm afraid you're right, Regina," Cara replied with as much dignity as possible. "There is little hope for this dress any longer. But I chose it today for its warmth and I will simply have to overlook its shortcomings."

Regina's face turned blatantly smug. "If I were you, I shouldn't worry about its loss. The gray coloring doesn't become you at all." She glanced to Cara's forehead. "And as I'm sure you know, yellow really doesn't suit you either."

Feeling a definite twinge of annoyance, Cara paused for the briefest moment at Regina's reference to her still-bruised temple, now various values of yellow. "This particular yellow wouldn't suit anyone," she stated evenly.

The composure Cara displayed irritated Regina. It was her intention to unnerve the chit, but that wasn't proving to be an easy task.

Setting her cup down, she spoke with deceptive nonchalance. "How did you manage to do that? From what I hear, Captain Reynolds found you in the companionway."

The mention of Justin brought a certain tension to Cara's stomach. "Yes, that's right. He found me unconscious," she explained, not liking the calculating gleam in Regina's eyes.

"And like a knight in shining armor, he swept you up and carried you off to safety."

At the mocking in Regina's voice, Cara grew wary. "Yes, you might say that."

With a condescending shake of her dark head, Regina leaned back in her chair, her perfectly manicured fingers clasped together loosely. "I applaud your efforts, you know. Quite dramatic, actually. But it really was all for nothing, wasn't it?"

"Excuse me?"

Regina laughed without mirth, smoothing a hand down over her skirt before gazing carelessly at Cara's perplexed face. "You can speak freely, we're alone. Come now, tell me."

Leaning back in her own chair, Cara blinked in confusion. She didn't have the faintest notion of what Regina was talking about. "Tell you what?" she asked cautiously.

"All about this little plan of yours. You get yourself hurt and Captain Reynolds comes to your rescue and you fall into his opened arms."

Cara was shocked. "You actually think I did this"—she waved a hand at her multicolored temple—"on purpose?"

"Don't worry." Regina leaned forward to whisper. "I won't tell anyone."

"There is nothing to tell."

"Oh, I don't believe that."

"Why not? It's the truth. I was foolish enough to leave my cabin during the storm. I lost my balance and hit my head. I didn't intend for that to happen any more than I schemed for Jus . . . Captain Reynolds to find me."

At Cara's slip, Regina's thin black brows rose in question and a good deal of the enjoyment she felt at goading Cara faded. "Justin, is it? My, my, my, isn't that cozy?" Her eyes narrowed. "You very well may not have staged this little charade of yours, but you certainly wasted little time in using it to your advantage."

Regina gave Cara no chance for reply. "Tell me, are you two lovers?"

The boldness of the question stunned Cara and a blush of anger suffused her cheeks. Up until now Regina had been irritating with her jeering comments and sneering attitude. But the crassness of her question, especially in its regard to her relationship with Justin, evoked the full force of Cara's temper.

"Why, Cara," Regina drawled acidly. She turned in her chair and, resting an elbow on the wooden arm, raised a finger to tap her smiling lips. "Your blush is giving you away."

Cara finally found her voice. It was right behind her outrage. "I am blushing at the rudeness of your question," she answered tightly. Her green eyes, lit like shards of green glass, mirrored the extent of her inner turmoil.

The sound of Regina's frivolous laugh filled the room. "What a little provincial you are."

Cara's chin came up in defense. "If nothing else, I am well mannered." Her voice was low and stiff, but held enough dignity to prick the other woman's ire.

The perfection of Regina's feline smile cracked at the edges. "Oh, you are a sly one, aren't you?"

"Meaning what?"

"Meaning you aren't going to kiss and tell."

Cara had reached the limit of her tolerance. She had no intentions of discussing anything more, least of all her relationship with Justin. And she was done with the verbal sparring Regina was reveling in. "I will not discuss this with you, Regina. In fact, I have very little else to say to you at all."

The finality of Cara's words didn't faze Regina in the least. "Do you know what I think, little Cara? I think you won't tell me anything because there is nothing to tell." She rose to her feet with a full laugh. "I have hit upon it there, haven't I? The good captain was right there for your taking and you let him slip through your fingers. And do you know why? Because you really aren't woman enough for him." She moved to the doorway with a rustle of silk. A hand on the latch, she turned back to Cara with a look of supreme confidence. "He needs a woman of experience. A woman of considerable talents. He needs a woman who knows how to please him." Her head tilted to an arrogant angle. "Do you know how to do that, Cara? I do."

As rigid as stone, Cara watched Regina swirl out of the room.

By the next morning, the skies had cleared and Cara was grateful to be outside again. After a restless night, brought on by Regina's insulting remarks, the endless spaces surrounding her proved to be a balm.

Cara ignored a great deal of what Regina had said. But her mind was still plagued with questions and vague impressions that she couldn't possibly begin to understand. Feeling ignorant, she wondered if Justin *did* need a woman to please him. But what did that entail? She was a good conversationalist, and he seemed to enjoy her company. But what kind of experience was needed for that? One simply talked. She pondered that. Perhaps if she were more witty or intellectual. She knew she didn't have a shrewish nature, but she did have to admit she was stubborn. He hadn't been overly pleased about that. And her talents? She didn't think keeping books or playing the piano or painting a watercolor would please a man like Justin. With a sigh, she concluded that Justin was just going to have to be satisfied with her just as she was.

She was finishing her solitary breakfast when Willie Carmichael entered the dining salon with a tray.

"Beg your pardon, miss, but are you finished?" The lad questioned unsurely while shifting his weight from one foot to another.

Wishing to put the twelve-year-old at ease, Cara smiled gently. "Yes, Willie."

With disproportionately long arms that appeared gangly,

he reached across the table and began stacking cups and spoons on the tray. "I don't want to be no bother to you, miss, but Percy says I's to get these to him five minutes ago."

"Heaven forbid that Percy not have his way," Cara whispered with such exaggerated horror that Willie grinned. "Don't worry," she continued in a normal voice, as she handed her plate to him, "I wouldn't do anything to see you get in trouble with Percy. I've been there, so you have my sympathies."

The brown, unruly curled head snapped up. "You?" Willie just couldn't imagine anyone as pretty and nice as Miss Fairchild doing anything to set off Percy.

"Yes, I have to admit, so I don't envy your position at this moment. You'd best hurry and get these to him."

When Willie began stacking the service platters from the sideboard, Cara quickly intervened. "Mr. Taylor hasn't had breakfast yet. Perhaps you might want to leave those."

"Oh, he ain't eating this morning. He's sick abed."

"What?"

"Mr. Taylor's feeling bad."

"Oh, dear," Cara murmured with a frown. "Do you know what ails him?"

"Nope," he answered shaking his head for emphasis. "But he catched me in the companionway earlier and asked for a pitcher of water. He didn't look so good. I asked if there was anything else he wanted, but he said there weren't. Just said he was going to rest some."

Cara suspected that Charles was more than mildly indisposed. He was usually quite spry, rising early each morning and spending nearly as much time on the decks as she. Even the coughing seizure she had witnessed hadn't deterred him to any great extent. For him to take to his bed was most unusual and she was truly worried.

Lunch came and went, and Charles had still not emerged from his cabin. Passing Regina briefly in the salon, Cara was tempted to inquire about Charles's health, but Regina's haughty glare stemmed any questions Cara had. She was left to wonder if perhaps she wasn't overreacting.

It was the sound of Charles's coughing that stopped Cara in the companionway late that afternoon as she came in from the deck. Just outside his door, she stood and listened to the wracking sound emanating from within the cabin. Her instincts told her something was terribly wrong. Regina was on deck while Charles was closeted, obviously not well. She raised a hand and knocked on his door. When he made no reply, she tried again, but only silence greeted her.

She didn't even stop to leave her cloak in her own cabin, but went straight to Justin's cabin and knocked on his door.

The few seconds she waited seemed like an eternity and gave her enough time to panic. In her mind's eye she could see herself on the other side of the door, wrapped in Justin's arms.

"Come." His voice sounded through the wooden portal.

Swallowing hard, she gave a mental shake. She was going to have to face him sooner or later. The door swung open at her push.

All her selfless resolve to help Charles fragmented momentarily at the sight of Justin clothed in dark pants, just shrugging into a white shirt. Sculpted muscles across his chest, covered with a matt of dark hair, a lean, flat stomach and wide shoulders, iron-toned arms, all flexed with his movements. Her senses were stunned.

"Oh . . . ex . . . excuse me." Her face flamed red as she helplessly absorbed the sight of him. "I didn't mean . . . to . . . to . . . I'll come back when you're . . ." Unable to get her words out, totally distracted and unnerved, she turned away, but a steely hand clamped down on her wrist with carefully controlled strength.

"Your pardon, Cara, I wasn't expecting you." His words were a deep purr, but heavily laced with humor.

Thinking he meant he was expecting one of his men, she quickly apologized. "I'm intruding." She chanced a quick look up at him. "Perhaps if you could spare me a few moments later."

Justin still hadn't released her wrist and he carefully pulled her a step closer. "I'm not expecting anyone, but since you've never come uninvited to my cabin, I assumed it was anyone else."

Her lame "Yes, well" was followed by a thick silence. She tried unsuccessfully to keep her eyes from straying to the portion of his chest exposed by his unbuttoned shirt, and Justin watched her watch him. He wished the order of their clothing was reversed and that it was she who stood there, partially uncovered, with his eyes feasting on her.

As if the very intensity of his thoughts assailed her, Cara blinked and collected herself. "My hand, please?" It was released immediately, then waved uncomfortably, indicating the general area of his shirt. "Do you think you could . . . button up?" She could feel her cheeks practically burning.

Justin finally took pity on her and turned away to complete his dressing. Cara busied herself by concentrating on taking steady breaths as she stared at her hands. Appalled, she found them shaking.

"All done."

She was greatly relieved to find all his clothing, including black boots, in place.

'Would you care for something to drink?" he asked, making his way to the bottles on the side table.

"No, thank you," she replied to his back. Without his penetrating gaze on her, she found it easier to compose herself. She took advantage of that and broached the subject that had brought her to his cabin. "I need to speak to you about Charles Taylor. I believe he is terribly ill."

Justin gave her a sharp glance over his shoulder. Saying nothing until he finished pouring his drink, he came to half-sit on the edge of his desk.

"What makes you think that?"

"He hasn't been out of his cabin all day, and for a good part of yesterday, either."

"I'm aware of that. But that doesn't signify that he's seriously ill or even mildly so, for that matter. Besides, if this were true, I would think he or Mrs. Taylor would have asked for Percy."

"That's not so." Feeling deeply about the matter, her eyes met his unflinchingly.

She took a deep breath and related the events of that breakfast weeks ago, when Charles had been so ill. "He tried to make light of it, but it was obvious he was not well. I heard him coughing in that same manner just moments ago, but when I knocked at his door, he didn't answer."

"Mrs. Taylor . . ."

". . . doesn't care a wit!" she cut him off in a scathing tone that proclaimed her dislike of Regina. "While Charles was too sick to leave his cabin yesterday, she was casually sipping tea and throwing insults at me. And this morning while he was too ill to eat breakfast, she was walking the deck as though she didn't have a care in the world." A frown of concern and annoyance creased her brow. "Charles is too proud to ask for help, and Regina doesn't care enough to even bother trying."

Justin needed no convincing of Regina's attitude concerning her husband. With as much subtlety as a brick wall, she had let him know that her favors could be his. At first he had been more amused that anything else, finding her efforts no different from those of scores of other women who sought to be his lover. But he had no stomach for cuckolding a husband and Regina's persistence had become a distinct irritation.

Setting his glass aside, Justin rose and came to stand before Cara. "I'll have Percy look in on him," he promised in a gentle voice meant to soothe. His hands caught at the collar of her cloak and snuggled it beneath her chin. Her eyes still flashed with the spirit of her feelings and once again he was amazed that she was such a wealth of passion lying dormant. "Was there anything else?"

Cara was touched by his concern for Charles. Gazing up, she sighed in relief, oddly comforted that he shared her same feelings. He stood close before her and, as always, she was helpless to keep her pulse from racing. The last time he had stood this close, he had taken her in his arms and kissed her until she was senseless. Half-afraid that he was going to do the same now, she was just as afraid that he wouldn't. Not trusting her voice, she shook her head.

His hands lightly skimmed her shoulders and for just a moment, as his eyes toured her face, Cara thought she saw that same glint of something that always seemed to appear when he was about to kiss her. She held her breath in anticipation, but the look vanished and he dropped his arms. Disappointed, she watched as he stepped away to the armoire and shrugged into a heavy, dark wool coat.

With a firm hand riding on the small of her back, he escorted her the few steps down the companionway to her cabin. As if in silent communication they both looked to the door of Charles's cabin.

"I'll find Percy," he told her, seeing the look of worry in her eyes again.

"Thank you."

"How did Mrs. Taylor insult you?"

The question could have come out of nowhere, as prepared as she was for the unexpectedness of it. Caught off guard, her face wore a quizzical expression as she tried to fathom his abrupt shift in mood. His face gave no answers. There was a short silence as she considered his question. She couldn't tell him of the conversation she had had with Regina. Groping for a calm she didn't feel, her mind scrambled for a suitable answer.

"It was all rather petty, actually," she explained with a dismissing shrug. "I shouldn't have even mentioned it."

"But you did." His words were as intense as the suddenly sharp blue gaze he leveled on her. "What did the two of you discuss?"

Cara glanced her toes briefly. "The weather, clothes, my accident the night of the storm."

He knew she wasn't telling him even half of it, and wanting to know what had transpired between the two women to cause Cara such unease, he pushed for more. "What did she want to know about that night?"

She had never been adept at making up stories, even worse at lying, and she found it impossible to fabricate something that would stem his inquisition now, before his questions had her revealing the entire embarrassing episode. "It doesn't matter, Captain . . ."

"Justin."

She blinked, regrouped, then continued. "Justin. Mrs. Taylor and I simply do not get along." She lifted imploring eyes to his. "I admit to you that I do not care for her. We have been at odds from the very start, although I do not know why."

Whatever the two women had discussed, Justin knew he wouldn't hear about it from Cara. And although he didn't know the specifics of what had occurred, he was certain Cara had been the victim in the exchange. Unexpectedly, rage boiled up inside him and an uncharacteristic surge of protectiveness that demanded he have the truth from her. But instead of exacting from her the answers he sought, he found himself relenting to the beseeching look in her eyes.

"You really are the most stubborn woman," he told her in the gentlest of accusations, a puzzled look on his face at how easily her silent appeal had neutralized his anger.

Days ago, he had hurled those same words at her in anger. Now he made them sound like an endearment. A lovely, dimpled smile formed on her lips as she gazed up at him. "No, just determined."

Chapter Six

The following morning found Charles's health no better. Exhausted from the painful coughing that drew increasing amounts of blood, he was too weak to rise.

Regina emerged on deck just before nine o'clock, long before she was accustomed to rising. Charles's coughing had kept her awake through most of the night and into the early morning hours. Since she had found it impossible to get any sleep at all, she dressed and left their cabin, tired and irritable.

The wind tore at Regina's velvet cloak and whipped at the fragile bonnet sitting cocked to one side of her head. With a crude curse she clutched the hat to save it from flying across the deck and gave full rein to her ill-tempered thoughts.

Damn Charles and his hacking! The last place she wanted to be was out on deck walking aimlessly in circles while the sea air made a shambles of her hair. But she couldn't tolerate being cooped up with that dying old man for one minute longer. He had just about driven her to distraction with his coughing, and if that hadn't been enough, there was all that blood. She shuddered then ground her teeth together, livid that Charles was putting her though this.

A biting gust slashed the ship, and Regina turned her back to the wind. With a hand gripping the deep burgundy ribbons of her hat, she muttered another curse. In self-serving interest she longed for sleep and gazed with a frustrated pout in the direction of her cabin. But just as quickly, her mind turned away from the thought. She simply could not endure another minute with him. Being forced into a close arrangement with Charles was barely tolerable when he was in a healthy state, let alone when he was so repulsively ill. For weeks she had been silently fuming about having to share a cabin with him, but thank God for small favors in that their cabin had two separate bunks.

She looked distractedly around the ship, and her thoughts skimmed over the past. There had never been any love between her and Charles. She admitted she liked him upon occasion, especially when it benefited her to do so. But overall, she found him boring, unappealing, and oh, so old. Even when they had first been married, he had been old, though at the time his enormous wealth had made his fifty years seem more stately than aged.

She had no regrets in having married him. He was so manageable and she knew there weren't many men who would have accepted the type of marriage she insisted upon.

They hadn't shared a bed since early in their marriage and even then, she had detested his wrinkled body next to hers. She had tolerated his "lust" for over a year, the thought of having unlimited access to his money sustaining her through his more passionate moments. In looking back, though, Regina wasn't sure how long she could have gone on like that, but as it was, in the second year of married life, Charles had suffered a heart seizure that had nearly killed him. It was the excuse she had dreamed of to discontinue the physical side of their relationship, saying that any exertion of that nature could easily cause another attack or even kill him.

Her refusal to share Charles's bed did not, however, keep her out of other men's beds. She gloriously indulged in as many affairs as suited her, shrewdly careful to keep her activities as discreet as possible. As Charles's wife she maintained a social status that pleased her and she made certain that her indiscretions did nothing to interfere with that standing.

She frowned at a sudden thought. Captain Reynolds was proving to be annoyingly moral. She had made it abundantly clear that she desired him, never doubting for a moment that he wasn't in full understanding of the meaning of her glances and carefully phrased invitations. And she had managed to do so right beneath Charles's nose. But it hadn't mattered at all because the good captain seemed to be preoccupied with that little snit, Cara. Well, so be it, that would soon end. Charles couldn't possibly last much longer and then she'd be able to pursue Captain Reynolds as she wanted. It was only a question of how soon the captain would tire of innocence and inexperience.

Heaving an aggravated sigh, she glanced around the deck, coyly searching to see how many men might be watching her. Satisfied that she had the attention of more than one man, she smiled to herself, her mood improving as she considered her situation. She'd be a widow soon. Anyone smarter than a clam shell could see Charles was dying and then everything would be hers and she'd be free at last.

Her black eyes darted toward her cabin again. She could not, absolutely would not, go back to that death room. But with only two other cabins, neither of which was available, she didn't seem to have a choice. Or did she? She paused for a moment, then a smugly feline smile grew on her lips.

Percy quietly closed the door behind him and stood for a moment outside Charles's cabin. The grim twisting of his lips and the deep furrowing of his forehead were evidence of the serious nature of his thoughts. He had checked the old gentleman the night before and had found him pale and weak with a mild fever. But during the night the man's condition had deteriorated to such a degree that Percy was now, as he made his way to Justin's çabin, truly distressed and saddened. And for more than Charles Taylor's sake alone.

"He's dying," he announced to Justin moments later.

Justin sat at his desk, his keen blue gaze sharpening in reaction to Percy's bald statement. With deliberate movements, he laid aside his quill and leaned back in his leather chair.

Long moments passed and Percy knew that his words slithered into Justin's consciousness and gnawed on the barricade that guarded certain memories. At Justin's insistence, those memories were usually kept securely isolated. It was only the intrusion of death into Justin's life that crumbled the barricade and freed the reminders of the past.

"Are you sure?" Justin asked at last, his voice edged in self-defensive anger.

Percy nodded. "I've seen it before. The man is burning with fever and coughing up blood. Got the shakes, too." Trying to gauge Justin's reaction, he could see his captain's carefully schooled expression. As he feared, he could detect the faint narrowing of Justin's eyes, the rigid set of his jaw, and the wave of tension that emanated from across the desk.

"Is there anything you can do for him?" Justin's voice was as controlled as his face.

"No. Just keep him as comfortable as possible in his last days."

"How long does he have?" Again, that collected voice.

Percy's massive shoulders hunched into a shrug. "A week, maybe less. This thing don't take long and it's been at him for a time already."

Percy waited as the finality of the situation permeated the cabin. He knew that jagged remembrances were eroding Justin's normal reserve, straining his self-control, but there was nothing Percy could say or do that would cure Charles Taylor's body or heal Justin's heart.

Finally, Justin spoke. "You are positive."

A look of sorrow filled Percy's eyes. "His heart's racing, he can barely breathe." His head nodded again, this time in a slow, sad movement. "I'm certain."

For just the briefest moment, the intensity of Justin's emotions flashed across his face and then just as quickly subsided. "All right then. Just do what you can for him."

"Aye, Captain."

"Where is Mrs. Taylor?" Each word was enunciated a little too precisely.

The look of regret in Percy's eyes dissipated instantly. "In the salon. She just come in from the deck," he answered derisively. He stopped to give vent to the mocking snort he couldn't contain. "Said she needed to rest a while and warm up." He jammed his fists on his hips and he glanced around the room as though the paneled walls would offer an answer to the questions in his mind. But whatever he would have said dwindled to a confused and pathetic shake of his head at the woman's callous lack of concern for her husband.

It was Justin's responsibility to break the news to Mrs. Taylor. Percy admitted to himself that she deserved no better than what she was about to get, for only death brought out the worst in Justin.

Peering at his captain, Percy could see the remote iciness already firmly in place in Justin's bearing, the haunting of his soul freezing his eyes. It had been this way with Justin, this hideous kind of seething that went far beyond the customary resentfulness that death inspired, ever since his mother had died. The coldhearted, treacherous bitch. Percy caught himself, then took his leave, damning all perfidious women.

The crisp, cold air on deck was a temporary balm for Percy's jangled emotions. His sorrow and frustration over Charles's health kept him on deck, soaking in enough of the swift sea breeze to help restore, to a small degree, his normal pragmatism. But not even the balmiest of Caribbean winds could ease the concern he felt for Justin.

An unusual bonding existed between the two of them, based on trust, respect, and a shared irreverence to a great deal of what life offered. After twelve years, their relationship was a peculiar sort of brotherhood that recognized the ranks of captain and cook, yet never strayed far from trusted friend.

"Is there anything I can do to restore your humor?"

Percy's head snapped to the side at Cara's gentle query. Wrapped in her worn cloak, she gazed up at him and, for a moment, Percy thought that if anyone's smile could cure the world's ills, it was surely Cara Fairchild's.

"Ah, lass, just the sight of your face does that."

Despite his ofttimes gruff, bearlike qualities, Cara thought Percy a perfect dear. She truly liked the man and it troubled her to see him so obviously burdened with some weighty problem.

"I would say in this instance that my face is not enough. You look troubled, Percy."

He didn't try to convince her otherwise. With a lowered head, he tried instead to decide the kindest way of telling her about Charles.

"It isn't good, Cara. Mr. Taylor is in a bad way."

A terrible foreboding clutched at Cara's insides, making her afraid to even consider the possibilities. She didn't want to hear what Percy had to say, but even the unconscious desperation in her eyes couldn't alter his next words.

"He'll not live out the week."

No, no, no, no, no! Cara's mind declared. Charles couldn't die. Not sweet, kind, dear, oh so dear Charles. In just a short while he had become her friend and now he was going to die. She just could not believe that.

"He can't," she pleaded, as though claiming so would make it fact.

"I'm sorry, Cara, but it's the truth of things," Percy said, unable to look at the awful pain in Cara's eyes.

There was only the sound of the wind whipping around them for the span of several moments. Acceptance was difficult for Cara, but it came and with it, the anguish of yet one more loss in her life. "Oh, Percy."

Percy's arms encircled her, drawing her close so her head came to rest against his chest.

When Justin entered the dining salon, Regina was standing before the window, one long white hand clutching the wooden sill. At his approach, she turned, remembering to keep her face as pitiful as possible.

"Captain Reynolds, what a welcome surprise."

Justin viewed Regina with dispassionate eyes. "Hardly, madam, since my presence on this ship is a given constant." His voice was coldly impersonal.

"Well, I was expecting your doctor."

He ignored the doleful look she cast him, and leaned against the paneled wall. "He has just finished with your husband."

"Oh, I can't tell you how relieved I am to hear that. I've been so worried about Charles, but proud man that he is, he refused my suggestion of help."

Her response galled Justin. Up until now, she had shown no obvious regard for her husband and it was absurd that she should attempt to do so now.

"He hasn't been his usual self lately," she continued with an overabundance of consideration. "I certainly hope Mr. Pettingill was able to administer to Charles's ailments."

"I am afraid there is little Percy can do for your husband."

Perturbed lines pulled at Regina's face. "Oh, I knew we should have waited until after the New Year before making this passage," she said, deliberately misinterpreting his words. "If we had remained in London, a proper physician could have seen to Charles." She wrung her hands in a show of agitation. "Now we'll have to wait at least another week to reach home, and the poor man is already suffering so."

The scene before Justin unfolded like a bad play. He crossed his arms over his chest and studied the exaggerated distress in her countenance. Cynically, he considered her overdramatic display and found her performance for sympathy transparent. Mentally he sneered. She was like every other woman he'd met. Faithless and selfish, intent only on satisfying her own needs. Uninvited, Cara's image flashed through his mind in contradiction to that thought, but he shoved away the mental image he had of her.

"You have misunderstood, madam. There is nothing Percy, or any other physician, can do. Your husband is dying."

Her eyes widened to enormous proportions. "What?" She dropped the single word with dramatic presentation, coming to stand beside the table.

"I offer my solicitude," he replied without the slightest softening to take the edge off his abruptness.

"But . . . but, I don't understand," she sputtered, "Charles cannot be dying. He's just ill. He's been sick in this manner before and did not die."

Brutally indifferent to what he considered to be tedious theatrics, Justin gave the shine on his boots his attention as he spoke. "I'm afraid that is not the case now."

For the first time, Regina neglected her own self-absorption and wondered about the state of Justin's temperament. However, she rashly ignored the frisson of uncertainty she felt that should have warned her to caution.

"Perhaps Mr. Pettingill is wrong."

"He isn't."

"Please tell me this is not so, Captain," she pleaded, taking a step closer in order to enhance her desperate-sounding plea.

His eyes cutting to hers in frigid disdain was all the answer he spared her.

"I simply will not believe that this is true." With hands pressed to trembling lips and tears coursing down pale cheeks, Regina advanced another step and then with practiced ease, collapsed in a torrent of weeping.

Instinctively, Justin's quicksilver reflexes closed the little remaining distance between them and he caught her up against him. Immediately, Regina rested her head on his chest, while one of her hands, in a pretense of distress, slid up the firm wall to clutch at his shirt. Behind her tears, her mind snidely challenged him to just try and ignore her as she leaned her weight into his, pressing intimately against his thighs. For a brief moment, Regina actually believed her scheme was successful, but in the next instant, Justin abruptly lowered his arms and she was dumped to the floor in an ignominious heap.

The copious sobbing ceased at once. From her lowly position at Justin's feet, Regina glared up, too incensed to heed the glacial look Justin directed at her. "How dare you!" she demanded.

A horrible excuse for a smile pulled Justin's face into taut lines. "I would dare anything, madam." His voice was a low growl. "Do not ever be so foolish as to forget that again."

Without a second glance, he stepped over her outstretched legs and stalked from the cabin.

Cara and Percy turned at the opening of the companionway door. Everything about Justin, as he stepped onto the deck, proclaimed a man in the grips of intense emotion. A half-formed breath caught in Cara's throat at the sight of him, and as he neared, she was hit by a wave of anger that seemed to radiate from him. Instinctively, she reached out a hand, but Percy wisely intervened, as Justin walked right past them both.

"Let him alone, lass."

With bewildered, troubled eyes, Cara watched Justin's retreating back, then turned questioningly to Percy. "Something is terribly wrong."

"There is," he answered.

"Perhaps I can help."

"You can't."

Cara turned toward the forward hatch where Justin had disappeared into the depths of the ship. "I don't understand. Why not?"

"You needs leave it be, Cara."

But she couldn't. "He's distraught over Charles?"

"Yes."

"Then somebody needs to speak with him."

"It isn't that simple."

"I can at least try," she persisted.

"He won't let you."

"Why not?" She was exasperated with being led in circles.

Percy scrubbed a hand over his chin, wishing he could say something to put her mind at ease, but he couldn't. The only thing that would make any sense at all to her would be the truth and he couldn't tell her without betraying Justin. It was something Percy had never done, something that was beyond consideration. No, she would have to be satisfied with whatever explanation he offered.

"Cara, if I thought being at his side would help him, I wouldn't be standing here talking to you," he said more forcefully that he had intended. He gentled his tone. "Justin's a lucky man to have your concern, but he wouldn't appreciate it right now. Trust what I'm telling you, and give him some time."

She didn't understand and her heart urged her to seek Justin out, but Percy's intense sincerity was enough to convince her to be patient.

The nightmare started as an obscure dream, strange and disjointed. A sea of laughing faces swam in meaningless circles. Out of nowhere, Charles loomed frighteningly real, then just as abruptly disappeared. Cara searched the swirling faces, but when she turned back, it was her father who stood there. Just beyond her reach, he called to her, trying to tell her something. She ran toward him, but never got any closer. Her legs tangled in the length of her skirt and frantically she yanked the folds out of her way. She called out for help, but he wasn't there any longer. Justin was at her side then and she could move again. Her face lifted for a kiss that never came. The walls of Fairfield suddenly surrounded her, and in the next instant they crumbled and she screamed as one of the mullioned windows crashed down upon her.

Cara jerked upright, her eyes wide, straining to focus on the reality of her low-lit cabin. Fully clothed, she had fallen asleep while trying to read. Almost as a second thought, she looked about the twisted bed covers for the volume of short stories and found it wedged between the wall and the pillow. The book gave her mind a focal point and with a sigh she came fully awake.

Troubled thoughts instantly assailed her. A profound sadness hung over the ship as Charles's health had worsened throughout the day. Percy went about his business in a close-mouthed fashion, a frown steadily in place across his forehead. Regina had taken to her bed, a hastily prepared cot set up in her temporary cabin, the dining salon. Cara herself had spent a melancholy day feeling helpless and heavyhearted. And if the crew seemed unusually cautious, it was only to be expected. Not only did they feel anxiety over the thought of an impending death, but they also walked an extremely narrow line for fear of displeasing their dangerously tense captain.

Veteran ship hands whispered to newer crew members to stay well out of the man's way if at all possible. It wasn't often that his disposition was so ominous, and every sailor accomplished his duties with one eye on his work and the other on Captain Reynolds.

Cara had heeded Percy's advice and hadn't attempted to speak to Justin, but she had worried about him all day. Loving him as she did, she wanted desperately to help him with whatever problem he had. And she was certain there was a problem, for Justin's reaction went far beyond the sorrow expected in such a situation.

A decision made, she stood. As far as she was concerned, she had been patient enough. With a determined tilt of her head that would have earned her Justin's accusation of stubborn, she donned her cloak and headed for the poop deck, where she knew Justin usually was at this hour of the night.

The ship, wrapped in a veil of moonless night, appeared a different place. Shapes that were solid forms in daylight now seemed to be dark, negative spaces that blended into the surrounding black sky. Even though the sound of the bow cutting through the ocean was still reassuringly present, as was the constant creaking of jute and timber, it took

Cara several minutes to reaquaint herself with the quarterdeck.

One of the nebulous structures detached itself from the shadows and made its way toward her as she stood before the companionway door. She watched its approach and by midship was able to recognize the silhouette. Her heart lurched. The figure quickly closed the distance between the mainmast and herself, and Justin came into stark, vivid perspective.

"I believe I told you never to be on deck, at night, alone."

His voice was tight, impersonal, but Cara was relieved that he was at least talking to her.

"If you will notice, I am not alone." She gave no ground, determined that he would not antagonize or bully or frighten her away.

"Do not mince words with me, madam."

"It was never my intent."

"Then return to your cabin."

"No."

It was as blatantly defiant as Cara had ever been. She held her breath. In his usual temperament, she knew he had no tolerance for defiance, and she could only guess what his reaction would be now. Considering his tension of the moment, she prayed that she had enough courage to see this through.

A day's worth of concentration had subdued the ungovernable emotionalism that had attacked Justin earlier. Back in seclusion was a part of his past that he normally never acknowledged. What remained of the deplorable state he had found himself in that morning was a bitter anger toward the temporary vulnerability he despised himself for feeling.

"You dare more than most sane men ever would," he growled, grasping her arms in a painful grip that brought a gasp to Cara's lips.

"I know," she answered, clinging to the bravado that had brought her this far.

Her admission, given so freely, so ungrudgingly, drew Justin up short and somehow, inexplicably, defused the tension of the moment. He gazed down in bemused disbelief. There she stood, knowing she was tempting his ire, yet she gazed back without a flicker of an eyelash.

"Would you please release me?" she asked gently, sensing that Justin was not about to explode in anger at her.

With a muttered curse, he stepped away. "What are you doing out here?" he asked.

Cara wasn't sure if his curse was directed at her or the situation. "I was looking for you."

"I am honored then," he replied, a snide twist of his lips drawing his face into a one-sided grin. "To what do I owe the pleasure of your company?"

"I was worried about you."

"Were you?"

"Yes."

"Why?" His question was voiced in genuine surprise.

A concerned frown creased Cara's brow. "Because you seemed so upset this morning. Percy would not tell me what was wrong." She paused as her expression turned tender, and in a gesture that felt as natural as breathing, she laid a gentle hand against the cool, hard planes of his face. "I did not want you to bear your discomfort alone."

It had been years since Justin had been the recipient of such purity of sentiment from anyone other than his grandmother. Only she had expressed such feelings toward him, and it always made him uncomfortable. He was no less uncomfortable now. In self-defense, he stepped back out of Cara's reach.

"Whatever 'discomfort' you believed you saw requires no further attention." He dismissed the topic. "Come, take the watch with me."

Without protest, Cara let him lead her forward, but the shift in subject was not lost on her. Casting a curious glance his way, she wondered why he chose to ignore the matter, but he obviously had no intentions of discussing it with her.

They stopped at the ladder leading to the forecastle deck, the rungs providing a perfect perch for Cara. Justin easily lifted her and set her so that they were at eye level.

"You are not subtle, Justin," she stated, once she had settled herself comfortably.

Justin took his place at the rail where he could watch both Cara and the ocean. "In what context am I to take your meaning?"

"You will not tell me why you have behaved as you have today." She paused, hoping he would take advantage of the opportunity she gave him, but he didn't. She continued in a somber voice. "I assume Charles Taylor was the cause."

"We are all affected by the matter," he admitted, yet Cara found the statement noncommittal.

"It really is quite sad," she whispered on a sigh, still trying to adjust to the situation.

"A choice of viewpoints, actually."

Shadows obscured the fine details of Justin's face, and Cara wished she could see his expression. "I am not sure I take your meaning."

"Death is just the natural, expected conclusion to life."

"Yes, you're right, of course. But logic has no bearing on how we feel, especially if it involves someone dearly loved."

"You are speaking from experience, I take it."

Cara hadn't realized she was. Glancing down at her lap, she lifted a shoulder in a shrug. "When my mother died, I was but a child of nine. I grieved as a child would. My father's passing was no less painful for the adult I am now."

"I would have thought you would have no great love for him."

Her head snapped up. "Why?" she asked, startled by his assumption.

Justin leaned into the rail, bracing his weight on a forearm. "The contents of his will have created a good deal of misfortune for you."

"Regardless of what he did, I love him no less." The words spilled out without thought, and once spoken, Cara realized how true they were. In the past months her feelings had been entwined with hurt, but time had somehow sorted through the confusion. She may never understand why her father had done what he did, but she would always love him.

"That is quite noble of you."

"Do you suggest that I forget my childhood?"

"No, I am merely curious as to your attitude."

"You find it strange?"

"I find it . . . unusual."

Cara was struck by his offhanded manner. She wondered why he was so cynical in this instance, that he should give family devotion such cavalier treatment.

'What of *your* family, Justin?"

Justin didn't reply at once, but Cara could see the overshadowed contours of his face regarding her. "What do you wish to know?"

Somehow she thought he would sidestep the issue and she was delighted that he didn't. She wanted to know about the people and events that made Justin the man she loved. It was important that she know about his past, his childhood, his youth. A glowing warmth filled her as she pictured a tousled-haired little boy, running through green fields, a muddied face with sparkling blue eyes and an adorable smile.

"Tell me of your parents."

"They are both deceased."

"Were you a child when they passed away?"

"Hardly. Father died seven years ago. Mother . . . Mother, when I was twenty-one."

"Justin," she claimed in a startled voice. "I don't even know how old you are." Her tone implied she had the right to know.

"Thirty-four," he answered, indulgent of her curiosity.

"Are you an only child?"

"No, I have a younger sister. Half sister, actually. Lenore was born when I was twelve."

Cara was creating a lovely picture in her mind of Justin as he must have been, surrounded by family members. "Was it your mother or father who had been married previously?" she asked, drawing the logical conclusion from his statement.

"Nothing that circumspect, I'm afraid. Lenore is the product of one of my mother's numerous love affairs. She got caught with the pregnancy, and by the time she realized her mistake, it was too late to handle the matter."

Confusion and shock swept through Cara simultaneously. She knew that fidelity was not a strong suit in some marriages, but Justin's blatant indifference to his mother's indiscretions held her speechless.

"Have I shocked you?" he asked, when her silence continued.

"I . . . I don't know what to say."

A short chuckle preceded his words. "There is little to be said. It's been twenty-three years now, water under the bridge, so to speak."

"How . . ." she began, still trying to collect her thoughts. "How did your father take it?"

"As I remember," he stated conversationally, "he wasn't particularly pleased, but he wasn't one to split hairs over it, either. He went about his business as usual and my mother, hers."

The pretty imagery Cara had naively produced withered into a muddied ruin. "Your parents had no love for each other, did they?"

Justin gave a short, mocking laugh. "That sentiment is extremely trite in most circumstances, positively ridiculous in my parents'. My father loved no one, least of all his wife. If there was a love in his life, it was money, how much he had and how much more he could acquire."

"Is that why your mother engaged in . . . affairs?"

"Do not endow my mother with false virtues. She was never so noble as to suffer through an unrequited love. She cared no more for my father than he did for her."

Cara was becoming increasingly sad with each passing minute. "Then, theirs was an arranged marriage?"

"Naturally." He paused, and even through the darkness separating them, Cara knew he was staring hard at her. "Cara, the sympathy you are feeling for my parents is misplaced. They both received what they wanted from their marriage. My mother was the very spoiled child of parents who indulged their child's every wish. Whatever my mother desired, she received. When she was seventeen, she received my father." He stopped and cast a glance out over the waters. "After they were married, she expected my father to take up where my grandparents left off, giving her everything she wanted. Since my father's main concern in life was making money and hers was spending it, they suited each other perfectly. My father, in return, wanted an heir. He received me to carry on the family name. After I was born, my mother was free to go her own way."

"She didn't raise you?" Cara asked in disbelief.

"Raising children was not one of her pursuits in life."

Cara was appalled. What kind of woman had a baby and cared nothing for it? What kind of father saw his son *only* as a means of continuing a name? His parents may not have cared for each other, but how could they not have loved their own child?

Cara had been raised in a loving, nurturing atmosphere. Justin's own childhood had been void of the very things that characterized hers. How he must have suffered, yearning for a parent's gentle care. She felt sick at heart and a huge rush of tears flooded her eyes and clogged her throat.

"Is the inquisition over?" he asked, half-playfully.

Cara couldn't answer. Silently, she sat and wiped the tears that slipped down her cheeks.

"Cara?"

When he again received no answer, he left the rail and joined her. "Are you crying?" he asked, completely baffled by her unexpected action. "Why are you crying?"

She raised her head, no longer trying to conceal her tears, or the outrage that had produced them. "Because some people do not deserve to be blessed with children," she stated emphatically. "Especially if they are incapable of loving them."

Justin's jaw dropped. It was almost beyond his comprehension that she was crying for him. "Cara, you absurd little champion, you needn't be upset. I assure you, I was adequately looked after."

She made a swipe at the last of her tears. "A child should not have to exist on just 'adequate.' "

Reaching out, Justin's hands slipped over her shoulders. "All has turned out quite well. Besides, I never wanted for anything."

Anything except love, Cara thought. Well, she had enough love for him to make up for his childhood and fill each day of the rest of his life.

"Captain." A disembodied voice cracked the silence.

"Yes," Justin called back over his shoulder.

"Change of watch, sir."

Justin called back his reply, then lifted Cara from the ladder.

No words were exchanged as they walked back to the companionway, but Cara had a hundred things she wanted to say. At the door, she turned, feeling the pressure of limited time, and she knew that she would have to wait to tell Justin of all the things in her heart.

With a yearning look that the midnight hid, she reached up and let her fingertips lightly skim his face. Those details—the firm edge of his jaw, the chiseled cheekbones, the strong line of masculine lips, obscured by the darkness—were lovingly illuminated by the image she carried in her mind.

Hesitantly, she rose to her toes and pressed her lips to his with a tender passion that originated in her heart. The kiss was warm, but fleeting, and then she returned to her cabin.

Justin stood in the night and smiled the only genuine smile he'd had all day.

Chapter Seven

Williamsburg, Virginia

From the pit of his belly, Bartholemew Smith forced a gurgling belch and shoved the chipped stoneware plate across the splintered tabletop. Wiping the back of his sleeve against his mouth to catch the traces of spittle on his lips, he ignored the cold remains of breakfast he had scattered on the grayed wood.

He greeted the dawn in the isolated backwaters of the James River with an unaccustomed sense of expectation. As a waterman, he normally viewed each day as being no different from the next. Only the variety of the day's catch accounted for any modification in his routine. But today was different. Today he had business to tend to, serious business.

He'd been into town the day before, a rare occasion, since he didn't associate with people he didn't trust and there was no one in Williamsburg he trusted. He'd overheard someone say it was one week from December. He didn't give a damn what name was tagged to the season. He knew that when the chub started running and the oyster harvest was its most plentiful, winter was nearby. But the townspeople named their months and this month of December had special significance to Smith. Sometime before that Christian day of Christmas, Captain Reynolds was due to return.

Reynolds. Smith mentally spat the name out in disgust. He had waited six long years for the bastard to return. Now it was just a matter of weeks before the bleedin' Brit got what he deserved.

Lifting his bulky weight from the stool that served as a chair, Smith opened the door and stepped outside to scan the marsh. The frost hadn't settled here on the reeds, but he could smell it on the inland air, the same way he could pick out the scent of Williamsburg almost five miles away.

Damn, he could still remember the smell of the air that night six years ago when he had crept onto the *Wind Dancer*. Every breath he had taken had been heavy with the odor of hickory smoke and hog dung from a nearby farm. And just like a piece of fatback, he would have sliced the hide from the high-and-mighty Reynolds, if he'd had the chance. Only it hadn't turned out that way. Reynolds had caught him trying to steal the casks of wine that brought such a pretty penny in town and had had him thrown into the gaol. Damn stinking, rotting place. It wasn't even fit for the lowest scum.

Cursing, Smith started down the dirt path leading out of the marsh. He needed to find his old friend, Olan Wright, and together they needed to make plans. If the British captain and his British ship were just a few weeks off, then he'd waste no time. There was no way of knowing how long the bastard would remain, but if Smith was successful, it would be eternally.

All it took in the end for Percy to capitulate and allow Cara to help care for Charles was a quietly spoken "please." Percy had been adamant in his stance that this particular sickroom was no place for Cara and no amount of discussion from Cara swayed him. But when she had finally uttered that single plea, the accompanying yearning look in her eyes, and the tearful catch in her voice, had broken down all of Percy's objections.

For two days they shared the duties of tending Charles, though there was little enough either had to do. Charles slept in an almost-unconscious state, barely able to drag in enough air to keep him alive. He woke infrequently to bloodied coughing spells and then would slip into sleep once again. Laying cool, damp cloths on his forehead and trying to feed him broth better served Cara's need to help than it did Charles's condition.

Regina was conspicuous by her absence. Languishing in a sham of despair that supposedly prevented her from accomplishing even the simplest tasks, she required almost as much attention as her husband. When she wasn't sleeping, she was calling on Willie to fetch her a pot of tea or to stoke the fire in the stove that was never quite warm enough to suit her. The ship's motion was too severe, the food offered upset her already-unsettled stomach, good money had been paid for a suitable cabin and not the makeshift one she'd been allotted; her complaints came in a steady stream.

Cara had just stepped from her cabin and was standing in the companionway as Percy emerged from the dining salon.

"That woman is cork-brained," he mumbled to himself between gritted teeth, as he intentionally slammed Regina's door behind him.

"I don't think I have to ask whom you are referring to."

He cast a dark glance at the door he'd just abused. "If she thinks for one minute that I'm going to prepare a special meal for the likes of her, then she's addled in her wits." He jerked the dinner-laden tray he was holding, before continuing in a sugary mimic of Regina. "Says she don't think her constitution could abide stew tonight. Perhaps a pudding or a light broth with some hen would rest easy on her distraught digestion." His voice dropped two octaves to its normal pitch. "Well, her digestion is as fit as mine, which, under the circumstances, says a great deal."

Personally, Cara agreed with Percy. She found it difficult to believe that Regina was so emotionally overwrought over Charles that she was completely incapacitated. But, for whatever reason, Regina seemed intent on her behavior.

"If I thought it would help, I would take the tray back to her," she offered in hopes of soothing Percy's temper.

"What? And have her make mincemeat of you? I've heard that tongue of hers, when she don't think anyone's listening, and you don't deserve to be on the receiving end of that." The tray rattled again. "A lady, she isn't."

"You're right, of course."

"She'll eat what's fit for the rest of us, or she can starve," he said more to himself than to Cara.

She could see that the worst of Percy's tirade was over. "I believe if you take the tray to Willie, you'll find a most appreciative diner there." She gave him a winsome smile, complete with dimples. "Besides, he deserves an extra reward for tolerating Mrs. Taylor as well as he has."

Percy scoffed, then broke into a contrite smile. "Another week, a fortnight at the most, then she'll be on her way."

The mention of time reminded them both of Charles and how limited his time was.

"How is he faring?" Percy asked, nodding his head toward Charles's cabin.

Cara gave a full sigh. "Same as this morning. He was sleeping when I was with him. I was about to sit with him again. Perhaps he'll be awake now."

Wishful thinking had its place, but Percy knew this wasn't it. He didn't have the heart, though, to stomp all over her optimism by telling her that the old gentleman would very likely never wake up again.

"I'll come by in an hour or so."

No more needed to be said and Cara entered Charles's cabin.

The hour passed in silence, a silence that lent itself to melancholy introspection. Sitting beside Charles's bunk, she thought how fragile he appeared in the low lantern light.

Ashen skin was sunken over newly prominent cheekbones. One blue-tinged hand lay on his chest that never drew in more than a small dose of air. Seeing him thus, she couldn't help but consider her father's death.

Prior to his demise, she had never given it a great deal of thought, but this is what she would have pictured. Her father lying ill, not from any specific malady, but from a lengthy, full life that had taken its toll. And she sitting by his side, offering comfort and companionship to ease his final days.

Hot tears stung her eyes. Turning her head away, she grieved that her father's last moments had been bereft of the solace and peace she could have offered.

A sputtering gurgle choked its way up Charles's throat, drawing Cara's immediate attention. The sound became a rattling cough that shuddered his frail body. It was the first time all day that he had done anything more than lie unconscious and in response, Cara laid a hand upon his. Surprisingly, his fingers twisted beneath hers to turn and hold and then, unexpectedly, his eyes gradually opened.

"Charles?" she breathed in wonder. As in her father's instance, she thought she was to be denied again the opportunity of last farewells. She smiled her joy.

Those blue eyes that had at one time twinkled with such gentlemanly charm, now gazed at her, strained with pain and burnished with fever.

"Cara." The word was a dusty whisper.

"Would you like some water?"

It took too much effort to speak, but the tiny negative shake of his head sufficed.

"Is there anything you require?"

Charles's lips formed the word, but no sound came out.

"Regina?" Cara asked. "You wish for Regina?"

She was about to leave for the dining salon when his hand tightened on hers and she remained seated.

Through his agony, Charles saw her questioning look. He forced his lungs to work. "Where?"

"She is in the dining salon." Wanting desperately to alleviate his burden of speaking, she tried to anticipate what it was he was trying to say. "Would you like me to get Regina for you?"

Again his head shook the slight negative response. "How?" he managed to get out.

For a moment, Cara wasn't sure she understood his question. "How is she?" she asked uncertainly.

His exhausted lids closed in a silent yes.

"She is bearing up. She is . . ." Her words dwindled. She couldn't bring herself to tell him that Regina was worried or beside herself or despondent, because she knew he would see that for the untruth it was. "We are all quite concerned, Charles," she finished.

A trembling smile wiggled his lips. "Tactful."

The embarrassment Cara felt was for Regina, not herself. Nonetheless, she glanced to her lap, not knowing what to say to a dying man who knew his wife didn't care. The thought tightened her throat with the tears she had been striving to hold back.

"That . . ." She swallowed past the ache. "That and honest. Percy has been in often to see to you."

"As have you."

"You knew? I thought you had been sleeping."

"At times."

And those other times? she wondered. Had he been too exhausted to even open his eyes? She was glad he had been aware of her presence. Hopefully, he had derived some comfort from her company.

"Marry him."

She didn't understand the seemingly disconnected command. "I'm sorry, I beg your pardon?"

"Marry."

"Who?"

"Captain Reynolds."

Caught off guard, she sat back in her chair and blinked in confusion.

"Love him."

"Charles, I . . ."

"Love him."

It wasn't a question, she realized, but a statement. "Yes, I love him," she admitted softly.

"Good."

She searched his face. "How did you know?"

"May be dying, but I see."

The very bluntness of his statement ate at Cara's self-control. She did not want to break down and weep in front of Charles, but she was helpless to keep her bottom lip from quivering. She started to protest, but he cut her off.

"As Ben Franklin said, 'Fear not death, for the sooner we die, the longer shall we be immortal.' "

The effort it took for Charles to speak cost him heavily. Pain ripped through him, expanding his chest in exaggerated heaving. Helplessly, Cara watched, unable to do more than take hold of his hands in support. The spasm was brief, but brought Charles all the closer to his quoted immortality.

"Charles, your Mr. Franklin would not want you to tax yourself so."

He lay still for long moments before he finally spoke. "Get captain."

Cara hesitated. She was loath to leave him, illogically feeling that her presence somehow kept him alive. Yet she could not deny him his request. "Yes, of course," she said, rising. At the door, she turned to assure herself that he was still breathing, then she left in search of Justin.

She found him with the help of Phillip. He took her urgent message to Justin in the hold and, within minutes, Justin joined her in the companionway.

"He's awake and wishes to speak to you," she said without preamble. The short wait had strained her composure to its limits.

Justin eyed her tensely fragile demeanor, her blue dress only adding to the pale quality of her skin. With fingers tightly entwined and her expression painfully expectant, she looked as though she were on the verge of fracturing.

"Wait for me in my cabin," he ordered.

Though reluctant to do so, there seemed little else for her to do.

Justin's cabin was as orderly as usual, warm and extremely masculine, and from the room as a whole, Cara derived a sense of control. Stepping to the desk, she was drawn to the mahogany piece that epitomized Justin's bolder traits of power and authority. She sat in the chair behind, the leather giving, but not to accommodate the softness of her contours. Unaccountably disappointed and feeling at frayed ends, she rose and leaned against the window frame, her distraught gaze oblivious to the ocean.

The minute Justin stepped into his cabin, he could feel the intensity of Cara's anxiety boring into him from her place behind his desk. He gave her a measured look, then crossed to the side table and poured a healthy amount of bourbon into a large, heavy glass.

"Drink this," he ordered as he came to stand beside her.

She ignored his outstretched hand. "Is he? . . ."

Her tension was a palpable thing. "No," he answered. "Drink."

Giving a relieved sigh, Cara looked at the glass. "What is this?" she asked, taking the cool cut-crystal in her hand.

"Bourbon."

"Justin, I've told you, I do not partake of spirits."

"You will tonight." He placed a long finger beneath the glass and with indomitable, understated strength raised the glass to her lips.

"Justin, I . . ."

"Quiet."

The rich liquor seared every inch of her insides between tongue and stomach. Coughing and sputtering, she leveled an accusing glare on him, miffed by his mildly amused smile.

"Why . . . how . . ." she began, when she caught her first good breath.

"It will help settle your nerves." He urged the glass to her lips again.

Cara took another swallow, Justin giving her no choice in the matter. She found the second sip little better than the first and determinedly handed the glass back.

"Enough," she declared, grimacing.

Justin thought it was not nearly enough by far, but he took the glass and set it on the desk. "That should make you feel better."

"I am not ill," she stated, wondering why he should think such a thing.

Taking her cold hand and stepping back, he sat in the leather chair and brought her down onto his lap.

Where Cara had found the chair nonconforming, the muscled length of Justin on that chair was a comfort not to be believed. She automatically leaned into his strength, her bottom finding a natural seat on his long thighs while her head eased into the crook beneath his jaw.

Weeks ago she would have been horrified to have found herself in such an intimate position, but now she welcomed the arm that supported her back and the hand that rested on her waist. The warmth of his body and the feel of its solidity permeated her senses with a contentment that was far more effective in restoring her calm than the strong drink.

"I did not realize my lack of composure," she admitted.

Justin tilted his head in order to view her face. "I know." Lifting the glass, he ordered again. "Another good sip."

Cara eyed the amber liquid skeptically. "I would prefer not to," she objected.

"Consider it medicinal treatment."

"It will only make me muddled."

"You need to be muddled."

Sitting upright, she gave him a bewildered look. Immediately, he tilted the glass to her lips, and short of having the contents spilled into her lap, Cara took another swallow. The sting was gone, but the flavor was no less distasteful.

"How do you drink this?" she asked, wrinkling her nose.

"An acquired taste."

"One that I have no intentions of cultivating," she assured him.

"Of that I have no doubt, but it will go far in easing your distress over Mr. Taylor."

The bourbon was forgotten.

"I didn't know what to tell him." She spoke quietly, with head lowered.

"Under the circumstances, there is nothing one can be expected to say."

"He wanted to know how Regina was faring. He was lying there, barely able to breathe, and *he* was concerned about *her*. I couldn't tell him that not once had she been in to see him. Or worse, that she hasn't even asked about him."

"Charles is no fool."

"I feel so badly for him. He does not deserve such disdain from his wife, especially so, now."

"No one is fortunate enough to choose the circumstances of one's death."

Cara knew this was true, but it didn't lessen her sorrow for Charles nor her dislike for Regina. "I should return to Charles."

"No."

At the implacable reply, her head snapped up. "He may need . . ."

"Percy is with him."

She considered this for only a moment. "I would feel better if I were there also."

"Your attendance on Charles has only served to upset you."

She took mild offense. "That is not true." Seeing his pointed look, she had to admit that, in part, he was right. "Well, perhaps it is disturbing, but my presence has been a comfort to him."

"One that he does not require at the moment." And before she could debate the issue further, he lifted the glass for Cara to take another drink. This time the bourbon made a smooth flow to her increasingly warm stomach.

"Why must you insist that I drink this vile brew?" she asked in exasperation, as he set the glass aside again. Her fingertips scrubbed across her lips as though to remove the taste. She was beginning to get annoyed with his overbearing nature and turned her head sharply to face him, intending to express her opinion on that issue. But while the movement brought her head around, it left her eyes behind and she quickly lifted a hand to her forehead.

"Oh dear."

"Muddled, are you?"

"Yes."

"Good."

"You need not sound so pleased," she said from behind her hand.

"Considering your normal lack of indulgence and your size, I am frankly amazed that you have consumed as much as you have." The tall glass was more than half-empty.

Cara lowered her hand. "Well, I shan't be having any more."

"Don't be too certain of that."

Ignoring his remark, she made a move to leave his lap, but his hands held her firmly in place.

"Let me up, Justin."

"No."

She gave him as direct a look as possible. "I will not sit here and become drunk while Charles is . . . while Charles . . ." Her words faltered, but Justin finished for her.

"While Charles is dying?"

She found it impossible to look away from the dark blue eyes that bore steadily into hers. In those clear depths she saw the truth, unwanted, but undeniable. In her mind she had accepted the situation. Now, finally, her heart did, too.

The strain of the last few days had taken its toll, and what little reserve of strength she had left was now eroded by the effects of the liquor. Dismayed, she felt her control slip away, helpless to prevent the tears from rising up in full force.

Closing her eyes, her head came to rest on Justin's shoulder and she cried softly. She cried for her mother and father and for Charles, for all those people dear to her but lost forever.

Justin could feel her body trembling, could feel the warm moisture of her tears dampening his shirt and found the experience strange. It wasn't in his nature to hold a crying woman, and up until now, he had rarely done so. The last time she had cried in such a manner, he had stormed out of the cabin. He didn't feel like doing that now.

Yet he wasn't certain what to do. Normally, when a woman was draped across his lap, it was for purposes entirely different than crying on his shoulder. But he didn't mean to take Cara to bed under the present circumstances. No, he liked his bed partners sober, and his only intention, after having taken one look at her outside Charles's cabin, was to get her drunk enough to cope with the old man's impending death.

Cold, instinctive cynicism told him to stand and let gravity resolve the uncomfortable situation, but somehow he just couldn't do it.

Muttering a curse at the absurdity of his reaction, Justin, nonetheless, eased his arms around Cara's shaking form. Without understanding why, indeed not wanting to understand why, he sat and silently rode out the storm of her tears.

Cara's weeping gradually dwindled, yet she remained where she was, firmly held within Justin's strong arms. With her forehead pressed to the base of his neck, she had no desire to move and relished the comfort his nearness provided.

"Better?" Justin asked, somewhat gruffly, when all traces of weeping had ceased. Beneath his chin, he could feel the nod of her head.

Neither spoke for several minutes more. Finally, it was Cara's shaky whisper that broke the silence.

"It is not right that someone as kind and gentle as Charles should die."

"Everyone dies, Cara."

"Yes, but that doesn't make it easier to bear." A huge sigh escaped her and she suddenly felt tired to the depths of her being. "I'm tired of losing all that I cherish." She closed her eyes, but her memories were in sharp focus. "First my mother, then Papa and Fairfield. Now Charles." Her voice became so quiet, Justin had to strain to catch her words. "Will you . . . will you also be lost to me forever, Justin?"

The moments passed. In the silence, the bourbon and spent emotions finally overtook Cara. With her head still nestled beneath Justin's chin, she fell asleep, never knowing her words had given Justin cause for serious consideration.

The silence in the cabin continued for long moments before it was disturbed by Justin's rising and carrying Cara back to her cabin.

Late that night, with only that same silence for company, Charles Taylor died.

Chapter Eight

Wednesday, 27th November, 1811

Committed to the sea yesterday eve, passenger Charles Taylor, who departed this Earth on the morning of Tuesday, 26 November, of causes related to hemorrhaging of the lungs. Ship's company was present for service. Also in attendance, passenger Cara Fairchild.

Present course puts us within seventy-two hours of Norfolk, Virginia. Easterly winds prevail.

Justin thrust his quill aside, snapping his log shut with a quick hand. He gave the book a long look. The last three and half weeks had sped by, but, if the truth be known, he was impatient for this particular journey to come to its natural conclusion.

His mind took a survey of all that had occurred from their parting London until the laying to rest of Charles. Much had happened, a great deal of it, he was surprised to realize, involving Cara. His thoughts turned sardonic. Not as much had happened on that score as he had intended.

With a dark frown, he muttered a short expletive. Who would have thought that he still hadn't bedded her? Certainly none of his associates at his club, who knew him for the womanizer he was, would have ever believed it possible. *He* even found it odd that once having set his mind to the task he hadn't made her his. He issued a string of curses, all at Cara's expense. She was the most damned puzzling, unique woman he'd ever met and the more he learned about her, the more complicated matters became.

That was the crux of the thing. He normally never bothered himself with really getting to know a woman. Yet somehow he had let himself be drawn into Cara's beguiling aura, her righteous air, her propensity for compassion.

"Christ," he swore. Now he was waxing poetic. Disgusted with himself, he shoved softer thoughts of Cara from his mind. Instead he remembered the feel of her sitting on his lap. Her softly curved derriere had nestled too enticingly against him to be ignored. He scoffed in annoyance. Lord, but he was hungry for her. He desired her more than he had any other woman and not, he admitted, because he had forced himself to wait. No, there was something about her, something he didn't give a bloody damn to try and fathom, that drew him to her, and he wasn't going to be satisfied until she was his.

He smiled suddenly, all dark, frustrating thoughts like brittle November leaves swept away in the wind. He'd given her more than enough time and he was through waiting.

A knock at the door pulled Justin from his musings. "Come," he called as he capped the inkwell and set aside his log. When he finally turned to the caller, one of his dark brows rose a fraction at the sight of Regina standing just beyond his desk.

Dressed in a rich yellow muslin walking dress, she gave no illusions of being the grieving widow. But then, Justin hadn't expected her to take up that route. He wasn't surprised either to see her here so soon after her husband's funeral.

"Mrs. Taylor," he drawled in a voice that was purposely

mocking. Leaning back in his chair, he rested his elbows on the chair's arms while his hands laced together on his lean stomach.

"Good afternoon, Captain." Regina struck a languidly seductive pose, her dark gaze drinking in the sight of Justin. Sitting in his relaxed manner, his body still appeared long and firmly muscled. His gaze slashed across the desk at her and she wondered what it would take to darken those eyes with passion. His lips were masculinely sensuous, and she wanted to feel them against her own. He was, without a doubt, the most handsome, virile man she had ever seen. He was also the most infuriating. She hadn't seen him since their disastrous meeting in the dining salon, six days earlier, when he had dumped her to the floor. She hadn't been able to forgive him for that for several days, but looking at him now made her glad that she had finally chosen to ignore his barbarous behavior. She wanted him. And she was now a widow, a status he was sure to find more desirable for a liaison between them.

"I hope I haven't come at an inopportune time, Captain."

Justin regarded Regina's carefully painted face. "I see you have recovered from your . . . indisposition."

She took a huge sigh, as though in distress, forcing the bosom she was so proud of to almost overflow the bounds of her shallow bodice. "I am recovered, thank you."

" 'Tis a pity your recovery was not timely enough for you to witness your husband's funeral."

The last thing Regina wanted was to be reminded of Charles. Nor did she want Justin harboring any such stray thoughts, either. "The entire matter was most distressing. I am only now well enough to venture out." She sauntered across the room to the bookshelves, wanting to move the conversation to one more inclined to her purposes. "I understand that my husband's cabin has been put to rights and that I am free to move back in."

"Yes, that was my order."

"Good, I am anxious to get on with my life."

"I have no doubt," he remarked dryly.

"Tell me, have you read all these?" She strolled along the line of books, pretending an interest she didn't feel.

Without blinking an eye at her shift in topic, he answered, "Yes."

"How impressive." Turning, she leisurely leaned back against the leather bindings, offering Justin an unobstructed view of her entire form. "But, then there is little about you that isn't."

In a casual move, Justin shrugged. "I assume this conversation is leading somewhere, Mrs. Taylor." His face looked as dispassionate as his action.

A well-practiced laugh curved Regina's lips upward. Pushing away from the books, she retraced her steps to Justin's side, standing close enough that her leg brushed his knee. "My, my, my, you are direct. Well, if that is what you wish. This conversation is going wherever you wish it to go."

With cool bluntness, Justin flicked his gaze over Regina, his inspection so brief as to be insulting. From her lace-turbaned head to her yellow velvet shoes, she epitomized the worst in the women he knew. Greedy and selfish to a fault. She was a widow of one day, and already she was sniffing around him like a bitch trying to take what she could.

Women were all the same, with their coy insinuations and laughing seductions. No different than his mother. Mentally he sneered. Just one thought of that woman, who had given him birth, and nothing else turned his mood dangerously dark.

"I believe it is time for you to take your leave." His voice was too quietly controlled.

Regina was taken aback. She hadn't anticipated any resistance and her self-confidence slipped a notch. Charles was dead. What possible objection could Justin have to their involvement now?

"I don't believe that," she said, unwilling to just give up and admit he didn't want her.

"Believe what you wish."

"I believe," she purred, "that you are just being obstinate, although I do not understand why." Reaching out, she ran her finger down the row of buttons on his shirt. When her hand encountered his, it detoured around to his midsection before continuing to the waistband of his dark pants. "We are both worldly people. You must realize that I can promise you infinite pleasures."

Justin's only reaction was to lower his gaze to her hand still resting at his waist and then to lock his gaze to hers. Regina interpreted the action as the acquiescence she had hoped for.

A giddy lust swamped her. With a carnal smile, she circled behind Justin's chair and, in a gesture meant to entice, slid her hands tantalizingly over his wide shoulders. Her caress wandered lower, drawing her body forward until the tips of her breasts teased the back of his head.

"We have wasted a great deal of time, you and I," she whispered near his ear. Slowly, she straightened, then continued around until she stood at his thigh and leaned against its hard length.

This time Justin made sure his eyes traveled slowly down the length of her voluptuous curves, moving sinuously along every line. Regina felt the look on her breasts, and her nipples hardened in response. The blue gaze descended to the juncture of her thighs and a familiar ache began to grow deep within her.

"Do you like what you see?" Caught up in the desire he was making her feel, her voice was a breathless whisper.

Justin's reply was an insolent smile.

"I am more of a woman than you are ever likely to meet again, Captain." She was heady with the knowledge of her own seductive powers. "I know what will please you."

Justin's brows rose in question.

"Would you like me to show you?" She extended a hand in invitation. "I see no reason for us to be coy with each other. After all, I want you and . . . you desire me."

Ignoring her hand, Justin stood. "No, Regina. You want me and I desire Cara."

Regina gasped, her eyes rounding in shock as his words truly struck home. The bastard! He'd been toying with her, making a fool of her once again. Rage exploded through her every vein. In a violent move intended to slap the nasty smile off his face, she swung her arm around with all her might.

In sneering indifference, he let her hand get close enough for her to think she would succeed in striking him. But in the last second, he grabbed her wrist in an iron grip and brutally yanked her arm behind her back.

"You bastard!" she snarled between gritted teeth.

Dropping all pretense, Justin's low voice growled, "You, Mrs. Taylor, are a pathetic, dried-up old slut." Disgusted, he shoved her away from him.

Regina stumbled, catching herself against the desk. Infuriated past reason, she righted herself then came around full circle with her arm thrown wide and her fist clenched. Her movement carried her forward toward her mark, but Justin easily sidestepped her attack, and her own momentum sent her sprawling to the floor.

From his great height, Justin looked in cynical amusement at the poor sight Regina presented. "Really, madam, this habit you have for trying to cosh one to my head is becoming tiring." He strode to the side table for a small shot of bourbon. "Frankly, I'm growing bored with your measures." He drained the drink in one swallow. "Actually, I've grown quite bored with you."

Eyes glittering maliciously, Regina struggled to her feet, wrath sizzling through her. No one had ever treated her in such a despicable manner. No one! He was the worst sort of scum to crawl the earth and she vowed he'd rue this day.

Exercising every bit of self-control not to fly at him and scratch his eyes out, she stalked to the door, hating him with every step she took. There she turned and threw a dagger-eyed look at him.

"So be it, Captain."

She slammed the door behind her as she left the room. Too furious to move, she stood in the companionway, shaking with anger as she tried to collect herself. Unconsciously, she tried to restore order to the hair and lace coiffure which had tumbled loose, but she took no notice as her mind began to plan her revenge. There was little she could do while she was on this cursed ship, but once she was home, oh yes, there she would have everything and everyone she needed at her disposal.

The sound of a door opening and closing snapped her back to reality. She was standing there for all to see, looking worse than the devil. Livid with Justin for making her forget everything, she glanced down the short hall. Fresh rage rose up and every foul curse she knew hammered in her brain at the sight of Cara. Of all the people to witness her at that moment, it had to be her!

To Cara, Regina appeared very much out of character. The woman was always impeccably groomed, yet the mass of her black hair now fell in complete disarray, tangled with a length of gauzy lace. The low-scooped neckline of her dress hung askew, its seams twisted haphazardly to one side.

Without wanting to, Cara became concerned. Regina deserved little in the way of compassion, her cruel ways abhorrent to everything Cara believed in. Yet she couldn't help but be affected by the sight and wondered worriedly what had occurred. Had she misjudged Regina? Was it possible that Regina really had loved Charles and she was so overwrought over his death that she was now reduced to a miserable state?

"Regina, is there anything amiss?"

Regina could have answered in a hundred different ways, each more spiteful than the next, but Justin's words slithered through her mind. The need for vengeance ate away at her, and she chose the most hateful way possible to respond.

"Why, Cara dear, how absolutely embarrassing," she said with a coy smile. She made a great show of tucking a loose curl behind her ear.

Something about Regina's flushed cheeks and sparkling eyes bothered Cara. "What's wrong? Do you need assistance?"

Smiling mischievously, Regina glanced over her shoulder

at Justin's door. "Good heavens, no," she trilled. "But you have caught us . . . me at an awkward moment."

Cara's wide green eyes followed Regina's meaningful glance.

"I am afraid," Regina continued, reveling in Cara's obvious shock, "I have been . . . shall we say, indiscreet. I suppose I am not as strong as I should be, but Justin is such a passionate man. Well, you know how that is, don't you, Cara?"

Too many thoughts assailed Cara at once. Regina's demeanor was that of a naughty schoolgirl who'd just been caught in some sly escapade. Her insinuations suggested that the escapade involved both her and Justin. With a sickening feeling cramping her stomach, Cara tried to deny the meaning of Regina's appearance.

Regina slipped past Cara to the cabin she had once shared with Charles, but stopped short of entering. "Oh, Cara, if you were thinking of calling on Justin, perhaps you might want to wait." She threw out a cunning laugh. "He might want a few minutes to collect himself."

Cara felt incapable of movement, too stunned to do anything except stare at Regina. The sickening feeling in her stomach had turned into an icy knot whose frozen strands spread to her limbs and wrapped themselves around her heart. Wordlessly, she continued to stand immobile, even when Regina's malevolent, jeering words scraped her raw nerves.

"You didn't actually think that a man like Justin would be satisfied with just one woman, did you?" She gave one more laugh and entered her cabin.

Without wanting to, Cara contemplated Regina's words, analyzed her appearance. Even knowing the widow could not be trusted, Cara couldn't explain away what she'd just seen. She swallowed painfully, a horrible hurt joining the iciness within her. For the past three weeks, she had been falling in love with Justin and he'd been chasing after Regina. No, it just couldn't be true. It broke her heart to believe that Justin could feel that cavalier about their relationship, but what, then, was the reason for Regina's behavior?

Without warning, Justin's door opened. Caught in her confused and painful suspicions, Cara whirled and faced him. Tall and incredibly handsome, he stood in his cabin doorway, a dashing smile on his face. Mutely she stared at that face, as though trying to find the answers there: high cheekbones and firm jaw, straight nose and crystal blue eyes. It was the face that filled her heart during the days and created her dreams at night. She loved him with every ounce of her being and the thought of him with Regina, any woman, was unbearable.

Justin found the sight of Cara like a clean breath of sea air, especially so after the putrid stench of Regina's advances. Even in the modest cut of her wine-colored dress, it was impossible to ignore her innocent sensuality that he found so alluring. Mentally he reinforced his earlier decision and his blood began to pound heavily, tightening his loins. His gaze traveled over her flawless features again and he realized then that she was under some duress.

She was standing perfectly still in the middle of the companionway, regarding him with wide, tragic eyes and parted lips. Her normally pink-hued cheeks were void of color.

"Cara, what's wrong?" He came forward with his words, wondering what had caused her rigid bearing.

It was the sound of her very words to Regina that pulled the numbness from Cara. Her gaze swerved away from Justin and darted around her as though trying to focus on something recognizable.

"Oh . . ." she murmured distractedly, suddenly conscious only of the need to be alone. She whirled around, intent on locking herself in her cabin before the hurt and anger she felt swamped her and reduced her to a ridiculous, humiliated fool.

She barely had time for two steps when Justin grasped her arms and pulled her around to face him. "I asked you a question," he enunciated carefully. His dealings with Regina had nearly depleted his supply of tolerance.

In all honesty, Cara didn't know what to say. But she

did know that she didn't want to discuss anything with Justin at the moment. "Let go of me," she stated stiffly, keeping her eyes firmly locked on his hand.

"Not until I have an answer from you," he demanded shortly.

"I don't have anything to say."

"Well, I do," he told the top of her head. He found her defiance puny but also unwarranted, and that was enough to set him off. "Damn it, look at me when I talk to you."

That stung and Cara reacted as much to his tone as she did her own disturbed, vulnerable feelings. "Don't you dare swear at me!" she declared, looking him straight in the eye.

He gave her a mocking laugh and an equally mocking bow. "I see I finally have your full attention. Now, what is this all about?"

The only words Cara wanted to say were lodged in her throat, too bitter to utter. She tried to imagine his reaction if she were to calmly ask, "Do tell, Justin, am I correct in assuming that all the while you were showering your attentions on me, you were also offering the same to Regina?" She groaned at the miserable thought, closing her eyes and mind against the possibility.

"There is nothing to discuss," she said, taking refuge behind a thinly veiled aloofness. "Now, please let go of my arm."

Never in his entire life had Justin expended as much energy, in or out of bed, on one woman. He had wooed and cajoled, teased and charmed, held and comforted her. Not to mention driven her half-wild with his kisses. By his standards he had gone to the limits of what any normal man could be expected to endure, and retain his sanity. Just two nights ago, she had sat upon his lap with her head on his shoulder and poured out her heart to him in the most trusting manner and now she was as withdrawn as some stranger, unwilling to even look at him. What in the hell had happened?

"Bloody hell," he grated out. With her startled gasp trailing behind them, he turned and stalked back into his cabin, pulling a shocked Cara behind him.

It all happened too quickly for Cara, and by the time her body caught up with her seemingly benumbed brain, she was standing in the middle of Justin's cabin and he was leaning against the door he had just slammed and locked.

Hurt, anger, and a certain amount of apprehension held Cara still. She'd seen that look on Justin's face before, the narrowed eyes, the tightly clenched jaw. It boded little good for her. Nervously she swallowed, then caught herself. He was demanding explanations of her, yet it should be the reverse. Her chin came up and she daringly met his gaze, despite the racing of her heart.

Justin was glad to see the show of spirit, for it told him that he had managed to get some reaction from her. But it also annoyed him because it was the surest sign that she had dug in her heels.

At any other time the prolonged silence between them would have been awkward, but it went completely unnoticed as they continued to regard each other. Finally, when the silence was broken, it was Cara's voice that sounded.

"Please unlock the door. I wish to return to my cabin." Her words were drawing-room polite, quiet, low, steady.

For Justin, they were too perfect, too remote, and his steely gaze said so. Cara's hard-won composure slipped a bit, but she yanked it back. "Justin," she began, putting more force in her voice. "I asked if you would please open the door."

"No."

The single word crashed into the room with deadly intensity. Cara licked her lips and blinked. "Justin, you can't just . . ."

"*Don't* . . . tell me what I can and cannot do," he warned in a dangerous voice.

"But . . . but, I don't . . . I don't wish to remain here."

"Well, you're going to."

"For how long?"

One of his shoulders rose in a deceptively casual shrug. "Until I'm ready to let you out."

Incredulous, Cara demanded to know, "When will that be?"

He ignored her question. "Let's begin with that little scene in the companionway."

Immediately her spine stiffened. Pride clamped her mouth shut and defiance flashed her eyes a sparkling green.

Grinning on a mirthless laugh, Justin pushed away from the door. "I've always liked your courage, Cara, but at the moment I find it bothersome."

Warily, she watched him advance, his smile brittle and somehow menacing.

"What, no righteous answer?" he taunted, coming to stand before her, so close she had to tilt her head back to see his face.

Instinct told her to step back, that he was more than just angry with her. She couldn't define what other element tinged his present mood, but she sensed it simmering just below his tensed muscles. Steadily, with only her trembling fingers to betray her, she held her ground. "I'm sorry you find me bothersome. You can alleviate that problem by allowing me to leave."

"Oh, bravo! A suitably high-principled remark, the type I've grown accustomed to hearing from you. Although it was a bit longer in coming this time."

"You're being insulting," she said tautly, offended by the nastiness of his sarcasm.

"Tell me, do you enjoy playing the virgin or do you find that it grows tedious?"

The impact of his question forced Cara away, but his hands shot out and hauled her right back. Horrified, she tried to shrug out of his punishing hold. "Let me go!"

"No, we're through playing your little game. It's time you began to understand exactly how things are between men and women."

Cara was outraged. How dare he accuse her of playing games, especially after what she had witnessed of Regina earlier. Caution had kept a firm rein on her temper, but now she threw caution to the winds. "You hypocrite! I've never been anything but honest with you," she declared, futilely pulling at his hands imprisoning her arms. "If anyone has been disporting, it has been you and Mrs. Taylor."

Justin drew back slightly and glared down at her. "Mrs. Taylor?"

"Oh, is it your turn to be confused now," she scoffed, giving him a dose of his own sarcasm. "Surely you are the expert in playing games. Well, I hope you enjoyed yourself while you trifled with me and . . . lusted after Regina."

"Lusted?"

"And stupid me," she continued, too angry to notice his incredulous expression. "You were right, though, I am a . . . a virgin and obviously too unsophisticated for your type of duplicity."

"Cara . . ."

"Don't take me for a fool any longer. If you find her so . . . so . . . wonderful, then so be it, but do not insult me with your attentions any longer!"

"What in the hell are you talking about?" he ground out fiercely.

"I'm talking about you and Regina." To say it so plainly brought a sharp pain to her heart. "I saw her out there, right after your afternoon tryst."

"What!"

"Three weeks ago, I wouldn't have understood. But even if I had, she would have told me as plainly then as she did today."

Justin studied her closely. "Told you what?"

"That you and she . . . that you . . ." Why did he have to make her say it right out? Her anger dissolved in the face of her humiliation.

"Cara." He tried to prompt her along.

"No," she declared, her voice a painfully tight whisper. She had been demeaned enough. Silently, she closed her eyes and turned her head away.

It was all suddenly clear to Justin. Cara had been in the companionway when Regina had left his cabin, looking like she could have just tumbled from a lover's bed. And that bitch of a widow, with her venomous tongue, had wasted no time in poisoning Cara's mind. Naive right down to her toes, Cara had been helpless but to interpret what she saw at face value.

Tipping his head back, he closed his eyes and ground his teeth together in a bid for control. He was furious with Regina and could very easily strangle her. But he was also so frustrated in his wanting of Cara that he was as close to contemplating rape as he had ever been. Opening his eyes, he watched her averted face as she struggled to stop the quivering of her lips and prevent the shedding of any tears.

He regretted his harsh words, but it was too late to recall them now. He sought to make amends and did so in the only way he knew how. He brought one hand up to her chin and tilted her face toward his. With surprising finesse, given the strain of his tension, he gently lowered his lips to hers, careful to keep his passion firmly in check.

Cara's heart wrenched and, on a sob of despair, she jerked her head away. "Don't," she croaked, her hands pushing against his chest in a flurry of movement. "Don't do this to me."

"Listen," he ordered, capturing hold of her arms to stay her attempts to flee. "What Regina told you was nothing but lies."

Cara was so intent on escaping that at first his words made no impression. Justin wondered if she had even heard him. Irritably he gave her a shake, just rough enough to gain her attention, then lowered his head until they were practically nose to nose. "She lied," he said slowly, distinctly, darkly.

Through her misery, Cara finally heard and quieted within his arms. Uncertainly, she regarded him. "What?"

Cupping her chin in his hand, he told her, "We did not make love." Gently, he slipped his other hand around to the small of her back. "I could be extremely angry with you for your lack of faith. Fortunately for you, I am constantly reminded of how ridiculously trusting you are."

Cara's brows snapped together at his backhanded compliment. "Ridiculous?"

"How else could Regina have accomplished all of this if you weren't so damned naive?" His gaze now fastened on her mouth, he lowered his head and captured her lips. This time, he gave his passion full rein and hungrily slanted his mouth across hers in a kiss of burning intensity. His tongue licked over her lips, demanding entrance into the sweetness of her mouth. He met with only momentary resistance before his tongue thrust forward to taste hers as his arms tightened around her. Deep in his chest, he groaned in pleasure at the feel of her lush curves held against him, and desire, instantaneous and devastating, surged through him.

At the first touch of Justin's lips on hers, Cara felt a shift in her equilibrium. Her emotions, still in a disconcerted jumble, collided with the passionate response he so expertly evoked within her. But as Justin's need increased, so did his ardor. Like a spectator observing from above, Cara watched her fears and hurt crumble before the onslaught of his desire. Pleasure, warm and languid, engulfed her, melting her doubts and turning her limbs to liquid.

It felt like years, not days, since he had last held her. For Justin, the sensation of Cara's body against his was like water to a parched man. Quickly, before he lost all control, he tore his mouth from hers, stilling the rampaging fires burning inside him by sheer will alone.

"Do you honestly believe I want this from anyone but you?" he asked in a rough, half-angry whisper against her lips. "Do you honestly believe I'd seek her out, when it's only you that can do this to me?" His arm lowered to her hips and pulled her tightly against his rigid arousal.

Yanked from her dream world, Cara dazedly looked into Justin's eyes, glazed hot with passion. She saw before her only a true burning need, a need for her. Miserably, she realized the extent of her mistake. How could she have ever doubted him? How could she have ever doubted her heart?

She lifted trembling fingers in a shy, humble gesture to his face. "I'm so . . . please forgive . . . I don't . . ." The rest was lost as Justin snatched her breath away in another kiss.

Cara gave herself up to the headiness created by his caresses. She needed no encouragement when his tongue searched for hers and joyously she returned the lush, ardent play. Of their own accord, her hands slid up his chest to encircle his neck, one slipping higher to tangle in the dark hair. With her breasts crushed to his chest, she could feel his heavy heartbeat and she pressed closer to the iron hardness of his lean body.

Justin was consumed by emotions he had never experienced before. As he swept Cara up into his arms, his only thought was to completely lose himself in her before he went mad with wanting. With his mouth covering hers, he carried her across the cabin and gently laid her down on his bed. Lying down beside her, with an arm braced on either side of her, he kissed her so thoroughly that Cara's pulse pounded in a mad dash through her veins.

As desperate as he was to claim her, Justin wanted to linger in the process, prolong the aching pleasure. With one hand, he slowly unfastened the row of buttons down her back. His lips left hers and hungrily caressed her slim neck and the sweet flesh not covered by her gown's bodice. He inhaled sharply, breathing in the flowered scent of her skin and wanted more. Brushing aside the worn fabric and thin cotton of her chemise, he bared her breasts and greedily pressed his lips to a rosy pink nipple.

Cara's breath caught in her throat at the moist heat of his touch. Tangling both her hands in his hair, she arched against him, never wanting the moment to end, wanting this magic between them to last forever. She was lost in the paradise he was creating, her boundaries defined by his lips and hands. The direction of her course had been charted by her love and it led back to Justin. Sighing in pleasure, her breath came out on a soft moan.

The sound drew Justin's head up. "There'll be no stopping this time, Cara," he told her thickly. "I want you more than I've ever wanted another." Urgently, he crushed his mouth to hers for a brief kiss. "Let me love you," he murmured against her lips.

Cara gazed at him knowing she wouldn't, couldn't put a stop to this, but where it led, she had no idea. They'd come this far before and always she'd been left wanting, of what was a mystery to her. Her voice, low with desire and hesitant with uncertainty, she said, "I . . . I don't know what to do."

The tightness in Justin's loins wrenched painfully at her answer and the last of his restraint broke. "I'll show you," he promised and kissed her with scorching intensity. With knowing fingers, he guided her garments off her shoulders and down to her waist. In the muted light of dusk, her skin glowed pearllike and he bent his head to the satin loveliness of her breasts, his tongue teasing the nipples to hardened buds. His hand came up to trace the delicate line of rib cage and smooth, sleek abdomen and his lips followed, trailing a hot path that inflamed Cara's blood and tightened the knot growing in the very core of her. Then, in one sure movement, he swept her clothing away, his hands brushing over her tiny waist, slender hips and down the subtle curves of her legs.

As drugged as Cara was with the riot of sensations coursing through her, she was unprepared to find herself completely bared before Justin's gaze. Instinctively, she stiffened, her hands seeking to shield herself from his view.

"Justin," she gasped.

But Justin would have none of it and moved her hands away. "Easy, love," he whispered. His darkened eyes drank in the lovely, sensuous sight of her and he groaned, knowing he was the first to see her this way. "Don't be frightened," he said, one hand riding possessively on her hip.

The gentle tone of his voice, as well as the warm strength of his hands, helped soothe Cara's fears, but it was the feel of his teeth nibbling their way over her shoulder that rekindled the flame within her. Her hands slid around his neck and back and she delighted in the strength of his corded muscles.

Unexpectedly, Justin sat up and quickly shed his clothing, wanting not a single layer of fabric separating them. Before Cara's mesmerized eyes, his body was revealed to her and she stared at the wonder of him: the powerful chest covered with a mat of dark, crisp hair, the lean, flat stomach. But there her innocent eyes were too shocked to linger and they hastily ran down the long length of his muscled legs.

All too aware of Cara's eyes upon him, Justin impatiently tossed the last of his clothes aside and lowered his body over hers.

Piercing jolts of pleasure shot through Cara when Justin nibbled at her ear and, helplessly, her body writhed with a restlessness she didn't understand yet couldn't stop. Urgently, she turned her head, seeking his lips, but his mouth devouring hers, his fingers kneading her breasts only increased the need within her. Driven by unbearable hunger, her tongue darted into his mouth as her hands explored the rippling muscles of his back.

The feel of Cara's hands skimming over his shoulders sent shudders through Justin. With each stroke of her palm and tease of her tongue, his blood pounded in a throbbing ache in his loins. Dimly, through the haze of his passion, he realized he had never in his entire life experienced desire this exquisitely fierce. He ran one hand over her smooth belly, lightly grazing the reddish curls below. With his mouth scorching kisses down her neck, his fingers unerringly sought and found the dampness between her thighs.

The intimacy of Justin's probing fingers was beyond anything Cara had ever experienced and an attack of virgin fright seized her. Alarmed, she clamped her hand over his wrist.

"Jus . . . Justin," she managed to get out, pressing her thighs together.

"It's the way of things," he reassured her, gazing deeply into her eyes. Slowly, his fingers resumed their caress, stroking the sensitive flesh, gradually building a new heat in Cara that took her breath away. She clung to him, nearly mindless with the need he was creating. Her hips pressed closer to his fingers, seeking more, and a soft whimper escaped her lips as she trembled with wanton desire. Watching her face, Justin could see the wonder of newfound sensations flicker in her eyes and he gloried in his being responsible for that look. His lips crushed hers and he knew he could wait no longer. He settled himself between her thighs, gently nudging her knees apart. As carefully as possible, he lifted her hips to receive him and eased his pulsing manhood forward. Against his lips, he absorbed her startled cry, his arms now gathering her stiffened body close.

Cara was stunned by the unexpected intrusion of pain into her bliss. Eyes filled with tears, she looked at Justin accusingly, pushing against the same shoulders she had just been clinging to.

"Stop! This hurts, Justin, I want you to stop."

Justin had no idea where he got the presence of mind to answer rationally at that moment. Tightly sheathed in the incredible warmth of her body, he was desperate for fulfillment.

"Easy, love. The pain will pass." He brushed a light kiss across her lips in a gesture more of comfort than passion and waited for her to become familiar with his body joined with hers. "I should have told you, but I had no wish to frighten you."

Already the pain had subsided, leaving Cara conscious of a feeling of fullness mingled with the aching need that even the brief pain hadn't diminished. Her hands curled over his shoulders once again as her body adjusted to accept Justin inside her. The very thought was bewilderingly lovely, and when she lifted her gaze to his, her eyes were filled with love and desire.

With gentle thrusts Justin began to move within her, gradually deepening his strokes. Cara's body pulsed tighter with each plunge and in absolute urgency, she arched her hips to meet his every move. Her tension grew unbearable and just when she thought she would splinter, the most incredible ecstasy burst forth, snatching her breath away.

Justin groaned and the sweet pulsing of Cara's body led him to the pinnacle of release. Kissing her with tender fury, his arms tightening around her, he drove into her one last time to join her in their privately shared heaven.

Slowly, as heartbeats calmed and the last light of day kissed entwined limbs, Justin eased his body from Cara's, but retreated no farther than to lay his head upon her breast. Cara gazed at his dark head and wrapped her arms around his shoulders, one hand lifting to comb through his damp hair. She was overwhelmed by what had just happened and lay in a euphoric haze. The cabin remained unfocused, time was a nebulous thing, but one thought was brilliantly clear in her heart.

"Justin," she whispered.

Wordlessly, Justin raised his head, his eyes finding hers in the near darkness.

She returned his gaze, then spoke softly with aching tenderness gracing every word. "I love you."

Chapter Nine

The creaking of timbers and an occasional flap of a sail stirred the ocean hush. The blending of grays created in the predawn stillness was roughly sketched in and shadows mingled freely with solid forms.

Lying awake within those obscured silhouettes of his cabin, Justin studied Cara's sleeping figure beside him, trying to find answers that were as ambiguous as the details of his surroundings. Physically, he was sated, more content than he had been in months. But his mind wrestled with an issue that he had kept at bay for the better portion of the night. Soundlessly, he slipped from his bunk, careful not to disturb Cara, and walked naked to the cabin's pair of windows.

Three softly spoken words played in his brain, frolicking with his peace of mind, and he was irritated with himself for being so affected. "I love you," she had said. He couldn't remember anyone actually saying they loved him.

Certainly none of his mistresses had ever made such a declaration, but then, they had all been shrewd enough to appreciate the benefits of an exclusively physical association with him. His parents had never even hinted at the sentiment, either by word or action. His grandmother? Lydia had come as close as anyone to expressing such tender emotions to him, but his skepticism on the matter had hampered most of her outward displays.

Love, and he doubted there actually was such a thing, had no place in his life. He would marry eventually and his wife would see to the bearing of his children while his mistress would see to his sexual needs. The remainder of his life would be occupied with investments, his stable, seeing to the upkeep of his properties, an occasional venture to one part of the world or another, the casual association with acquaintances. Love did not signify in any of that. No, love had never existed in his life and it never would.

What, then, to do about Cara? He was amazed that he even cared. He had no desire to treat her cruelly, but she obviously believed herself afflicted with this paragon of emotions. How best to deal with what she was sure to view as unrequited love?

Turning his back to the windows, he made his decision. Come morning, in as careful a manner as possible, he would put a distance between them. The day ahead would see the *Wind Dancer* at the mouth of Virginia's treacherous bay. The business of navigating into the James River would spare him little time from the upper decks. Once they were docked, he would see to it that Cara was safely placed with her cousin and he would retire to his plantation for the winter. In March he would return to England and that would be the end of the entire matter. Briefly, he contemplated his choice, then returned to the bunk, satisfied with his planned course.

Cara woke from the most blissful sleep of her life with a long, lazy stretch. In the early morning light, she was aware only of a languid peace, and then her foot brushed a muscular calf and her elbow bumped a sturdy rib cage. Instantly, she realized where she was and her eyes flew open as her hands instinctively drew the sheets up to her chin. She peeked shyly at Justin. Thankfully, he was still asleep and she relaxed to gather her thoughts.

Memories of last night flooded her with a lovely headiness. She hadn't been prepared for the ecstasy Justin had given her and she wondered about her body's uncontrollable response to his. She still wasn't certain what had happened to her, but each time they had made love, that same shattering explosion of feeling had claimed her.

In his sleep, Justin readjusted his position, laying his arm across her waist to draw her closer. Cara gazed at his long, tanned fingers and helplessly remembered how those same fingers had explored her body's most intimate secrets. Blushing furiously, she also recalled how her hands had traced the hardened planes and steely muscles of Justin's body.

A warm ache grew deep within her and astonishingly, her nipples hardened. Once again, her body was reacting of its own volition and she was powerless to control her response. Surprisingly, she realized, she didn't want to.

Amazed at her newfound boldness, she reasoned that love was responsible for the changes in her outlook. With a glowing smile, she snuggled against Justin's warmth.

Yet despite the near perfection of her morning, a persistent worry blemished her contentment. Her love for Justin was all-consuming and telling him so had been as natural as breathing. Last night she hadn't anticipated what his reaction might have been, but in retrospect, his lack of response left her wanting.

With a frown, she examined her feelings. What she wanted, she admitted, was the same profession of love that she had made to him. Unfortunately, she realized that wasn't about to be forthcoming. From everything Justin had told her, it was easy to see that his life had been singularly devoid of love. It stood to reason, then, that he might not know how to express such emotions.

Feeling contrite, she gazed at him. In sleep, he appeared oddly vulnerable and she suddenly found herself wanting to protect him. It made no difference, she told herself, that he hadn't actually said the words. They had made love three times during the night, each time more exquisitely beautiful than the last. Obviously he had been declaring with his body what he couldn't with words. She could find no other explanation for the depth of what they had shared.

All doubts banished, her world was once again a blissful heaven. With thoughts of a glorious future with Justin warming her heart, she wondered curiously if there was some sort of etiquette that dictated one's behavior upon awakening beside a man. If there was, she concluded, she was sure Justin would see to those amenities.

When Cara woke again, it was just past ten o'clock. Disappointingly, she discovered that Justin had already left the cabin. For a brief moment, she gave into a playful pout, then laughed at her self-indulgence. She was anxious to find Justin and set about washing and dressing.

Her fingers made quick work of laces and buttons, but her hair required serious attention, so she returned to her own cabin.

With a hard-won patience, she sat on her bunk and combed the tangles from her hair. Reminiscing about how the tangles got there brought a smile to her lips and she wondered if she was going to have to do this every morning from now on. Not that she would mind. Mussed hair was an insignificant consequence for the passion she and Justin had shared.

Her hands stilled and suddenly she hugged her arms about her, laughing in pure joy as her thoughts took flight. In just a matter of days they would be docked in Virginia, and Justin would find a minister to marry them. Perhaps her cousin would be present for the ceremony. And certainly Percy. Her only regret was that her parents would not be there to share her happiness.

As quickly as she could, she braided her hair into a single plait, then went in search of Justin. Despite the sun's brilliance, the air was cold on the outer decks and Cara snuggled into her cloak.

"Morning, Miss Fairchild." Willie's voice came from behind Cara and she turned to face him.

"Oh, it is a good morning, Willie," she replied, beaming a radiant smile at the lad. "I hope you find it so."

Willie's jaw went slack. He had never seen Cara looking more beautiful. It was several moments before he remembered his manners. "Is there anything I can be helpin' you with?"

"Yes. Could you tell me where I might find Captain Reynolds?"

"He's at the wheel this morning, sailing us through this last leg of water. It gets a mite tricky from here on, but he's the one to handle it."

Cara's gaze flew to the poop deck and found Justin just where Willie said he'd be. Standing tall and bronzed, he worked the ship's wheel with ease and Cara felt her heart swell with pride.

Across the distance, their eyes locked. A breathless wonder seized Cara, a joy so profound that tears came to her eyes. Here was the man who brought all her hopes and dreams to life. Here was the man who had brought her love.

"Miss Fairchild?"

With a start, Cara looked to the cabin boy.

"You all right?" he asked in concern, the sight of her tears causing him to worry.

"Yes, I'm better than all right." She blinked back her emotional display. "Might I be allowed to join him?"

Willie shook his head emphatically. "Sorry, miss, that deck ain't no place for passengers right now. Captain's got serious business to tend to."

For the second time in an hour, Cara faced disappointment. This was not at all what she had imagined her morning to be like. She and Justin should have been exchanging tender words of devotion. They should have been privately secluded in his cabin, passionately reaffirming their love.

"You hungry, miss?"

"Excuse me?"

"You hungry? You didn't have no breakfast and I was

wonderin' if you might be wanting tea or something to tide you over till the next meal."

Consternation was clearly evident on Cara's wide-eyed face. If Willie was aware that she hadn't eaten, was it possible that he knew where she had spent her morning, her night? She wasn't ashamed of what she had done, but the situation was extremely private.

"No, thank you, Willie. I'll . . . I'll be fine."

With a tip of his finger to his hat in a parting salute, Willie went off in search of other duties. Cara was left to her own thoughts, all of them centered around Justin.

For the remainder of the day, the *Wind Dancer* claimed Justin's time and attention. Cara had to content herself with only brief glimpses of him as he oversaw his ship with the same masterful authority that typified everything he did. Dusk approached, and while Cara understood the necessity for his presence at the wheel, it didn't make her evening any less lonely. She spent her last night on board with only the sweet torture of imagining herself in Justin's arms to keep her warm.

The Virginia air was cool when Cara stepped onto the quarterdeck the next morning. The ship was docked at College Creek, just outside Williamsburg; however, Cara didn't scan the area for a first impression of America. Her attention was focused entirely on Justin as he made his way toward her.

"When did we dock?" she asked, her eyes drinking in the sight of him.

Justin came to stand before her. "Just after dawn. The tide was right, so I took advantage of it."

"You look tired." She ached to reach out and smooth the lines of fatigue from his face. But most of the crew was bustling about, allowing little privacy. "Were you out here all night?"

"Most of it. We could have laid off the shoals until light, but I was anxious to dock."

There were a hundred things Cara wanted to tell him. She started with, "I missed you yesterday."

Justin didn't miss the warm look in Cara's eyes or her intimate smile. "Have you packed your things yet?"

Taken aback, Cara regarded him curiously. Wasn't he just the smallest bit desirous of a moment alone with her?

"Captain," Phillip called from the forward hatch. "When you've got a moment, you're needed in the hold."

Annoyed with yet another matter that kept her and Justin apart, Cara sighed in resignation. Obviously now was not a good time to try and discuss anything with him. The ship had just docked, goods were being unloaded, he was needed in ten places at once.

Raking his hand back through his hair, Justin said, "I'm going to be tied up here for a while. Percy will take you to your cousin."

Disappointment engulfed Cara. She started to protest, but Justin's attention was already claimed by one of the barrels being lifted ashore. Lamely, she glanced about and suddenly felt like the odd man out.

Justin looked back to her and she gave him a brave smile. "I will speak to you later, then?" she asked hopefully.

For a moment, he studied her lovely features, then gently ran his knuckles over her cheek. Then, he turned and made his way to the hatch and disappeared into the hold.

Cara's first impression of Williamsburg was that of a town sadly neglected. Through the tenacious midmorning fog, dingy, weather-worn buildings and crumbling brick structures proclaimed a town in its decline.

Sitting on the seat of a short-bed wagon, beside a brooding, more than usually taciturn Percy, Cara gazed at the scene around her. So far, nothing on their short ride down the road from the College Creek wharves had given her cause to change her initial opinion. Dense forests, thick with undergrowth even in December, crowded in on the town from all directions. Roads and houses alike were deteriorating. And while the town itself was laid out in a neat, symmetrical fashion, few people appeared to actually inhabit the place. Overall, the effect was sad.

There was one building, however, that gave Cara pause.

Even two blocks away, its impressive size and dignified design hinted at a grandeur that was promising.

"Percy," she said, pointing to the large brick structure that had caught her attention. "What is that building?"

Percy spared the subject a cursory glance and answered in clipped tones. "The lunatic asylum."

Cara stared openmouthed. A bedlamite house? She drew her cloak more snugly about her, as though to ward off the sensation of gloom that seemed to hang with the fog.

"Not what you thought." Percy's voice bordered on snide.

Cara didn't pretend to misunderstand. Williamsburg was a far cry from what she had imagined. Still, she ignored Percy's disdain and tried to be optimistic. "No, I admit it is . . . different."

Percy snorted his opinion of that. "It's different, all right. And no place for the likes of you." With a muttered curse that drew Cara's puzzled gaze, he handled the reins to guide the two stocky horses around a crag in the rutted road. "This blessed road gets worse from one year to the next." He eased the team to the right, but not quickly enough, and one of the rear wheels caught a deep hole.

Abruptly, he grabbed both reins in one hand as his other arm shot across in front of Cara to keep her from toppling off the wooden seat. Irately, he blasted the dirt highway.

"Damn this mud trap! The bowels of hell have better roads that this!" He lowered his voice, but only marginally. "Bloody Americans. Give them a country, and look what they do to it. Let it go to ruin. They needs come east, the whole lot of them, then they'd see proper roads and a proper town, not this sorry excuse they call a God-damned city!"

Shocked and embarrassed, Cara listened to Percy's tirade, her eyes wide and uncertain. She had never seen him in such a state. He had been in a temper ever since they had left the ship and no amount of good-natured teasing on her part had eased his mood. She couldn't help but wonder if she was somehow responsible.

Strained silence stretched between them. Cara sat and

stared at her tightly clasped fingers, hoping the quiet sounds of horses and wagon would dispel the tension. But, instead, as the minutes passed, it only increased.

"Percy," she said quietly, unable, unwilling to bear any discord with this man who had become her friend. "Have I upset you in any way?"

Percy shook his head in self-disgust, silently berating himself for being such a boor. His anger lay with Justin, yet, in Cara, his frustration had found an easy target.

"Ah, missy, you've done nothing to fret over. You'll have to be forgiving my tongue. I have a lot troubling my mind, but it has naught to do with you."

But Percy knew that wasn't true. His thoughts had everything to do with Cara. And Justin. He shook his head again. In all the years he'd been with his captain, he'd never had cause to question the man's judgment. Until now.

"It's been a long voyage," he offered as an explanation. "And to tell you the truth of things, I'm worrying about your welfare in this place."

Relieved and pleasantly surprised by his remark, Cara regarded him warmly. "Percy, I'll be fine. I have family here and a place to live. That's more than I had back in England." She paused before continuing, her face breaking into a smile. "And I'll have Justin nearby."

Percy's jaw clamped into a rigid form. "I suppose he told you that." His gaze was fixed straight ahead.

"He didn't need to. I may not be familiar with Virginia yet, but even I can tell that the ship is only a short distance from here."

Percy ground his teeth together. "Missy, we're only docked here for a matter of days. Once the cargo is seen to, he's sailing upriver."

Startled by this information, Cara frowned. She had assumed Justin would be in Williamsburg. "Upriver? To where?"

"Justin owns a bit of property on the James River. Half-hour ride, maybe, that way." He tipped his head westward.

With a sigh, Cara relaxed. It wasn't as perfect as she would have liked, but half an hour was no great obstacle.

"That's still nearby. But I'm glad you told me. As busy as Justin has been, I haven't had a chance to talk with him."

The wagon came to a halt before a faded, olive green building. Cara gazed to the tavern sign posted in front even as Percy announced their arrival.

"Here you are, missy, Hawthorne Tavern."

The one-and-a-half-story inn was set back from the road, nestled cozily among the trees. Dark green shutters that had seen fresher coats of paint accented windows below and dormers above, while centralized double doors were fashioned of deeply tanned wood.

Percy climbed down and retrieved Cara's valise from the wagon bed, while Cara took a moment longer to familiarize herself with her cousin's home. The tavern was located on the fringes of Williamsburg's westernmost boundary, and although it was set within the municipal limits, the building and accompanying grounds had a quality of being quite separate from the rest of the town. Cara wondered if it was the location itself that enhanced the feeling of being once removed from Williamsburg's bleak air. Or perhaps it was the reddish brown bricks of the three chimneys puffing smoke, or the borders of holly and pyracantha bushes that added a touch of cheer. In any event, Cara felt warmly welcomed by Hawthorne Tavern.

At that moment, the tavern's doors flew open and a petite, plump woman rushed down the steps.

"Cara Fairchild! Welcome. Oh, if we had only known exactly when to expect you, we could have been at the docks."

Accepting Percy's help from the wagon, Cara got her first look at her cousin Beatrice. The two women stood equal in height, but while Cara carried her five feet three inches with slender grace, Beatrice Hawthorne's silhouette was made up of generous, convex curves. Dark brown hair, lacking the auburn glints present in Cara's, was pulled into a tidy, braided bun. Small but smiling lips, dimpled cheeks, and a rounded chin comprised a pleasant face, though one bearing no resemblance to its cousin's. The only similarity that declared Cara's mother and Bea's mother had been sisters was the eyes. Cara discovered that looking into Beatrice's vivid green eyes was like peering into her own.

"I am so pleased to finally meet you, Beatrice," Cara said, coming forward with a smile. "I cannot thank you enough for your generosity in having me here."

"Bea, please, and don't thank me," Bea exclaimed, meeting Cara at the bottom of the steps. "After all these years of posting letters across the ocean, having you here is just too thrilling for words." In a gesture of genuine affection, Bea slipped her arms around Cara in a warmhearted hug, and an instant rapport was struck up between the two women.

"Let me look at you," Bea said, standing back. Her gaze leisurely roamed over Cara's features, then she announced without a trace of envy, "Oh, my heavens, but you are lovely. Even when I was your age, I was never such a sight. Although John, bless his heart, has always found me to his liking. You have to be the image of your mother." At the thought of Cara's parents, Bea's expression turned somber. "We received your letter last month," she continued kindly, linking her arm with Cara's and turning to climb the steps. "We were all quite saddened to hear of your father. Has it been an awful trial for you?" Without waiting for Cara to reply, she went on. "Yes, I'm certain it has been. The best thing to do right now is get you settled and rested from your long voyage."

It was obvious that Beatrice Hawthorne had a tendency to ramble, but Cara found it oddly comforting. Where matters of her life in England were concerned, it was a relief to let someone else do the talking.

"I'll have one of the servants come out and fetch your luggage."

"Percy." Cara turned to face him with a sheepish grin. In the excitement of the moment, she had nearly forgotten his presence. "Percy, I beg your pardon. Please let me introduce you."

Greetings were exchanged and in true Virginia hospitality, Bea invited the huge man in for a meal, however, Percy was quick to decline.

"I've got to be getting back to the ship," he explained. Reading the disappointment on Cara's face, he patted a hand on her shoulder. "I've got pressin' matters to tend to, but I'll be by." He winked, then added, "Just to keep an eye on you."

"Will Justin be busy with the ship all day?" Cara couldn't help but ask. The words just slipped out and a slight flush colored her cheeks.

Unable to look at the trusting faith in Cara's eyes, Percy glanced at the tips of his boots. "I doubt you'll be seeing him today."

Inwardly, Cara sighed. There was so much she and Justin needed to discuss. The matter of their future had yet to be settled, but it seemed it was going to have to wait. Ruefully, she realized she was going to have to get used to sharing Justin with the demands of his being a sea captain.

"Well, please tell him . . . that is . . ." Her words faltered. She couldn't think of a message for Justin that was suitable for Percy's ears. All her thoughts concerning Justin began and ended with "I love you."

"Tell him I hope all is well with him," she finished lamely.

The glowing love written all over Cara's face drew Percy's brow into a frown. Quickly, he caught himself then hurried his farewell before he found the situation any more uncomfortable.

The wagon rumbled back down the road and only after it was out of sight did the two women enter the tavern.

Light-green-painted walls above knotty-pine wainscoting lined the roomy foyer. The large tavern room lay to the right while a small sitting room for ladies was situated to the left. The stairway leading up to the second story was directly ahead, flanked on its left by a narrow hall that ran from the front of the inn to the back.

"I just can't tell you how glad we are to have you with us." Bea spoke over her shoulder as she preceded Cara down the hall to the rear door.

"No more so than I," Cara said, following behind. "Without your generosity, I shudder to think what my circumstances might have been." A ripple of tension ran down Cara's spine. If she hadn't come to Virginia, she could very easily have been living with that odious earl's grandmother. If Bea hadn't opened her doors to her, she would have never met Justin.

"This is the private entrance to our part of the house." Bea stopped at the rear entryway, indicating a door to her left. "The parlor and office are downstairs and three bedrooms upstairs. They're quite separate from the guest rooms, of course." Her tone became a whisper. "For privacy, you know."

Cara expected to be led into the Hawthorne's wing of the building, but Bea continued her way out the back door and into the brick-paved courtyard.

The laundry, kitchen, dairy and smokehouse stood in a neat, orderly row facing the back of the tavern. Beyond the dependencies, Cara could see a garden, now tilled under and a small orchard, whose limbs were bare.

Bea linked her arm through Cara's once again and ushered her down the brick walk. "I hope you don't mind," she said, pulling Cara's attention from the fenced-in pasture and stable that lay beyond the orchard. "We thought you might be more comfortable having a cottage to yourself. We have six rooms upstairs and, believe it or not, they're all usually occupied every night."

"Why wouldn't I believe that?" Cara asked curiously.

Bea came to a stop with a startled look. "Why, because Williamsburg just isn't a bustling community anymore." Her tone implied she had stated the obvious. "What with Richmond being the capital now, and Norfolk growing up as it is, Williamsburg is fairly overlooked these days. Most people who come this way are passing through to somewhere else." She paused for a sigh. "Of course, there is the lunatic asylum, but I don't think that counts as an attraction, do you? Not like a fair or a theater. Did you know we used to have a playhouse here? Of course, there is the college."

With a smile, Cara listened to Bea ramble as they approached a small cottage sitting on the edge of the orchard. The single-story, steep-roofed dwelling was painted and trimmed out to match the main house.

"John, bless his heart, had this built ten years ago to serve as his office. But Mother Hawthorne came to live with us right after that and used the cottage for her own until two years ago. Since then, we've let it stand as a room for rent."

Stepping into the single-room cottage, Cara set her valise down and looked about the sunny interior. The walls were a pale yellow to complement the green-and-ocher quilt spread over the canopied tester bed. Opposite the bed, on the wall to the right, was the fireplace, and before it stood a wing back chair. A clothes press and dry sink were the only other furnishings, but they were finely crafted pieces and completed the room nicely.

Bea busied herself opening the cottage's only window. "We're having a warm spell just now, so we haven't kept any wood in here for the fireplace. But just in case, I'll have Custis bring some down for you."

"I'm sure I'll be fine, Bea." After the frigid cold Cara had experienced on the ship, the mildly cool air felt wonderful.

"Oh, my heavens, it's no bother." Bea moved to the bed to fluff the already-plumped pillows. "And I'll make sure to get you another blanket. I don't want you to be cold in your bed at night."

At that moment, Cara's mind chose to recall the warmth she had found in Justin's bed. With his body pressed intimately to hers, she had slept soundly, blissfully. A heated blush rose up her cheeks as she thought of the other things she had done with his body pressed closely to hers. A pang of yearning swept through her. She ached to feel his firm muscles beneath her fingers, his lips against hers, snatching her breath away while his caressing hands stroked and teased. Unconsciously, her fingers skimmed over the intricately stitched quilt, her inward gaze seeing only Justin at her fingertips.

Straightening the perfectly level mirror, Bea caught the

reflection of Cara's intense expression and quickly turned. "Cara, what is it?"

Startled by Bea's worried voice, Cara realized where her wayward thoughts had been. Immediately, her blush turned scarlet. Stammering for a reply, she pressed trembling fingers to her overheated cheeks.

"Bea . . . oh, dear . . . I mean . . . my mind just wandered away with me. Please forgive me."

Bea's eyes filled with sympathy. "Oh, you poor thing, you must be exhausted. Perhaps if you lie down for a bit. I can have Ophelia make you up a pot of tea. That might help."

Cara gathered her wits as best she could. "I think I'll unpack," she replied lamely.

Bea decided her young cousin might need some time to herself. "Of course, dear, take as long as you like. When you feel up to it, I'll be in the kitchen."

Not trusting her voice, Cara simply nodded.

"I'll be helping Ophelia with tonight's chowder. Not that I don't trust her with the recipe, mind you. She is the best of cooks, but I do like to make certain of the seasonings. You know how that is." Swirling out of the cottage in a rush of skirts and petticoats and nonstop monologue, Bea continued to speak even as she closed the door. "Rest easy now and don't worry about a thing."

The door shut and still Cara could hear Bea's voice as she bustled down the walk, at that point talking only to herself.

Thirty minutes later, a collected Cara left her cottage in search of Bea and the rest of the Hawthorne family. After having taken herself firmly in hand, relegating her more intimate musings to the safekeeping of her heart, she had unpacked her belongings and washed up. In deference to the mild day, she donned the burgundy dress with short, capped sleeves. She pulled her hair into a simple arrangement that left the long tresses free to flow down her back from the crown of her head.

The sound of children's gay laughter reached Cara as she neared the smokehouse. Scampering into view almost immediately came a raven-haired little girl. She was doing her best to run in one direction while yelling back over her shoulder in another.

"You won't catch me, you won't catch me," she taunted her playmates in earnest, but one look at Cara and she promptly forgot her game.

Wide green eyes that had all the promise of one day rivaling the sparkling vividness found in Cara's solemnly regarded the beautiful stranger from her round little face.

"Good day to you," Cara said, kneeling down so she was eye level with the adorable cherub.

"Good day to you, mistress." The four-year-old replied with all the mannerly advice her mother had ever given her.

"Which little Hawthorne are you?"

"Sarah Beth."

"How do you do, Sarah Beth. I am your cousin, Cara."

"Your servant."

"And yours, Sarah." Cara couldn't help but smile at the child's seriousness.

"You're pretty."

Cara raised a hand to her throat in mock surprise. "Oh, not nearly as pretty as you."

Sarah dissolved into giggles, forsaking all formality. "You talk funny."

"Everyone where I come from sounds like me."

"Where's that?"

"England."

"Where's that?"

"Far away, across the ocean," Cara explained.

"I've been to Elizabeth City," Sarah stated emphatically.

"You have? Perhaps one day you'll take me there."

"Are you going to live with us now?"

"Yes, for a while."

"How long?"

"At least until springtime." After that, Cara thought, she would be returning to England with Justin. "Would you like to play a game with me?"

"Oh, yes," Sarah squealed, clapping her hands. "What shall it be?"

"We'll see who can be the first to find your mother."

"I win!" Sarah turned and dashed off toward the kitchen. "Mama, Cousin Cara has come from England!"

From the deep shadows beside the far corner of the tavern, Bartholemew Smith watched Cara follow Sarah into the kitchen. His gaze lingered on the alluring curves of her trim figure. Once she was out of sight, he turned to glare at the cottage he had just seen her leave, and a satisfied smile jerked at his lips.

Chapter Ten

"Why you smilin' at dem apples like dat?"

Cara looked up from the fruit she was peeling and threw an impish grin at the lanky cook, Ophelia. "Was I smiling?" she asked innocently, knowing full well that she had been.

"Don't you give me none of yo' fine lip, Miz Cara. You been smilin' like a cat fo' a week now."

"Maybe that's because I'm happy."

"I'm sho you is, but dat ain't what's puttin' dat look on yo' face."

Cara gave Ophelia her full attention. "What look?"

"Dat look like you got some secret you ain't goin' to share wid nobody." Ophelia put her weight into rolling out a crust, but her sidelong gaze was fixed on Cara. "I didn't know better, I'd say you got yo'sef a man."

The blush that stained Cara's cheeks betrayed her, and Ophelia was quick to pounce on the unspoken disclosure.

"Miz Cara!" she exclaimed, abandoning her pastry. "You put dem apples down right now and git over here." Cara started to protest, but the cook cut her off. "Don't you argue none wid me."

After a week of listening to Ophelia issue her orders, Cara knew it was useless to try and argue. The woman had a will of iron and ruled her kitchen—and anyone who came into its proximity—with near tyrannical authority. Despite the idiosyncrasy, Cara liked Ophelia for her generous nature and teasing ways.

Resigned to the fact that the black cook would not be satisfied until she heard what she wanted to hear, Cara crossed the warm kitchen and sat in the proffered chair. On a defiant whim, however, she gave in to a bit of her own stubbornness and brought her bowl of apples with her.

"Now, what dis about some man?" Ophelia started right in with a determined gleam in her big brown eyes.

Cara wasn't sure where to start. Up until now, she had kept all that she shared with Justin hugged close to her heart. It was difficult to tell someone of her own private dream come true.

"I have met a man of whom I am . . . fond," she began hesitantly.

"Where? Here?" Ophelia scoffed. "You ain't been in Williamsburg long enough to meet any man worth knowin'."

Cara picked up an apple and applied her paring knife to the fruit's peel. "No, he isn't from Virginia."

"From dat England of yo's?"

"He is the captain of the ship I was on. Captain Reynolds."

"Justin Reynolds?"

At Ophelia's tone of recognition, Cara looked up from her work. "Do you know him?" Her voice carried an anxious note.

The cook went back to rolling out her raw dough. "He own dat property on de river, over by de Miller place. He stop by de tavern now and again, but he ain't round too much." She pursed her lips before continuing. "Dat some man."

Cara couldn't have agreed more. "Yes, I think so," she admitted shyly.

Cara's reaction did not go unnoticed by Ophelia's sharp eyes. "You ain't a babe no more. It's 'bout time you found a man." Her dark head nodded sagely. "I was fifteen when my Pheobus and me got married, sixteen when he got my first child on me. By de time I was yo' age, I'd had three." She laughed at some private remembrance. "Oh, my Pheobus, he was full of de pepper, struttin' round like he did." In a tight circle she stepped out a hip-swaying swagger. "Lord, he was a fine man."

Cara regarded Ophelia with wonder. "I didn't know you had children."

"Five. Four boys and one girl. Dey all live up to Massa Hawthorne's farm."

Inside, Cara shriveled up at Ophelia's casual reference to her slave status. If she lived to be a thousand, Cara knew she would never understand, nor condone, the owning of another human being. She had been appalled when she had first learned that all the black servants at the tavern were actually slaves, owned by Bea's husband, John. The fact that John was as nice a person as his wife, or that he did not mistreat his slaves, did not, in Cara's mind, excuse the practice.

"And your husband?" she asked.

"He died some years back," Ophelia answered easily. "Just got old in his bones one day and stopped."

"I'm sorry, Ophelia."

"Dere ain't no need for you to fret. We had a good life, better 'n most and I still got my babies."

"Grandchildren?"

The toothy smile came back to Ophelia's face. "Thirteen," she proclaimed proudly. Setting her rolling pin aside, she dusted the flat crust with flour. "So, when you and Mr. Reynolds goin' to make some babies?"

Despite the blush that stained her face, Cara managed to reply. "After we're married, of course."

"When you plannin' on doin' dat?"

Cara took a quick sigh and gave a delicate shrug. "We haven't had time to actually discuss that, but Justin will be by any day now."

Ophelia cast a shrewd, speculative look at Cara's radiant face, but kept her thoughts to herself. "You done wid dem apples?"

"Yes."

"Good. You keep slicin' away like dat and I'm goin' to end up wid applesauce. Now git."

Cara left her bowl on the table and retrieved her cloak from a peg beside the door. The weather had turned cold and she bundled up even for the short walk to the tavern.

"Save a piece of pie for me?" she asked, as she opened the door.

"Don't I always make sho you get fed? You ain't nothin' but a pretty package of bones. I ain't goin' to let you starve, no sir."

With a smile and a quick step, Cara crossed the courtyard to the tavern and entered through the rear door. At two o'clock in the afternoon, all was quiet. Opening the Hawthornes' private door to her right, she was about to call out a greeting when she heard Bea's scolding voice and the dismayed pleas of her son, Stephen.

"Mama, that hurts."

"I have no doubt, young man."

"Ow!"

"Hold still, Stephen."

Following the voices, Cara entered the parlor. The scene was what she might have expected. Eight-year-old Stephen was perched on a low stool, a basin of water on his lap, while Bea stood before him, dabbing at one of several scrapes on her son's face.

"Stephen, what happened to you?" Cara asked from the doorway.

The eldest Hawthorne child was quick to twist around on his seat, but Bea's firm hand held him fast in his place.

"Cousin Cara, I got him good." The boy spoke from behind a wet washcloth held to his upper lip.

"Who?"

"Boaz Booth."

Bea clicked her tongue in annoyance. "I wouldn't be so proud of myself this day, young man."

"Yes, ma'am," he said contritely, but above the towel his eyes were alight with excitement.

The washcloth was dipped and wrung out again before making one last pass over Stephen's minor bruises. Having done as much as she could, Bea gathered up the bowl and cloth and sent her son on his way.

"Upstairs with you, change out of those filthy clothes and then present yourself to your father."

Even at his tender age, Stephen recognized the no-nonsense tone of his mother's words. The sparkle left his eyes and with shuffling feet he left the room.

Cara watched his slumped-shoulder retreat with a barely controlled smile. As soon as he was out of sight, she gave full rein to her chuckle.

"Poor, sweet thing. He was so proud of himself."

Bea sighed dramatically. "Don't let him hear you say that, Cara. Good heavens, he'll be impossible. Although, I dare say, that Boaz Booth can be vexing at times."

"Who can be vexing?"

Both ladies turned to see John Hawthorne enter the room, accompanied by a tall, sandy-haired man.

"Oh, John, you startled me," Bea exclaimed, laying a hand to her chest.

The physical contrast between Beatrice and her husband was as great as any Cara had ever seen in a couple. What Bea lacked in the way of height and slenderness, John more than made up for. Standing six feet, he towered over his wife. His frame carried only a moderate weight and his hair was coal black, threaded with strands of white. Light gray eyes were his most outstanding feature in a face that was more masculine than handsome.

"Who can be vexing?" John repeated, coming forward.

"That Booth boy," Bea explained. "He and Stephen have tussled again. I don't know who got the worst of it this time. Judging from our son's face, I simply will not hazard a guess, but to listen to him, he was most definitely the victor." She paused only for a breath and lifted pleading eyes to her husband. "I don't know what we shall do about this, John. This is the third time the two have gone round and round. I've told Stephen he is to speak to you, and you will, of course, impress upon him the seriousness of the matter. Yes, I know you will."

John gazed down at his wife in the midst of one of her digressions. In the ten years they had been married, he had never been able to effectively halt her once she got started, least ways not in public, and he didn't try now. Instead, he shifted his weight to a comfortable stance, crossed his arms over his chest, and waited for her to finish.

In fascination, Cara watched John and Bea and was suddenly aware of a subtle current that passed between them. The lovingly tolerant look on John's face, his attentive, yet relaxed, acceptance of her wordy discourse, her unconsciously adoring gaze as she looked up at him, the gentle laying of her hand on his arm, all declared a couple finely in tune with each other. Cara wondered if she and Justin would in time share such an unspoken communication, ripe with devotion and awareness. It was a strangely intimate exchange to witness and, self-consciously, Cara looked away.

To her surprise, she found the gaze of John's companion boldly fixed on her face. Her self-consciousness escalated to embarrassment, washing her face with rosy color.

"John," the companion quietly interrupted.

At the sound of the man's voice, Bea's flow of words stopped, but only for a moment. "Oh, Hunter, good heavens, we've practically ignored you. You'll think us sadly lacking in manners."

"No more so than I," Hunter Rollins said, still making a close scrutiny of Cara's delicate features. "I'm afraid I have embarrassed your guest."

"Guest?" Bea trilled happily. "Cara is no guest, I assure you. She is my cousin." It was impossible not to recognize Hunter's avid regard of Cara, and Bea quickly made the introductions.

"My pleasure, Miss Fairchild." Hunter bowed formally.

"Mr. Rollins," Cara replied, having regained enough of her composure to answer courteously.

"Ah, do I detect your British ancestry?" he remarked, enjoying the sound of Cara's accent.

Bea immediately explained. "Cara has come from England to live with us."

Hunter's smile was its most charming. "Virginia is graced by your fair presence, Miss Fairchild."

With her face mirroring everything from wonder to a very feminine contemplation of the situation, Bea glanced between Cara and Hunter. The moment presented a host of possibilities.

Cara found Hunter's continued study of her to be disconcerting. Politely, she turned to the matter that had brought her in search of her cousin. "Bea, if this is still a convenient time, perhaps we might pay a visit to the dressmaker."

Bea thought Cara's timing was perfectly horrendous, and could only marvel at her young cousin's ineptitude in recognizing Hunter's interest for what it was. Nonetheless, she had promised the day to Cara.

"Yes, this is a perfect time," Bea replied, sounding anything but convinced. "Peachy is watching over the little ones, and John will be closeted with Stephen."

Within minutes, Hunter had taken his leave, John repaired to a closed-door meeting with his son, and the ladies were walking toward Williamsburg's Main Street. The icy cold day was saved from being intolerable by the absence of any wind and the presence of a clear blue sky.

"I do think Hunter is quite smitten with you," Bea announced a little too casually, after only a short while. The prospect of a romance tinged her words with a hopeful note.

Comprehending that tone, and the underlying message that accompanied it, Cara shook her head in good-natured exasperation. "One can hardly judge from that interview. We barely exchanged words."

"Words were not necessary," Bea insisted. "He couldn't take his eyes from you."

"Mine is a new face, nothing more."

"Oh, good heavens, Cara. Your lack of vanity is amazing. You are far more than lovely."

Cara had no reply, and a brief silence ensued before Bea continued the discussion. "You must admit Hunter is a striking man."

"Yes, I suppose," Cara replied, although she hadn't noticed.

"He has gentle eyes, wouldn't you say?"

But they are not cobalt blue, Cara's mind answered.

". . . and his hair is such a nice shade of brown . . ."

But not the deepest blendings of rich umbers.

". . . and, of course, many women are quite taken with the figure he cuts . . ."

But he doesn't stand well over six feet, with wide, powerful shoulders and long, muscled legs.

". . . and he has a sizable plantation not far from here . . ."

He isn't my sea captain! "Please, Beatrice," Cara said, hoping to stem any further declarations her cousin might have on Hunter's behalf. "I am sure Mr. Rollins is a nice man, but I truly have no interest."

"That is all right, dear," Bea remarked, undaunted. "As you said, you've only just met him. Give yourself time. All couples need time."

For half the length of Main Street, Bea extolled the virtues of a prolonged engagement between a man and a woman and its lasting benefits on a marriage. Cara had little chance to assure Bea that time would have no bearing on her feelings for Hunter Rollins.

Just past the courthouse, Bea directed their path down England Street and then onto Nicholson Street, to a modest house of graying clapboards. The sight of the posted sign, decorated with spool and thread, brought a tingling excitement to Cara that only increased when she and Bea drew near the cluttered shop. It had been four years since Cara had had a new dress, and she was grateful that Bea had convinced her to replenish her wardrobe.

Unfortunately, Cara's anticipation faded when she and Bea entered the shop just as Regina Taylor was making her exit. The three came to a halt just inside the door, and for a few seconds Cara was taken aback by the unexpected meeting.

Memories of their last encounter on board the *Wind Dancer* flashed through Cara's mind. They had stood together outside Justin's door and Regina had done her utmost to insinuate that she and Justin had been intimate. The thought of that ignited Cara's ire.

"Regina," Cara coolly acknowledged.

Regina's black eyes flared. "Cara," she returned with an air of indifference she was far from feeling. Just the sight of the younger woman was enough to make her blood boil.

Glancing bemusedly between the two women, Bea asked, "Do you two know each other?"

"Yes," Cara replied, glad for Bea's presence. "We sailed together on the same ship."

"Well, isn't that just wonderful?" Bea exclaimed, oblivious to the tension simmering between the two women. "Introductions won't be necessary at all then, will they? Not that I wouldn't have minded. After all, everyone in Williamsburg knows everyone else. Isn't that right, Regina?" Suddenly, Bea frowned, her expression becoming grave. "I was so sorry when I heard of Charles," she whispered. "I know his passing must be a trial for you."

A picture of a permanently gagged Beatrice Hawthorne formed in Regina's mind. Mentally, she cursed the woman's prattle. "Yes, it was," she replied smoothly, careful to keep her thoughts from reflecting on her face.

Knowing the lie for what it was, Cara ground her teeth together. "Charles was most dear," she managed to get out, staring at Regina pointedly. "However, I am glad his suffering has come to an end."

Regina nearly choked on the subtle insult. If they weren't in public, she'd show the brazen little twit just what it meant to cross words with her. Quickly, she cautioned herself to patience. She would have her revenge on Cara. Just as she was going to have it with Justin. She had been planning it all quite carefully and only a few more details remained to be seen to. She nearly laughed. Beatrice was right about one thing, everyone in Williamsburg did know everyone else. That included the less than savory types, like Bartholemew Smith.

"Strange how one person's suffering ends and another's begins." She smiled knowingly at Cara. "If you will excuse me, ladies?" With a nod of her head, she swept out of the shop.

The brief encounter couldn't have ended a second too soon for Cara. Taking a deep breath, she pulled her seething emotions under control.

"Now, what do you think she meant by that?" Bea wondered aloud, closing the door.

Cara didn't know and she was not going to waste any time speculating. "One can never tell with Regina," she replied, her voice thankfully calm.

The sound of voices drew the shop's rotund proprietress from the fitting room. Waddling forward, Mrs. Gates beamed a huge smile at one of her more regular, and extravagant, patrons. "Good day, Mrs. Hawthorne. How may I serve you today?"

Moving about the shop with an ease that spoke of familiarity, Bea answered over her shoulder. "With your usual splendid fashion, Mrs. Gates. My cousin is in need of several new dresses and I know you shall be able to assist us."

Mrs. Gates was only too happy to comply.

Cara set aside any lingering twinges of pique and immersed herself in the matter of her wardrobe. The process of considering patterns, selecting styles, and choosing fabrics occupied the women for the better part of the next two hours. Bea's natural inclination to spend was tempered by Cara's inherent practicality, and more than once during the afternoon, Cara found herself having to restrain her cousin's exuberance.

"Bea, I know the pelisse made up in the red wool would

be beautiful," Cara protested during an interval when Mrs. Gates had stepped out of the fitting room to wait on another customer. "But my own cloak will suffice."

"But, Cara, the coloring would so become you," Bea insisted.

Not wanting to hurt Bea's feelings, Cara patiently reminded her of the original purpose of the excursion. "Bea, my intent is to purchase only two dresses. It is what we agreed upon."

"Well, yes, that is true, but you have so little that is suitable for our climate."

"Two dresses, Bea. Your monies will make the purchases now and I shall work at the tavern to repay you."

"I wish you would not insist upon paying me back."

"I will accept the dresses under no other circumstances."

"But you are family and I cannot abide the idea of you wearing rags."

Knowing Bea meant well, Cara did not take offense at the unintentional insult. Nonetheless, her chin came up. "My wardrobe has seen me through thus far."

Seeing the unshakable resolve on Cara's face, Bea gave in, though not graciously. "Well, so be it, but I for one am going to fetch that shriveled-up gray thing you call a dress and feed it to the fires."

Glad for the compromise, Cara slipped her arm around her cousin's plump shoulders. "And I will help you."

In the end, Cara decided upon a gown of forest green cotton, with long sleeves à la mamluk and a high ruffled collar. Also, a much more serviceable dress of lightweight wool, woven in beige-and-white stripes. Both pieces promised to be flattering and Cara was anxious to have them completed.

The walk home was accomplished in a comfortable silence. After having spent the entire afternoon in conversation, the only words either woman felt inclined to offer were greetings to passersby. Bea seemed content with the serene arrangement, until she and Cara approached a glamorously attired woman near the end of Main Street. Cara extended a friendly hello, however Bea did not even acknowledge the other woman and in return was completely ignored. Puzzled by the mutual snub, Cara turned to Bea.

"Good heavens, Cara," Bea remarked stiffly, having read her cousin's questioning look. "You shouldn't have spoken to her."

"Why ever not?" Cara's brow pulled into a frown, especially so at Bea's frosty demeanor.

"You had no way of knowing," Bea explained with a roll of her eyes and a sound that was practically a groan. "And it certainly isn't something one brings up in polite conversation."

Thoroughly confused, Cara asked, "What isn't? Who was that?"

"*That* was Yvette Bouchard."

It was obvious to Cara that the name held some special significance of which she was unaware. She waited for Bea to continue and finally had to prompt her along. "Who is Yvette Bouchard?"

Seemingly pained by the matter, Bea's normally pleasant features took on a pinched look. "Yvette Bouchard . . . is a harlot."

Cara gasped and quickly looked back behind her to Mrs. Bouchard's retreating figure. "A . . . harlot?"

Having broached the subject, Bea cast off her initial reticence and eagerly gave in to her gift for gab. "Well, she owns a brothel on the other side of the hospital and that makes her as good as a whore."

"A brothel?" Cara gasped again, her eyes growing wider by the second.

Bea's head nodded emphatically. "Yes, if you can imagine such a thing. Oh, she gives herself airs, claiming to only own the house and professing that she merely oversees the business." She sniffed disdainfully and pulled her cloak tightly around her. "That still makes her as much a hussy as the rest. And she has the nerve to walk around in broad daylight, right down Main Street, mind you. But I suppose she's too frightened to stray from that house of hers at night, after the murder several weeks ago.'

Her senses still in a whirl at actually having seen a strumpet, Cara had to mentally shake her head to grasp this last tidbit Bea dropped. "Someone was murdered?" she questioned in an awed whisper.

"Not just someone, but one of Mrs. Bouchard's whores, Martha Trent. She was found in the backwoods one morning with her neck broken."

Cara shivered at the thought. "Who killed her?"

"We don't know and it has us all quite leery. But John, bless his heart, says I'm not to worry. He thinks Martha Trent was killed because she wouldn't . . . I mean, some man was . . . oh dear." Bea finished in a pitiful voice, flustered by her own lack of decorum in discussing something so scandalous.

Shrouded in the midst of the lengthening shadows, Williamsburg's dingy appearance took on a new, sinister cast. To Cara, the sight of Hawthorne's Tavern as it came into view was especially welcome.

Justin stood at one of the long windows in his library and scanned the afternoon scene before him. The carefully tended lawn sloped gently to the river where the *Wind Dancer* lay at anchor. Absently, he watched the ship shift easily with the water's motion.

"You see any problem with that?" Percy asked from behind him.

The sound of Percy's voice jerked Justin's mind back to the topic at hand. Irritably, he realized he had no idea what Percy had just said. "What?" he asked, pushing away from the window and striding back to his desk.

Standing before the desk, Percy squinted curiously at Justin's scowling face. The man was in a rare mood, that was for sure. They had been struggling through a stack of paperwork for the better part of an hour and making very little headway. "I asked if you have any problem with the price we were quoted for that list of supplies you got there before you?"

"No, none," Justin snapped, glaring at the offensive document in question.

"Good," Percy returned, "because the way you're looking at the thing is likely to set it on fire."

From his seat, Justin regarded the man irately. "Then you better have a bucket of water at hand, shouldn't you?"

"Ha!" Percy crowed, not in the least affected by Justin's show of temper. "You sure got some bug bitin' at you today."

"And if I do, it's none of your damn business. Now, can we please finish this up?"

Percy wanted nothing more than to do just that. "We got to see to repairs to the ship. She made it through the trip all right, but the carpenter says this last storm weakened most of the yardarms."

Leaning back in his chair, Justin focused his attention on his ship, but it was only a matter of minutes before he found his mind wandering again. Percy's words, bulkheads and masts were all replaced by thoughts of Cara.

Bloody hell, Justin swore to himself. She was like a fever in his blood, interfering with his life until he was behaving like a besotted simpleton. Foolishly, he had thought that once he had taken her to his bed he would be rid of the need he felt for her. But damn, he wanted her more now than he had last week.

Ever since she had left the ship he had been tormented with the thought of her. The sound of her laughter plagued his days, the sight of her winsome smile chased him into his nights, the memory of her yielding softness invaded his sleep. She was constantly in his mind.

And, he admitted, his conscience nagged at him. She had been a virgin, for Christ's sake, not some trained courtesan. He could have made their parting more gentle for her.

Mentally, he cursed again. For the first time in his life he seemed to have no control over himself where a woman was concerned. He found the experience both uncomfortable and annoying. And, he'd be damned if he was going to let it continue. Cynically he reminded himself that Cara was a woman, perhaps more beautiful than some, more witty, more passionate, more clever, but a woman nonetheless. He would put her out of his mind just as he had every other woman he had known.

Snapping out of his private musings, he glanced up to find Percy silently watching him with an expression of fine exasperation on his face. "Are you finished?" he asked shortly.

Percy shook his head in astonishment. "I could be asking the same of you. I've been standing here growing roots."

Justin shoved himself out of his chair, his piercing gaze slicing across the desk. "I don't need any lectures from you."

No, Percy didn't think so, either. He had a good idea what was bothering his captain and it would take more than any lecture to get the man back on an even course again. He shrugged his massive shoulders. He knew when it was useless to deal with Justin and now obviously was one of those times.

"Suit yourself. When you're ready to finish this up, you just let me know." Turning, he headed for the door. "Me? I got better things to do, like get me a mug of ale."

Justin glared at the door Percy slammed shut, and considered his own affairs. He too had more immediate matters to tend to, first and foremost ridding himself of the hold Cara had on him.

Angrily, he realized that was going to be easier said than done.

By the end of the week, Cara was firmly established in the routine of the tavern. Working beside the tavern's hired barmaid, Lucy Dooley, she easily adjusted to the busy schedule of serving meals and drinks. Waiting for Justin, however, became increasingly more difficult. Every morning she rose absolutely certain he would show up on her doorstep. Every night she retired having to reassure herself that some important matter had kept him from her side.

A low-grade fear took root within Cara when Justin was still absent after three full weeks. During the lonely nights, her mind played a nervous game, imagining any number of tragedies to have befallen him. She pictured him lying gravely ill, too weak to leave his bed. Recalling his description of the watermen and their extreme dislike of the English, she saw him suffering an ill fate at their hands. And of course, there was still a murderer who hadn't been caught. The possibilities seemed endless. Yet despite her worries, Cara steadfastly kept faith with her heart, knowing instinctively that Justin was well and would arrive soon. She continued her wait and optimistically set her sights on Christmas as the day of their reunion. What better Christmas present, she reasoned, could she ever have?

Christmas Eve morning dawned over Williamsburg with a solid sheet of gray clouds looming overhead. The wind dashed brittle leaves over the frozen ground that was sure to be covered with snow before nightfall.

Ignoring the uncomfortable chill of her cottage, Cara rose and dressed, not even bothering to stoke the coals in the fireplace. Knowing Mrs. Gates would have her new green dress ready before noon, Cara was anxious to start her day. She hurried through her chores, grateful that the holiday had kept most travelers at home. A hurried breakfast followed and then a quick change of clothes. With noon still more than an hour away, she was walking down Main Street, a bubbling Bea beside her.

"Cara, I don't think I have ever seen you this excited." Bea's breaths emerged into the wintry air as small, white puffs.

Snuggling into her cloak, Cara smiled at her cousin. "It has been so long since I have had a new dress." The explanation was true, but Cara knew that the real reason for her expectancy lay in the fact that she was planning to wear the new gown tomorrow for Justin.

"Well, then," Bea replied, "we shall have to make certain that more new dresses are forthcoming. Just this one has put the most lovely sparkle in your eyes and a delightful lilt to your step."

Cara laughed. "Bea, you are absolutely poetic."

"It's Christmas, dear. I shall lay the blame there."

"This Christmas shall be the most wonderful I've ever had," Cara declared with certainty.

"I agree. Our family is together, we are in fine health and spirits. There is little that could spoil this day." Unexpectedly, Bea's expression cooled, her gaiety freezing. "Except perhaps that."

Bemused, Cara looked to her cousin. "Bea, is there anything amiss?"

"Only that," Bea indicated with a nod of her head.

Cara followed the direction of Bea's frigid stare to a carriage on the other side of the wide street, drawn up in front of an eatery. Just stepping down, with the help of a footman, was Yvette Bouchard.

"This type of thing would have never happened ten years ago," Bea snipped in hushed tones. "But there she is, entering a public place."

That issue aside, Cara admitted that Mrs. Bouchard was a beautiful woman, somewhat reminiscent of Regina Taylor. Like Regina, Mrs. Bouchard possessed a buxom-lined figure, with dark eyes and hair. Even at a distance, Cara could discern the distinct arch of the woman's brow and the engaging smile she offered to her escort, just now emerging from the conveyance.

"I should like to see what man is bold enough to flaunt proprieties in our very noses," Bea exclaimed.

In the next fraction of a second, every nerve in Cara's body seemed to explode. The force sent the blood pounding through her body with a sickening rush, twisting her stomach and constricting her lungs.

Before her green eyes, grown wide with panic, Cara faced a horrible, *horrible* reality. *Justin.* It was *Justin* who stood beside Yvette Bouchard, *Justin* who bent low to listen to some remark she made and then laughed in carefree response. It was *Justin* who extended his arm and ushered the woman into the building.

The blood that had coursed wildly through Cara just seconds before froze in her veins. Her steps faltered.

"Whatever it is, dear?" Bea asked in alarm, shocked by Cara's ashen face and trembling lips.

Cara remained motionless. The meaning of Justin's appearance with Mrs. Bouchard seeped into her brain like a hideous acid that ate at her hopes and dreams, leaving in its wake nothing but a truth too wretched to bear. He had betrayed her. She loved him with all of her being, her heart and her soul and he . . . didn't love her.

The alarm on Cara's face frightened Bea. "Cara! What is wrong?"

It was the near shout of Bea's voice that penetrated the thick, tormenting shroud that threatened to engulf Cara. Absently, she gazed at her cousin, fighting desperately not to collapse right there on the street.

"I . . . I . . . am ill, Bea." Her words were barely audible. "Please . . ." She swallowed past a sickening lump in her throat as tears flooded her eyes. "I need . . . to go home."

Chapter Eleven

Yvette Bouchard rarely permitted herself the luxury of taking a lover. However, when the lover involved happened to be Justin Reynolds, she eagerly allowed herself to indulge.

Sitting before her mirror, she brushed the shining length of her hair. Surreptitiously, she studied the reflection of Justin's frame as he reclined against the padded headboard of her bed. He had removed his boots and jacket and, she noticed with an inward smile, was openly watching her.

"It has been a long time, Justin," she said, laying aside her brush and strolling languidly across her opulent bedroom.

Justin lifted his snifter of brandy to his lips, his eyes taking in the seductive play of Yvette's diaphanous yellow dressing gown swirling about her voluptuous figure. The weak afternoon light, filtering in from between heavily curtained windows, created mysterious shadows on her lavish curves. Justin felt the tension that had been riding him begin to dissolve.

For weeks he had worked himself to the point of exhaustion, personally helping with the repairs to the ship, cramming as much activity as he could into each waking hour, in an effort to purge himself of the stranglehold Cara retained on him. He had risen early each morning, retired late every night, but his efforts had been in vain. He had still wanted Cara with a need that bordered on desperation.

He had found it inconceivable that one slip of a woman could make a mockery of his, up until now, perfectly disciplined life. It was intolerable, and infuriating. And there was only one cure, he had reasoned. A woman had created the havoc in his life. Another woman would see its order restored.

"How long has it been?" he asked, not really caring to know the answer.

Coming to perch beside Justin's raised knee, Yvette draped her arm across his thigh and made a show of trying to remember the last time they had shared a bed.

"Four, perhaps five years?" she returned, knowing full well it had been over six. There were some things a woman never forgot. Making love to Justin Reynolds was one of those things.

Taking his time, Justin let his eyes travel down the white column of her throat to the plump breasts tantalizingly displayed, then silently cursed as he had to shove away the mental image of brilliant green eyes and auburn hair. "Time has been good to you," he replied in a gruff voice.

"Like a fine wine?" she asked with a laugh, liking the compliment. "I must confess, my friend, I have missed you. And . . ." she drew the word out meaningfully, "I was most surprised you decided to pay me a visit."

One of Justin's dark brows quirked upward. "Is that a complaint?"

"No," she assured him, shaking her head to make certain the dark waves of hair spilled teasingly over her left shoulder. "You are always welcomed into my room." Leaning forward, she pressed her full lips to his in a luxuriant kiss meant to entice. "But you have been back for almost a month now," she murmured against his mouth. "I thought perhaps you had forgotten me."

"I didn't realize you were keeping track of me these days," he said, very aware of her breasts pressed to his chest. Reaching out, he toyed with the heavy cloud of dark hair cascading sinuously about her shoulders.

A guilty smile stretched Yvette's lips. "We have known each other too long for me to deny it. I admit, I have been waiting for you."

Taking the snifter from him, she set it on the nearby table before once again settling comfortably against his bent leg. "Thank you for taking me to lunch earlier. That was most pleasant."

"My pleasure," he replied.

Devilry sparkled in Yvette's eyes. "I haven't even begun to see to your pleasure."

Her transparent invitation was just what Justin wanted. It was the only reason he was there. Sliding his hands up her arms, he pulled her forward until her body was reclining on his.

Purring in anticipation, Yvette coiled her arms around Justin's shoulders. Eagerly, her lips sought his and as his arms closed about her, she melted into his embrace.

The kiss was potent, as tantalizing as Justin had ever received. Ardently, her tongue teased his, while her hands caressed their way to his chest and her hips rhythmically pressed against his. She knew her art well, Justin thought distractedly, his hands cupping her rounded bottom.

"Do you know how good you feel, Justin?" Yvette whispered against his lips.

It was a rhetorical question, Justin knew. But suddenly, as he waited for desire to lick at his senses, he realized the most appalling answer. While Yvette was already entwined in passion, he was still coldly unaffected. And he did *not* feel good. Not about Yvette or what he was doing with her.

Without warning, his mind took him back to that night on board the *Wind Dancer*. Suddenly, it was Cara who he held, Cara who was returning his kiss, Cara who was sighing in trembling need against him.

Roughly, he grabbed hold of Yvette's shoulders and thrust her back, his hands retaining their firm grasp as he silently searched her features. "Bloody hell," he ground out in a murderous voice.

Startled, Yvette found herself set aside. Coming out of her short-lived sensuous haze, she watched Justin push himself off the bed and stalk to the side table to pour himself a drink. He filled a glass with bourbon, then set the crystal piece down without even touching its contents. For several moments, Yvette silently contemplated his rigid stance.

"Justin?" Her soft inquiry floated across the room.

As though he had been pulled from the depths of grave thought, his head snapped to one side, but he offered no reply.

Yvette studied him closely and felt a nervous tremor pass through her. This was not like Justin. "What is it?" He remained silent and she tried again. "Is there something wrong? Did I . . ."

Turning abruptly, he silenced her inquiry with barely leashed fury glittering in his eyes. The sight was so unexpected that Yvette hastily rose from the bed and faced him warily.

Justin recognized her nervous reaction and tried to get a grip on his temper. "I'm sorry, Yvette," he growled, running a hand over the back of his neck. "You don't deserve this."

Yvette's eyes rounded. She had never known Justin to be contrite over anything. Apparently, he had changed to a certain degree since his last trip to America. Her nervousness faded, to be replaced by concern and a great deal of curiosity. In an easy manner she shrugged. "I don't mean to pry, but you are not yourself."

The understatement of the century, Justin thought caustically. Some of his opinion showed on his face, prompting the return of Yvette's puzzled frown.

"How long have we been friends, Justin?" she asked in genuine concern.

Almost resentfully, he answered. "Fifteen or so years."

Nodding, Yvette strolled forward to stand directly before Justin. Carefully, she smoothed her fingertips over the angry lines of his face. "A long time. Some friendships never last that long."

"Make your point, Yvette," he stated, impatient to know where this was leading.

Her hand dropped to rest lightly on his chest. "My point is that you and I have always been friends, as well as lovers. I can't help but worry about you."

"Thank you, but you don't need to worry about me," he said stiffly.

"No?" she returned with a look that clearly said, prove it. "Then why aren't we in my bed?"

Because I cannot rid myself of her memory! Growling low in frustration and fury, he returned to the bed and sat to jerk on his boots. That done, he snatched up his jacket and pulled it on. Only then did he glance to Yvette. Her troubled frown made him pause.

"I will be all right," he assured her, although he knew he was lying.

Tipping her head to one side, she gave him a hopeful smile. She knew better than to try and push the subject. "Remember that I am here for you."

He nodded, then stepped forward to cup her chin in his hand. With a disgusted shake of his head, he turned and left.

Outside, the cold air hit him like a slap in the face. Glancing to the heavy sky, he muttered a pithy curse.

The snow that had threatened all day fell from the midnight sky, coating Williamsburg with a thick layer of white. In the still hush, the town assumed a fairy-tale quality as bushes became misshapen mounds and roads disappeared. Light spilling out from unshuttered windows created an absurd, shifting lacework on the dancing flakes, only enhancing the fantasy feeling the night possessed.

Inside Cara's cottage, reality hung with an oppressive weight. Yellow-and-blue flames snapped in the fireplace, sending eerie shadows across the space of the single room. Seated on the floor before the blaze, wrapped in a quilt, Cara shivered despite the heat and the cover that should have been more than sufficient to keep her warm.

Cara felt a weariness settle on her shoulders, a tiredness of both body and spirit. Slowly, she closed her eyes and lowered her forehead to her drawn-up knees. Absently, she wondered about the time and guessed it to be past midnight. She had lost track of how long she had been sitting thus, trying to combat the chill that permeated her body. But no matter how many logs she had fed to the fire, it had been useless in thawing the cold that ran to the very depths of her soul.

With that same absent sense of distraction, she wondered if she would ever be warm again. Sighing heavily, she was inclined to think not. Just as she doubted she would ever feel whole again. Her heart was gone, torn apart and left in tattered shreds.

Behind closed lids, the tears came up again as they had since the moment that afternoon when she had finally gained the privacy she had so desperately needed. Before Bea's worried eyes, she had somehow managed to keep a firm grip on her control, had even convinced her cousin that the physician was not needed. Admitting to a sudden pounding head that would best be cured by sleep, Cara had been left alone.

Now, hours later, in a solitude she found dismal, the truth was no easier to bear than it had been that morning when she had seen Justin step beside Yvette Bouchard.

Without wanting to, she saw him smiling down at the curvacious woman. Repeatedly, she pictured his hand slipping to the small of her back. There could be no denying the meaning of his presence with the woman. And even if their association was innocent, completely without fault, his absence over the past three weeks had finally been explained. He hadn't been ill or injured or harmed. He had simply not cared.

A pitiful, heart-wrenching sob escaped Cara's lips.

Throwing her head back, she gazed unseeing to the rafters, the firelight glazing the tears on her face.

"He doesn't love me." Pain ripped through her as the words repeated themselves again and again in her mind.

Once-pleasurable images of all those weeks on board his ship choked her mind and lit the fuel of burning rage within her. Like a naive child, she had misinterpreted his actions. And he had let her. No, he had helped her! A whispered word here, a penetrating glance there, shared confidences and tender embraces; he had played her like an untried violin, with a master's hand, plucking the strings of her heart. And stupidly, she had gloried in every moment, feeling alive and beautiful . . . oh, so loved.

The heat of fury exploded in her veins and she threw off the quilt. She had given Justin her trust and her love and in return had received deception! Mentally, she squirmed in enraged regret as she thought about what else she had given him. Her virtue. It had been the only thing that she had been able to truly call her own. From her heart, with all her love, she had gladly offered it to Justin.

The fire before her had burned down, casting a red glow on her shaking form. Outside, the snow continued to drift and pile. Distantly, the strains of a Christmas carol, sung by celebrants, reached Cara's ears.

Bitterly, she wished herself a happy Christmas, then shook her head in disgust. She had had such faith in the day, just as she had held such belief in Justin. In humiliation and anger she watched her dreams drift up the chimney, like so much smoke. All that was left were the ashes of betrayal.

Cara awakened the next morning feeling exhausted both physically and mentally. Within her was a sensation of emptiness, but she refused to allow herself to wallow in self-pity. Anger and hurt had carried her through the night. It was up to her pride and determination to see her through the days ahead.

When she appeared in the Hawthorne's parlor an hour later, no one was more surprised to see her than Bea.

The elder cousin rushed forward in concern. "Good heavens, Cara, I was just about to come out and check on you." Her discerning eye took in Cara's ashen face. "Whatever are you doing up and about?"

Cara lowered her hood before tucking errant curls back into place. "I am here to accompany the family to Christmas service."

"Are you well enough?" Bea asked, but didn't wait for a reply. "You don't look at all well." Over her shoulder, she queried her husband. "John, do you think she should be up?"

Shrugging into his jacket, John approached the ladies. The blue smudges beneath Cara's eyes were not usual and her face lacked its normal healthy color. Still, she was here and that said a great deal.

"If Cara says she is fit, then I am inclined to agree with her."

"I *am* fine," Cara insisted. "I experienced a passing malady, nothing more. My strength has returned."

"And it could just as easily take its leave," Bea exclaimed, her brow furrowing. "You can never be too sure."

Cara felt a little inclination toward humor, but the ironic words brought a wry smile to her lips. Two months ago, two weeks, even yesterday morning she would have disagreed. Now she could only berate herself for her own simplemindedness.

"You are right, of course. Only a fool trusts blindly. However, I would not lie to you. I wish to attend the service."

If Cara's resolute words weren't enough to convince Bea, then the look of unwavering determination on Cara's set face was. Sighing, Bea capitulated.

"Well, I'm sure you know what is best for you."

Know what was best? Cara nearly laughed at the notion. She thought she knew, once, before she had met Justin. She had thought loving him had been the best thing for her, for them both. Now it seemed that the best thing, the only thing for her was to rid herself of his memory. Resentfully, she realized just how difficult that was going to be. Gritting her teeth, she forced back the wave of pain and fury that washed over her.

"If we don't leave soon," John interjected much to Cara's relief, "we shan't have to worry about it at all. It is nearly time we departed."

In a flurry of motion, Bea gasped and whirled out of the room in search of the children.

"She only has your welfare at heart," John said quietly. "We both do."

Startled from the intensity of her thoughts, Cara gazed to John. His rugged features were softened by concern. The sight of such tender sentiment went far in diffusing her ire. "Yes, I know," she whispered.

"You will be all right, won't you?"

Raising her chin, she took a long, steady breath before answering firmly, "Yes, I will be fine."

It was only by sheer determination that Cara held true to her word. As the weeks passed, she suffered all the heartache of a woman truly scorned. In self-defense, she kept as busy as possible during the days, avoiding thinking of Justin. Unfortunately, the nights were too lonely and too quiet to keep the memories at bay. It was more often than not that Cara's pillows soaked up her hot, bitter tears.

On a clear, frozen morning, near the end of January, she emerged as usual from her cottage. Wrapped in her cloak to combat the winter chill, she hurriedly made her way up the walk, eager to reach the kitchen's fireplace. But the sight of little Sarah sitting in the courtyard, crying, detoured Cara's steps.

Worriedly, she knelt before the tearful child and gathered her in her arms. "Sweetheart, what is it?"

The four-year-old sniffed loudly and presented a pudgy hand for inspection. "I fell coming down the steps and hurt my finger."

Taking the cold little hand in her own, Cara examined the fingers with all the serious intent of a skilled surgeon. All the digits moved easily and not even the slightest scrape could be seen. Nonetheless, Cara lifted sympathetic eyes to Sarah and raised the dimpled hand to her lips for a healing kiss.

"Better?" she asked with an encouraging smile.

Not quite ready to relinquish Cara's loving attention, Sarah shook her head solemnly. "I don't think so, Cousin Cara. The finger still hurts."

Cara patted the soft palm and let herself be taken in by the child's adorable, albeit, woeful face. "Well, the best cure I know for a finger like this is a piece of cobbler."

Sarah's green eyes widened in surprise. She had never, ever heard of that remedy before. "It is?" she asked in wonder.

"Yes, it is," Cara replied with a nod. "And you are most fortunate because last night Ophelia mentioned that she was going to bake a cobbler this morning."

"Truly?"

"Oh, yes indeed."

Forgetting all about fingers and grievous injuries, Sarah scampered out of Cara's arms and raced for the kitchen.

"You are shameless, Cara," Bea announced gaily from the tavern's back door, where she had silently witnessed most of the exchange.

Rising, Cara pulled her cloak snugly about her before shrugging, "I admit it, but she is easy to spoil."

"You know Sarah has grown quite attached to you," Bea said, descending the steps to join Cara.

Cara did indeed know, and was equally fond of not only Sarah, but Stephen and Mary as well. They were intelligent, polite, beautiful, and honest as only the young can be. They were children to be proud of.

Unexpectedly, Cara pictured children of her own, the children she would never have with Justin. Regret stabbed at her, and out of the pain she tried to withstand came a full-blown resentment. How long, she asked herself, would it be before she could get through a day without some reminder of Justin? How long must she endure his intrusion into her life? Mentally, she berated herself for having fallen in love with a man who didn't understand the meaning of the word, let alone the emotion itself.

Watching the brittle look settle on Cara's face, Bea grew concerned. "Oh, dear, have I said something amiss?"

With a shake of her head, Cara struggled to pull herself together, "No," she replied, unable to keep the sharp edge from her voice. Grimacing, she tried again. "No, Bea, you've said nothing wrong."

"Well, thank heavens," Bea declared, relieved. "I would hate to think I had said or done anything to cause you distress. And you did look quite troubled there for a moment."

"Sarah is a sweetheart," Cara replied a bit lamely.

Beaming proudly, Bea agreed. "I think so. She is the joy of my life, as are her brother and sister. And of course, John, bless his heart. I don't know what I should do without him." She paused to stare off dreamily for a second or two, then collected herself with a chuckle. "Good heavens, here I am, going on like a silly schoolgirl, when I am a married woman of too many years. It's your head that should be filled with romantic notions."

As though they were standing in the warmth of her parlor instead of the middle of the cold courtyard, Bea expounded on a germ of an idea that had taken root in her mind.

"Just think of all the fun you'll be having once spring arrives. Of course, the social season isn't what it was when I was your age, but there are still men aplenty who will be flocking to our door once you've been introduced properly."

The thought sent chills down Cara's spine. She had no desire to meet any men, especially for the purposes of courtship. She knew it would be impossible for her to love another man as she had Justin. And even if by some miraculous chance she could ever come to care for another man, marriage was a moot point. She was no longer virtuous. How could she go to a husband after having given herself to Justin? A man deserved an unsullied wife.

Bea's voice pulled Cara from her miserable reverie. "Oh, I cannot wait for certain young men to meet you. They will give Hunter Rollins a run for his money. Before you know it, we will be having a wedding on our hands."

The words poured like salt into the open wound of Cara's heart. However, in the midst of her fanciful tangent, Bea missed the trembling of Cara's lips and the wince that crossed her face.

"We shall have Mrs. Gates create the most beautiful bridal gown imaginable and John, bless his heart, can give you away. In no time at all, you will be having children of your own."

Having mapped out a perfectly splendid plan, one that was sure to dispel the gray winter gloom of anyone's day, Bea smiled expectantly at her cousin, anxious for her reaction.

And it came. Without warning, Cara burst into tears, the anguish she had been striving to control overflowing the bounds of her restraint. Mortified, angry, and confused, she turned and fled to her cottage.

For several seconds, Bea could only stare, bewildered by Cara's behavior. A multitude of questions raced through her mind, but she wasted no time waiting for answers. Quickly, she followed her cousin.

"Cara?" she called, knocking on the cottage door and opening it simultaneously.

Lying on her bed, her arms cradling her head, Cara sobbed with a force that shook her slender form.

"Cara. Dear. Whatever is it?" Bea rushed to Cara's side, shaken by the pitiful sight before her.

For two long weeks, Cara had tried to cope with her pain, had tried to keep her despair locked deep within her where it wouldn't afflict anyone else. But the burden of shouldering such misery had become too great for her to bear. Needing comfort, she resignedly turned to Bea.

In a halting, tearful voice, Cara poured out the events of her passage from England. From her first meeting with Justin to her seeing him with Yvette Bouchard, Cara wept out every last detail.

Ever since Christmas, Bea had been wondering what had been troubling Cara. Cara had shrugged off her lack of spirit and distracted manner with the excuse of not feeling well and being homesick, but Bea had never been totally convinced. Now it all made terrible sense.

The tears finally dwindled and Cara raised herself to a sitting position. Smoothing the hair back from her face, she raised tired eyes to Bea.

"Do you think me a fool?" she asked, fully expecting recriminations.

Bea saw no purpose in casting moral judgments on a woman who had fallen deeply in love, and unfortunately had followed her heart's dictates. Quickly, she reached out and took one of Cara's shaking hands between her own. "No, Cara, you must not think that," she insisted. "We all make mistakes."

Gazing at their clasped hands, Cara murmured, "Thank you for understanding."

"You should have told me sooner."

"I had no wish to tax you with my troubles." Cara scoffed. "Here I am doing just that."

"As well you should. It is not right that you should suffer through this alone."

Cara's panicked eyes flew to Bea's face. "Please, you will not tell John of this, will you? I could not bear to have him know. I truly did not wish for anyone to know of this."

Unable to meet Cara's gaze, Bea glanced away. "That may not be possible."

"Why?" Cara asked.

Her face drawn into troubled lines, Bea broached a subject that could not be ignored. "Cara, is it possible that you are pregnant?"

Cara's jaw dropped. "Pregnant?"

Silently, Bea nodded, unconsciously holding her breath.

"Pregnant?" Cara repeated, thoroughly baffled. "Why on earth would you think such a thing?"

"Then you're not?" Bea asked hopefully.

Confusion and doubt and a genuine innocence all flashed across Cara's face. She had no idea how one became pregnant, other than it somehow involved one's husband and she wasn't married. But for some reason, Bea had felt the need to ask. Suddenly, she sensed that something was very wrong. "Well . . . no, that is . . . I'm not sure. How could? . . ."

Bea mentally groaned. The girl was simply too innocent for her own good. But that was hardly Cara's fault. With no mother to give her counsel, it was little wonder she was making all kinds of embarrassing blunders.

"Cara, the night you spent with Justin," Bea began slowly. "The results of your . . . union . . . with him could have resulted in your being . . . with child."

Stunned, Cara's eyes rounded enormously.

"So you see," Bea said, "it is imperative that I know. And if . . . you are . . . then we will have to tell John."

Pregnant. With Justin's child. Cara found the idea overwhelming. "How would I know?"

As simply as possible, Bea explained, then practically melted with relief when Cara knowingly confirmed that she was not pregnant.

"Thank goodness for little favors," Bea sighed.

Despite her own relief, the issue still pounded in Cara's head. She was far from finished with the matter. "I am obviously horribly uninformed in certain aspects of life, so I am no standard to judge anyone by. But what of you, Bea? How did you come to know all of this?"

Bea's heart went out to Cara. "You mustn't blame yourself. My mother told me a little, at least what to expect on my wedding night." Blushing delicately, she shrugged. "John, bless his heart, taught me the rest. Most husbands do."

"Are all men so informed?"

"Yes, I would imagine so."

Cara lowered her head, resentment back in full force. Stiffly, she voiced her conclusion aloud. "Then Justin would have known. He knew I . . . what might have happened when he took me to his bed." Ire glazed her eyes a vivid green. "I could have been carrying his child . . . and he never bothered to find out."

Not wishing to say anything to add to Cara's bitterness, Bea silently nodded. Sadly, she patted Cara's hand, offering what little comfort she could.

* * *

The sound of a stoneware plate crashing to the wooden floor jerked Ophelia's head up from the pot she had been stirring. With a squint she watched Cara shake her head and regard the mess she had just made.

The cook frowned. That was the third dish in as many days that the girl had dropped. That wasn't like her. Cara Fairchild was the most careful person, always taking extra pains with dishes and trays and pans. With just about everything and everybody, for that matter. Not a single day went by where she didn't offer a kind word or a helping hand.

Ophelia's frown deepened into a full-fledged scowl. Something was wrong with the girl and she aimed to find out what it was. "You been churnin' butter dese days?" she asked, placing a lid atop a heavy cast-iron kettle.

Stooping low to gather the fractured pieces of crockery, Cara sighed in self-disgust at the thoughts that had kept her distracted. *I could have been pregnant and he never bothered to even find out. A baby, an innocent child, and he didn't care.* "No, just clumsy, I guess," she replied at last.

Chuckling dryly, Ophelia left her fireplace and came forward. "Dat ain't no way to start de New Year, wid yo' brain sayin' one thing and yo' fingers doin' another. Seems to me, you best have a talk wid dem hands of yo's."

"Believe me," Cara replied, shaking her head again. "If I thought it would help, I would."

"Den maybe it's yo' head you need to have a chat wid."

Cara looked up and found herself to be the recipient of Ophelia's pointed gaze. Feeling awkward beneath the shrewd stare, she concentrated on the broken dish. "Do you suggest I walk about having conversations with myself?"

"I'm sayin' dat might not be such a bad notion."

"Someone might think I belong in the lunatic asylum." Cara stood, her apron gathered to hold the plate's remains.

Ophelia snorted. "Shoot, you ain't crazy, but you ain't been yo'sef lately, neither."

Not bothering to deny it, Cara fixed her gaze on the

fragments in her apron, but not before Ophelia saw the pain in the young green eyes.

"Lord, child, I ain't tryin' to hound you none, but you been carryin' some heavy load inside you for close to a month." Ophelia stretched out a dark, wrinkled hand to lovingly stroke Cara's shining head. "You a fine person, Miz Cara, always carin' 'bout folks. It breaks my heart to see you hurtin', especially when it comes to some man."

Cara's head snapped up, but Ophelia cut her off before she could say anything.

"It was a man dat used to put dem smiles on yo' face. It dat same man dat took dem smiles away."

"Have I been that obvious?" Cara asked, appalled to think she may have been wearing her heart on her sleeve.

Ophelia shrugged. "Dat depends on how hard someone's been lookin'."

With a sigh, Cara relaxed. "I have told only you and Bea of . . . Captain Reynolds."

Nodding her head knowingly, Ophelia moved to her simmering kettles. "Didn't think you told nobody else." She paused to check the stew for the night's meal. "What you plannin' on doin' now?"

This was a matter that Cara had given a great deal of thought over the past few weeks. Before she had met Justin, her original intention had been to come to Virginia and begin a new life for herself. That was once again her plan, and toward that end she had been formulating her ideas.

"I've been thinking I might like to establish a private school for girls. There doesn't seem to be a great deal of attention paid to a girl's education in Williamsburg. Unless you're a boy, and of age to attend college, you have to be content with very little knowledge."

Looking back over her shoulder, Ophelia caught the expectant look on Cara's face. "Dat some idea you got dere."

Encouraged by even that small degree of support, Cara continued. "I believe it is a splendid idea."

"Where you goin' to have dis school?"

With eyes alight for the first time in nearly a month, Cara

explained. "For now, I thought I could use the cottage. The furniture can be moved and a few benches brought in. That would suffice until I can save enough money from the tuition to rent a vacant building in town. There are certainly no shortages there."

"Sounds like you got dis all figured out."

Cara's expression turned sheepish. "Not entirely, actually. I have yet to speak to John and Bea. The cottage is, after all, theirs."

"Shoot." Ophelia chuckled as she shifted a pot from one wrought-iron trivet to another. "Massa John ain't goin' to say no. From de day he built dat cottage to be his office, it ain't never once seen no work of his in dere. And 'sides, Miz Bea is goin' to love dis notion, have her girls schooled proper."

It was Cara's turn to chuckle. "I hope you're right."

"I's always right," the older woman replied irreverently. Turning back to Cara, she nodded her head, indicating the broken shards gathered in Cara's apron. "Why don't you go dump dat mess in de old well, 'fore you cut yo'sef. Den git back here and tell me more 'bout dis school."

Feeling better than she had in a long while, Cara gave Ophelia a genuine, unrestrained smile.

Chapter Twelve

Bea was ecstatic over Cara's idea for a girl's school. John was equally positive, finding a certain degree of merit in not only the plan itself, but also in Cara's industriousness in attempting such a project.

While the organizational details remained to be seen to, Cara continued to work in the tavern. Lucy Dooley proved to be a wonderful companion in the afternoons when the tavern made few demands on the two young women.

"Do you think there will be room for me to attend school?" Lucy asked, drying a mug and setting it on the bar.

Seeing her friend's big blue eyes light up with expectation, Cara quickly offered assurance. "You'll be my very first pupil."

"This is just grand." Lucy beamed, reaching for another mug. "But you don't think I'm too old, do you?"

"Of course not. You're only twenty, and besides, one is never too old to learn."

Lucy laughed, then unexpectedly groaned beneath her breath. "Oh, no."

Standing on the other side of the bar, Cara glanced up curiously. "What's wrong, Lucy?"

Lucy's reply wasn't immediate. Her attention was riveted over Cara's shoulder on the two men who had just entered the empty tavern room.

Cara sent her gaze in the direction of Lucy's, wondering what had caused the other young woman's distraction. She was immediately taken aback by the odd-looking twosome.

"Who are they?" she whispered, turning her back to Lucy.

Lucy hesitated, as though reluctant to explain. "The maimed one is Olan Wright," she murmured with a visible shudder. "The big one is Bartholemew Smith."

Reacting instinctively to Lucy's wariness, Cara was careful to keep her voice low. "I haven't seen them before."

"That's not surprising. They rarely come into town unless it's to stir up trouble of some kind." Glancing cautiously past Cara, she added, "Lord only knows why they're here."

"Girl!" Bartholemew Smith's heavy voice rang out across the room.

Cara and Lucy exchanged nervous glances for a moment.

"Well, we'll find out," Lucy mumbled, stepping from behind the bar.

Bartholemew Smith settled himself in his chair as comfortably as his bulky weight would allow. "Girl," he called out again, already aggravated by what he considered to be less than cordial service.

Three years of serving drinks had taught Lucy that aggressive men were best handled with a show of bravado. Anything less and they'd turn an evening's work into a nightmare. Not about to put up with any kind of harassment, especially from the likes of Bartholemew Smith, Lucy made sure her voice was firm.

"Mr. Smith. What are you drinking this afternoon?"

Smith's fat palm slammed against the table. "Rum, and none of that local swill, neither. I want the Jamaica stuff."

Lucy leveled a jaundiced eye on the man while she briefly contemplated telling the oaf that the only swill in the place was seated before her. "And you, Mr. Wright?" she asked, prudently keeping her thoughts to herself.

Olan Wright's one good eye peered up at Lucy's curly blond hair before lowering to her pretty features and finally to her petite, buxom figure. "Same." The word slithered out from between his twisted, scarred lips.

If his appearance wasn't enough to give Lucy the shivers, the sound of his strangely hollow voice was and unconsciously, she rubbed the nape of her neck. When she returned to the bar, she did so with a sigh of relief.

"Are you all right?" Cara whispered, seeing Lucy's set face.

Placing the pewter tankards on a tray, Lucy poured a serving of rum into each. "Yes, I'm fine. But I don't mind telling you I'll be glad when John gets back."

With a frown, Cara joined Lucy at the far side of the bar. This time of the afternoon was usually never busy, and John and Bea had used the opportunity to go out to the farm to bring back chairs for Cara's school. They weren't expected back for another hour.

"Are they dangerous?" she asked quietly, resisting the urge to stare at the two.

"No, just permanently angry," Lucy replied, picking up the tray. "A word of warning, though. Those two have little love for the British, so try to stay out of their way, if you can."

Wide-eyed, Cara watched as Lucy served the drinks and collected payment. Without meaning to, she studied the men. The one called Smith was a huge, fleshy bear of a man whose unkempt appearance indicated a marked dislike of soap. But it was the other man, Olan Wright, who drew and held Cara's attention. His dirty, disfigured face bordered on grotesque, with one eye missing and most of his upper lip gone. Blackened teeth showed prominently against pasty skin and his matted hair was a wild tangle. The contours of his spindly body created awkward angles while his movements seemed disjointed. He was a hideous sight and Cara could only wonder what had befallen the man.

"Ain't I pretty?" Wright's voice called out loudly.

Startled, Cara's gaze snapped to the man, then immediately dropped to the tankards in front of her. Quickly, she picked up a mug and applied her cloth to the wet pewter surface.

A murmured remark from Wright produced a chorus of crude laughter that echoed in Cara's ears even after Lucy came to stand beside her.

"Don't worry," Lucy said. "It's hard not to stare at him. Best thing to do is try to ignore them both if you can. Hopefully, they'll drink up and be gone."

But Lucy's wish wasn't realized. The two showed no signs of leaving and, within minutes, called for more rum.

"Hey, you."

Together, Cara and Lucy looked up at Smith's call.

"Bring us a bottle this time."

It was Lucy who bent to retrieve the bottle, but Smith's voice halted her before she took another step.

"No, not you." Thrusting a thick finger in Cara's direction, he indicated his choice of maid. "You, with the red hair, you bring us the bottle."

There was something about the man's snide look that was blatantly threatening and Cara felt her pulse trip. Realizing it was going to be impossible to avoid the men as Lucy had advised, Cara drew a deep breath to steady her nerves.

Taking the bottle, she set it on the table, thoroughly repulsed by the rank odor that emanated from the men. "That will be two bits," she told them, determinedly keeping her chin up.

Insolently, Smith poured himself a drink and swallowed nearly a third of the tankard's contents before he even acknowledged Cara's presence. When he did, it was with a derogatory gaze.

"That's some accent there, girl. Where'd you get it?"

Cara knew she was being baited. Unless the man was a complete idiot, which she seriously doubted, it was perfectly obvious where she came from. Proudly, she replied, "You know as well as I do, Mr. Smith, that I come from England."

Smith took another swallow, his eyes behind the tankard growing hard. "Yeah, I know. I just wanted to hear you admit it."

"Regardless of my place of birth, you gentlemen still owe for the bottle."

With clumsy movements, Wright reached into the pocket of his filth-encrusted jacket and tossed the necessary money onto the table. "What you doin' in America, pretty little British girl?" The sound of his voice was just as mutilated as his face.

The pressure of Wright's one eye bore into Cara like a dull drill and she tried not to shudder. "Serving rum," she replied crisply. Deftly, she picked up the money before returning to the bar and a worried-looking Lucy.

"Maybe you should go out to the kitchen," Lucy suggested in a hushed voice, her eyes flicking to Smith. The men seemed intent on badgering this afternoon and Cara was obviously their target.

"And leave you to fend for yourself?" Cara whispered incredulously. "Absolutely not."

"I can take care of the place for a while. It won't be busy until dinnertime."

The opening of the tavern's front door proved her wrong. Three squalid-looking men sauntered into the room, taking a table near Smith and Wright.

"Oh, my," Lucy whispered, her eyes fastened on the trio.

Cara looked between Lucy and the newcomers. "Who are they?"

"Some of Smith's friends. They all work the water."

Cara's heart sank. It was going to be difficult enough dealing with Smith without having his friends present. The afternoon did not look promising.

With each tankard downed, Smith became increasingly boisterous, spewing out offensive remarks about life in general, the British in particular, much to the glee of his friends. Cara ignored the insults as best she could, but with Wright making a show of following her every move, her nerves were quickly stretched thin.

Anxiously, she awaited John's return, but by dark it was obvious that something was amiss. It was unlike him to ever be absent from the tavern at night. And Bea would never leave the children for such an extended period of time, even under Peachy's watchful eye. All Cara could do was wait, her anxiety growing with each passing minute.

The room gradually filled, as it usually did at night. Cara and Lucy adjusted their routine as best they could. Those patrons passing through for the night did not recognize any slack in service, but Smith and his cohorts took special pleasure in taunting the two beleaguered maids.

"Girl," Smith growled as Cara moved by. The excessive quantity of rum the man consumed had made him flagrantly belligerent. A ripple of trepidation shuddered through Cara as she cautiously stepped near.

"What do you think of my friend here?" His words were a slurred grumble.

Despite her apprehension of these men, Cara's forbearance was rapidly coming to an end. The last thing she was going to do was stand there and exchange pleasantries with them.

"Do you wish to order, Mr. Smith?" she asked, making no effort to hide her annoyance.

His eyes narrowed at her defiance. "You got somethin' against Olan here, little Miss English?" he asked loudly.

"Not anything more than I have against you," Cara replied.

From one of the other tables, one of the watermen called, "Well, I got somethin' against you, and all your British kind."

A mumbled assent sounded throughout the room.

"Damn sick and tired of all ya bleedin' Brits," another voice called. "Ought to take the whole lot of you and ship ya back to where ya came from."

"Can't," another declared sarcastically. "American ships don't sail to hell."

Raucous laughter erupted, the sound flaying Cara's nerves. When it died down, Smith glared a poisonous smile at Cara. "My friends don't like you, little Miss English. Why don't you go back to that England of yours. Go on back home."

"Get the hell out," someone ordered harshly.

Dread snaked its way up Cara's spine, yet she felt the need to take a stand against Smith and his group. "This is my home now, Mr. Smith."

Wright gave a cackling laugh. "Just because you say so?"

As sickening as the sight of Wright was, Cara forced herself to look at him. "I don't need your permission," she informed him with disdain. It wasn't the wisest thing she could have said, but it went far in fortifying her courage.

Smith slammed his tankard down in anger. Furious, he made a move to shove himself out of his chair, but Wright's clawlike hand stayed him in his chair.

"Oh, you're real brave, little Miss English," Wright muttered mockingly to an ashen-faced Cara. "But then, that's the way you Brits are. Thinkin' you own the world and everyone in it. Sailin' round these waters, firin' on our ships, killin' folk."

From somewhere in the room, someone voiced a loud agreement.

Wright continued. "We ain't goin' to stand for too much more, little Miss English." His glazed eye made a deliberate trail over Cara's figure. "Not from you, not from your kind."

Cara's heart was pounding heavily. These men were drunk and they were angry.

Trying to alleviate the tension that filled the room, Lucy rushed forward and pushed a laden tray into Cara's hands. "Why don't you take this to the gentleman in the far corner," she stated emphatically. "I'll see to Mr. Smith's table."

Gratefully, Cara accepted the tray, but as she made her

way to the far table, she could feel the eyes of every waterman boring into her back.

With shaking hands, she placed the plates before the gray-haired stranger sitting quietly in the shadows. With her eyes averted, and her concentration focused on keeping her alarm under control, she missed the intense look he gave her.

The room quieted, but the mood among the watermen steadily worsened. Cara tried to go about her business with some semblance of normalcy, but the snide remarks and condemning glares that followed her made her feel as though she waited for the ax to fall.

And it finally did.

"Bring us another bottle," Smith yelled to Cara. "And be quick about it. I been dyin' of thirst waitin' on your lousy service."

Standing behind the bar, Cara sent a nervous glance across the room to Lucy. She swallowed hard, then raised her chin as she brought Smith and Wright the ordered rum.

Smith filled his cup, gulped down a mouthful, then angrily slammed the mug onto the table.

"You watered down this rum!" he accused loudly, his malevolent gaze stabbing at Cara.

"I did not," she stated through set teeth.

"I say you're lyin'. This here rum's been watered."

The room was suddenly hushed, but Cara tried to ignore the ominous silence. "Everyone knows Hawthorne's is an honest establishment. We don't tamper with the drinks."

"No one 'cept you."

Wright laughed crazily, licking the spittle from his lips. "Just another one of your damn British tricks to try and cheat us Americans."

Fear gnawed at Cara's stomach, but she refused to play Smith's pointless game. "I did not water the rum," she insisted in a low voice. "But since you are displeased with our liquor and our service, you may take your business elsewhere." Reaching out, she retrieved the bottle, but Smith's beefy hand clamped down on her slender wrist with bruising strength.

"Why you little bitch," he snarled.

In the far corner, the gray-haired stranger sitting quietly in the shadows rose to his feet.

Wide-eyed, Cara twisted her arm in an effort to free herself. "Let me go," she demanded, her heart racing.

Surging to a swaying stance, Smith cruelly yanked her up against him. "I'll teach you to . . ."

"Let her go."

Even through her fright and anger, Cara heard the steely-voiced words, her mind instantly recognizing the one who issued the command with such authority. Astonished, her head snapped around to find Justin standing within arm's reach.

Despite his drunken state, Smith was still capable of some pragmatic thought. He understood interference when he heard it and he didn't like it any more now than he did when he was sober.

"Shove off . . ." he began, then came up short when he realized who stood beside him.

His face a rigid mask, Justin regarded Smith and his hold on Cara with deadly cold eyes. "I'm not asking you, I'm telling you. Let her go."

Revenge and hate and a blood lust all scrambled through Smith's sodden brain. He wanted to take care of Reynolds here, now; could practically feel his own fist smashing into the bastard's face.

"I ain't one of your slimy sea dogs, *Captain*. I don't take orders from you. I don't take orders from no one."

A nasty smile drew Justin's lips into a thin line and when he spoke, the air fairly sizzled with the dangerous energy that emanated from him. "You'll take orders from me . . . or be dead in the next five seconds." Without warning, he drew a razor-sharp knife and had it expertly held against Smith's neck in the space of a heartbeat.

Caught between the two adversaries, Cara's skin crawled with fear. Her gaze clung to Justin and she could see the barely leashed fury ready to explode. In that second, she had no doubt that he would not hesitate to kill Bartholemew Smith.

Apparently, Smith's brain was lucid enough to realize that, too. Growling angrily, he shoved Cara away to land against Justin, and stalked his way out of the tavern.

From her secure place against Justin's solid form, Cara watched Olan Wright take one last gulp of rum before limping after his friend. When the door slammed behind him, she wearily sighed in relief.

Yet the threat of danger had not been entirely eliminated. With exacting precision, Justin sent his glacial gaze to every man in the room in a silent challenge. Seconds crawled by. Two of Smith's friends shoved out of their chairs and left. The remainder turned sullenly back to their drinks.

In the far corner, the wary stranger watched the entire episode. Satisfied that he'd seen enough, he quietly slipped out unnoticed.

Lucy quickly rushed to Cara's side.

"Cara, I was so frightened for you. Are you hurt?"

Shaken, but otherwise unharmed, Cara levered herself away from Justin. "I am all right."

But she wasn't. Every nerve in her body was quaking. Justin had just walked into her life and she was torn between wanting to run out of the room and soundly slapping his arrogant face.

All of her resentment and hurt surfaced as she watched him sheath his knife beneath his dark jacket. She had finally gotten to a point where she could make it through a day without crying, she was finally able to keep her heart from yearning for his gentle touch, she had at last begun to think about a future for herself. . . . And now, here he was, rescuing her, making himself her hero when that was the last thing she could cope with. If she thought she even had a tear left within her, she would shed it in pure frustration.

Her eyes scanned his handsome features. Absurdly, she hadn't expected him to appear the same. But the blue of his eyes was still as deep, the angle of his jaw, just as lean, the mold of his lips, as sensual as she remembered.

"Thank you, Justin," she said levelly. She was going to

get through this with her dignity intact. She wanted neither gratitude nor animosity evidenced in her manner.

One of Justin's dark brows flicked upward. He looked at Cara as she stood straight before him. With her lustrous hair twisted to the crown of her head and the lush curves of her figure revealed by a faded blue dress that looked vaguely familiar, she looked as beautifully desirable as ever. Yet, her jade green eyes were blazingly cold in her pale face, her finely sculpted lips compressed into an uncompromising line. The look was a too-ready reminder of that streak of righteousness that ran deep within her.

"You are most entirely welcome," he replied. Matching her tone of civility word for word. "I'm glad I happened to be near."

That was about all the politeness Cara could stand. Forcing a smile to her lips, she excused herself. "I must return to work now." Careful to keep her shaking hands hidden in the folds of her apron, she glided with regal elegance to the bar.

Justin moved to the corner table near the door. Taking the seat closest to the wall, he was assured of an unobstructed view of the room, and Cara.

For all the tension Cara had felt at Wright's obstructive stares and Smith's belligerent comments, it was nothing compared to the effect created by Justin's subtle perusal. The weight of his eyes clung to her as she cleared tables and served drinks. It tore at her composure when John finally arrived with explanations of a broken axle on the wagon. It stabbed at her heart when the call came for the last round of the evening. And when Justin rose and left, taking his disturbing gaze with him, Cara ached with a sense of loss.

Once she gained the sanctuary of her cottage, she stoked the coals in the fireplace and fed the flames to chase the chill from the room. Only then did she remove her cloak and take down her hair. Her thoughts were somber, and despite the fatigue that encompassed her, she knew the night would allow her little sleep. Her mind was already struggling with new images of Justin.

A quiet tapping sounded at her door, pulling Cara from her musing. Too tired to even stop and consider the possibility that Smith or Wright might be paying an unexpected call, she answered the summons. But the second she saw Justin and her heart began thudding in her chest, she realized she should have been more cautious.

"Justin," she said in surprise.

Leaning against the doorframe, he gave her a wry smile. "Were you expecting someone else?"

His arrogance was provoking. It would serve him right to let him think so, she thought. "What are you doing here?" she replied, not answering his question.

Forsaking all social niceties, he crossed the threshold and walked into the cottage. "I think that's obvious. I've come to see you."

Now? her mind screamed. *After two months you finally remembered I even exist?* She shut the door forcefully before crossing her arms against her breasts and facing Justin.

"You saw me at the inn earlier. I would have thought that would have been enough."

Standing before the fire, Justin studied the smooth perfection of Cara's skin, the shimmering highlights in her tumble of curls. "You don't know me very well then," he remarked smoothly.

"Oh, I know you, Justin. Better than you think. What I don't know is why you're here."

"I've already told you."

"Yes, I know what you said, but what did you mean?"

Justin covered the distance between them in three long strides. "I'll just have to show you then, won't I?"

Before Cara had time to react, he slipped his arms around her and pulled her soft form against his large, muscled length. With devastating hunger, his lips captured hers in a lush, molten kiss. It was bittersweet agony to be in his arms again. The feel of him was as glorious as she remembered, the impassioned delight as magically wonderful. Helplessly, she arched against his hard body, her hands sliding up his broad chest to cling to his powerful shoulders.

Justin's blood pounded at the torturing feel of her breasts crushed against him. His mouth sought the sweet, trembling flesh of her neck, where her pulse beat frantically. "Damn, I want you," he muttered hoarsely, nibbling a fiery trail to her ear and taking Cara into that sensual paradise she had striven so hard to forget. Her hands caressed the corded muscles of his back, and with desperate urgency his mouth returned to hers, parting her lips as his tongue plunged into her mouth. At the touch of his tongue against hers, Cara groaned low in her throat, unable to control the desire that shot through her.

Breathing hard, almost dazed at the speed with which she had ignited his passion, Justin dragged his mouth from hers. "Lock the door, love," he growled thickly against her heated cheek.

Love. Hearing that one word jerked Cara back to reality. This had nothing to do with love. This was lust. Pain knifed through her as she realized the folly of the moment and her own helplessness in resisting his touch. The truth of what existed between them was encompassed in his single command. She was nothing more to him than a target for his desires. Pushing against his shoulders, she turned her head away.

"Justin, stop," she whispered, her throat tight and aching.

At the stiffening of her body and the cold tone in her voice, Justin's head snapped up. Catching her chin in one hand, he turned her face back up to his. "The hell, you say," he grated out, unwilling to let her go.

"I do say," she replied determinedly, ignoring his fierce scowl. "Now, let me go."

He recognized that stubborn look of hers and mentally cursed. Angered by her latent resistance, he released her. "You have a strange way of *not* welcoming a man," he said coldly, his blood still running hot.

"You have a stranger way of remembering a woman," she shot back.

His eyes narrowed. "Is that what this is all about? Some temperamental display to assuage your pride?"

All the hurt and rage Cara had been carrying within her exploded. "How dare you! How dare you reduce my feelings to mere theatrics. How dare you walk in here and order me into the nearest bed! Just who do you think you are? You dumped me on the docks without a backward glance and now expect to just stroll back into my life."

"As I remember," he remarked darkly, frustrated and angered by her refusal, "I saw that you were safely settled with your family."

"Only because you couldn't wait to have me gone! You used me like the cheapest doxy. You were cruel and heartless, and I despise you!"

"No, you don't," he assured her with an arrogance that was infuriating. "You forget, I just kissed you, and I felt your response."

An embarrassed flush colored her cheeks, but she refused to admit that he had had any effect on her. Clamping her jaw shut, she jerked open the door. "Get out. Go prove your masculinity to Yvette Bouchard. I'm sure she's had a great deal of experience in dealing with men like you."

With an icy glare, he stepped to the door, but stopped and leveled a cutting glance on her. "I intend to prove something, Cara. I'm going to prove to you just how much you *do* want me."

With that challenge, Justin left, the resounding bang of the door escorting him up the path.

In the shadows of the lunatic asylum, the quiet stranger from the tavern shoved his hands into his pockets to ward off the damp iciness that hung in the air. From deep within the walls of the building a hideous cry rent the night, yet the stranger ignored the chilling sound.

Out of the shadows, a cloaked figure emerged. The stranger watched warily, deciding whether to reach for the knife sheathed in his boot. The man approached and the stranger relaxed.

"Well?" the cloaked man asked in a low voice.

"Things are getting out of hand," the stranger from the inn replied.

"Where were you tonight?"

"At the inn. Smith and his band were there, making things difficult for her."

The cloaked man gave a vicious curse. "Any trouble?"

"Almost. They've been hounding her, giving her a bad time. Thought I was going to have to step in, but Reynolds showed up."

"The captain?"

"Aye."

"What the hell was he doing there?"

The stranger said nothing for a moment, and his partner gathered a great deal from that silence. "He came for her," he finally said.

"And?" The single word was sharp, demanding.

"He went to her cottage, but didn't stay."

Another silence fell between the two until the cloaked man issued his order. "It's time to move."

"Aye," the stranger agreed.

"I can have my man ready within the month."

"Do your plans include her?"

"Definitely. And I want you to keep an eye on her from now on."

The stranger nodded. "Wright was making threats."

"Keep him away from her, and Smith, too."

"And Reynolds?"

The man in the cloak considered that. "Let that run its course."

"All right. Anything else?"

Again the cloaked man paused for thought. "No."

"Then I'll meet you in five days," the stranger said.

"In five days."

The two parted as stealthily as they had arrived, leaving only the moaning human sounds from the lunatic asylum in their wake.

If there was one thing Cara was absolutely positive of, it was that she would grow a second head before she would let Justin seduce her again. She admitted she had been helpless to fall in love with him, but she wasn't about to sacrifice her self-respect by succumbing to his charm a second time. Just let him try and work his ways on her and he'd find out exactly what "temperamental displays" were all about. And with that conviction, she went about her business the following day.

Of course, she hadn't planned on Justin being just as resolute. The fact that he was as determined in his own convictions became obvious when he arrived at the inn for lunch. With a lazy smile, he doffed his coat and took a seat, his bearing that of a confident man who had all the time in the world.

It was enough to make Cara grit her teeth.

"Justin." Her voice was pleasant but cool when she approached his table. Doing her best to ignore the thorough inspection he gave her, she put a smile on her face.

"I don't remember that dress," he murmured, his appreciative gaze caressing the swell of her breasts beneath the beige-and-white-striped gown. "It's very becoming."

A month ago, Cara had yearned for just this reaction from Justin. Now she was annoyed with him because he did notice her new dress, and with herself because she was, in part, glad that he did.

"We have ham or mutton for the meal," she informed him with overstated cordiality.

Justin would have preferred tasting something sweeter. "The ham will do just fine . . . for now."

Beneath his amused gaze, Cara turned and made her way to the kitchen. Justin watched the seductive sway of her hips and the amusement left his face. She had the most incredible effect on his body, she always had. Irritably, he shifted in his seat and gave full rein to his thoughts.

His coming to the inn last night had been no mere coincidence. He had finally reached the conclusion that he could no longer ignore Cara as he had tried to. He had to have her again, despite the problems he knew were sure to arise.

He hadn't expected to find her working as a tavern wench. That idea did not set well. A dangerous light gleamed in his eyes at the thought of her attracting the attention of Bartholemew Smith. He'd allow no one to abuse what was his. And Cara *was* his. Of course she was too angry to admit it now, but he would change her mind.

Within minutes, Cara was back with a heaping platter of ham, greens, and biscuits. Not bothering for Justin's request, she also brought a mug of ale.

"Join me," he said, as she placed the meal before him.

Poignant memories of another lunch they had shared swamped her. He had invited her to dine, just as he had now. She had trusted him enough to accept and to tell him of the Earl of Ellsworth and all that had happened as a result of her father's death. "I'm afraid I can't." She fought back the pain and forced a calm into her voice. "I'm working."

Justin glanced pointedly around the empty room. "With the exception of your barkeep, we're the only two in here."

It would have been easy to have given him some other excuse, but that's all it would have been. An excuse that he would see right through. A surge of pride came to her rescue. Well, she wasn't about to give him the satisfaction of watching her take the cowardly way out. Giving him a derisive look, she took a seat.

"I think you'll enjoy the ham," she remarked casually. If he was determined to play this game, then so was she. "The cook has a way with pepper."

Although he found the food well prepared, Justin couldn't have cared less about the meal. "What have you been doing with yourself, other than fighting off the likes of Bartholemew Smith?"

Cara's eyes rounded. That he should inquire of her activities was almost as surprising as his knowledge of Mr. Smith. "How do you know him?"

"I make it a point of knowing who my enemies are," he remarked casually, cutting through the ham with ease. "But you have not answered my question."

"Oh, I've been busy," she said lightly. "I have met quite a few people."

Over the rim of his mug, Justin studied Cara's smug smile. "By that, I take it you mean other men."

Her look turning innocent, Cara demurred. "You're

being indelicate, Justin. What I have done in the past months is hardly your affair."

"That may be true," he returned, unperturbed. "But I intend to have a great deal to say about how you spend the months ahead."

"Why?" she shot back heatedly before she could get a grip on her frustration. Collecting herself, she continued in a quiet voice. "Just because I was once naive enough to be your m . . . mistress doesn't mean you have proprietary rights."

Laying his fork down, Justin propped his elbows on the table, his fingers forming a tent. "If you would discard your pride long enough to see reason, you would admit that what we shared is hardly over. You cannot deny that you have always wanted me."

It was true. She had wanted him, but only because she had loved him and had thought herself loved in return. Defensively, her chin came up. "I will not 'discard' my pride, Justin. That and my self-respect are all I have left." Rising, she kept her voice low as she glared into his eyes. "I will not give them to you as I did my virtue." Turning, she swept out of the room.

Cara hoped she had seen the last of Justin. Yet she couldn't suppress the jolt of expectancy she felt when he arrived the next day. As she was leaving the tavern for her cottage, she spotted him leaning against the smokehouse and quickly caught her surprised gasp. It wasn't as easy controlling the flutters of excitement in her stomach. Disgusted with her reaction, she mentally scolded herself for her own foolishness.

"I have been waiting for you." He pushed away from the wall, his great caped coat flaring as it caught a stiff breeze.

"And you expect me to be honored," she replied dryly.

Justin expected a great deal more but knew better than to say anything. The last thing he wanted was to raise her hackles. "I thought we might talk."

Cara eyed him warily. "About what?"

"To begin with, us."

Shaking her head in disbelief, she laughed ruefully. "There is no 'us,' Justin. There is you and there is me."

Grasping Cara's elbow to prevent her turning away, Justin scrutinized the emotions flashing in her eyes. "It needn't be that way," he said quietly.

Helplessly, Cara found herself yielding to the exquisite enchantment he was so effortlessly weaving around her senses. The touch of his hand was a gentle bliss, the look in his eyes a mesmerizing joy. Against her better judgment, she capitulated. But not unconditionally. If they were going to have this conversation, they would do so on her terms.

"Where are you off to?" Justin asked, when she did not stop at her cottage door, but continued on toward the pasture at the back of the property.

"To that fence," she explained, nodding ahead. "Do you have any objections?"

A roguish grin creased Justin's face and he couldn't resist goading. "Don't you trust yourself to be alone with me in your cottage?"

Her heightened color threatened to betray her. "No, it's you I don't trust."

Justin's rich laughter floated away on the wind, but not before it pulled at Cara's heartstrings.

She stopped at the edge of the small orchard where it bordered the pasture's fence. There, she leaned against the wooden rails and waited as Justin stepped beside her, his tall, solid form shielding her from the wind.

"I had hoped for more privacy than this," he began, eyeing with distaste the stable hands coming and going on the far side of the field.

The public nature of the spot was the very reason Cara had chosen it. "Whatever we have to say to each other can be said here."

As though in surrender, he raised his hands. "You always were the most stubborn woman."

"In light of the source of that comment, I will take it as a compliment."

"Only you would."

"Are you complaining?"

"Oh, never," he replied, caught between irritation and laughter. He enjoyed the easy banter, but he had more pertinent matters he wished to discuss. "Has Smith bothered you again since the other night?"

Caught off guard by the unexpectedness of his query, Cara hesitated for a moment. His seeming solicitude was disconcerting. "No, just that one day."

"You antagonized him." Concern made his voice sharper than he had intended. "That wasn't wise."

Neither was the underlying note of censure in his words. "That man was drunk," Cara informed him haughtily. "There was no reasoning with him and, frankly, I was tired of trying."

"Nonetheless, it was foolish. The man is dangerous and he could have hurt you. You're lucky I arrived when I did."

Cara's eyes popped wide open. The irony of the situation was galling. Justin had done more to hurt her than anyone ever had, yet he was worried about her welfare. "Why did you come back at all, Justin?" she asked, irritably. "Why couldn't you have left well enough alone?"

It was something Justin had asked himself repeatedly, but to no avail. His brow creased. "I couldn't," he admitted with some trouble. "You left the ship, but not my mind."

Feeling her defenses slipping, Cara closed her eyes, afraid to let herself hope. He hadn't forgotten her at all. He wasn't cold and unfeeling as she had imagined. But he wasn't declaring everlasting love, either. She opened her eyes to harsh reality.

"So you decided you needed me in your bed again," she scoffed.

He knew her stubborn streak was hard at work here and frustration rode him hard. Had they been out of sight of curious eyes, he would have swept her into his arms and demolished every last one of her objections.

"Yes, I want you," he ground out harshly.

"That's not enough for me," she replied, angered by his answer.

"It could be."

"If I were a whore!"

"You make sharing my bed sound repulsive."

Glaring into his angry blue eyes, she bit out, "It would be, if you felt no love for me."

Cara watched a remote stillness settle over Justin's features and she shook her head sorrowfully. Even as objective as she had tried to be, some tiny part of her had dared to hope. Disappointment crushed her. Again.

Trying her best to keep a grip on her hurt and anger and the swirl of conflicting emotions making a muddle of her peace of mind, she struggled to keep her voice low and steady. "It's time for honesty between us, Justin." She paused to swallow past the burning lump in her throat. "What we shared was a mistake. I was too naive to understand what was happening, and you didn't care enough to explain." Taking a steadying breath, she searched the sky for control. "I didn't even know that you could have put a baby in me. But you knew what you were about. From the very start I was nothing more than a conquest."

A child. The thought crashed into Justin's mind. Children had never held a place in his life, but the idea of his baby, nestled within Cara's body, was overwhelmingly gratifying.

Surprised by his own reaction, he grasped her by the shoulders. "Are you with child?"

"No," she murmured, her voice edged with a certain amount of regret. "Which is most fortunate. Children should be conceived in love, not lust."

No child. Unexpectedly, Justin experienced an odd sense of loss for something that was never his. For the first time in his life, he felt true remorse. The sensation left him irritated and defensive. Uncomfortable with what she was making him feel, he shoved a hand through his dark hair as he tried to push the irksome feelings away.

Cara fully expected a caustic remark from Justin, but when none was forthcoming, she continued in a gentle command. "Leave me alone, Justin. Please do not come here again."

"Why the hell not?"

"Because you hurt me, every time you come here wanting my body, but not me."

Her lower lip quivered, but Cara kept her eyes fastened steadily on his. "You want me to be your mistress and I can't do that. I wanted you to love me and you don't know how."

For no reason, for all the reasons, she rose up on her toes and pressed her trembling lips to his. For a fleeting second, she let herself pretend before she turned and walked down the empty path.

Chapter Thirteen

"Cara." Bea's voice called from the far end of the path.

Emotionally spent, Cara watched her cousin scurry toward her.

"Good heavens," Bea proclaimed in an outraged whisper, when she had reached Cara's side. "Please tell me that wasn't Captain Reynolds just now. And what on earth could you have been thinking, allowing him to kiss you like that?"

Cara could almost find a bit of humor in Bea's indignation and fierce scowl. They went far in easing her pain. "Yes, that was Captain Reynolds."

"Well," Bea declared, a fiery gleam in her eyes. "I hope you told him that his actions have been of the vilest nature. I hope you soundly upbraided him for his treatment of you. I hope . . ."

"Bea," Cara interrupted, a small smile actually touching her lips. "Rest easy. I did tell him all of that, and then some."

Surprised, Bea blinked in confusion. "And his response was to kiss you?"

"Actually," Cara admitted, coloring lightly, "I kissed him."

"Whatever for?"

"I was saying good-bye."

That gave Bea pause, but only for the briefest moment. "I should certainly hope so. I do not wish to tell you what to do, but if I were you, I would have nothing more to do with that scoundrel."

Cara had privately called Justin far worse, yet she hated to hear another refer to him in such a derogatory manner. It was equally difficult to believe that her instincts had been so poor in judging his character.

"He won't be bothering me again. We have . . . we have parted ways."

Bea saw the wash of regret that cast a pallor over Cara's face. Immediately, she set aside her own anger. "I am so sorry, Cara, and here I am going on, probably making matters worse. But it really is for the best this way." She patted one of Cara's hands sympathetically. "Now, what you need is to take your mind off the entire matter."

"You're right," Cara agreed with a sigh.

"Well, of course I am, and I have the perfect solution."

Cara regarded her cousin's no-nonsense suggestion with skepticism. "Oh?"

"Hunter Rollins is at this very moment waiting in my parlor to see you and . . ."

"Bea," Cara complained plaintively.

"Yes, I know, dear, but he is most desirous to see you."

"I do not have the heart for this, especially not right now."

"Which is precisely why you should march right up there and pass a most pleasant afternoon with him." Bea was not deterred by Cara's miserable face. "Cara, you cannot go on letting the memory of *that man* interfere with your life."

That man. Cara knew that for as long as she lived, she would never be able to forget Justin. But she had to admit to the wisdom of her cousin's statement. If she was truly going to put Justin out of her life, once and for all, she might as well begin now. "Very well," she concluded.

"Excellent." Bea practically bubbled over with satisfaction. "Why don't you change into your new green dress and I will tell Hunter that you shall be up in a moment. And perhaps if you twist your hair up," she added, lifting a strand off Cara's shoulder. "It always looks so becoming arranged that way. And tea. I'll have Ophelia make up a pot of tea."

Dismayed by her cousin's too-enthusiastic reaction, Cara protested. "Bea, please do not make a fuss over this. I agreed only to visit with the man."

"Oh, it's no bother," Bea replied lightly, wondering if Ophelia would be able to whip up sweet biscuits in record time. "Just a little refreshment for an afternoon call."

"That is all it will be," Cara insisted. Taking hold of Bea's hand, she made sure she had her cousin's full attention. "I have no wish for a suitor. I do not know if I will ever feel differently. To encourage Mr. Rollins to entertain false hopes in my direction would be cruel. I would not see him hurt in that manner."

Bea fully understood the reasons for Cara's sentiments. However, she had her own ideas concerning Cara and Hunter. The two would make a perfect couple. Of course, given Cara's present frame of mind, it would undoubtedly take time for her to realize it.

Happily anticipating a most romantic, albeit lengthy courtship, Bea stated innocently, "I have no intention of causing Hunter, or you, any upset." She shrugged her matchmaking shoulders for good measure. "It will be a friendly visit, nothing more."

For the next hour, Cara put forth her best effort to try and enjoy herself. If her efforts fell short of their mark, none were the wiser. She poured tea with true British expertise, despite the trembling of her slender fingers. Her smiles were genuine even though they were somewhat crooked. And while her conversation was attentive, it was altogether very, *very* polite.

It didn't help matters to have Bea sitting beside her, exuding an aura of expectancy trained on a possible romance. Nor was Cara's composure settled by Hunter's admiring gazes, which had a tendency to drop below her chin. More than once, Cara sent up a silent prayer of thanks for the long sleeves and high neck of her green dress.

"Cara, dear," Bea prompted during a lull in the conversation. "Why don't you tell Hunter of the plans for your new school."

"What's this?" Hunter inquired. Facing Cara from his seat opposite hers, he was glad for the opportunity to direct his attention solely to Cara.

Seated beside Bea, on the formal settee, Cara lightly blushed under Hunter's avid regard. Throughout the entire visit, Hunter had made his attraction to her exceedingly obvious. It was exactly what Cara had not hoped for. "I am establishing an academy for young women." She kept her tone impartial yet courteous.

Hunter smiled broadly, but then he would have smiled even if she had said she intended to sprout wings and fly. Cara Fairchild was the most lovely woman he had ever met and it behooved him to further his association with her. "Quite a noble venture, Miss Fairchild. We're long overdue for a school of this nature."

Somewhat taken aback by his response, Cara considered Hunter curiously. "I must confess, Mr. Rollins, that I am surprised by your reaction. Most men do not deem a woman's education to be of any significance."

"Hopefully," he replied, his brown eyes peering meaningfully into hers, "you will soon realize that I am not like most men." He watched the color flare back into her cheeks while her eyes dropped to her lap. "Are you yourself planning to tutor?" He asked, aware of the effect he was having on her.

Cara took a sip of her tea and willed her discomfiture away. "Yes, I will teach," she replied carefully. "I have had an extensive education and will base the school's curriculum on my own course of study."

Hunter's gaze discreetly traveled the sweet curves of

Cara's figure. Personally, he thought she would be far better suited to be a wife than to teach. "I have no doubt that you will make a most splendid tutor. When does your school open its doors?"

"Within the month, if all goes as it should." Cara turned to Bea for confirmation that the benches and chairs and slates would be ready soon.

"Good heavens, Cara, we should have all in order long before then," Bea declared happily. "And I know the school shall be such a wonderful success that you'll be looking for a building in town before you know it."

As Bea had intended, her hint struck its target. "Why, I own several vacant shops in town," Hunter offered. "I'd be honored to show you any number of buildings that would be suitable."

Bea quickly spoke up before Cara could say a word. "Oh, Hunter, that is just too kind of you. Isn't that wonderful, Cara?" She glanced innocently to her cousin's incredulous face. "Hunter can be of such help to you."

Cara dearly loved Bea, but at that moment she fervently desired that her cousin be struck mute. Forcing her expression into an affable facade, she replied, "I would not wish to impose on your generosity, Mr. Rollins."

"The only imposition would be to my self-esteem should you refuse my assistance."

Caught between not wishing to offend and having no civil way of refusing, Cara was forced to accept Hunter's offer. "I would welcome your help."

By the time Hunter took his leave, Cara's head was pounding. But that didn't stop her from turning exasperatedly to Bea. "Beatrice Hawthorne, what could have possessed you?"

To Bea, who was marvelously pleased with the outcome of the afternoon, Cara's vexation was befuddling. "Whatever do you mean?"

"I mean the way you maneuvered Mr. Rollins into helping me find an empty site for the school."

"Oh, that," Bea returned airily. "It seemed a good idea, since he does own property and you are in need."

Cara pressed cool fingers to her thumping temples. "That was a contrivance meant to place us in each other's company."

Bea had the grace to look sheepish. "Well, I see nothing wrong with that. Hunter is a fine man, and you could stand a dose of gentlemanly deportment."

With a sigh, Cara shook her head. "The last thing that I desire is for any man to further complicate my life. And Mr. Rollins is going to do just that."

"He wishes to be your friend."

"Judging from the looks he was giving my bosom, he wishes to be an intimate chum!"

Cara's impetuous words caused a blush to rise in both women's faces. They stared at each other in mutual surprise, then without warning, burst into laughter.

"Oh, Cara, that was too bad of you." Bea's chiding was ruined by her chortles.

Cara didn't even try to suppress her glee. The unexpected humor had diffused a day's worth of tension and brought her the first honest laughter she'd had in weeks.

In the wake of their merriment, Cara tilted her head to one side, a smile gracing her lips. "You are right, I shouldn't have said that. And I didn't mean to sound sharp with you."

"There is nothing to forgive. And perhaps I did push a little."

"I know you mean well."

"I only want to see you happy again. And from the sparkle in your eyes right now, I'd say you're feeling at least better than you were."

"I am feeling better," Cara said, realizing just how true it was. It was as though her laughter had broken through the dark clouds which had been hanging oppressively over her, letting in the first weak rays of hope.

That feeling was still with her the next day when Hunter arrived at her door. It was just after the morning breakfast trade had departed and Cara had returned to her cottage to freshen up. Mentally she was making lists of mathematics problems she would give to her students, when Hunter knocked at her door.

"Mr. Rollins," she said, surprised by his presence. Even though she had known to take him seriously when he offered to show her his shops, she hadn't expected him to make good on his promise quite so soon.

"Miss Fairchild." Hunter gave a short bow and a long smile. His eyes made a quick, enjoyable inventory of her features. "I hope this is not an inconvenient time for you."

"No, not at all."

"In that case, I've come to whisk you away from your work. I thought you might like to examine an empty store of mine on England Street."

Cara's brows rose. She looked at Hunter's pleasantly handsome face, a mixture of anticipation and doubt flashing quickly and repeatedly in his eyes. He clearly expected her to refuse, even though she had agreed to accept his help.

"I think it would be most apropos, Mr. Rollins, if my school were to be named England Girls Academy." She smiled kindly. "Thank you, I would like to visit the shop."

The vacant milliner's was all Cara could have hoped for. Two small rooms occupied the lower level while the upstairs was one large chamber. She envisioned rows of benches in the front room, where windows let in dappled sunlight. The back room could be used for an office and the upper room would easily suffice for storage.

Stepping outside after she had made a complete inspection, Cara snuggled into her cloak and smiled back at Hunter as he locked the front door.

"I think it's just perfect, Mr. Rollins."

Pocketing his key, Hunter contemplated Cara's radiant bearing and thought *she* was absolutely perfect. "I hoped you would like it. When you told me of your plans, I immediately thought of this place."

At a leisurely stroll, they walked back to Main Street. Cara's mind was well ahead of their pace. "It will be several months before I will be able to afford a lease," she explained. "I'm not certain yet how many students I'll have, or if I'll even have any, for that matter."

With a light touch at Cara's elbow, he guided her along. "Of course you will. I know several planters who have been contemplating sending their daughters to Richmond. Female schools are quite the thing there these days. I'm sure parents would rather have their girls schooled closer to home."

Cara was grateful for his endorsement and his help. Bea was right, Hunter was a kind man, a perfect gentleman. He'd made no untoward overtures, he was congenial and attentive. Surreptitiously, she studied him, wondering if Bea's remark that he wished merely to be her friend had any merit. She rather hoped it did, she liked Hunter, as a friend. He could never be more than that to her. But she couldn't discount the look of desire that flared in his eyes with amazing frequency. No, sadly, Hunter Rollins had more than friendship on his mind.

An unexpected notion struck Cara just then. Two months ago she hadn't even known what desire was. Now she could recognize it in a man's eyes when she saw it. If that was an accomplishment, she thought wryly, she had Justin to thank for that.

As though her thoughts had somehow conjured him up, she caught sight of Justin across the street. Her heart flipped over in her chest, but she clamped down on her response. Her brain was annoyingly more recalcitrant in its behavior. Wistfully, she recalled their parting yesterday and the brief, wonderful feel of his lips against hers. Their last kiss. If she could choose any kiss to remember him by, she would pick the sweet, honest, caressing touch of that one.

With poised dignity, she met his gaze and even allowed a shadow of a smile to pull at her lips. Then, with a courage she congratulated herself for, she continued on her way with no threat of tears, only a melancholy ache touching her deep inside.

"Are you still with me?" Hunter asked teasingly as they gained the tavern's drive. "You've gone suddenly quiet on me."

"I was just caught up in my thoughts," she offered.

It was Hunter's hope that those thoughts included him,

but he hesitated in admitting that to her. He sensed a reluctance in Cara, a prudence that precluded eagerness on his part. He scanned her lovely face, then smiled inwardly. All good things were worth waiting for.

Cara entered the tavern with her sincere expression of gratitude to Hunter. Closing the door, she removed her cloak and made ready for the lunch trade.

As expected, only a few people arrived for lunch, but one patron brought a smile to Cara's face and brightened her day.

"Willie Carmichael," she exclaimed. "How are you?" Until now, she hadn't seen any of the *Wind Dancer*'s crew and she was genuinely glad to see Justin's cabin boy.

Whipping his knit cap from his head, Willie stared at Cara in sheepish awe. She always had been the prettiest woman he'd ever seen. "Hello, Miss Fairchild."

"Oh, Willie, it is good to see you again. How have you been?"

"Fine, just fine as can be, miss."

"And Percy? Is he still the same old tyrant?"

Willie shifted from one foot to the other as he grinned at Cara's teasing. "Yes, miss, he ain't never goin' to change."

"Well, what brings you here? Lunch?"

"Uh, not exactly. I already had my meal. I was lookin' for the captain. I thought he might be stoppin' by here."

Cara wondered why Willie would draw that conclusion. "No, Will, he isn't here, but I happened to see him in town a while ago. In front of the cooperage as a matter of fact."

Willie's face scrunched up as he pondered that, prompting Cara to ask, "Is there anything wrong?"

"Oh, nothin' like that, miss. I just needed to get with him on a matter or two and since he's been stopping here lately, I thought to try here first."

"I'm sorry, Willie, he hasn't stopped by." Nor would he ever again.

In obvious indecision, the gangly teen hesitated. "Do you think I could wait here, maybe, for a bit and see if he does show up?"

"Of course. And I'll get you something to eat to help pass the time."

"That's real kind of you, Miss Fairchild." Now that he thought of it, he really could stand another lunch.

Cara brought him a bowl of stew, its portion suited to a growing boy's appetite. She also brought a small bowl for herself and joined Willie at his table.

"You don't mind, do you?" she asked, noting his look of astonishment.

"Gosh . . . I mean, no, ma'am . . . miss."

It was a companionable time. Willie filled her in on all he'd been doing since their arrival in Virginia. He was living on board the *Wind Dancer,* which was anchored in the James River where Justin's house was located. Some of the crew was scattered on leave while others were assigned to the ship. Phillip Collinsworth was in Norfolk.

"And Percy?" Cara asked.

"Oh, he has a room at the captain's house. Takes care of him, he does, not that the captain needs to be took care of, mind you. I never met a man who could do anything the way Captain Reynolds can."

At Willie's blatant hero-worship, Cara bit down on her smile. "You admire him greatly," she commented easily.

Willie looked up as though she'd gone daft. "Well, o' course I do. What man wouldn't? I seen him sail around the world, through the worst storms you can imagine. But you know about that."

She did indeed remember the storm that had rendered her unconscious. As a result she had ended up in Justin's bed, after he had removed every last article of her clothing.

"He's been in tough scrapes," Willie elaborated, oblivious to Cara's red cheeks. "I can tell you that, but he just snaps his fingers at the danger. He's tough, if you know what I mean, but fair. Always treats his men squarelike. The bravest man you'll ever come across, which beats all, his being that fancy Ellsworth Earl and all."

A bite of potato slid down Cara's throat in one painful lump. Incredulously, she stared at Willie in horror.

"What?" she whispered.

Upset by his loose tongue, Willie stared back, his hands gripping the table tightly. "Oh, miss, I shouldn't o' said that."

"But you did," she insisted.

As though the table wouldn't suffice, the boy grasped his head with both hands. "I wasn't suppose to tell no one. There's only Percy and me that knows." Groaning, he squeezed his eyes shut. "I gone against his trust, and God only knows what he'll do to me."

Too stunned to think clearly, Cara stood, her eyes unfocused as she glanced around. *The Earl of Ellsworth.* Justin was the *Earl of Ellsworth.* It was beyond rational thought. She had left England, refusing his arrogant orders and monstrous dictates, only to end up on his ship and in his bed!

Hysteria was rapidly rising up within her, bringing with it a wild urge to laugh uncontrollably. *The Earl of Ellsworth,* her mind repeated. She had detested him for his callous lack of regard for her feelings and she resented him for owning the only home she had ever known. And she had told him so! Standing in his cabin, believing he was Captain Reynolds, she had hurled out her insults and contempt for the earl. And he had responded by kissing her, savagely hauling her into his arms and demolishing all of her anger and rage. Knowing how she felt about the *earl,* that very same captain had made her desire him until she had been a mass of trembling, yielding flesh.

Willie took one look at Cara's pale, frenzied face and forgot his own problem. "Miss Fairchild? Miss Fairchild," he repeated, trying to get her attention. "You going to swoon or something?"

Swoon! Swoon? She was very likely going to lose her sanity right here. Without a word, not giving a damn what Willie might think of her absurd behavior, she fled the tavern to her cottage as though chased by the devil. Justin was a devil. Dark and cynical and wicked. And she had loved him. Oh, God, she had *loved* him.

She barely heard the knock at her door; in her agitation, she wasn't sure if she had imagined it. On instinct, she flung the panel wide, then gasped audibly, positive her wits were going to desert her.

Justin recognized emotional trauma when he saw it. Urgently, he grasped Cara's slim shoulders. "Cara?"

Fueled by the strength of her rage, she wrenched out of his grasp and retreated halfway across the room. There, she whirled around to face him, her fists clenched at her sides.

Uncertain of her state, Justin kept a careful eye on Cara as he closed the door. "What is it?" he asked, concern lending a gentle note to his words.

"You!" she grated, hating the sound of tenderness in his voice. "You lecherous, lying, mean-hearted, despoiler of virgins!"

One dark brow flicking upward was the only sign Justin gave to her tirade. "I've been called worse," he assured her. "Now, suppose you tell me what this is all about."

"Still giving orders, always issuing commands," she sneered. "Do you enjoy your despotism more as Captain Reynolds or as the Earl of Ellsworth?"

Stunned silence crashed into the space between them. Abstractedly, Cara noticed the tense tightening of his jaw.

"What, nothing to say, *my lord?* No orders, no mandates to fulfill your every desire?"

Ignoring her biting sarcasm, Justin asked, "How did you find out?"

"What does it matter?" she spat. "It's enough that I know, but you obviously meant to keep me ignorant of your little secret."

"I saw no reason for you to know." His words were clipped.

"You saw nothing beyond your own lust," she hissed, her eyes blazing. "You knew how I felt about the earl, you *knew*, and yet you deceived me so you could get me into your bed."

Justin had no defense. He had done exactly that. But he would have done anything to have made her his. He'd been obsessed with her from the very first moment in his cabin when she had lifted those glorious green eyes of hers to him. No, her damnable hold over him had preceded even that. It went back to that moment when his solicitor had first uttered her name. Even then, he had acted out of the ordinary by trying to assure her welfare.

"I'm sorry," he said, quietly. It was one of the few times in his life that he'd apologized for anything he had done.

Shaking with fury, Cara verbally lashed out her wrath. "I don't want your apologies, I don't want anything from you."

Unaccustomed to asking anyone to excuse his behavior, he bristled at her rejection. Snidely, he raked her figure with cold eyes. "Are you getting everything you 'need' from Hunter Rollins?"

Cara gasped at his crude remark. "At least he treats me honestly, which is something you've never done. You play with people's lives for your own amusement. And that's all I was to you, a game. I refused to go to your grandmother's, so you tricked me onto your ship. You knew I despised the earl, so you charaded as the captain."

His own anger beginning to ignite at her insults, Justin's eyes narrowed dangerously. "I did not put you on my ship. Your solicitor arranged that."

"And you took advantage of it." She paused to draw a breath into her heaving chest, condemning herself a thousand times for her own stupidity. "Did you enjoy making a fool of me, my lord Captain? Did you enjoy your little tryst?" she bit out, irrationally needing to punish herself as much as him. "I wouldn't have thought gullible virgins were quite your thing."

"They're not," he snapped.

"But you condescended to ruin me anyway."

"You willingly came to my bed."

"And I've regretted it ever since!" she blazed back. Infuriated past caution, she sought to hurt him as he had hurt her. "It has been my misfortune to have ever set eyes on you. You are cold and incapable of feeling, made that way by your colder, mercenary parents. Your father should never have been allowed to have created someone in his own image."

With the speed of striking lightning, Justin was across the space separating them, ruthlessly yanking her up against him with punishing force.

In all her life, Cara had never witnessed an anger to match Justin's fury. The sharp lines of his face were drawn into a frightening mask. His blue eyes shone black, like lethal daggers stabbing at her. Instinctively, she shrank back, but his fingers bit into her tender flesh as his arms clamped around her, holding her captive.

Through the red haze of his rage, Justin saw the fear in her eyes. "You should be afraid," he ground out, satisfied to see her wince when he tightened his hold on her. "Be thankful you are a woman, Cara."

Unwilling to admit he frightened her, Cara raised her chin. "The only thing I'm afraid of is that you will continue to inflict yourself upon me."

Gritting his teeth, Justin thrust her away. "You needn't worry about having to fend off my advances again," he mocked cruelly. "The last place on Earth I want to be is buried deep inside your sanctimonious little body."

Cara's open palm slapped against Justin's lean cheek with all the enraged strength she could muster.

"You . . . bastard!" The words were ripped from her chest. Too hurt, too incensed, too wounded to say anything more, she marched past Justin and yanked open the door. In blazing contempt, she glared her last words at him.

Get out! her pain-filled eyes screamed. *Get out and don't* ever *come back.*

Reading the command as clearly as if she had hurled the words at him, Justin stalked from the cottage, his own eyes returning a message of their own. *With pleasure, madam.*

Chapter Fourteen

Regina Taylor let the curtain slip between her fingers. Sighing in disgust, she turned away from the window, annoyed with the steady fall of rain and snow that covered the plantation's rolling lawn. Her peacock blue skirts rustled with her movements as she moved to the sofa and lounged back. The heat from the fire, blazing in the parlor's fireplace sent the temperature in the room to that of a summer day. Idly, she fanned her fingers before her face.

She liked this room, she decided, glancing critically about her. Of course, she had removed every reminder of Charles that had ever occupied not only this room, but the entire house. Gone were his clothes, his chess set, and even that ridiculous painting of him when he was fifteen.

She gave a scoffing laugh, rolling her black eyes. Lord, but she was glad to be rid of him. It was true, he had served his purpose, in that he had always been a most indulgent husband. But his feeble, repulsive body had been enough to make her gag. Now she was free, answerable to no one except herself. And with the fortune the old fool had left her, she was now able to indulge her every whim.

A nasty smile yanked her lips to one side as she considered a desire that had yet to be satisfied. She had a score to settle with Captain Reynolds. All humor drained from her face and blistering rage spewed into her veins, when she remembered his vile treatment of her. He had let her make a fool of herself, not once, but twice. She had promised to exact revenge on the bastard and it would be hers.

"Miz Taylor?"

Regina glanced to her slave housekeeper standing uncertainly in the doorway. "What is it, Aggy?"

"There's some man here, says he's got business with you, but I ain't never seen his sort come round here before."

"Who is it?"

"Says his name is Bartholemew Smith."

At the name, Regina's eyes glittered. Oh, yes, Justin Reynolds was about to pay dearly. "You can send him in."

Aggy did as she was told and Bartholemew Smith lumbered into the room.

Smith felt at a disadvantage when he walked into Regina Taylor's parlor. He'd felt distinctly uncomfortable in just coming to the house. City folks were a breed unto themselves, the rich ones stranger than most. The few times he'd done business with any of them, it had left him with a vile taste in his mouth. But it had also lined his pockets heavily.

The initial sight of Smith gave Regina a start. Standing in the middle of the room, dripping discolored drops of melted snow from his filthy clothes, he was a repugnant eyesore. For a moment, she considered changing her mind and finding someone else to carry out her plan. But his reputation had preceded him. She had chosen the right man.

"Good afternoon, Mr. Smith," she remarked coolly. "Thank you for coming."

Smith eyed Regina without the least bit of subtlety. "Got your message."

"Yes," she replied, ignoring the inspection he was giving her silk-covered breasts. "There is a matter I wish to discuss with you."

"How much?"

He was to the point. Regina liked that. She wouldn't have to waste time playing games. And the less time she had to be around Smith, the better. Already his stench was nauseating her.

"You are direct, Mr. Smith. I think we will deal well with each other." She rose and went to stand upwind of him. With her back to a window, she gave him a bland look. "Five hundred," she announced coolly.

His thick lips compressing into a rigid line, Smith considered the amount. "I'm listening."

The pressure against Cara's face invaded her sleep as part of a dream. As a heavy, burdening cloth it stifled her breathing before transforming itself into an iron band, whose grasp was almost painful. The band became a hand, and substance joined with illusion to jerk Cara to comprehension.

Suddenly thrust awake, Cara lurched against the hand clamped tightly over her mouth and frantically pushed at the weight of a man's body pinning her torso to the mattress. Terrified, her hands clawed at anything she could connect with, her wide eyes straining into the pitch black of her room.

Instinctively, she gave a scream, but it was forced back into her lungs and in the briefest part of a second, she saw her own death. *Justin, help me!* her mind cried. Writhing and twisting in mindless terror, she tried to break free.

"Be still." The throaty, male whisper ordered roughly from only inches above her.

The sound of the voice somehow made the intruder's presence more real, more threatening, filling Cara with such dread that her entire body quaked uncontrollably.

"Be still, I said." The grating, muted voice came again, impatient this time.

Too frantic to do as she was ordered, Cara fought desperately against the hands holding her prisoner, silently praying for deliverance from whatever was about to befall her.

From out of the concealing darkness, the strange, implacable voice commanded, "For your own protection, madam, cease and listen well. I have no desire to harm you."

Through the rush of blood pounding through her head, Cara heard his assertion. She didn't believe him for an instant, but neither did she possess the strength to escape him. Reluctantly, having no choice, she stopped struggling and lay rigid, expecting the worst.

"As I said, I have no desire to hurt you. Indeed, you are most precious to my cause. But make no mistake, I will do what needs be done to insure your compliance."

Cara found the fact that he was not going to hurt her only a mild relief. His presence itself was still a gruesome threat.

Proof of that was immediate. His weight shifted and Cara felt the edge of cold metal held to the trembling edge of her jaw. She needed no light to know that the metal was a knife. Beneath the imprisoning hand, she swallowed a moan of abject fear.

"Not a sound, madam," the man warned, "unless you wish to test the blade."

The pressure across her face gradually lessened and then was gone completely as the intruder took his hand away. Free to breathe normally, Cara dragged in labored breaths of air.

"The knife is my insurance that you will remain quiet . . . and pay close attention to all I have to say. Your life . . . and that of others depends on your strict attendance to my words."

Every ounce of Cara's trembling being was riveted on the mysterious trespasser. More frightened than she had ever been in her entire life, she was loath to even blink for fear of antagonizing the man.

"I have little time to spare, Miss Fairchild, so heed my

words. Your acquaintance with Captain Reynolds is of special significance to me. It is apparent that the two of you are on a . . . familiar basis. I have decided it would be to my advantage . . . ultimately to yours . . . to utilize this association."

Cara flinched. The mention of Justin in the midst of this mad scene was an added shock to her already-stripped nerves. Her mind skidded over the question of who this stranger was, that he knew of her relationship to Justin. She squinted through the darkness. Only the vaguest silhouette was discernible and from that she found no clues as to the man's identity.

"Take a message to your captain." The voice was low, abrasive, implicit in its demand. "Tell him that all is proceeding as scheduled."

Chaotic thoughts tumbled over themselves in Cara's alarmed mind. She was being forced into a situation of which she had no understanding, other than this dangerous man was somehow involved with Justin. And she was to act as a go-between. But that was impossible. She and Justin had parted, forever. After what they had said to each other, all ties had been severed. He would never concede to listen to her and, if by some miracle he did, he wasn't likely to believe her.

"I can't," she blurted out hoarsely.

Immediately, the knife was pressed closer and Cara's icy hands gripped the sheets by her sides as she shrank back from the lethal edge.

"You will."

"No, no, you don't understand," she pleaded. "He'll have nothing to do with me."

Again the knife demanded obedience. Cara squeezed her eyes shut as a moan of pain escaped her lips.

"You play me false, madam. Captain Reynolds has spent considerable time here. I have seen the two of you together, have even been witness to that touching scene by the pasture."

Who was this man? Who was he that he had been watching Justin, observing her, assessing their actions? Her skin crawled to think that someone had been spying on her every move.

"Things have changed between us," she tried to explain through stiff lips.

"Then you will have to change them back."

Cara realized no excuse she offered would alter this man's course or extricate her from the predicament. Swallowing to clear her throat of the dread she was barely constraining, she asked, "What do you want me to do?"

"I'm glad you have chosen to see reason, but then you always did have a mind that appreciated logic. Your task is simple. Give your captain the message, tomorrow. Tell him it is from Liverpoole's man. He'll know what it all means."

There was a moment of silence as he let her absorb this. When he spoke again, his voice had taken on the ominous tones of a warning. "Tell no one else of this meeting. A stray word to the wrong ear could mean your captain's life . . . or worse, yours."

How could her life be in danger? What was Justin involved in that would be a risk?

"I will seek you out again when Captain Reynolds needs to be contacted.

"What!" Cara could hardly believe her ears. She hadn't thought past conveying the one message. This madman planned to engage her for God only knew how long. "But . . ."

"You thought your service would be required only this one time? Hardly, Miss Fairchild. I would not go to such lengths for such a paltry encounter."

"I don't understand."

"Your understanding is not necessary, only your compliance."

Unexpectedly, defiance surged up in Cara. To be used, against her will, like a mindless idiot was intolerable. She hated being forced, under any circumstances, and if this cur hadn't been holding a knife to her neck, she would be tempted to tell him exactly what she thought of his clandestine affair. Frustrated, but nonetheless cognizant of the precariousness of the situation, she restrained an angry retort.

"I will take my leave, madam. Remember what I have told you. It would be the ruination of my life should you fall victim in this."

Before Cara took her next breath, the man was gone, slipping soundlessly out into the night. Immediately, she scrambled to the door, her shaking hands searching for the latch. She found the cold metal, and even as she set it into place, she realized how useless her action was. The wrought-iron catch had done nothing to prevent the man's entrance. The implications of that were horrifying.

Her mind went numb, as if finding the answers to how or why or what if would take it over the edge. With groping hands, she stumbled her way back to the bed. Huddled in its middle, she pulled the covers around her and gave in to the tremors that shook her entire body. And then the tears came. Huge, wracking sobs, formed in terror were released on choking breaths. In the chilled, dark room her pitiful cries sounded like those of a wounded animal.

It was the first pale light of dawn, filtering around the shutter that woke Cara. Sometime during the night, as she had striven to stay awake, too fearful to sleep, her exhausted mind and body had finally given out on her. Now, curled on her side, wrapped tightly in a quilted cocoon, the soft, muted light delivered a brutal, jabbing reminder of all that had occurred in the inky darkness of the night.

Groaning, she buried her face in the pillow, trying to block out the memory. But it all came back, the sounds of the man's grating voice and her own harsh breathing, the indistinct shadow of his body looming over hers, even the smell of horse and leather that clung to his hand and clothing.

She shoved away from the bed as she jerked away from the haunting images. Yet the movement brought her face to face with an issue that was as dreadful to face in reality as the mental images were to confront in her mind. She was going to have to go to Justin. Today. She wrapped her arms about her stomach, trying to ease the pain that suddenly shot through her.

In the mirror she caught her reflection, and what she saw was enough to produce a bubble of hysterical laughter deep in her throat. Her hair was a wild tangle of twisted strands, surrounding a face dominated by red, puffy eyes and bruised lips. Her fingertips traced the blue smudges beneath those eyes, skimming lightly over the pale skin of her cheeks to her neck. Involuntarily, she winced as she touched the spot just below her ear. Turning her head, she saw an angry scratch run the line of her jaw.

Her face in the mirror may have been cause for a tinge of warped merriment, but the evidence of the knife's work brought forth a roiling, storming anger. Glaring at the reflection of that red mark, Cara damned whatever skulduggery Justin and his "Liverpoole's man" were involved in. And, she vowed silently, *she'd* be damned if she was going to idly let those two walk all over her.

Armed with fury, she dressed to do battle. In minutes, she was wearing her reliable blue dress, her hair left loose to hide the ugly scratch. A whipping motion flung her cloak about her shoulders and a quick, irate stride sent her up the brick path.

She pulled in the reins of her anger only when she knocked at Bea and John's door.

"Cara." John's face, when he opened the door, registered his surprise at seeing her up so early. "Come in."

"I'm sorry to bother you this early, John." Stepping into the parlor, she kept her voice low, not wishing to disturb anyone who might still be sleeping. "But I know that you're up with the dawn."

Seeing the intense look on Cara's face, John was compelled to ask, "Is there something wrong?"

Cara detested lies. She had never knowingly told one, nor had she ever wanted to. But the intruder's warning had been implicit, "*Tell no one else of this meeting*."

"No, there is no problem," she replied, her resentment

of the situation escalating with the falsehood she was forced to tell. "But I have come to ask a favor."

John eyed her shrewdly. "It must be some favor to bring you here at this hour." He glanced over his shoulder to the clock on the parlor mantel. "It's barely six o'clock."

"Yes, I know, John, and I would have never bothered you if it weren't important."

"What is it?"

"I . . . that is . . ." Suddenly the words clogged in her throat at her deception. She swallowed hard and felt the reminding sting along her jaw. "I need to pay a visit to Captain Reynolds," she stated firmly.

Blinking past his confusion, John peered questioningly at her. "Now?"

"Well, yes, that is, if you wouldn't mind." Seeing his puzzlement, she tried to explain. "There is a matter of . . . of a personal nature that I need to speak to him about." Her face colored hotly and she hurried on. "I know you are aware of his assistance to me the night you were away from the tavern. I have some concerns that I need to settle with him."

It was one of the stranger elucidations John had ever heard. Add to that Cara's obvious nervousness, and he was immediately suspicious. However, he had no cause to mistrust her, but he was concerned for her safety.

"You know this is a strange request you make?"

"I know. And I'm not asking that you take me. Perhaps Sam or one of the other stable hands can drive me over in the wagon."

He searched her face, hoping to see something there that would ease his concern. Instead, he became aware of the signs of her fatigue and a grave tension shining in her clear green eyes. She had obviously lost sleep over whatever this issue was and it still weighed heavily on her mind.

Gently patting her shoulder, John gave her a reassuring smile. "I'll have Sam hitch up the wagon and take you on out."

Ten minutes later, Cara was seated beside Sam on the high perch of a covered buggy, trying to anticipate the scene ahead. And a scene it was going to be. Justin owed her a great many answers and she knew him well enough to know that getting those answers from him was not going to be easy.

Justin's house was what Cara might have expected it to be. Set in a clearing of the surrounding forest, it dominated a slight bluff sloping to the James River. Of rust-colored brick, the three-story Georgian dwelling was of an imposing size, meticulously appointed with marble pilasters and dentiled cornices.

The intricately carved front door opened before Sam had even drawn the buggy to a halt before the brick steps. The huge, indomitable figure exiting the house could only belong to Percy.

"Well, look at you," his voice boomed, as he came down the steps.

Percy Pettingill was a treasure to see. Forgetting her dilemma for a moment, Cara gave vent to her sudden laughter and leaned down into the enormous man's waiting arms.

"Oh, Percy, I've missed you so!" she exclaimed as she was engulfed in a tremendous hug.

"Ah, missy, you are a rare sight." Putting Cara at arm's length, Percy scrutinized her from head to toe. "Has Virginia been treating you fair?"

"More than fair, now that I've seen you." She couldn't resist laying a gentle hand against his leathery cheek. "And you? I hear you are as cantankerous as ever."

Appreciating the teasing glint in her eyes, Percy allowed her the backhanded compliment. "Stuff and nonsense. But what brings you here?"

The smile dropped off Cara's face like a lead sinker. "I need to speak to Justin."

The grin left Percy's face just as quickly. "Ah, missy, I'm not sure that's such a good notion."

Watching Percy scrub a hand across his chin in a gesture that was achingly familiar, Cara grinned ruefully. "No one knows that better than I, but I have no choice. And frankly, neither does he."

There was serious doubt etched all over Percy's worried

face. He couldn't ever remember seeing Justin in as black a mood as he had been in the last few days. And Percy was convinced that this little miss before him was very much the cause.

"I don't think he'll see you," he advised as kindly as he could.

Cara glanced awkwardly to her toes before replying. "If the truth be known, I have even less desire to see him." A bit of her hard, repressed ire crept into her voice. "I wouldn't be here if it weren't of the utmost importance."

Just the thought of subjecting a fragile thing like Cara Fairchild to Justin's evil temper made Percy shiver. He shook his head emphatically. "You don't know what you're asking, Miss Cara. He ain't been himself lately."

"Neither have I," she shot back. Immediately she regretted her hasty remark and shook her head in chagrin. "I know that you have been privy to most of what . . . what has transpired between Justin and myself. So you, more than anyone, should realize that I would not make this request lightly." Some of the fear and anger and desperation surging within her flashed in her eyes. "Please, Percy."

If her words hadn't been enough to convince Percy, then her look of dread was. "Come on, then." He tipped his head back toward the house and put a firm hand to her elbow.

Cara paid little attention to the rich surroundings as Percy escorted her past a curving stairway and down a long hall. They stopped before a closed door at the far end, but Percy hesitated before knocking.

"Are you certain you wish to do this?"

Silently, she nodded.

Taking a strained breath, he knocked, then waited for Justin's call. When it came, Cara felt her heart lurch.

As if by mutual agreement, Cara entered alone. Closing the door quietly behind her, she found herself in a library with floor-to-ceiling shelves filled with books. Her eyes flew to Justin, seated at a formidable-looking desk set before twin windows.

An agonizing memory of their first meeting assailed her. It had been just like this, that day in his cabin with her standing nervously at the door and him, seated at his desk, engrossed in his work. She had waited for him to look up from his map, and when their eyes had finally met, he had stolen her heart.

But that had been when she was young and naive, before she knew him to be the despicable, lying cad that he was. Before she had helplessly fallen in love with him.

Fiercely yanking herself away from the tormenting past, she made her way toward the desk. Halfway there, Justin looked up and she froze in her steps.

"What the hell are you doing here?" His voice lashed across the short space separating them.

Struck by the cold, savage look on his face, it was difficult not to cower. But if anyone had a right to be angry, Cara mentally declared, it was her. "I am not here," she said tightly, managing to keep her chin up, "by my own volition."

"Nor by my invitation," he bit out.

She resolutely ignored his insult. Instead, she concentrated on the matter at hand. "I have no desire to be here, Justin, so let me say what it is I have to say so I can leave."

With rigid movements, Justin shoved himself out of his chair and stalked to the fireplace. There, he turned and glared back at her.

"Oh, do tell," he scoffed hatefully. "What little pearls of wisdom can I expect to fall trippingly from those scathing little lips of yours?"

"Don't, Justin," she fumed quietly. "Don't for one minute think I will tolerate your reproach."

"And don't think for a second that I won't have you thrown out." The derisive look he gave her matched the caustic tone of his voice.

Cara flinched inwardly, but the thought of her hideous night sent the anger back into her veins. "Then I'll just have to tell your *friend* you couldn't be bothered listening to me," she informed him furiously. "I'm sure he's going to be extremely disappointed, but then it won't be my fault when I end up carved into little pieces by that knife of his. And I certainly won't shed a tear when you end up dead."

"What the hell are you talking about?"

"I'm talking about this," she cried, thrusting her hair aside to reveal the vicious-looking scratch. "And I'm talking about someone who calls himself 'Liverpoole's man' breaking into my room last night and threatening me with death if I don't follow his orders!"

Justin's body went perfectly still. His fathomless eyes snapped to the injury on Cara's neck, studying it with chilling intensity for long moments. "Sit down," he finally told her in a deadly calm voice.

"Don't you dare tell me what to do!" she rallied back, absolutely at her wit's end with being ordered about.

"Either sit yourself down," he warned, each word a chip of ice, "or I'll pick you up and do it for you."

And he would, and Cara knew it. Infuriated, she took a seat before the fireplace. Not trusting himself not to shake her soundly, Justin strode away to a side window. Only after he had gained control of his temper did he return to stand before her.

"Now, tell me what has happened," he requested neatly, after a moment's silence.

Cara, too, had obtained a firm grip on her ire. "He came to my room last night." Her words sounded flat, her gaze was fixed on her knees. "I was asleep, and the next thing I knew, there was a hand over my face and knife at my neck." Her voice shook at the recounting of this. "I thought he meant to kill me, but that was never his intent. In fact, now that I think of all he said, he was most anxious not to hurt me."

"But you said he threatened you with death," Justin stated, finding a flaw in her statement.

"He said my life would be at stake if I didn't do as I was told."

"But he didn't harm you in any other way."

She briefly glanced up. "Not physically, no."

"What did he want?"

"He wanted me to tell you that all is going as scheduled." She expected some reaction at that, surprise or shock or at least some indication of interest. After all, if the midnight "visitor" believed that message was important enough to threaten her life for, Justin should at least act accordingly. But not so much as a flicker appeared on his face.

Shaking her head, she ground her teeth together, the hold on her anger slipping. "I assume you know what that means."

His gaze bore into hers. "Yes."

"Then will you please explain it to me?" she asked with exaggerated patience, as though she were speaking to someone who was dim-witted.

"No."

"Yes!" she insisted, surging to her feet as his curt denial ignited the short fuse of her temper. "I deserve to know what's going on. I didn't choose to be here, but your *friend* insisted." She flung a hand wide in a furious gesture. "And for some reason, which he refused to tell me, I am to be his only means of communication with you. So, whether you like it or not, you're stuck with me."

Cara had the satisfaction of seeing the brick veneer of Justin's face crack just the tiniest bit, and she gained strength from that. "I have been frightened beyond my wits, threatened with my life, and injured by some madman's knife. I am being forced to participate in a scheme that smacks of danger, with the one man who has been the plague of my existence. And it's all your fault!"

Raking his fingers through his hair, Justin swore liberally. His temper waged an obvious battle with his better judgment, debating whether or not to toss her out on her ear. With narrowed eyes, he studied her set face, before examining her neck. "Very well," he relented rudely, "sit down." At her sharp glare, he sardonically added, "Please."

Only marginally mollified, Cara sat. It was a small victory, but she would take it nonetheless.

A full minute passed in silence as Justin fought to gain possession of his self-control. Only when he was reasonably sure he wasn't about to grab hold of her arm and drag her out of the house did he begin. "What do you wish to know?"

"To begin with," she started right in, "who is this . . . this . . . detestable blackguard who accosted me?"

"I don't know."

"What do you mean, you don't know?"

"I don't know his name."

"But he knows you," she insisted.

"He knows only to contact me."

"In regards to what?"

There was a thick silence before Justin replied. "In regards to war."

Cara's eyes widened in shock. "War?"

"That's right."

She glanced around in confusion. "Which war?"

"The one that will in all likelihood begin here very shortly."

Cara tried to take it all in. "America is going to engage in a war? With whom?"

"With England."

Her mouth formed a silent O. "Why? I thought Mr. Jefferson lifted that embargo on trade three years ago. Relations between our two countries have been routine."

"But not without incident. Madison continues to play France against Britain in a bid for trade. At the same time, he is doing everything within his power to gain supremacy of the seas for America. No ship, regardless of its color, sails without a risk from the American Navy."

"Including yours?"

He nodded.

Cara digested what he had just told her, but was still in the dark as to how this related to him. "What does all of this have to do with you?"

Justin turned away and let his gaze fall to the flames in the grate before him. To confide in Cara was to step over into that shadowy realm where safety would no longer be guaranteed. If left to him, she would still be ignorant of his affairs, but for some God-damned reason, his contact had chosen to involve her. *Her*, of all people.

He was not accustomed to relying on anyone. With the exception of Percy and his grandmother, he trusted no one. To be forced to depend on Cara was so intolerable as to be ludicrous. Unfortunately, he hadn't been allowed a choice.

Irately, he swung back around to glare down into her upturned face. Mentally, he damned her stubborn, proud, merciless, self-righteous little hide. Just looking at her made him want to wring her neck, or worse, carry her upstairs, strip her naked, and take her a thousand different ways.

Disgusted with his reaction, he accepted the inevitable. "I assume you have heard of Lord Liverpoole?" he asked snidely.

Cara immediately bristled at his tone. "Yes, I believe he is a member of the prime minister's cabinet." Her voice dripped with sarcasm.

"War secretary, to be exact. I have had several dealings with him, on a purely political level. Upon occasion, he has requested my services and upon occasion, I have complied. I am here at his request."

"Are you a spy?" she asked, drawing a logical conclusion.

"Hardly, madam, nothing so melodramatic. But you have come close in your assumption that a spy or two is heartily involved in this scenario. One in particular is of major importance to Liverpoole and he wants the man out of Washington and back to England posthaste."

"On board the *Wind Dancer*." Cara supplied the bit of information as the puzzle pieces came together in her mind.

"Exactly."

"And the man in my room?"

"He is the gentleman who is orchestrating the entire matter of delivering our agent to me, with the least possible suspicion."

It all made terrible sense to Cara. Everything except the reasons for her unwilling involvement. "What do I have to do with this?"

Justin scoffed. "I'll be bloody damned if I know."

"You needn't sound so offended," she exclaimed, reacting to his manner as much as his words. "My sensibilities have been far more abused than yours."

"Then I suggest," he snapped, "that we get through this with as little infringement on each other as possible."

His sneering rancor cut painfully though her. Unwilling to admit he still had the power to hurt her, she pasted a look of cool detachment on her face. "I couldn't agree more. What do you suggest?"

A nasty smile grew on Justin's lips, the wicked gleam in his eyes darkening the blue to the deepest cobalt. Lazily, he crossed his arms over his chest and grinned down at her. "I suggest we pose as lovers."

Chapter Fifteen

"Lovers?" Cara shot to her feet as embarrassment and indignation surged through her. "Of all . . . how dare . . . why, I . . ." Her words halted as her face flushed and her fists clenched.

"Am I to take that as a no?" Justin asked sarcastically.

"That is most definitely a no!" Cara exclaimed, finally finding her voice.

Unfolding his arms, Justin strode across the room. "I'm afraid you have little say in the matter," he informed her coldly. "If my man needs to communicate with me and he chooses to do so through you, then we will have to accommodate."

"Fine, we'll accommodate," she stated, watching Justin take a seat behind his desk. "But not by posing as lovers. Or anything else for that matter."

"It's the only way."

"No, it is not," she insisted. "He can tell me whatever he needs to tell and I'll pass it on to you."

Justin casually lit a thin cigar and leaned back, drawing deeply on the rolled tobacco. "And how do you intend to do that?"

"Just the way I did today."

"No."

"Why not?" she demanded to know.

"First and foremost"—he paused to exhale a fine stream of gray smoke—"your coming out here on a regular basis will raise suspicions, and doing that is out of the question. Second, I'll be able to keep an eye on you. You've already attracted the attention of the likes of Smith and you'd be a too-easy target traipsing all the way out here."

In mounting frustration, Cara stepped before the desk and leveled an accusing look on Justin. "Don't ask me to believe you're concerned for my welfare," she scoffed.

"I'm not," he snapped back. "But you have suddenly become indispensable to this mission. Your safety is therefore imperative."

His words stung. "Thank you for the honesty," she said with a lethal load of graciousness. "But posing as lovers is out of the question. There must be some other way to go about this."

"There isn't." He regarded her through a veil of smoke. "As your lover, I can call on you each day. No one will have cause to question my activities if they think I am your devoted suitor."

"But you aren't and I do not wish to deceive my cousin by pretending otherwise. And she will find it very strange to suddenly have you calling on me."

Justin's eyes narrowed. "Why?"

Glancing down at her toes, Cara drew a steadying breath before answering. "Because she knows all that has happened between us."

"You weren't very discreet," he accused darkly, not liking the particulars of his personal life bandied about.

"I was far more privy than you were honest," she retorted in sheer self-defense. Sighing in disgust, Cara pressed cold fingers to her throbbing temples. She detested this hurling of accusations. It was demeaning and accomplished nothing.

"Justin, this will not work. We cannot even be in the same room without attacking each other. How do you expect to convince anyone that you have developed a tender inclination toward me?"

"I will manage," he assured her blandly.

But I won't, her mind cried. Just coming here had been difficult enough. How could she possibly endure seeing him on a daily basis, pretending an affection that was only a horrid reminder of all she had once felt?

Seeing the indications of refusal in her eyes, Justin silkily prodded, "What are you really afraid of, Cara?"

Her head came up sharply and she regarded him warily. "I'm not afraid of anything."

"Oh, yes, you are," he murmured with an arrogant smile. "And it's more than your involvement with this scheme." He let his gaze slide assessingly over her figure. "It's me you're afraid of, or rather the idea of falling back into my bed that has you so defensive."

She felt the weight of his gaze like the physical caress it was meant to be. But his haughty assumption obstructed any response she might otherwise have experienced. "You flatter yourself, Justin," she said tightly, galled by his audacity.

"Oh?" He was warming to the lunacy of the entire matter for the first time. "Then you should have no objections to my being the gallant for a while."

She had serious objections. She knew for a fact that there was no chance of her, as he put it, falling back into his bed. But she admitted that where he was concerned, she was extremely vulnerable and being in his company again was going to be painful. She ground her teeth together, her eyes searching his face for some sign of compromise. Finding only self-assured contours and unyielding lines, she turned away from the desk and walked to one of the windows, all too aware of Justin's unwavering gaze on her back.

She lifted a shaking hand to her forehead in an effort to

ease the headache pounding behind her eyes and silently examined the situation. As much as she wished to deny it, his idea was sound. He could call on her without anyone finding it odd. Anyone, except Bea. Cara closed her eyes in remorse. The thought of deceiving her cousin ate at her heart. Sweet, caring Bea did not deserve to be treated so. She had done nothing except offer love and support and guidance and in return Cara was going to have to betray that devotion by lying. The bitterness of that wrenched at her stomach. But Justin's contact had made it painfully clear that she had no alternatives.

Scalding resentment and anger boiled in Cara's veins. Turning, she marched back to the desk. "I do not like this madness," she bit out, her green eyes flashing. "I hate being coerced into deceit. And I detest being forced into a position of having to lie to those I love."

From his seat, Justin watched Cara fight to control her outraged emotions as she declared all sorts of noble sentiments in that righteous air of hers. Cursing, he leaned forward and ground out his cigar in a silver dish before standing and crossing his arms over his chest.

"Your likes and dislikes have no relevance in this matter," he told her with bald indifference.

Exercising all of her strength on refraining from slapping his face, Cara clenched her hands into fists. "That has become abundantly clear, but know this, Justin. I will accede to this blackmail only because I have no wish to go to my grave and I have an equal aversion to the thought of having to live with the guilt of your death hanging over me for the rest of my life." She leaned forward in her vehemence, her whole body trembling with suppressed fury. "Now, if you will excuse me, I am anxious to take my leave. The sooner we begin this charade, the sooner it will be over and I can rid myself of you once and for all."

Twirling on her heel, she stalked out of the library.

Even though Cara knew what to expect, she was truly not prepared to actually see Justin waiting for her the next morning when she emerged from the inn. Having just finished serving breakfast to the morning patrons, she descended the back steps to the courtyard with one last platter that needed to be returned to the kitchen.

Her steps slowed as she approached his tall figure negligently leaning against the dairy wall. The morning was unusually warm and his casual dress of white shirt, dark pants, and polished boots only accentuated his relaxed stance. However, the penetrating look in his blue eyes told Cara he was a long way from feeling as offhanded as he appeared.

"Good morning," she said rigidly.

One of Justin's dark brows flicked upward at her implacable greeting. He shoved away from the whitewashed building and strode forward to meet her.

"Good morning," he returned, letting his eyes touch briefly on each of her features before raking his gaze down her slender length.

Given the awkwardness of the moment and the hideous state of affairs between them, Cara found his close scrutiny insulting. "If you are quite finished with your inspection, I need to take this tray in to Ophelia."

Justin ignored the contempt underscoring her words and gave a mocking smile. "I hardly think that is any way to greet a swain of intimate standing."

His words provoked instantaneous ire. "I don't care what you think," she informed him in a low, icy voice.

"Careful, Cara, you're pique is showing around the edges." He spoke lightly enough, but his unyielding bearing was a clear warning. For appearances' sake, they were to seem the courting couple.

"If I am in a mood this morning," she remarked as levelly as she could, "it can only be attributed to my lack of sleep of late." She turned toward the kitchen then added over her shoulder, "And the company I have been forced to keep." With a swish of striped wool and white apron, she disappeared into the cook house.

Justin watched the door close behind her and mentally cursed. He could see that she was going to make this as difficult as possible. Well, he would disabuse her of any high-minded ideas right now.

Annoyingly, he was forced to wait. It was several long moments before Cara finally emerged. Having gained a modicum of sangfroid, she determinedly ignored his dangerously narrowed eyes and faced him with a cool, artificial smile and one disdainfully arched brow.

"Save your contempt for someone else, Cara," he bit out, irritated by her defiance.

"No one is as deserving," she quipped, "my lord."

The line of Justin's jaw sharpened as his teeth clenched. "I think there are several matters we need to discuss. Now." He took hold of her elbow in a none-too-gentle grip and started off toward her cottage. "In privacy."

Cara found herself being towed away, and while she had no desire to be alone with Justin, she doubted she could continue to stand there and appear to be pleased to see him. She quickened her pace to match his long, irate strides. However, once they had gained her cottage and Justin was leaning back against the closed door, she had second and third thoughts as to the wisdom of being closeted with him. Even from her place across the room, she could feel the menacing air he emanated. Helplessly, her heart began to beat nervously, yet she stubbornly clung to her courage.

"What is it you wish to discuss?" Her steady, quiet voice betrayed none of her unease.

"You are going to have to do better than you did, just now," he informed her in equally measured tones.

"It is the best I can do, under the circumstances."

"It isn't good enough."

"*I* am not accustomed to practicing deception."

"Do not fling your insults at me, madam. And never," he warned darkly, enunciating each word with icy precision, "never again make any reference to my true identity."

The blast of his frigid rage hit Cara like a physical blow. She swallowed hard, and Justin was quick to notice her unnerved response.

"You would do well to proceed cautiously with me,

Cara. This is no game of wounded pride or lover's revenge that we're embroiled in. The stakes we play for are real and the only winners are those who remain alive."

Cara needed no reminders of the peril they faced. During the interminable night just passed, she had lain awake, too frightened to sleep. He mind had recounted the scene played out in the dark with Justin's contact. The man was a spy and her helping him, whether willingly or not, technically made her a spy also. The Americans would not hesitate to hang her or Justin, especially in the event of war. Unconsciously, her hand covered the scratch along her jaw.

"Does it hurt?"

Justin's query snapped Cara from her private reverie. She looked up questioningly.

"The cut," he clarified shortly, "does it still pain you?"

She regarded him for a moment, relieved to find that the worst of his anger was fully under control. "Minimally."

"It must have drawn notice. How did you explain it?"

"I lied," she told him honestly. "I said I had scratched myself on the splintered edge of a door."

"Were you believed?"

"There is no reason for anyone not to trust me." The bitterness she felt crept into her words. Suddenly, it was just too much to bear and she turned away to pretend an interest in the graining of the clothes press. She was tired and frightened and lonelier than she could ever remember being. She longed to be held and comforted. Some tiny part of her mind realized that it was Justin's embrace she yearned for and that made the ache within her all the more agonizing.

She walked to the fireplace and faced him squarely, needing this interview to end now. "I see no need for you to prolong your stay. Your man did not contact me last night."

From outside, Bea's urgent voice interrupted, accompanied by a rapid tapping at the door. "Cara. Cara, may I come in?"

Cara's gaze flew to Justin's. This was the one encounter she dreaded. She knew Bea harbored a healthy dislike of

Justin, and as overprotective as her cousin was, there was no telling how she was going to react. Justin was committed to his pretense of beau and would brook no interference with his plans. Miserably, Cara acknowledged that she herself was going to be caught in the middle.

"Yes, Bea, come in," she called, waving Justin away from the door.

Justin swung the panel wide, stepping back as Bea anxiously swept into the cottage.

"Good heavens, Cara, are you all right? I thought I saw . . ."

Before Bea could finish, Cara gestured lamely to Justin. Bea swung around, her face a picture of surprise and concern. However, like the washes on a watercolor, her expressions quickly ran together and blended until what remained was a vivid, transparent indignation, complete with a stiff, haughty bearing.

Cara stepped into the uncomfortable silence with an attempt at introductions. "Bea, I don't believe you have met Captain Reynolds."

"No. No, I haven't," Bea replied, her gaze fixed accusingly on the man she considered a cad. She refused to say a word to him and another awkward silence threatened. Quickly, Cara turned to Justin.

"Captain Reynolds, may I introduce you to my cousin, Beatrice Hawthorne."

The line of Justin's lips stretched into its most charming smile and the short bow he offered was as polished as it was polite. "Madam, it is a pleasure."

Bea had an arm load of disparaging thoughts about that, but she firmly kept her mouth clamped tight.

"Captain Reynolds has just stopped by," Cara explained, trying to pick up the ends of the conversation. "He . . . he came to pay a visit."

Bea peeled her gaze from Justin and peered curiously at her cousin. "How . . . nice."

"Yes . . . I thought so." Belatedly, Cara remembered to smile.

"But I was about to take my leave," Justin announced,

coming forward with his words. "Cara, I will call again tomorrow."

Before Bea's wide, indignant eyes, Justin lifted Cara's hand and placed an intimate kiss on the inside of her wrist, his gaze warm and devouring. Cara's own eyes rounded and instinctively she tried to snatch her hand free, but Justin retained his firm hold for a few seconds more. It was but a flash of time, still long enough for Cara's heart to begin a mad pounding, her face to heat with a blush, and her nerves to stretch tightly.

With one last look at Cara, Justin gave Bea a departing nod and took his leave. As soon as the door closed behind him, the words Bea had bottled up came flowing out.

"Cara! What on Earth was *that* man doing here? The nerve of that scoundrel. And what could you have been thinking to agree to even speak with him, let alone allow him in here? I hope he behaved himself. Oh, good heavens, he didn't make any untoward gestures to you, did he?"

Cara could barely keep up with the rush of words. "Bea, please do not fret."

"Well, someone has to!"

"There is no need."

"But what did he want?"

"He wished to talk." Cara was grateful for the truth of that.

Skepticism pulled Bea's forehead into a trouble frown. "Talk? That kiss was beyond all that is proper. And from the looks he was giving you, he did not wish to discuss picking the lint from the rug!"

It was exactly the impression Justin had wished to give. Silently, Cara fumed at how easily he had achieved his task, and how readily he had left her to make the explanations.

"We spoke only briefly. His behavior was quite circumspect."

"But what of tomorrow? He said he would call again. I tell you, this is intolerable. I have half a mind to tell John to get his musket and shoot that black-hearted villain."

"No," Cara nearly shouted. At Bea's startled look, she

gentled her tone. "No, please do not go to John with this. It would only lead to questions and you know the answers are too embarrassing."

Cara's genuine look of distress was too potent for Bea to withstand. Her indignation died swiftly in light of her cousin's obvious misery.

"I shan't say a word," she murmured kindly. "But I do worry so."

"And I appreciate it. Truly."

"What shall you do, when he calls again?"

"Talk with him."

"Is that wise?"

Cara shrugged. "Probably not, but I cannot deny that there are . . . forces that bind us."

"Yes, I understand," Bea commiserated.

Sighing heavily at the half-truths she was telling, Cara's words dwindled to a mere whisper. "This is a situation that only time can resolve."

Time for Cara, however, refused to cooperate. Each ensuing day was a sluggish advance of hour upon hour; the nights, a frozen, nerve-wracking limbo that seemed eons long.

Justin routinely showed up in the early morning hours, occasionally in time to be served breakfast in the tavern room. His warm, courtly manner and obvious attention toward Cara raised more than a few eyebrows. Within a week's time, there were few in the Hawthorne establishment who didn't believe a serious romance was developing between Cara and her sea captain.

Nothing could have been further from the truth. Once out of sight of curious eyes, Justin was coldly impersonal, his resentment of the situation infuriating him to a dangerous level. Cara was no less frustrated. Trying to maintain an air of normalcy for her family while dancing her way around Justin's dark mood was so ludicrous as to be laughable.

After an entire week, Justin's contact had not returned and the situation began to take its toll on Cara. The thought of once again being awakened by "Liverpoole's man" made sleep nearly impossible. She would lie awake in dreadful anticipation of his arrival, dropping off to a fitful slumber only after exhaustion had claimed her. Tired and drawn, she would arise at dawn and go about her duties, only to have to face Justin, who gave every indication of having spent more than enough time in the arms of Morpheus.

As much as Cara dreaded another meeting with Justin's contact, she was just as anxious for the occurrence to take place and have it done with. When he did finally make another appearance, it was again during the darkest hour of the night, long after her fire had dwindled down to coals.

His method of arrival was less extreme than that of his initial visit, but no less alarming to Cara who had been, for the first time in two weeks, sound asleep. At the gentle pat on her shoulder, she came awake with a startled gasp, instantly aware of who sat on the bed beside her.

"Couldn't you just knock?" she cried, scrambling as far from the man as possible.

"I apologize if my measures are clandestine," the raspy voice answered. "However, secrecy is imperative."

Leaning back against the headboard with her knees drawn to her chest, Cara took several deep, steadying breaths to slow her racing heart. "How do you manage to get in when the door is locked?" she asked in exasperation.

A brief, whispery laugh preceded the man's explanation. "A trick of the trade, Miss Fairchild. A skill I managed to pick up in France years ago."

"I must tell you, I do not appreciate it." She raked her hair back from her forehead and tried to glare at the shadowy figure.

"If I could alter my manner, I would, but for your own safety, the less you know of me, the better."

He shifted his weight, and Cara carefully pulled the covers to her chin.

"You have nothing to fear from me, madam," he assured her, detecting her movements even in the dark. "I am here strictly on business."

"Then please state it, sir," she implored, impatient for this man to be gone.

"An earnest woman, if there ever was one. Very well. I assume you did as I asked and contacted Captain Reynolds."

"I did as you ordered."

He ignored her obvious dissent over the phrasing of his remark. "And his reaction?"

"He was not pleased by my participation in this affair."

"Did he explain the circumstances of the matter?"

"Yes," she replied bitterly. "You are a spy helping another spy."

"And did he also caution you to discretion?" he fired back sharply. "Be warned, Miss Fairchild, one stray word and we will all see our Maker before it is our desire."

"Sir," she said distastefully, "I have no need of your reminders. I carry your knife's mark as a token of the danger I face."

As though caught off guard, he remained silent for a minute. "Again, my apologies," he whispered in what sounded like genuine regret.

Cara reluctantly acknowledged the sentiment. "Sir, your promptness would be far more appreciated than your apology. I assume you are here to convey another message to Captain Reynolds. Please, do so."

"So that I will leave you in peace." He finished her thought for her. "As you wish. Tell your captain to have his ship ready to sail in three weeks. I will have my man here in Williamsburg by that time."

Three weeks. There was suddenly a time frame, a foreseeable end to this madness and Cara took heart. Just as unexpectedly, her spirits crashed. In three weeks, Justin would be sailing back to England. He'd be gone. Irrationally, anguish flooded her at the thought and try as she could, there was no controlling the sense of loss she felt.

It was absurd, she knew, to lament his leaving. She had wanted this very thing for weeks now. There was nothing left between them except rancor and disdain. Anything else they had ever shared had been brutalized by his betrayal and deception. And what had they ever truly shared? her mind cruelly asked. One night of passion where she had given her love and he had taken her body.

Justin did not know how to love, she told herself. His parents had seen to that. Unfortunately, she had been the one to pay the price.

"I will tell him tomorrow," she murmured, trying to come to grips with the finality of it all.

"Then I will take my leave."

His weight lifted from the bed and Cara squinted to follow his path to the door. He lingered, then turned toward Cara again. "The mark, left by the blade. Did it . . . are you scarred?"

Perplexed by his concern, Cara gazed back at his obscured silhouette. That he should be troubled over the matter was extraordinary. "No. It fades each day."

She thought she saw him nod and then he left without another word.

Justin's arrival the following morning was later than usual. Breakfast was long since over, and as he made his way to Cara's cottage, his thoughts were ominous. His night had been a disaster; his morning a study in futility. He detested being forced to tolerate the entire scheme and he had finally come to the end of his patience. He damned Liverpoole, he damned his contact and, as he gained the brick path and spied Cara at her door in the company of Hunter Rollins, he God damned her to hell.

His pace halted as he watched Rollins bend low over Cara's hand and press a kiss to her slender fingers. The contact was brief, but given Justin's more-than-ready fuse, it was enough to ignite a burning rage deep in his gut.

"Thank you for calling, Hunter," Cara said, unaware of Justin standing at the far end of the path.

Sighing heavily, Hunter retained his gentle hold on Cara's hand. He had known she was reluctant for an association of any sort. Still, he had come here today hoping to change her mind. He hadn't. "I am sorry you feel disinclined toward my suit, Cara."

Wistfully, not wishing to cause him any hurt, Cara

regarded the gentle man before her. "No sorrier than I, Hunter. But please know that I will always consider you my friend."

With a shake of his head, Hunter gave a wry laugh. "I'm not sure that will suffice."

"It will have to."

Seeing her unwavering resolve, Hunter accepted the inevitable. "You know of course that you are still free to use the shop for your school."

Smiling, Cara said, "Thank you, my friend."

With one last fond look, Hunter took his leave. Cara followed his departure with a troubled frown, then turned and spotted Justin out of the corner of her eye. One look at his formidable face as he bore down on her, and her heart leapt into her throat.

"Justin . . ." was all she managed, before he grabbed her arm and unceremoniously yanked her into her room. Anything else she might have said was cut off by the sound of the door slamming shut.

Almost as quickly as Justin had taken hold of Cara, he thrust her away. Stumbling slightly, she righted herself against the bed. With a shaking hand braced on the mattress, she warily regarded Justin as he came to stand near. Unable to fathom the cause of his dangerous mood, she felt the distinct urge to shrink back.

"For whose benefit was that display?" he snarled at her.

"What . . . what display?" She truly had no idea to what he referred.

"Do not mince words, Cara."

"I'm not," she replied cautiously, all too aware of the depths his anger could reach.

"I mean that little farewell gesture you just received from Rollins."

Her eyes widened in comprehension. "The kiss on my hand?"

"Yes."

She gazed around the room, as though searching for reason and sanity on the walls. "It was an innocent expression, nothing more."

"You always were," he ground out in excruciating exactness, "and to this very moment remain the single most naive woman I have ever met."

The ends of Cara's own temper began to fray. He was being purposely antagonistic and she had done nothing to warrant such treatment. "What are you going on about?"

"If that kiss was innocent, then I am God Almighty."

"Well, it was and you aren't. Hunter Rollins is my friend."

He raked her slender figure with an insolent gaze. "Exactly how are you defining friendship these days?"

"As I always have," she snapped back. "Hunter is a fine man. He has offered me nothing but kindness and respect. I will not have you discredit what honest emotion we share."

"I can well imagine what you are sharing with him."

Cara stiffened in outrage at his crude implication. "This is none of your business."

"It is my business when it interferes with my mission."

"Damn your mission," she cried. "If I choose to have Hunter call on me, then he shall."

The blue of Justin's eyes sparkled with frustration and ire. "He wants to get under your skirts."

"And you never entertained that exact thought?"

Before Cara had time to blink, Justin's hands shot out and grasped her by the arms. In the next instant, she was imprisoned against the firm wall of his chest, an arm wrapped securely across her back, while one hand captured her chin.

"If you remember, Cara," he said thickly, "I did more than just think about it."

Cara's outraged gasp was silenced as Justin's mouth came down on her with punishing force. With a moan of protest, she strained desperately against his unyielding strength, struggling to free herself from his hold. But his arms only tightened and his lips slanted fiercely across hers.

Goaded past logic, Justin absorbed Cara's struggles, forcing her soft body against his until he could feel every inch of her boring into him. Those lush curves belonged solely to him, his mind declared.

But Cara wasn't agreeing. As his hand came up to boldly caress a breast, his thumb tracing teasing circles across its nipple, she twisted away from the betraying sensations spiraling through her.

"No, Justin," she gasped, tearing her mouth from his, her hands pushing at his shoulders. "I won't let you do this."

Her words penetrated the torment and anger clouding Justin's mind. Lifting his head, he glared down into her wide, infuriated eyes. For endless moments, they stared at each other. And then with a nasty curse, he pushed her away and stalked out of the cottage.

Trembling with the turbulent emotions racing through her, Cara squeezed her eyes shut in a bid for control. Like someone who had withstood the battering winds of a storm, she stood motionless, too exhausted to move or think.

That hollow feeling clung to Cara through the days that followed. Justin did not return and for that she was grateful. Their encounter had robbed her of some of her spirit. She had no desire to deal with him and even less energy to do so. Unfortunately, she realized he would not remain away long enough to jeopardize his mission. He would seek her out, of that she was certain. What she wasn't sure of was how she was going to bear up when he did.

The need to escape the pressured atmosphere sent her in search of a tranquil setting. With chores completed and lunch not due to be served for several hours, she wrapped up in her cloak and set off for the copse of trees beyond the stables.

Even bare of their leaves, the sheltering oaks and elms provided a buffer from the sights and sounds of the tavern, as well as from the burdens that plagued Cara. A blithe little stream defied the winter's chill and gently ran a curved path. Having no destination in mind, Cara followed its lead until she found herself at the edge of a pond. Serene and lovely, the wooded spot was a balm for her nerves.

She observed the clearing with a biased eye. She could just imagine the beauty of the place in the spring. It would be an easy task to sit here and forget her worries.

There was only one real worry that beset Cara. For days now she had refused to dwell on it. As she picked up a twig and idly toyed with its rough surface, she made herself face the truth. She still loved Justin. Despite all that he had done to her, regardless of everything that had occurred to put them at odds with each other, her heart and body had responded to his kiss even when her mind had raged against it.

"Ain't this a pretty sight."

Startled from her musings, Cara's head snapped around to find Bartholemew Smith standing indolently beside a large pine. Just the sight of his huge, burly body caused the fine hairs on the back of her neck to prickle. Carefully, she stood and regarded him intently.

An expression that could easily have passed for a sneer split his thick lips in a travesty of a smile. "What you doin' all the way out here by yourself?"

Instinct warned Cara not to confront this man. Memories of his drunken assault in the tavern tripped though her mind and caused a shudder to run down her spine.

"I was just on my way back to the tavern." She kept her tone as neutral as she could.

"Now, ain't that somethin'," he laughed. "So was I."

Had she said she was on her way to the moon, Cara knew he would have chosen the same as his destination. "If you will excuse me then."

"I ain't in no hurry. And besides," he added with an abhorrent leer, "I got a thing or two to discuss with you."

Cara had no intentions of remaining there with him for a second longer. Bartholemew Smith was a dangerous man. "Perhaps another time, Mr. Smith. I am already late as it is."

Sauntering toward her, Smith cocked his head to one side, smirking at her polite manner. "You got yourself a pretty way of talkin', little Miss English. And you got yourself a real pretty face."

He was too close for comfort, and Cara stepped back, every fiber in her being alerted to his threatening presence.

"What are you afraid of?"

"Leave me alone, Mr. Smith," she declared, retreating another step.

"I ain't finished my business with you," he returned mockingly, advancing yet again.

"I have nothing to say to you."

"Well, I got plenty to say to you."

Withdrawing again, her foot caught the edge of a fallen branch and she stumbled slightly. Almost frantically, she gained her balance, her gaze never wavering from his beefy face.

"You know you ain't goin' nowhere," he taunted. "You and I are goin' to stay right here and see if that body of yours matches that pretty face."

Incredibly, Cara felt her panic evaporate. In its place was a solid fear, but more surprisingly, an all-consuming rage that fed her courage and brought a trembling to her limbs. To rationalize at that point would have been absurd. It would have also done nothing to change her course.

"How dare you!" she yelled, her eyes glittering heatedly. "Your actions have been of the vilest nature and I am not going to stand for any more."

Caught off guard by her outburst, Smith stared at her. but only for a moment. "You uppity little bitch," he spat just seconds before he lunged for her.

Cara saw his movement and tried to evade his seeking hands. Her attempt was futile and with a gasp she felt him take hold of her and haul her up against him.

"Take your hands from me," she hissed, twisting wildly.

"I ain't even started," Smith vowed on a chuckle.

His foul breath made her gag and she jerked her head away. Without warning, his hand clamped in her hair and yanked her face back to his. Smiling evilly, he gave the auburn mass a cruel twist and Cara cried out in pain.

"Let's just see what you got." His tongue flicked out to wet his lips, a crazed cast glazed his eyes.

Despite her frantic struggles, Smith found the ties of her cloak and broke the laces with a quick snap. He flung the garment aside, then reached for the bodice of her dress and tore the fabric downward with a mighty wrench.

Cara's scream pierced the forest's hush, yet she was barely conscious of its echoing sound. Her mind was deaf to all except the suffocating fear and dread within her and the vital need to escape. Pushing and shoving, she freed one hand and raked her nails down his face as she delivered a kick to his leg. Jolted by the unexpectedness of the attack, Smith loosened his hold and Cara frantically shoved away.

Her effort was in vain. Snarling in rage, Smith grabbed her arm and shoved her to the ground, throwing his bulky weight on top of her.

The impact of his body jarring against her knocked the breath from her lungs. She gasped on sobs and fought for air, just as she fought to keep Smith's mouth from capturing hers. In hideous agony, she felt his hands grasp her skirt, pulling the fabric up to bare her legs, and a wailing moan rose up in her throat. One cold, vicious hand was on her thighs, kneading the flesh, while the other groped ruthlessly at her breasts.

Panic choked her and even as she writhed and resisted with all her strength, she realized how hopeless it was. Tears of rage and pain spilled from her wild eyes. There was nothing she could do to stop him.

Chapter Sixteen

Little Sarah Hawthorne gazed in fascinated rapture at the tall captain. From her four-year-old perspective, he was the most handsome man she had ever seen. It had been her secret for a little while now that she loved the captain, and someday, when she was older, she was going to marry him.

From her place beneath the fruit trees, she watched him knock on Cousin Cara's door. Sarah could have told him not to bother. She had seen Cara walk out through the backwoods just a while ago.

"She's not home," she piped up.

Justin swung around at the sound of the sweet voice and found its owner standing several yards away. Large green eyes, reminiscent of Cara's, regarded him with serious intent.

"Do you happen to know where she is?" he asked with a smile that made Sarah blink.

"Yes. She just left."

Sarah wondered if she had said something wrong, because the captain stopped smiling and frowned in the same way Papa did when she had been up to mischief.

"Did she, by chance, mention where she was going or when she would return?"

She gave the question serious consideration. She didn't want to say anything that would make him angry. "No, she didn't tell me those things." She hoped that would make his smile return, but when it didn't, she tried again. "But I don't think she'll be gone for very long. There's nothing back there except trees."

Justin's eyes narrowed as he gave Sarah a discerning look. "Where?"

Turning, she pointed toward the forest on the far side of the stables. "The backwoods." A quick glance at the look of interest on her captain's face told her she had said the right thing. Encouraged, she went on. "I don't know why she would want to go walking there now. The berries aren't out and it's too cold to take your shoes off and put your feet in the pond."

"Was she with anyone?"

"No, all by herself."

That, Sarah concluded, must have been a terrible thing to say. In dismay she watched his face turn fierce, while he whispered something to himself. Suddenly, he started for the woods, without even saying good-bye.

From the depths of her being, Cara gave a shrill scream as Smith's wet mouth slobbered its way down her neck and his coarse hand slid over her hip. Writhing away, she clenched her eyes shut, gulping on her terror. Her mind saw the inevitable, anticipated the worst and in its frenzy, pictured every gruesome detail. She screamed again . . . even as Smith's body was forcefully pulled away.

Smith felt himself hauled to his feet by a powerful grip. For a dazed moment, he was standing upright and then in the next instant, he was spun around. A second later, Justin's fist crashed into his face.

With blue eyes blazing in fury, Justin watched Smith drop to the ground. Not waiting to see how effective his first blow had been, he crouched low over the huge waterman, flipped him over onto his back, and once again delivered a mighty punch.

Smith's head jerked backward, slamming against the ground with crippling force. He grunted in pain, trying to shake off the dizziness of the unexpected attack. Instinctively, he lifted a hand, attempting to strike a blow, but his swing was impotent, missing its mark by a wide margin.

With brutal indifference, Justin took hold of Smith's neck and leaned his weight forward onto the man's throat. "I could kill you right now, Smith," he drawled quietly. "All I have to do is press a little harder."

Smith's eyes, still whirling in an unfocused state, managed to converge on Justin's menacing features. That sight, and the beating he had just received, should have been sufficient to convince him he'd had enough. But the roots of his hatred ran too deep and restraint had never been his strong suit.

"You bleedin' English dog . . ."

His words choked off in a gurgling cough as Justin brought all his weight to bear on Smith's neck. Desperately, Smith tried to pry the vicelike grip away, but his hands, like his eyes, were practically useless.

"It's been a long time since I've killed a man with my hands," Justin remarked casually. "It was in Spain and I had to snap the fellow's neck. Have you ever heard a man's neck break?"

Smith's eyes bulged as he gasped for air. His mouth worked, but only harsh croaks resulted.

"It's not a particularly pleasant sound, yet it does have its advantages. No blood." He paused to smile mirthlessly, his tone turning icy cold. "I don't really care how I kill you, Smith, but I will, if you even come close to her again. And I won't care if I spill your blood or not." He let his words sink in, then rose to his feet.

Slowly, Smith came to his knees, gulping in air. A swaying motion took him upright as he chafed his sore neck. It hurt to swallow, it hurt to breathe, it even hurt to stand there. Muttering a vicious curse, he threw Justin a scowling look before glancing to Cara's quaking figure.

He never saw the blow coming. Without warning, Justin's fist landed squarely on his jaw and he crumpled in an unconscious heap.

"Don't even look at her, Smith," Justin muttered. Without a second look at the prostrate hulk, Justin crossed to Cara. Kneeling, he gently took her shaking body into his arms, gathering her close, unconsciously murmuring soothing endearments.

He buried his head within the silken strands of her streaming hair, overjoyed and relieved that he had arrived in time. All the animosity he had harbored in the past weeks evaporated, the feeble residue of his wounded pride at her rejection withered to nothing. She was safe, that was all that mattered.

The scene he'd come upon flashed before his clenched eyes. Smith's loathsome body, sprawled over hers, his hands and mouth defiling her sweet flesh. When she had screamed, an inhuman urge to kill had enveloped Justin. Somehow, it had been tempered with just enough sanity to prevent murder, because Smith was still alive.

He gazed down at Cara, her face half-hidden against his chest, and his stomach wrenched. He had come close to losing her. Smith would have seen her dead after he'd finished with her. Just the thought of that bastard made him want to forsake sanity and give in to his earlier impulse.

"Easy, love," he murmured, bending low to press a kiss to her brow. "It's all right, now."

Cara was dwelling in a detached realm of shock. From the moment Smith had been pulled from her, she had withdrawn into herself, her arms moving unconsciously to cover her naked torso. One part of her mind had realized that it was Justin who had saved her, but she had viewed everything from a peripheral perspective, detached yet cognizant.

It was the touch of Justin's lips to her forehead that snapped her back to reality. Immediately, she became aware of his arms around her, of being held close, almost lovingly, and she curled into his strength. Her shaking hands slid up his chest and over his shoulders to cling tightly.

"Hold me, Justin," she whispered raggedly, weak tears of relief flooding her eyes.

Needing no encouragement, Justin tightened his embrace, responding to the wounded sound of her voice as much as her plea. "Are you . . . hurt?" He knew there was a need for the question, yet he dreaded the answer.

"No . . . no, just . . . so frightened."

He acknowledged that with a sense of immeasurable relief. Satisfied, for the time being, he wrapped her in her nearby cloak, then stood, holding her securely in his arms. There would be time for questions later. The most pressing need was to remove Cara from this place, now, and see her safely cared for.

Smith wasn't given even the most cursory glance as Justin quickly strode away. Within minutes, the forest was behind them, yet once the stables were in sight, Justin's route to the cottage became less direct. The fewer people to witness Cara's return, the less burdened she would be by their idle speculation.

Sarah Hawthorne's presence was, however, a blessing. Still playing beneath the orchard's limbs, she paused to watch her handsome captain carry Cara up the path and push open the cottage door. Over his shoulder, Justin leveled a no-nonsense look at the child and sternly ordered, "Go fetch your mother."

Four-year-old love was instantly forgotten in the face of such an adult command. Sarah ran to do as she was told.

A well-placed heel shut the door behind Justin. Carefully, he laid Cara on the bed, but when he would have withdrawn his arms, her hands clung resolutely to the front of his jacket.

"Hold me, Justin . . . please, just . . . hold me." Her face was a mask of misery, shock adding sharp edges to each feature. Regardless of the discord between them, she couldn't bear for him to release her. Her eyes searched his, the beseeching look betraying the frailty of her state of mind.

There was never any question of Justin refusing. Every instinct he possessed demanded he take her in his arms and hold her quivering body close to his. Not in lust or desire, but solely for the sake of offering comfort.

He followed his instincts. Gently, in the single most selfless act of genuine compassion he had ever committed, he held Cara close. His arms slanted across her back, one hand coming up to carefully cup the back of her head and ease it into the crook beneath his chin. It was a simple gesture, but for Justin it was so highly charged with honest emotion that he closed his eyes against the sheer force of it.

Seconds ticked by, becoming minutes with silent progress. Cara let herself float on the bliss Justin's arms provided. But try as she may, she couldn't block the ugly scene from her mind. Smith's face loomed up behind her closed lids and a ripple of fear shuddered through her.

Justin felt the tremor and pulled her closer. He could well imagine her thoughts as his own were fervent with images and questions.

"Are you certain he did not hurt you?" he asked, his tone low and quiet. Beneath his chin, he felt her nod. "Your little cousin said she saw you leave just moments before I arrived at your door. Can you tell me what happened?"

"I went for a walk," she replied with a calm borrowed from the strength of Justin's arms. "I didn't even know he was there. He said he had matters to discuss with me."

Her voice dropped off and Justin mentally completed the picture.

"What were you doing out there?"

Fleeing from the thought of you. Suddenly, the horror of Smith's attack combined with the exhaustion of the past few weeks, and what little control she had crumbled. Without warning, she was wracked by sobs, tears spilling down her cheeks and soaking his shirtfront. "I . . . I wanted some privacy. Just a . . . a moment or two . . . without the fear." Her slim shoulders shook with her crying, her hands clenched the fabric of his shirt. "I can't go on, Justin . . ." she cried. "This . . . all of it . . . has to stop. I cannot bear to go on this way . . . living with the terror and the lies . . . and your hatred."

His chin resting atop Cara's head, Justin stared unseeing at the wall, her words cutting into him like sharp razors, her sobs filling him with remorse. During the entire time they had been executing their parts in his assignment, she had been living in abject fear, while he had callously ignored her anxieties and had used her as a target for his own frustrations.

Her words echoed in his mind. She believed he hated her, and who could blame her for feeling that way? From the very start, he had treated her abominably, and she had reacted by doing the unbelievable, she had fallen in love with him. That had been before she had learned the truth of his identity. Since then, she had regarded him with open hostility. Yet, in spite of her feelings, she had not betrayed him. It would have been an easy matter for her to have confided the affair in her cousin and thereby lay a trap for him and his contact. But she hadn't. Instead, she had placed herself in jeopardy to protect him.

"I don't hate you, Cara," he murmured close to her ear. Admired her, desired her, been angered to his very limits by her, but he had never, *never* hated her.

Cara blinked at the declaration, uncertain she had heard correctly. Choking on a sob, she levered away from his chest, her gaze lifting questioningly to his. "I thought . . ."

"I can well imagine what you thought. I am only sorry it has come to this."

Through the remnants of her tears, Cara carefully regarded Justin. His face was tender with emotion, his voice hoarse with regret. She had never known him to offer such genuine sentiment and it had her both confused and amazed.

It had Justin appalled. He yanked in his wayward emotions and rose to make his way to the foot of the bed. "I have sent for your cousin." He didn't sound as unaffected as he would have liked.

Still watching him intently, Cara nodded. "Thank you." Remembering suddenly the message she had never given him, she gave a mental shake and said, "If Bea is to be here shortly, then I must hurry. Your man was here several nights ago."

Justin's gaze snapped to her in silent question, his brows slanting into a frown, and Cara explained.

"He says you are to have your ship ready to sail in three weeks. And he will have his man here by that time."

"When was this?" Justin asked, glad to be able to direct his attention to something less treacherous than his feelings.

"Three days ago." She glanced to her lap, drawing her cloak more snugly about her. The same day he had seen her with Hunter and then accused her of all sorts of vile things. The same day he had kissed her, and her heart had . . . she didn't have the strength to prevent her eyes from filling up again.

"That was all he said," she announced abruptly, annoyed with the futility of hoping.

The door burst opened at Bea's entrance. One look at Cara's disheveled appearance and woeful expression and Bea turned wrathfully to Justin. "*What* have you done?" she demanded to know in her most imperious tone. Not waiting for a reply, she rushed to Cara's side, wrapping her arm protectively around Cara's shoulders. "Oh, Cara, what has he done to you?" she asked, her gaze never leaving Justin.

"Madam, had I done anything to her I would have hardly sent for you," Justin declared, irritated by the woman's assumption that he was to blame for Cara's present condition.

Bea showed no signs of believing him and Cara quickly intervened. "Bea, Justin . . . saved me."

With wide eyes, Bea looked to her cousin. As best as she could, Cara explained, but when her voice soon faltered, then ceased altogether, Justin continued for her. At his conclusion, Bea sat speechless and white-faced.

"I think it would be best if I left you now to tend to Cara," Justin added quietly.

As though coming out of a daze, Bea blinked. "Yes, you are quite right, Captain. I will send for a bath immediately."

Miserably, Cara watched Justin turn to leave. "Justin," she called.

He paused to gaze back at her forlorn countenance.

"Thank you."

Silently, he opened the door and left.

There was a great deal of discussion that night between John, Bea, and Cara as to where Cara was going to be spending her nights from now on. John insisted that she move into one of the tavern's upstairs rooms and Bea heartily agreed. Cara, on the other hand, politely, but firmly, refused. She was sincerely touched by their concern and she even admitted to herself that she would indeed feel safer under the Hawthorne's roof. But there was still the matter of her being available for Justin's contact that she could not ignore.

"I wish you would change your mind," John implored. "I don't like the idea that Smith is out there somewhere."

Propped up in her bed with the blankets pulled neatly to her shoulders, Cara smiled tiredly. "Smith will not bother me again. Justin saw to that this afternoon."

"We can only be thankful that Captain Reynolds happened along when he did," Bea said, fluffing an already-fluffed pillow behind Cara's head.

"I will be fine," Cara insisted. Noting neither John nor Bea looked convinced, she added, "Please, let me continue on in here. If you still feel the same in a few weeks, then I will move into the tavern."

John was far from satisfied, but he knew there would be no dissuading Cara. "Very well," he agreed, throwing up his hands in surrender. "But make sure you lock the door."

Readjusting the fall of Cara's blankets, Bea asked, "Are you quite certain, dear?"

"Yes, quite certain."

Exchanging a worried glance with her husband, Bea shook her head, then patted Cara's hand. "Good night then, Cara."

After the two were gone, Cara slipped from her bed to lock the door. Her fingers lingered on the cool metal of the lock. It had not prevented Justin's contact from entering. She could only pray it would be more effective against Bartholemew Smith should he decide to ignore Justin's warning.

That thought plagued her each night as she prepared for bed. But as the week progressed and Smith was not to be seen anywhere in the area, Cara began to relax. Determinedly, she refused to be intimidated by the memory of his attack, which hovered in a back corner of her mind. Not so easy to overlook was the thought of Justin's arms around her, his gentle words, the look on his face when he had said he was sorry. She took those memories to bed with her each night and slept, if not contentedly, then soundly.

Unfortunately, it was only a matter of days before that unbroken sleep was shattered by the arrival of "Liverpoole's man." It had been just over one week since his last "visit," and since his plans were set for two weeks hence, his presence was more alarming than usual.

"I didn't expect you for some time yet," Cara said, coming awake instantly at the urgent shake of her shoulder. She sat up, barely able to discern the man's position at the foot of her bed. "Is something wrong?"

"I wish I could tell you otherwise, but all our plans have gone awry."

Fear gripped Cara. "Justin?"

"He remains well, but not for long." Impatience edged the raspy voice. "I have no time to couch my words with niceties, madam, so listen well. There is a plot that would see your Captain Reynolds dead. We must act with all possible haste. Do you know of a man called Smith?"

Cara went still at the name. "Yes, yes, I know who he is."

"Then you must also know he is a dangerous man who is capable of any foul deed."

Cara needed no reminders. "Yes."

"He acts with the help of a group of other watermen, and a man named Olan Wright."

Shivers ran up Cara's arms when she remembered Wright's grotesque, one-eyed face.

"They mean to kill Captain Reynolds . . ."

"No!"

". . . and take his ship."

"What!"

"Once on board, they will train the guns back on the houses that line the James River."

It was almost too unbelievable for Cara to grasp. "They mean to fire on their own countrymen? Why?"

"It will have the appearance of a British attack. No one here is likely to stand for one more act of aggression by England. Smith, and especially Wright, will do anything as a means of killing the British."

"This doesn't make any sense," she declared. "How can they possibly think to get away with this? Justin won't allow them to take his ship."

"Captain Reynolds won't be available to protect his ship. A widow by the name of Taylor will see to it that he is lured from the scene. Without his command, the skeleton crew that safeguards the ship now won't be able fend off the attack."

"Taylor?" Cara gasped. "Regina Taylor?"

The whispery voice turned sour. "I see you know of her."

"Yes, we sailed together from England. She is a spiteful woman, but . . ." She struggled with disbelief. ". . . but I never thought her capable of something like this."

"Then think again, Miss Fairchild. This entire nasty scheme is of her making. Smith and Wright together don't have one quarter the brains needed to have conceived this plan, let alone carry it out. They follow her lead."

It was all too amazing. "Why?" Cara asked. "*Why* would Regina do this?"

"I have yet to find a rhyme or reason for her actions and I am unlikely to do so by Friday night."

"That is when this is all to take place," she concluded.

"Yes, so as you see, time is scarce."

Cara mentally ticked off the days. It was the early morning hours of Wednesday. Justin would have only two days to ready his ship. "I will tell Captain Reynolds of this as soon as it is light."

There was only a short silence before the man broached another matter. "There is one more thing, Miss Fairchild. You must be on the *Wind Dancer* when she sails."

Cara didn't think she could have possibly heard correctly. "I beg your pardon?"

"You are to leave with Captain Reynolds."

"Me? Whatever for?"

"You are in danger here, madam. Once Captain Reynolds leaves, you will be at risk. Smith is only biding his time to strike again. He will do so once the captain is no longer here to protect you . . . as he did some days ago."

Stunned, Cara stared through the darkness at the silhouette. "You . . . you know of that?" Her voice was a weak murmur.

"Yes," he replied harshly. "Mark my words, Miss Fairchild, I will see that he pays for this outrage to you."

That this man knew of Smith's assault was incredible. With the exception of herself and Justin, only Bea and John were aware of what had occurred. "How did you know?"

"Be on that ship," he ordered, ignoring her question.

"I can't possibly go back to England. I have nothing, no one to go back to."

"If you remain here, your safety will be forfeit," he insisted. "There must be someone who cares enough to see you provided for."

Justin had once demanded that she live with his grandmother, but his edict had been issued for the sake of his own convenience. And he certainly hadn't offered marriage after their one night together.

"Yes, someone cares. An entire family, and I am presently living in their cottage."

From the shadows came an exasperated grunt and Cara needed no light to know the man was becoming aggravated. "Miss Fairchild," he stated succinctly, "war is inevitable. As hot as things are in this area, the fight will very likely break loose over your stubborn little head."

She actually smiled, a sad, wistful grin. "As I have been told so often of late, I don't have a choice."

The man thought to argue, then changed his mind. "So be it, madam, but I urge you to have a care for yourself." He moved to the door. "I will not need to call upon you again." He paused, then finally added, "I hope . . . someday you will understand."

His parting left Cara sitting in complete confusion. Long after she was once again alone in the room, she pondered his cryptic statement.

Sleep was impossible, she didn't even try. By first light she was dressed, and by the time the sun had cleared the horizon, she was sitting beside Sam as he steered the buggy up the drive to Justin's house. The vehicle came to a stop before the steps and Cara hoped her hastily scrawled note to John would be explanation enough for her taking the buggy without his permission.

"Miss Cara," Percy declared, coming to the door in response to her knock. He cast a jaundiced eye first to her and then to the early morning sky. "What are you doing here?"

"I need to speak to Justin," she stated with an undeniable sense of purpose. "I know it is early, Percy, but I must see him. Now."

It took only one look at her set features to know something was wrong. Taking hold of her hand, Percy drew her into the foyer. "He's gettin' himself up. I'll tell him you're here."

"Percy." She stopped him at the foot of the stairs. "Tell him it's urgent."

The grizzled red brows lowered into a frown as he scanned her anxious face. He gave a single nod, then bounded upstairs.

Within minutes, Cara's gaze traveled two stories up and

found Justin on the landing. Wearing only a pair of black pants, he made his way to the stairway, applying a white towel to the lower half of his face as he went. Behind him came Percy, carrying boots and an assortment of clothing. Halfway down the stairs, Justin handed Percy the towel in exchange for a fresh white shirt.

Unable to help herself, Cara watched his powerful arms flex as he shrugged the garment on, hiding the broad expanse of chest with its mat of dark hair. She swallowed, hard, then hastily looked away.

"What's wrong?" he asked, coming to stand before her.

She gazed to his piercing eyes, her own filled with dread. She started to explain, halting when she remembered Percy's presence.

Seeing her glance hesitantly to Percy, Justin allayed her fears. "Say what you will, Cara. Percy knows it all."

She swallowed again, this time in dismay. "You are in grave danger, Justin."

Cara recounted all the information she had received early that morning. Sitting in Justin's study, with a cup of tea provided by Percy, she related every last detail of the plot to the two men. Her only omission was the contact's warning that she also leave. That, she decided, was something Justin did not have to know about.

When she had finished, the room was ominously quiet. Nervously, she nibbled on her lower lip, her eyes fastened on Justin, who stood leaning back against his desk, his arms crossed over his chest.

"Get everyone together," he ordered suddenly. "We sail as soon as it's dark on Friday. But keep it easy, I want no one to know what we're up to."

Percy didn't waste a minute. He strode from the room immediately.

In the wake of his departure, Cara felt like an intruder. Setting her cup aside, she murmured, "I . . . I should also leave." She lifted her gaze to Justin's and it came to her then. The crushing realization that this was the last time she would ever see him.

Justin openly studied her, his expression enigmatic. "Are you all right?" he inquired in a low voice.

No! You're leaving and I'm staying. "Yes."

"I want to thank you for all you have done."

I don't want your gratitude. I want your love. "You are welcome."

Cara felt her control slip, and she knew if she didn't leave now, she was going to make a fool of herself. But she lingered for just one more minute, drinking in the sight of him, memorizing his image to carry in her heart.

"Have a safe journey back," she whispered in a suffocated voice.

Stiffly, he nodded, his eyes boring into hers.

Please, say something, her heart cried. She waited for an eternally long second . . . hoping.

His silence was eloquent.

"Good-bye, Justin."

No matter how many times Cara told herself that Justin's leaving was for the best, she had to repeat it yet another time in order to convince her wayward heart that it was true. And when she was tempted to contemplate what might have been, she brutally reminded herself of their parting. She had stood there, dying inside, and he had let her walk out of the room, the house, his life. No, she was better off without Justin Reynolds. She was certain that if she repeated that thought to herself enough times, she would eventually believe it. However, by Friday night, it was still more an opinion than a conviction.

Business was unusually slow at the tavern that night. There were barely enough patrons to keep Lucy busy. At John's suggestion that Cara return to her cottage, Cara gratefully agreed. Her mind was distracted with images of the *Wind Dancer* sailing away and she doubted she would be of any use to John or Lucy.

Feeling dispirited and at odd ends, she entered the dark cottage, leaning back against the door for a brief moment. The routine of her night stretched before her, urging her to light the fire, take down her hair, change out of her dress.

With a sigh, she crossed to the fireplace and stoked the coals to a healthy glow before adding wood. Flames quickly caught, snapping and crackling. Satisfied, Cara turned, then gasped.

"Justin!"

"If you hadn't shown up in the next minute, I was going to go up there and drag you out of that tavern."

Shocked, Cara could only stare at his tall figure standing across the room. "What? . . ." Too many thoughts assailed her. "What are you doing here?" she finally managed to get out. "Why haven't you left yet?"

Justin's gaze sliced through the short space between them. "You made that impossible," he said grimly.

Her eyes widened. The tense line of his jaw, the implacable set of his features appeared ominous. "What do you mean?"

"I mean," he stated in a clipped tone, "that my ship is ready, my men are aboard, I was ready to sail and I couldn't." He stepped closer, his voice lowering. "Not without you."

Cara's insides wrenched. He wanted her to go back to England with him. But in what capacity? "You know how I feel about living with your grandmother. I won't be anyone's charity case."

"You won't be living with my grandmother," he told her in a growl.

Her heart sank. "I refused to be your mistress here. Do you honestly believe I will accept being kept in London?"

He took another step closer. When he spoke his voice was solemn. "I thought you might accept being my wife." In one stride, he closed the distance between them, taking her in his arms, staring down into her eyes. His mouth hovering above hers, he murmured, "Damn you, Cara, your answer had better be yes."

Through tears of joy, she smiled into his tense face. "Yes," she whispered. "Oh, Justin, yes."

The words had barely passed her trembling lips, and Justin's mouth came down on hers, caressing, demanding, wanting more than her yes, wanting all of her. With an urgency that betrayed all the pent-up emotion that had been playing havoc with his peace of mind, his arms tightened their hold, molding her slender curves against him.

Cara gave herself up to the headiness of his kiss, the enchantment of his embrace. Her hands curved over his shoulders, drawing him to her in a need to share all the love bursting within her heart.

"I love you," she whispered against his lips.

For a long moment, Justin remained silent, his darkened blue eyes taking in her radiantly glowing face. "I'm not sure I know what love is, Cara, but if it's this agony you've put me through for the past three months, than I am as afflicted as any man can be. All I know is that I want you with me, forever."

Smiling radiantly, Cara murmured, "That is love, Justin."

He bent his head for one more kiss, a meshing of lip and tongue, then reluctantly drew back. "We have to go."

As quickly as possible, they collected Cara's belongings, placing them in the same valise she had brought with her from England. With the threat of Smith's attack hanging over their heads, they hurried to the tavern for explanations and good-byes.

"Good heavens, Cara," Bea exclaimed. "This is so sudden." She turned to her husband as though seeking insight into some great mystery. "John? She's leaving."

John smiled broadly, and while he didn't quite understand the need for such a hasty departure, he was genuinely pleased for Cara. "Good luck to you both."

"Thank you, John," Cara returned. "I am going to miss you terribly."

"What shall I do without you?" Bea asked, still trying to grasp the situation.

"Cara," Justin interrupted kindly. "We must hurry."

Taking Bea's hands in her own, Cara smiled. "Thank you, Bea, for everything."

Bemused, but convinced by Cara's obvious joy, Bea said, "I'm sorry we will miss the wedding." She wrapped her arms about Cara for a hug, sniffing back the tears. "Take care of yourself, dear."

"I will," Cara promised. "Say good-bye to the children for me."

"Yes, yes, of course."

Moments later, Cara and Justin made their way down the familiar brick path to the stables where Justin's horse was tethered. Deftly, Justin tied Cara's bag behind the saddle, then mounted easily. Bending low, he lifted Cara before him, his arms holding her securely.

The ride to the *Wind Dancer,* moored in the James River behind Justin's house, was completed in near silence. Justin urged his steed swiftly down the dirt road, ever conscious of Smith's impending attack. Not wishing to disturb Justin in any way, Cara remained quiet, a mixture of happiness and apprehension rioting through her.

From a distance came the muted sound of a gun being fired. Pulling back on the reins, Justin drew his horse to a halt, listening. Under his suddenly tense weight, the animal danced nervously.

For a long moment, there was only silence, and then the night echoed with more gunfire, seemingly ripping through the surrounding trees.

Silently cursing, Justin sent his horse into a thundering gallop. Within minutes the house came into view, and beyond, the *Wind Dancer* still tied up to its dock.

The moon cast its light to a scene that brought a cry to Cara's lips. Men, too many to count, seemed to be everywhere. A mass, crowding the dock leading out to the ship, hurled lighted torches over the ship's rails and into its rigging. From the decks, Justin's crew returned gunfire and fought off the attackers trying to board. At the river's edge, men grappled in the reeds, and even as Justin's horse drew them closer, Cara couldn't discern friend from enemy.

Wasting no time, Justin urged his horse into the bordering woods, the sound of the animal crashing through the tangled underbrush combining with the shouts of wounded men and blasting guns. Cara tried to block out the wild sense of chaos that surrounded them, but the acrid smell of smoke mixed with the pungent odor of the sweating, frightened horse forced a reality too overwhelming to deny.

Justin drew his mount to a halt near the edge of the forest. There, he dismounted and lifted Cara down beside him. "Stay here," he ordered sharply. Capturing her chin, he lifted her face and drilled his gaze into hers. "Whatever you do, don't leave the cover of the trees." Quickly, his mouth covered hers in a fierce kiss, then he turned and raced for the dock.

A horrible sense of doom assailed Cara as she watched Justin's retreating figure. Her mind was held terror-stricken by the idea of losing him, especially now when they had so newly come to share their love. With horrified eyes, she saw Percy come to Justin's side, handing him both sword and pistol. Immediately, he was set upon by two men, but he deftly fought them off, leaving them both slumped on the ground.

"You and me got some unfinished business, little Miss English."

The voice came from just behind her. With a gasp, Cara whirled around, recognizing Smith's voice even before she saw his ugly face. Beside him lurked Olan Wright. And behind them both stood Regina.

The sight of the vicious woman momentarily snatched Cara's breath away. Ignoring both men, her gaze riveted on the one responsible for this catastrophe.

"Regina," Cara whispered, amazed and appalled by the woman's depravity.

Regina sauntered forward, her face contorted by hatred and a grim satisfaction. "Cara," she acknowledged darkly. "I was beginning to wonder when you two were going to show up."

Shaking her head in muted denial, Cara tried to make sense of it all. "Why, Regina?"

Unbelievably, Regina threw back her head and laughed, a harsh, grating sound, perfectly suited to the frenzied circumstances. "Because, you simple little bitch, you made a fool of me. You both did." Without warning, rage twisted her features into an ugly mask. "No one makes a fool of me!"

Scurrying forward, Wright interrupted. "We ain't got

time for no chat.'' The fight around him brought a crazed light to his eye.

''He's right,'' Smith agreed. Turning to Cara, he sneered. ''Your captain ain't goin' to be able to save you this time.''

It was a nightmarish repeat of their last encounter, only a hundred times more horrifying because Cara knew that in the end, Smith would see her dead.

Fear snaked up her spine, gripping her stomach and sending her heart to pounding. But she knew better than to try and talk her way out of this as she had done before. And she knew she had only one chance. Mentally apologizing to Justin, she lifted her skirts, turned and darted through the trees.

Regina's infuriated scream followed her as Smith, caught off guard, belatedly gave chase. Instinctively heading for the last place she had seen Justin, Cara broke free of the trees and ran for the river's edge. Heading straight into the thick of the fighting, she dodged fallen bodies, and sword clashing against sword, searching for some sign of Justin, but in the shadows of the ship, it was impossible to detect one man's identity from another.

Smith caught up just as Cara reached the river and she screamed in pure terror. His arm cruelly caught her around the waist and hauled her toward the dock. Her clenched fists striking out wildly and her legs kicking determinedly slowed Smith's progress enough to enrage him.

''You little bitch,'' he spat.

Angrily, he set her down, resorting to the one strategy he knew best. Savagely, he drew back his arm and backhanded Cara across the face.

Sight and sound coalesced in Cara's brain, producing a bright, flashing light and a dim, muted uproar. Unable to withstand the blow, she reeled backward, hitting the ground, dazed. The thought of trying to run actualized only after Smith was once again hauling her toward the dock, and a small boat tied to the pilings.

Justin fought like a man possessed. He had emptied his pistol only moments after Percy had handed it to him. With his sword and a wicked-looking knife, he fended off one waterman after another, fighting furiously to save his men and his ship.

From the left another man came at him, swinging a huge wooden club in a deadly arch aimed at his head. Deftly, he threw himself to the side, turned and pivoted low, then caught the man from behind, shoving him off the dock into the dark, frigid river.

Immediately, he turned and scanned the dock.

Olan Wright caught up with Smith and Cara. Clambering into the small, waiting boat, tied to the dock's pilings, he extended his gangly arms to take Cara from Smith's hands. Realizing their intent, Cara reacted with a violent thrashing of her legs, nearly catching Wright in the head and upsetting his precarious balance. His awkward movements nearly capsized the vessel.

Out of the darkness, Justin suddenly appeared on the dock beside them. His features set in a deadly mask, he snarled, "I told you once before what I'd do to you, Smith, if you ever touched her again."

Smith glared at his adversary, incensed with the lust to kill. Despite the feral gleam in the man's eyes, there was a score that had to be settled between them. Without warning, he flung Cara aside, then charged headlong at Justin.

Cara landed on the reed-covered bank as the two men crashed onto the dock. Scrambling up to solid ground, she watched, horrified, as they fought furiously. Vicious blows landed with crippling accuracy. Smith thought to use his greater bulk to his advantage, but Justin was possessed by an overpowering obsession to avenge the anguish Cara had suffered at Smith's hands.

With a pistol drawn, Olan Wright viewed it all from below, his stance bobbing with the boat's motion. Like a puny, ineffectual cyclops, he cackled a crazy laugh and leveled his weapon on the struggling duo, waiting for a clear shot at Justin.

Rolling across the wooden planks, Smith's hands locked around Justin's neck. Blood pounded through Justin's head, blurring his vision, but he repeatedly sent his fist into Smith's face. The powerful blows loosened the hold around his neck and he shoved the waterman aside. With painful breaths, Justin came to his feet and not waiting for Smith to make his next move took hold of the huge, bear of a man and delivered a devastating punch, just as Wright aimed and fired.

The ball seared Smith's head and he toppled backward off the dock, falling onto Wright. The force of the dead weight split the boat's flimsy hull, filling it with water. With the massive body bearing him downward, Wright screamed as he sank below the surface of the icy waters.

Cara rushed forward and threw herself into Justin's arms. Sobbing, she clung to him, unconsciously reassuring herself that he was alive and unharmed. "I thought he was going to kill you," she said in a distraught whisper, caressing his bruised cheek and dabbing at the blood on his chin with shaking fingers.

Realizing that the attack had ceased and that the remaining watermen had withdrawn, Justin held her firmly against his chest. Gently, he eased her tumbled hair back from her smudged face and gazed lovingly into her teary eyes. "Have you no faith in your future husband?" Grinning carefully, he said, "Let's go home."

Chapter Seventeen

Cara rolled over in bed, stretching languidly. Sleepily, she viewed the bedroom she was temporarily using as her own and mentally shook her head.

She sat up in the ornate four-poster, with its pierced and gilded cornice round the canopy and its yards of delicate, pink silk taffeta hangings. The inlay in the satinwood posts matched the intricate design on the armoire and dressing table. The pieces were beautifully crafted, complementing the highly embroidered pink drapes and the floral pattern woven into the plush carpet. All in all, the decor was light and airy and wonderfully feminine. It truly epitomized the Lady Lydia Gray.

Cara chuckled ruefully. After months of adamantly refusing to live with Justin's grandmother, she was doing just that. Of course, the circumstances were entirely different from those under which she had previously been expected to take up residency. She was staying with the Lady Gray not as a destitute orphan, but as Justin's fiancée.

At the thought, she gazed lovingly to the ring on her left hand and her heart swelled with love. A magnificent emerald, chosen by Justin to especially match her eyes, was surrounded with glittering diamonds. She had been astounded and deeply touched when he had placed it on her finger. She had never expected, nor did she need, such an extravagant symbol of their betrothal. His love was, would always be, all she could ever desire.

Slipping from beneath the covers, she stepped to the windows and eased back the drapes, letting in the bright May sunlight. How different, Cara thought, this promise of spring was from the rainy gloom she had witnessed when she had first pulled the curtains aside and peered into the garden below.

That had been a month ago. After a treacherous, six-week crossing, the *Wind Dancer* had docked in London, none the worse for wear. Justin had brought her to his grandmother's town house at once and had promptly introduced her as his wife to be. In her mind, Cara could still picture the scene . . .

"Justin!" the Lady Lydia Gray exclaimed, rising from the settee upon which she had been sitting. Joyously, she watched her grandson enter her parlor, escorting a lovely, but unknown young woman. "When did you return?"

"Just this moment," Justin replied, placing a light kiss on her cheek.

Taken aback by the gesture, Lydia stared in surprised confusion to her grandson, who in all his thirty-four years had studiously avoided such displays of affection. "How absolutely wonderful to see you."

"Well, I am sure we are a sight. We have just come from the ship, but I wanted to introduce you." Turning, he caught Cara's hand and drew her forward. "Grandmother, may I present Cara Fairchild."

The name struck a chord in the elderly woman's mind. "Yes, yes, from Fairfield, wasn't it? How do you do, Miss Fairchild?"

"Very well, madam," Cara replied politely.

Openly curious on several counts, Lydia took her seat, waving a hand in graceful invitation for Cara to sit beside her. "I confess, Miss Fairchild, that I was disappointed when I was informed by your solicitor several months back that your plans would be taking you to America."

Justin laughed wryly, taking a seat opposite them. "I am afraid I made those arrangements before I was aware of Miss Fairchild's intentions."

Cara smiled uncertainly, hoping she had done nothing to offend this woman who was held in such special regard by Justin. "I hope my decision did not in any way inconvenience you."

"No, not at all," Lydia assured her graciously, shrugging prettily. "I had anticipated the company, that is all." Her faded blue eyes shifted from Cara to Justin, then back. "Have your plans once again changed?" she asked, doing nothing to hide the note of expectation in her voice.

"You are being obvious, Grandmother," Justin chided warmly. "But yes, Cara's plans have changed." He openly regarded Cara with an intimate look. "With your permission, Cara needs to reside here temporarily. I didn't think you would object."

"Object? Of course not," Lydia declared happily, not missing Justin's distinct interest in Cara or his use of her first name. She turned to Cara again. "I would love to have you as my guest for as long as you wish to visit."

"Thank you, madam," Cara returned, sincerely grateful for the woman's thoughtfulness.

"Her visit will not be all that long, Grandmother," Justin advised with an ill-concealed smile.

"Oh?" Lydia gave him a questioning look.

"No, for several weeks at the most. Just until we can arrange to be married."

He dropped the announcement like a bomb and Lydia reacted accordingly. With a cry, she pressed her blue-veined hands to her lips. For too long she had dreamed of this for Justin. Could she dare hope that love was involved?

"This is wonderful, Justin, simply wonderful." She smiled, her voice full of emotion. Taking Cara's hand, she patted it affectionately. "I can't tell you how pleased I am. And I will have to have the whole story from you, but not until I have seen you properly settled in. . . ."

Cara let the curtain fall back into place. It had taken her no time at all to settle in. Lydia had seen to that. Cara smiled. Justin's grandmother was a treasure, and in the past few weeks, Cara had come to genuinely care for the gentle lady.

For Cara, Lydia was the doting grandmother she had never had, while in Cara Lydia had found a kind, compassionate young woman who made her grandson happier than she had ever known him to be. The perfect recipient for her penchant to pamper and spoil.

With a tug at the bellpull, Cara rang for Molly, the personal maid assigned as her own. Within minutes, the curly-headed young woman answered the summons.

"Good morning, miss. I didn't think you would be up as yet. It's barely seven o'clock."

"Mmmm, I know," Cara replied, already brushing out her hair before Molly had a chance to get to the brush. "But the morning sun was so bright and beautiful that I was anxious to start my day."

"You say that every morning," Molly said, beginning to lay out clothes. "Even if it's raining."

Cara couldn't deny it. "That's because I do so look forward to each day."

Molly smiled to herself, knowing full well that Miss Cara really meant she looked forward to being with the earl. And who could blame her? Every day when he came to the house, it took Molly's breath away just to look at the man.

"Which dress do you wish to wear today, miss?"

Pursing her lips, Cara mentally considered her choices, and there were a great many now. Lydia was responsible for that.

Cara had arrived with only her meager assortment of clothing, most of which were in terrible condition. Lydia had taken one look at the worn and faded garments, which even a thorough laundering couldn't revive, and declared the entire lot ready for the fires.

With all the panache of one accustomed to wealth and its resulting privileges, Lydia had sent for her dressmaker to create an entire new wardrobe befitting the future Countess of Ellsworth. Cara had protested adamantly, uncomfortable with such an expensive gift.

"Cara," Lydia had remarked, on the verge of looking hurt. "This is something I wish to do for you. I have wanted Justin's happiness for so long and you are the answer to my prayers. Please, do not take this joy away from me."

Cara had detected a certain degree of blackmail in the entire matter, but to have refused would have been akin to pulling the wings from a butterfly.

And, there was also Justin's position in London society to contend with. Once it became known that the Earl of Ellsworth was betrothed, invitations of every sort came flooding in. Cara had the sense to realize that no ordinary dress, the kind she was accustomed to wearing, would suffice for the type of functions she and Justin would be attending. She learned quite quickly that Justin occupied one of the more elite positions among the *ton,* and in doing so, was expected to maintain a certain image. She would do nothing that would reflect poorly on him or cause him embarrassment.

Knowing Justin wold be joining her for breakfast, she chose an elegant morning gown she had not as yet worn. Of forest green muslin, it had short, puffed sleeves, slashed with lace. Its high waist fitted snugly beneath her breasts, accentuating their fullness revealed by the low, square-cut bodice.

"Oh, miss, you are a sight," Molly sighed, putting the finishing touches on Cara's hair, which was swept up into intricate twists and fastened with jade clasps.

Sitting before her mirror, Cara silently contemplated the effect of the dress's décolletage, cut lower than those of most of her dresses. Even though she had become accustomed to the revealing style of her more fashionable gowns, this dress made her hesitate and consider if perhaps she shouldn't change in favor of a more modest neckline.

"The earl will just love this gown," Molly offered, seeing the reflection of her mistress's troubled gaze fastened on her curves.

Startled, Cara glanced up to Molly's image in the mirror. "You don't think . . . it's just a bit . . . revealing."

"That I do, which is just why his lordship is going to like it," the plucky maid declared. "With him leaving for his home until the wedding, this will give him something to remember you by."

Pinkening, Cara nonetheless rose from the table and went below, deciding it was too late to change now.

At the foot of the stairs, she was greeted by the butler and informed that Lady Gray had not yet arisen, but that his lordship had just arrived and was waiting in the dining salon.

Delighted, Cara thanked him, then walked down the short hall and quietly let herself into the room Lydia reserved for private meals.

Justin was standing at one of the windows, something outside having caught his attention. For a few moments, Cara simply stood back and let herself admire the magnificent man who would soon be her husband. The thought swelled her heart with love. She still found it difficult to believe that she and Justin were going to be married in less than two weeks. At times it seemed less than real, and if she were to pinch herself, she would awaken and find it all nothing but a dream.

There was nothing dreamlike, however, about the man before her. Justin was very, very real. Dressed in a dove gray jacket that accentuated the breadth of his shoulders, and snug black pants delineating the long line of his muscular legs, he was the epitome of bold masculinity. His pure white cravat framing the sharp line of his jaw, and his hair rakishly falling about his forehead, intensified his sensual looks to such a degree that Cara felt her heart begin to race.

"Is it interesting?" she asked from across the room.

Justin's head snapped around, his smile indicating just how glad he was to see her. "Is what interesting?"

"Whatever has caught your attention out that window," she remarked, coming forward with her words.

His gaze dropped to her lush curves enticingly displayed above her bodice. "Nothing so interesting as what I see in this room."

Beneath the heavy weight of his stare, she felt herself blush.

Justin strode forward to meet her. "You might want to learn to control that," he drawled.

"Control what?"

"Your tendency to blush."

Her hands flew to her cheeks. "Justin, it's something I've never been able to regulate. Is my face all that bright?"

His eyes dropped pointedly. "It wasn't your face that concerned me."

Cara's gaze plunged to her chest and she groaned in mortification. She was blushing from her breasts up.

Justin's arms slipped around the small of her waist to draw her close. "Not that I mind, love, but I would just as soon this charming little reaction be reserved solely for me."

With his arms holding her so near, the feel of his firm chest pressed to the softness of hers, it was impossible to concentrate on the matter at hand. Her hands linked behind his neck. "All my responses are reserved for you," she murmured distractedly.

"There is one in particular that I am most impatient to receive," he whispered thickly, his mouth hovering just above hers.

Her blush intensified, but riding on the extravagant longing he was so effortlessly making her feel, she gazed steadily into the heated blue depths of his eyes. "They say patience has its own rewards."

Forsaking patience for the moment, Justin captured her lips, slanting his mouth over hers. With little coaxing, his tongue parted her lips, thrusting within her mouth, teasing, tormenting, until Cara thought her insides would melt and her knees would buckle. Her hands clung tightly to the corded muscles of his shoulders as she instinctively pressed her body to his. Deep in his throat, Justin groaned at the exquisite torture that demanded to be assuaged. One hand slipped to the small of her back to press her intimately to his hardened length.

"How many days until the wedding?" he asked hoarsely, his mouth trailing a molten path down her neck.

"Twelve," she choked, her head tipped to one side, her eyes closed at the rapturous sensations shooting down into the pit of her belly.

"I could arrange to make it tomorrow." His long fingers cupped one breast.

"Justin . . ." She was rapidly losing control. "The servants . . . Lydia might come in any minute."

"I'm not done," he growled. And having said so, he freed her breast from the confines of her clothes. Bending his head, he drew the taut nipple into his mouth.

Cara arched uncontrollably. Desire licked at her insides, building with each kiss and caress. "We . . . shouldn't even be in here alone." She tried to sound stern, but her words were more of a sigh.

Justin heard the throaty reminder and clenched his eyes in a bid for control. Concentrating on bringing his desire to heel, he was amazed at his own self-restraint. Then again, he was truly astounded with his own actions of late. Ever since he had asked Cara to marry him, he had been besieged by the most incredible attack of propriety. As his future wife, his countess, he suddenly wanted her to be treated not as some common mistress, but with all the dignity and honor of a cherished spouse. And that meant, much to his own regret, consummating the marriage *after* the wedding.

Needless to say, the journey back to England had at times felt like a quest. And it didn't make the situation any easier to bear when the gowns she wore had only an excuse for a bodice.

Wrapping his arms loosely about her shoulders, he declared, "If I live through the next fortnight, it will be either a miracle or a testimony to my ability to withstand pain."

"Pain?" Cara asked, searching his face with eyes still glazed with passion.

Justin chuckled, shaking his head ruefully. "There is only so much of *this* a sane man can endure," he explained.

Understanding dawned in Cara's mind and she smiled sheepishly. "In that case, my lord, I suggest we have breakfast."

Lydia joined them a few minutes later, lovely in a heavily frilled gown that only she could possibly wear, and get away with. The coral silk complemented her coloring, but it was Justin's presence that put the sparkle in her eyes.

As could be expected, the major topic of discussion was the upcoming wedding, which was to take place at Wyndham, Justin's country seat. The invitations had been sent out weeks before; Cara's gown had been created in record time and sent on ahead; menus, flowers, and endless details had been seen to by Justin's experienced and capable staff.

"When do you leave for Wyndham?" Lydia asked Justin, as the footman removed the last of the plates and soundlessly exited the room.

"In about an hour, which makes me late," he replied, laying aside his napkin and pushing back his chair. "My things are being packed and loaded even as we speak."

Cara let her gaze linger on his handsome features. "I'm going to miss you."

"But not for long," he assured her. "You two will follow next week." He winked broadly. "Besides, someone has to make sure your gown arrives safely." Rising, he came around the table to stand beside her chair. Gently, he pulled her to her feet and gave her a tender kiss good-bye. "Take care, love," he ordered quietly.

Her eyes shining, Cara whispered, "I love you."

In answer, he lightly skimmed his knuckles over her cheek.

"And you, my dear grandmother," he added, stepping to her seated figure. "Behave yourself." He bent low to kiss the top of her head.

Cara watched from the window as he drove off in his coach. In his absence, the room was suddenly empty. Hugging her arms about her waist, she wondered how she had ever thought she could live without him.

With a wistful smile, she turned back to Lydia and found the faded blue eyes overflowing with tears. Alarmed, Cara rushed to kneel at her side.

"Lydia, what is it?"

Through her tears, Lydia took in Cara's anxious expression. "Nothing, Cara. Absolutely nothing."

"Then why are you crying?"

Lydia tried to collect herself. "I told you once that you were the answer to my prayers. But the truth is, you must be an angel sent by God."

Cara shook her head in denial. "Lydia, I am far from being an angel."

Dabbing at her eyes with her napkin, Lydia disagreed. "You don't know, you just don't know the change that's come over Justin, and it's all your doing." She sniffed back the last of the tears and took a watery sigh. For a moment she gazed at Cara, then shook her head. "I feared for him, Cara. I feared that he would go through life cynical and angry and incapable of loving anyone."

Cara nervously toyed with the fabric over Lydia's knees. "I know he loves me, Lydia. I can see it in the way he looks at me." She gazed up with suddenly troubled eyes. "But he has yet to tell me. I know it has something to do with his parents and how he was raised."

Lydia's shoulders slumped and for the first time since Cara had known her, she looked tired. "I'm not certain he'll ever be able to actually say the words, Cara. I suppose I am to blame for that."

"You?"

"As much as I would like to deny it, I am in part responsible for Justin being the way he is today. If I hadn't been such an indulgent parent with his mother, perhaps she would have loved Justin. I loved my daughter, my husband and I both did. She was the joy of our lives and we did whatever we could to grant her every wish." She gave a humorless laugh and her voice turned flat. "Unfortunately, after she was married, she didn't wish to be a mother."

Lydia was silent for a long moment, and sensing that she was struggling with shadows from the past, Cara gently squeezed her hand. Finally, Lydia continued, her voice marginally stronger.

"It's a terrible thing to say about one's own daughter, but Margaret was not a . . . faithful wife. It broke my heart to see her engage in all her nasty little liaisons. And poor little Justin so desperately wanted and needed the love and attention of his parents, especially his mother. I did what I could, whenever I was about, but it wasn't enough. Margaret never told him she loved him. Not until it was too late and she . . . she didn't know what she was doing."

Cara's eyes searched the pale, distraught face and saw some terrible secret reflected there. "What happened to your daughter?" she asked quietly.

Unexpectedly, Lydia drew herself up straight, sitting back tall in her chair, her chin elevating disdainfully. "She got the pox. Does that shock you? I can tell you it did me. It shouldn't have, considering her behavior, but it did. It affected her mind and in her last months, she had to be confined to her bed. By then, she had lost all touch with reality, babbling, crying for hours on end for no discernible reason. But worst of all, she began telling Justin she loved him, pleading with him to be her lover. He was only twenty-one at the time, and rarely around, but during those few times he came to check on her, she created the most terrible scenes."

Cara closed her eyes in remorse. All his young life, Justin had wanted his mother's love. What he had received was a mad version of what he had so desired.

"I know Justin blames himself for his mother's death," Lydia said.

Cara's eyes snapped open in shock. "What?"

"I don't suppose he told you of how Margaret died."

"No," Cara whispered. "He has only ever spoken of her once and then very briefly."

"That is understandable. He carries such burdens because of her."

"What happened?"

Lydia's lips twitched at the memory. "Margaret was dying, the doctor had said it would be only a matter of days. We all felt compelled to be near. You understand that Margaret had no idea what she was doing." She hesitated, her face crumbling in anguish. "She tried to seduce Justin."

In stunned surprise, Cara's mouth fell open.

"He was retiring for the night. She left her room while the nurse had gone to fetch more water and came upon Justin at the second-story landing. He did what he could to ward her off, but Margaret became angry, shouting that she loved him. She attacked him. In the struggle, she fell down the stairs and broke her neck."

"My God," Cara whispered.

Lydia nodded in agreement. "He was never a demonstrative person, always aloof and proud. But after Margaret's death, he became almost detached from others, cynical and arrogant, using people. He poured all his energies into his ships and his properties, but never into people, least of all women. And he had to control everything about him. The only thing he found he couldn't control was death."

Kneeling at Lydia's knees, Cara thought back to Charles Taylor's passing. At the time she hadn't understood Justin's distressing reaction, but now it all made terrible sense. He was still fighting the private demons of his mother's death. Charles's dying had only intensified his already profound feelings.

"I'm sorry I had to tell you all of this, Cara," Lydia murmured with a sad smile. "But now you know why I think you are the very best thing to have ever happened to Justin. Somehow, you broke through to his heart and made him whole again."

With tears shining in her eyes, Cara returned Lydia's smile. "All I did was love him, Lydia. I will always love him."

* * *

The day of the wedding dawned bright and clear over Wyndham. Servants bustled about in preparation of the momentous occasion. The hundreds of guests that filled all the guest rooms in the ninety-room house waited expectantly to witness the gala event. The groom's grandmother flitted from one spot to another, like a lovely butterfly, checking and double-checking on every last detail. The groom took a morning ride on his favorite horse, some said to alleviate a case of prewedding nerves, before retiring to his apartment to bathe and dress for the late afternoon ceremony in the ancient twelfth-century church.

Only the bride seemed unaffected by the excitement going on around her. Cara floated through the hours on a cloud of bliss as maids scurried in and out of her rooms, readying her toilette. A smile of utter contentment graced her lips while Molly arranged her hair and then helped her into her gown of flowing lace. And when she serenely walked down the long aisle of the church to join Justin, her face positively glowed with a radiant beauty that brought a collective sigh from most of the assembled guests.

Cara had waited for this day for months. Justin had waited a lifetime. When the minister pronounced them man and wife, they gazed into each other's eyes and saw all their hopes and dreams realized.

The dinner that followed was sumptuous; the music and dancing, delightful. Justin and Cara thoroughly enjoyed the celebration and accepted congratulations from all. But as soon as it was politely possible, Justin filled two long-stemmed glasses with champagne, gave one to Cara and led her from the ballroom.

"I feel as though we're deserting them." Cara chuckled as they ascended the winding stairway.

Slipping his arm around her waist, Justin said with a wicked grin, "We are."

She turned a shaming glance on him and he pulled her closer.

"If we didn't desert them, love, they would think I was not in full possession of my wits. As it is, I'm not certain after having seen you that half the men don't already think I'm touched for waiting as long as I did."

At the top of the stairs, they turned down the hall to the left and entered Justin's bedroom. Curiously, Cara looked around, noting the twin sofas placed before the marble-tiled fireplace. Her eyes touched briefly on the tables and cabinets, but studied with interest the huge four-poster bed on the far wall.

"Your things have been moved into your room next door," Justin said, nodding to the door that connected his chambers to hers.

Suddenly, the reality of the wedding *night* hit Cara and a multitude of questions ran through her mind. The last time she and Justin had made love, they hadn't been married. Now she was his wife and she wondered if she was supposed to do anything differently. Uncertainly, she took a sip of champagne.

Wondering at the hesitation he saw on her face, Justin came to stand beside her. Setting both glasses down on a nearby table, he took her cool hand in his and led her to one of the sofas, where he drew her down onto his lap.

"Are you nervous?" he asked gently.

She smiled sheepishly, lifting one shoulder in an elegant shrug. "No. But I was wondering if there is some custom or social dictate that I should be performing now."

In dubious humor, one of Justin's dark brows flicked upward.

"Not that," she explained hastily, her face taking on a rosy hue. "I . . . I mean, I don't know what I'm supposed to do now."

Justin smiled indulgently. "You could start by relaxing," he suggested. Unable to resist, he traced the curve of her lips. "And by kissing me."

Cara needed no coaxing. Sliding a hand up his chest, she leaned forward to press her lips to his. The warm pressure of his mouth was reassuring. It was also arousing, stirring up the heat of desire within her. Unconsciously, she deepened the kiss.

"Your maid is waiting in your room to help you with

your clothes," he murmured thickly, that one kiss igniting his long-starved passions.

Cara remained where she was, reluctant to leave his lap. If etiquette dictated that she retire to her room and have Molly help her out of her clothes, then she supposed she ought to go. In a moment or two. After one more kiss.

Her gaze lowered to his firm mouth, lingered, then rose to his eyes. At the innocently seductive glance, Justin groaned low in his throat, but the sound was absorbed when Cara pressed her lips to his again.

Desire ripped through Justin and he immediately pulled her tightly against him. After six months of waiting to claim her again as his own, he was not about to stand on ceremony and send her off to her room to change into a gown that he was only going to remove. Her hair would come down, her dress would come off. He would see to that.

Cara had initiated the kiss, but Justin quickly took control. He slipped a hand up to cup the back of her head, while his lips teased and caressed. One by one, he pulled the pins from her hair until the silken mass tumbled around her shoulders and down her back like the shimmering veil she had worn that afternoon.

Leaning back, he took in the seductive picture she made and the ache in his loins increased. Against the backs of her thighs, Cara felt the evidence of his arousal and a corresponding need grew within her.

Acting purely on instinct, she untied his cravat, unwinding the white cloth then letting it float to the floor. She experienced a twinge of doubt at her boldness, but Justin, highly attuned to every flicker of emotion that crossed her face, raised her hand back to the buttons on his shirt.

The surge of feminine power Cara felt was like a heady wine, acting on her senses, adding to her courage. With a grin flirting at her lips, she unbuttoned his shirt and waistcoat before spreading both garments wide to bare his chest. Lovingly, her fingers slowly slipped through the mat of dark hair, sending delicious ripples through Justin, and against her palm, Cara felt the rapid beat of his heart.

He sucked in his breath at her touch and instantly made

a decision. He lifted her from his lap, set her on the sofa, and strode through the connecting door into her room. Within minutes, he was back.

"What did you do?" she asked.

Justin made his way around the room, extinguishing the candles until only two were left glowing. "I dismissed your maid," he said, coming to stand before her.

Cara had no way of knowing that Molly had been utterly shocked by not only Justin's curt dismissal, but also his half-unbuttoned clothing. But even if Cara had known, she wouldn't have cared. Her only thought was of her husband.

Justin removed his jacket and waistcoat and laid them aside. Gently, he pulled Cara to her feet and turned her around to unfasten the row of tiny buttons down her back. Ever so lightly, he trailed a line of kisses down her neck, easing the gown off her shoulders to pool at her feet. With expert hands he removed her undergarments until she was clad in only a clinging white chemise, her lush curves and tempting shadows seductively displayed to Justin's heated gaze.

For a moment he stood mesmerized by her beautifully flushed face. With exquisite care, he traced a finger over her cheek and down her neck to the fullness of her breast, drawing a delicate circle around the nipple until it hardened beneath the gossamer fabric. Waves of pleasure washed through Cara's entire body, creating an almost painful ache too luscious to bear. Almost desperately, her hands came up to stop the intimate teasing, but rather than ease his hand away, she pressed it firmly against her breast.

Justin's pulse pounded in his veins and he suddenly wanted her free of the last of her clothes. With a pull of the ribbons he removed the thin chemise.

Self-consciously, Cara tried to shield herself from his view, but he moved her hands aside and drank in the sight of her. Her skin glowed, the mellow light touching on her high breasts, flat belly, and slender thighs.

"My wife, my beautiful wife," he whispered, as though he couldn't believe she was really his. Tenderly, he picked her up and carried her to his bed, laying her on the cool sheets.

Cara lay back and watched as Justin removed his clothes. As each article fell to the floor, she was reminded of how magnificent he was. She remembered, too, how wonderful it was to be held close to that tall, lean body and she held her arms out in a silent beckoning.

All the love and desire Cara felt was reflected in that one gesture and Justin reacted to it like a moth to a flame. Lowering himself beside her, he gathered her close, her arms circling his shoulders and clinging tightly. His mouth covered hers, slanting insistently back and forth as his hand came up to caress her breast, stroking and teasing the nipple to a hard little bud.

Delicious sensations swirled into Cara's belly and she arched upward seeking more. And Justin gave it to her. His mouth left hers to kiss the pulse beating at the base of her throat, while his hand slid along her ribs to her belly and circled her waist. Lowering his head to the soft roundness of her breasts, he kissed one and then the other until Cara thought she would die from wanting. He sensed her longing and took one of her nipples into his mouth, lavishly stroking it with his tongue. A low groan sounded deep in Cara's throat, passed over her lips, and was captured by Justin's mouth as his lips came back to hers.

Cara's senses were reeling. Her hands caressed Justin's broad shoulders and lean-waisted back, trying to draw him as close as possible. Her lips clung to his, her tongue delving into his mouth driving Justin mad with longing.

As much as Justin wanted to prolong the torturous ecstasy, his restraint was rapidly dwindling. His body was ravenous for hers and demanded that he take her soon. His hand slipped down to the juncture of her thighs and gently parted her legs. His fingers unerringly found the soft, warm center of her and he knew he couldn't wait another minute. Carefully he stroked the tender flesh, caressing intimately, knowing she was more than ready for him.

Bracing his weight on his forearms, he eased his hips against hers. Cara felt a moment of fear at the thought of the pain that was to come. She instinctively started to tense, then sighed in rapture when she felt the hard, warm length of him enter her and begin a slow, rhythmic thrusting that brought only pleasure. She clung to his back, her hips rising to meet his, and the tight knot of pressure grew within her. Her breaths came out in frantic little gasps that matched Justin's labored breathing. He deepened his thrusts and Cara felt the tension increase unbearably, tighten and finally burst within her.

Justin gloried in her pleasure. Urgently, he thrust into her arched body one last time, then lost himself as the feel of her sweet pulsing took him over the edge.

It was a long time before Justin eased himself from Cara's body. When he did, he rolled to his back and pulled her into the crook of his arm. Tenderly, he caressed the small of her back, the satin skin of her arm, and finally kissed her forehead.

Looking up into his eyes, Cara smiled, awed by the fact that he was hers. "Husband," she whispered.

"Wife," he returned.

Closing her eyes, she shook her head at a sudden memory.

"What is it?" he asked, wanting to know what was going on in her mind.

Shyly, she looked back. "I never thought I would ever be saying that to you. At times I believed it was all quite hopeless."

Justin truly regretted his treatment of her and cursed his own stupidity. Hugging her to him, he asked, "Can you forgive me, love? I was a complete fool."

"I think you are the wisest man I know," she returned loyally. "After all, you had the sense to marry the one woman who loves you more than life itself."

Her declaration shot to Justin's heart and he tightened his arms about her. He had thought to live his life void of any real emotion, but here she was in his arms, giving him all the good that was in her.

He faced a truth at that moment, a truth he had tried to

avoid, ignore, and even run from. Lying naked with his soul stripped bare by her words of love, he realized that she was his destiny. From the moment his solicitor had first mentioned her name, he had been destined to share her life, forever. He pressed another kiss to her forehead and vowed he would have it no other way.

Chapter Eighteen

Cara lay on her side and stared at the man who had only the day before become her husband. Sleep, she decided, did not in any way detract from his masculine appeal.

She eased herself higher on her pillow and winced at a twinge that reminded her of the night just past. She and Justin had made love repeatedly, taking each other to glorious heights, until replete and exhausted she had fallen into a deep and dreamless sleep. It had been the most perfect night of her life.

She gazed at Justin's sleep-softened features and a wistful smile touched her lips. Only one thing could have made the night more wonderful than it had been, and that would have been for Justin to have told her that he loved her. She had no doubts that he did. Despite her limited experience, feminine intuition told her that Justin had been expressing with his body what he couldn't with words.

Unable to help herself, she placed her hand on his chest,

directly over his heart. Love was new to him, and like anyone dealing with the unfamiliar, Justin needed time to understand love, to learn from it and to trust in it. And while he discovered all there was to know, she would be by his side, showering him with her own love.

"Why are you awake?" he asked, his sleep-roughened voice breaking into Cara's reverie.

She looked up to find him openly watching her. "I couldn't sleep," she murmured contentedly.

"You should be able to. I thought I wore you out last night."

Draping herself over his chest, Cara rested her hand on his firm muscles and propped her chin on the back of her hand. "That was last night," she replied with a coquetry she had found during the early morning hours.

Amused interest danced in Justin's eyes. "And this morning?" he drawled suggestively, brushing a long strand of hair back over her shoulder.

"I think I might need some help falling asleep."

Justin's arms circled about her. Smiling wickedly, he promised, "I can help you with that."

After a thoroughly self-indulgent morning, Cara and Justin rose to retire to their separate dressing rooms to bathe and dress before leaving on their honeymoon. By the time they were ready, it was nearly noon, and since neither had feasted on food for breakfast, they met in Justin's private study for lunch.

Cara entered the book-lined chamber just off Justin's bedroom, and found Justin already sitting at a small table set formally for two. At her entrance, he stood and held out a hand in invitation.

"I was beginning to wonder if you had gotten lost between your room and mine." He placed a kiss on the corner of her mouth before holding her chair for her.

"I'm sorry if I am tardy, but Molly was all thumbs this morning. Actually she seemed quite nervous."

Justin smothered a laugh at the thought of the poor

maid's shocked expression last night when he had suddenly appeared in Cara's bedroom instead of Cara.

"I'm sure it's just postwedding jitters," he informed her knowingly as he took his seat opposite hers. "It probably has something to do with the fact that she is now maid to the Countess of Ellsworth."

She wrinkled her nose at the use of her new title. "That is going to take some getting use to. All I wanted to be was your wife."

He plucked a bottle of wine from the wine table and filled their glasses. "Yes, well you now have other responsibilities."

During the course of the past few months, Cara had learned of the extent of Justin's enormous wealth, including his possession of five estates and a town house. The idea of being the mistress of all those properties was mind-boggling.

"You do intend to lend your support," she hinted broadly, one of her brows lifting inquiringly. "After all, I've only been a countess for one day and you are very much the landed gentry. It will take me some time to become familiar with all your homes."

"Actually, I was referring to another matter."

"Oh?"

With his elbow resting on the chair's arm, Justin's hand came up to idly stroke his chin. "Yes. What I was referring to was your obligations as a property owner."

Cara's brow knitted with a frown. Nonplussed, she regarded his serious face.

From beneath his chair, Justin lifted a flat, rectangular box, all neatly tied up with an elegant gold ribbon. Without a word, he placed the small package on Cara's plate set before her.

"What is this?" she asked, his suddenly solemn mien as surprising as the gift before her.

"My wedding gift to you," he said quietly.

Deeply moved, Cara gazed at her husband then to the box. With her lower lip clenched between her teeth, she drew the ribbon away and lifted the lid. Inside, she found a packet of papers and curiously she lifted them out to examine them more closely.

Suddenly, her eyes filled with tears and her hands began to tremble. "Oh, Justin," she whispered incredulously, rereading the documents that made her sole owner of Fairfield.

"Since it was Fairfield that brought us together, I thought it only fitting that you should have it back."

Laying the papers aside, Cara left her chair and threw herself into Justin's arms, tears and laughter making speech impossible. Half-sitting, half-lying against him, she wrapped her arms around his neck and kissed him full on the mouth. Absently, she thought there really was something special about expressing love without words.

For Cara, who wished to savor every minute of being Justin's wife, the first two months of marriage flew by. They honeymooned at Justin's most isolated estate on the northernmost shores of Scotland. In the small, sixteenth-century castle, the newlyweds disengaged themselves from all the trappings of society. They explored the local rivers, played in the tempestuous sea, rode over the green pastures, and reveled in each other's joy. They made love with a frequency that made Cara blush, but which left both her and Justin contented and happy.

It was a time of great discovery for Cara. She saw every facet of Justin's personality, from the businessman who managed each detail of his fleet of trading ships, to the considerate husband who was solicitous of her every comfort. It became apparent to Cara rather quickly just how complex her husband truly was. And whether he was the demanding entrepreneur, a lusty lover, or her best friend, she loved him with all her heart.

For the first time in his life, Justin learned what it meant to love and be loved. In all that she did, Cara gave of herself totally and without reservation, and he was amazed to realize that she derived her greatest pleasure from making him happy. Astonishingly, he found himself obsessed with doing all he could to insure *her* happiness. It was a delightful circle, one that was reflected in all they did.

By the end of August, Cara was knee-deep in her plans to renovate Fairfield. Justin had set up an account entirely for that purpose and she put it to use immediately. The small parlor off Justin's study in their town house in London became Cara's office where she met with architects, decorators, and bankers.

On a particularly beautiful September morning, Cara woke later than usual. Justin had kept her awake into the early morning hours making love and she was still pleasantly tired.

She glanced to the empty place beside her. Justin had risen hours earlier, placing a light kiss on her lips before leaving for a morning of meetings with several investors. She had roused briefly, noted the time on the nearby clock, and then promptly fallen back to sleep.

According to that same clock, Cara realized it was now past ten, and since she was supposed to meet with Lydia for a late lunch, she had better start her day.

Bathed and dressed, she descended the stairway and was greeted immediately by a perturbed-looking Daniels, the butler, who came hurrying down the hall.

"Good morning, my lady."

"Good morning, Daniels," Cara replied, noting the man's flustered face. "Is there anything the matter?"

"There is a . . . gentleman here who insists on seeing you." Daniels's expression became disapproving. "He refused to give his name, but he said it is imperative that *you* speak to him."

At the oddly phrased request, Cara's eyebrows rose. "Did he state his business?"

"Only that it involved Fairfield. I tried to tell him that you were not receiving yet and that he should call back at another time, but he said that this was a matter that could not wait."

Pursing her lips, Cara frowned. Perhaps it was one of the masons or painters who had come to speak with her about some problem. But why wouldn't he give his name?

"Where is he?"

"I put him in your parlor." Daniels sniffed disdainfully.

Bewildered, but nonetheless curious, Cara shrugged a shoulder and made her way down the hall to the small room off Justin's study. Entering, she closed the door behind her, then glanced around in surprise to find the room empty. She was about to leave and find Daniels, when she turned and saw that the door leading into Justin's den was ajar.

"Of all the nerve," she muttered, irritated by the man's effrontery in trespassing. She didn't care what business at Fairfield had brought him here, she wasn't about to stand for this kind of intrusion, especially into Justin's personal retreat.

Intending to deliver a stinging tirade before having the cad thrown out, she started across the room at the same time the connecting door swung fully open.

In that second, Cara's mind went completely numb. Her nerves and muscles became absolutely still, rooting her to the floor. All the blood seemed to drain from her head as her heart began a furious pounding and her eyes strained wildly at the person before her.

"Papa," she whispered.

"Hello, sweetheart," Henry Fairchild said quietly, his eyes moist with tears.

It wasn't possible. It couldn't be true! But there he was, looking a little thinner than she remembered, his thin brown hair streaked with gray. Tears of shock and joy flooded her wide eyes and suddenly she raced across the room and into his waiting arms.

"Papa . . . Papa," she sobbed, against his chest. "I thought you were dead. They told me you were dead."

Henry hugged her tightly, standing silent while she cried, giving her comfort and strength the way he did when she was a little girl. For long moments, they stood thus, until Cara's tears dwindled to watery sighs and she looked into the eyes.

"Where have you been," she asked, shakily. "Are you all right?"

"All is well, Cara," he promised. Cupping her face between his hands, he gazed down at her. "Let me look at you. Oh, as beautiful as ever."

With an effort, Cara tried to pull herself together. "I cannot believe this is true." As though to verify he was indeed there, she laid a shaking hand on his chest. "Where have you been?"

Henry hesitated. "Perhaps you had best sit down, sweetheart. What I have to tell you is, well, it is complicated."

Concern clearly written on her face, Cara sat on the sofa, growing even more worried when her father began to pace slowly before her.

"First of all, let me tell you how glad I am that you married the earl. He is a fine man."

Surprised, Cara asked, "You've met Justin?"

"In a manner of speaking, yes. About two years ago."

She frowned. "Justin never told me that he knew you."

Henry's pacing halted and he scrubbed his forehead with his fingertips. "Actually, he doesn't." Seeing her obvious confusion, he held up a hand. "Cara, let me start at the beginning. I think that might be easier."

"All right, Papa," she said, nodding slowly.

Sighing heavily, Henry resumed his pacing. "You know that for the last ten years my business dealings were going badly. After your mother died, I couldn't seem to do anything right. I tried to recoup what losses I could by investing in various trading companies. But bad seemed to go to worse, especially with this trouble in France." He kneaded his forehead again. "I tried to put it all to rights, but even my traveling to every port city I knew of didn't insure my fortune. Fairfield was going to end up on the auction block."

Cara didn't need to be reminded. She better than anyone else knew how desperate things had become.

"Well, about five years ago, just as I was making ready to take one last trip to America, the oddest thing happened. I was approached by some members of the War Ministry."

"Why?" Cara couldn't help interrupting.

Henry shook his head in memory. "I asked myself that

same thing. What did they want with me? But it seems they were aware of my frequent travels, especially to America. They believed I could be of use to them."

"How?"

Spreading his hands wide, he shrugged. "In all manner of ways. To carry letters, deliver messages, make observations."

Cara's jaw actually dropped. "Papa, you're a spy?"

It was a term Henry himself rarely used, but Cara was quite right. "Yes, yes, I am. And a rather good one, I might add." He grinned ruefully. "I am a far better agent than I am a businessman."

Cara's head was whirling. There was just too much to absorb and she sensed she'd only heard the half of it. "Papa, where have you been for the last year?"

Grimacing, Henry pulled uncomfortably at his cravat. "I was coming to that. The truth is, I've been in America."

Remembering all the pain and sorrow she had experienced thinking him dead, Cara was suddenly exasperated. "Why didn't you write and tell me?"

"It was imperative that everyone think I was dead."

"Why!"

Seeing her frustration and confusion, Henry sat beside her and took one of her hands in his. "Cara, you have to understand. What I do is dangerous. I have made a number of enemies in the last few years who would like to see me dead. When it had become known in certain military and political circles in Washington that I was working for the British government, I was a marked man. I booked passage to return home, but at the last minute changed my mind. The ship went down and, as my enemies believed, so did I. It was the perfect opportunity for me to resurface elsewhere safely." He lifted a hand to lightly stroke her cheek. "Oh, sweetheart, I know you must have suffered thinking me dead, but there wasn't anything I could do."

Cara gazed into the face she had never thought to see again and recognized the harsh regret that was there. It didn't matter what he had done, or why. All that mattered was that he was back.

"Oh, Papa," she murmured, hugging him tightly.

"Am I forgiven, then?" he asked, his voice suddenly strained with emotion.

Holding him at arm's length, she gave him a wondrous smile. "Of course."

"Good, because there is more that I want to tell you."

"Papa," she exclaimed, not certain she was ready to hear anything more.

"Since I am making a clean breast of things, I might as well get it all out in the open at once."

"You are making me nervous again."

Henry patted her knee and grinned. "Nervous might not be the right word when you hear what I have to tell you."

"What word would you choose?"

"Angry might be more appropriate."

Rolling her eyes, Cara pleaded, "Papa, please just tell me."

Despite her earnest request, Henry paused while he stood and turned to face her. "I . . . am 'Liverpoole's man.' "

Silence. For seconds, not a single sound and Henry began to think he had bypassed the storm. Then . . .

"What!" Cara shot to her feet, arms akimbo, green eyes blazing.

"I was Captain Reynolds's contact who paid you all those midnight visits."

"How . . . could . . . you?" she cried. "How could you have terrified me the way you did?"

"Cara, let me explain . . ."

"Why?" she demanded to know, throwing a hand wide in an irate gesture. "Why did you make me take those messages to Justin? You could have done that yourself."

"True, but . . ."

"And that knife of yours. I had nightmares about that thing. I had nightmares every night, when I wasn't too frightened to sleep. I never knew when you were going to suddenly appear in the darkness, getting past a locked door. And how did you manage to do that?"

She waited for him to answer her questions, but when

he didn't she prompted, "Well, aren't you going to say anything?"

Hiding the smile that threatened to break across his face, Henry lifted a brow in mild inquiry. "Are you finished?"

"Yes," she replied, insulted by his barely concealed humor.

"You, young lady, were not supposed to be in Virginia."

"What does that mean?"

"That means that I willed everything to the earl knowing he would provide for you, here in England, not in America. Imagine how I felt when I saw you blithely strolling down Main Street with that cork-brained cousin of yours?"

"Beatrice? You saw us together?"

"Yes, and I had one of my men watching you at all times. As well as one keeping an eye on Justin and another on Regina Taylor."

At the name, Cara shivered and grew somber. "Papa, she was so eaten up with hatred. The last time I saw her, she was very nearly evil. I can't imagine what her life is like now."

"She has no life, dear. She was killed the night Smith and his bunch made their attack."

"Killed?"

Henry nodded. "Her body was found in the woods near Justin's house. Her neck had been snapped. In much the same manner of a woman several months earlier." It was a gruesome thought, one that neither wished to dwell on. "Now can you understand why I wanted you in England? Even without the possibility of war hanging over your head, Williamsburg was the last place on Earth I wanted you to be. So I did what I did to make sure Captain Reynolds would take you out when it was time for him to return to England."

"You couldn't be certain he would do that," she returned.

"He knew what risks you faced and I knew him well enough to know he wouldn't leave you to face that danger all by yourself, especially with Smith and that bunch running wild. If you *hadn't* been involved, he might very well have left you there, especially the way things were falling apart between the two of you."

Cara was caught off guard by the scope of his knowledge. "What . . . what do you know of all that?"

"I knew that there was something going on between the two of you." He cocked his head to one side and gave her a cool, very paternal look. "Anything beyond that, I do not wish to be privy to. Suffice it to say, it's a good thing he married you."

A heated blush rose into Cara's cheeks, yet her ire was rapidly cooling. After all, his plan had worked and she was the last person to complain about the results. If he hadn't forced her and Justin into his scheme, they most likely would have remained parted forever.

Still, there were a few things she didn't understand. "Was it necessary that you go to the extremes that you did in Virginia? I was terrified of that entire scheme."

Henry glanced heavenward. "I have known for some time now, Cara, that you can be a most stubborn woman. I needed to impress upon you the seriousness of my endeavors. A gentle coaxing on my part would not have sent you back to your captain."

"You do have a point," she admitted. As angry as she and Justin had been with each other, nothing short of imminent danger would have brought them together.

"Papa, you said you knew Justin well, well enough to be assured of his character. Yet you say Justin doesn't know you."

"And he doesn't," he said, relieved that her temper had abated.

"Not as Henry Fairchild. If he remembers me at all, it is as a passenger of another name, bound for Charleston on board his ship two years ago. We had a great many conversations during that voyage. I was impressed by the man."

"Did you know then that he was the earl?"

"Oh, yes, thanks to my contacts in the ministry. But your husband wasn't aware that I knew."

"Is that when you decided to make out your will?"

"Yes. When I returned home, I had it drawn up here in London." He laughed wryly. "I can well imagine old Nigel Bennett's face when that piece surfaced."

With a prim lift of her chin, Cara gave him a shaming glance. "Imagine my look, if you please."

The smile left Henry's face. "I am sorry, Cara. But I knew it was only a matter of time before I lost Fairfield. And I couldn't bear to imagine what would happen to you then. I knew the earl would take care of you."

For the next hour, father and daughter caught up on all that had happened in the past year. Cara was ecstatic at the reunion and couldn't wait to introduce Justin to her father.

"No," Henry declared, surprising Cara with his vehemence.

"Why not?" she asked, unaccountably hurt by his refusal to meet her husband.

"There are matters that I must still tend to. Until I have completed this assignment, I must insist on your silence. No one must know of my return, Cara. As it is, I shouldn't have even come here, but I gave into my own weakness to see you again."

"But Justin would not betray you," she insisted.

"No, I don't believe he would, but the fewer people who are aware of my presence, the better. Please, Cara, do not make me regret having come here today."

She looked so forlorn that he laid a gentle hand on her shoulder and tried to coax her to smile. "It will only be for a few weeks."

Gazing at her lap, Cara wrestled with her father's request. She did not like the idea of having secrets from Justin. "Where will you be?" she asked, glumly.

"France."

In the emotionally charged moment, neither heard the door in Justin's study open, nor saw the shadow of movement of the person who had entered and now stood listening to their conversation.

"France?" Cara cried. "But you've just returned. How

can I let you go when you have only now come back to me?"

"Patience, sweetheart, that is all I ask and then we can be together again."

"But I don't wish to wait." Emotionally drained, Cara had no defense against the tears that clogged her throat. "You went off and left me and it took me months to recover. Now you're back and expect me to gladly bide my time while you leave yet again." Morosely, she took a sigh and realized the futility of the situation. It would do little good to debate the issue. He obviously had no choice. "If having you back didn't make me the happiest woman alive, I could be very angry with you."

Henry smiled at the grudging acceptance on his daughter's face. "That's my girl."

She crossed her arms over her chest and glanced to the toe of her shoe she scrubbed over the carpet. "What am I going to tell Justin?"

"Don't tell him anything," he suggested.

"No." Cara shook her head emphatically. "That won't work. If Daniels let you in, he's sure to say something to Justin and Justin is bound to be curious." Distractedly, she chewed her lower lip for a moment, then shook her head. "I'll think of something, but please do not be away for long. I will be on pins and needles waiting for you."

Henry gathered her close for a brief hug. "I will return with all haste."

"You will take care of yourself, won't you? I couldn't bear it if anything happened to you."

"You have my word."

"And you have my love."

Cara hugged her father in a final farewell, then linked her arm with his and escorted him to the front door.

In his study, Justin stood silent, his face a mask of rage and anguish as the tableau he had just witnessed pounded through his head. He tried to deny it, tried to reject all he had seen and heard, but there was no blocking out the sight of Cara clinging to some strange man, the sound of Cara pledging her love to someone else.

A harsh laugh erupted from his chest. *Love*. What a fool he had been, allowing Cara to make him believe in its existence while she blinded him with her lies. She had told them so convincingly, those declarations of devotion, that he had let down his defenses and had come to place his trust in her. And in return, he had been betrayed, deceived by a lying little bitch who was waiting breathlessly for the return of some other man. He cursed his own stupidity for not trusting in his instincts.

And he cursed Cara. It was all too classic; the husband coming home to find his wife in the arms of another man. He could just imagine who the bastard was. Obviously, someone from her past who had left her. Only now that she was the Countess of Ellsworth, he had come crawling back, probably thinking to live off her money.

With icy cold anger, Justin fought against the devastating hurt that threatened to engulf him. In defense of the pain that wracked his mind and heart, a lifetime of cynicism flooded back into his body. His *wife* thought to keep her liaison a secret from him. He would see to it that she understood just how foolish she was.

Chapter Nineteen

Cara returned late that afternoon from her luncheon with Lydia and was greeted immediately at the front door by Daniels.

"His lordship is in his study, my lady," the butler intoned, "and asked to see you as soon as you returned."

Standing in the spacious foyer, Cara removed her hat and gloves and handed them to Daniels. "Thank you," she replied with a wide smile, smoothing errant curls back into place. With a light step she made her way down the hall, trying to school her features into some semblance of normalcy.

After the shock of seeing her father had finally worn off, she had been besieged by an attack of nervous happiness. All during lunch a seemingly permanent grin had settled on her face. She had explained her barely restrained excitement to a curious Lydia with a noncommittal shrug and something about how beautiful the day had turned out.

However, Cara knew Justin would never be satisfied with such a flimsy explanation. As discerning as he was, he would take one look at her and know she was keeping something from him. And frankly, she didn't want to try doing that. She wasn't about to lie to him, but neither could she betray her father. After a great deal of thought, she had decided to tell Justin that she had a surprise, of sorts, for him, one that she would be ready to share with him in a few weeks.

"I have been informed that you wished to see me," she announced cheerfully, as she stepped into his study and closed the door behind her.

Seated at his desk, Justin looked up at her entrance, his expression unreadable. "Yes," he replied in a too neutral tone.

"Well, *I* have been waiting to see you all afternoon, my darling." She slipped onto his lap and pressed a quick kiss to his lips.

"That's odd," he murmured sardonically, not returning her kiss. "I've been home since before you left to have lunch with Lydia."

Surprised, Cara studied his set features. There was a hard glint in his blue eyes and she wondered if he was annoyed with her. "I didn't know you had come home then. Why didn't you find me?"

Leaning back in his chair, he leveled an icy look on her. "Oh, but I did find you."

It had been months since Cara had seen that tight, accusing expression on Justin's face, but she remembered it all too well. Apprehension gripping her stomach, she stood and regarded him warily.

Suddenly, her eyes widened. He said he had returned before she had left to see Lydia, yet she had departed almost immediately after her father had. Which meant Justin must have come home while she had been talking to her father.

"Why are you angry with me?" she asked uncertainly.

Justin's body tensed, his eyes frigid with contempt as he sneered softly. "How do you expect me to react when I come home and find my wife in the arms of her lover?" Without warning, he surged to his feet, his hands snaking out to grasp her painfully by her arms.

"Justin!" she cried, as he gave her a rough shake that sent her hair tumbling down her back. Frantically, her mind tried to make sense of his accusation. He had seen her with her father and assumed he had caught her in some nasty little assignation. "Oh, Justin, it isn't what you think."

"Oh, isn't it?" he ground out. "You certainly looked convincing enough, clinging to the bastard, declaring yourself the happiest woman alive now that he has returned to you." With a violent shove, he flung her away, watching dispassionately as she stumbled against a leather chair.

With trembling hands, Cara righted herself and stared, horrified at her husband. How could he think she would give herself to another man? Didn't he know how much she loved him?

"That man this afternoon . . ."

"Yes, who is he?" he taunted. "Some miscreant from your past who now finds you worthy enough to take to bed because you have a title?" He raked her shivering figure with a condemning glare. "Tell me, is that why he left you in the first place, because you wouldn't spread your legs for him?"

His accusations seared into Cara's heart, piercing her with pain. He was wrong, yet how could she explain without divulging her father's secrets? She reached for him in a pleading gesture. "You don't understand."

He ignored her outstretched hand. "I understand perfectly," he declared hatefully. "You, my slut of a wife, are a liar."

"No!" she cried. "I have never lied to you."

"Then tell me you didn't pledge your love to that bastard!"

Cara closed her eyes in agony. She had told her father she loved him.

"Get out," he snapped.

Terrified, Cara shook her head in denial.

"I want you packed and out of here within the hour."

"But . . . I . . ." *love you.* But he wouldn't believe that, he wouldn't believe anything she had to say, because as far as he was concerned, she was guilty.

The torture of disillusionment ripped through her, constricting her lungs and wrenching her stomach. She had thought that in the last months he had come to realize the meaning of love and trust. Yet he was so ready to believe the worst of her, he was ordering her not only from the house, but out of his life. He didn't want her, he didn't love her.

Wracking sobs choked her. Through her tears she searched his face for some indication that he might relent, but all she saw was an awful hatred wounding her.

Too hurt to stand there any longer, she turned and fled the room.

Night descended on the town house like a suffocating blanket. Sprawled in a chair in his study, Justin raised his drink to his lips and listened to the stillness surrounding him. It was funny how he had never noticed the quiet before. But now it seemed a tangible thing, irritating him with its obtrusive presence.

He took another swallow of his bourbon, grimacing slightly, and slouched farther into his chair. The whole house was like a tomb and it was her fault. Three hours ago she had left as ordered and since then a deathlike silence had permeated the rooms. Even the servants crept about without making a sound.

Suddenly incensed, he threw his glass into the fireplace, the amber liquid making the low flames sputter and dance. The sound of shattering glass was strangely satisfying, but only for a moment. Before he even settled against the back of his chair, the firelight flickered on the harsh anguish etched into his face.

Memories assailed him from every angle and he ground his palms against his forehead in a useless attempt to block them from his mind. He remembered the first moment he had looked at her and how his body had instantly responded to her innocent, beguiling air. He scoffed. She may have been untouched, but she was far from innocent. He had seen proof of that this morning when he had watched her make a mockery of their marriage.

He swallowed with difficulty. Their marriage. For the first time in his life he had *loved* someone. His very existence had gone from an empty void to a lavish profusion of laughter and devotion. It was but a travesty now. And all the nights of shared passion, with their bodies and hearts joined in total union, were nothing more than a cruel pretense.

Absently, he glanced to the crystal decanters of liquor on the side table and knew blessed numbness could be found in those bottles. If he chose that course, he could obliterate her image from his mind. But it would only be a temporary cure. Tomorrow and for the rest of his life, he would have to face the tormenting truth that he had been a bloody fool for ever having believed in Cara and her promises of love. Tomorrow, he was going to have to resume his life as he had once known it, before she had turned her smiles on him and become the center of his universe. Tomorrow, he would gain control of the pain twisting his insides mercilessly. Tomorrow.

Lydia Gray was worried and it clearly showed on her lovely face as she sat in her coach on her way to her grandson's town house. Not more than an hour ago she had sent a note around to Cara, asking that she and Justin join her for an impromptu dinner party she was giving that evening. She had already begun anticipating the seating arrangements when her man returned with the message that the Countess of Ellsworth had departed three days ago and would no longer be in residence.

Nervously, Lydia tapped her fingers against her lips. She couldn't imagine why Cara had left London, especially without Justin. They were still newlyweds and a separation at this point in their marriage could only be construed as an indication that something was wrong.

She was even more convinced of that minutes later, when

she was led into Justin's study to find him working at his desk, deeply engrossed in a stack of papers.

"Good morning," she said, searching his taut features.

"Good morning," Justin snapped without lifting his gaze from the paper he was sprawling his signature across.

Taken aback by his brusque manner, Lydia regarded her grandson for a startled moment. This was *not* the same content and happy Justin who had returned from America. That man would have greeted her with a kiss, or a smile at the very least.

"Justin, the most peculiar thing just happened," she began, trying to keep her tone as light as possible. After all, what had transpired between Cara and Justin was none of her business. However, she couldn't help but be concerned.

Justin glanced up briefly. He knew why she was here and he bitterly resented her intrusion into his privacy. He had been informed of the note she had sent over and assumed she was now here for some sort of clarification of the message she had received.

Mentally, he cursed. He could have refused to have seen her, but this discussion was inevitable. And the sooner he had this over and done with, the sooner he could put it, and all the acidic memories of Cara, behind him.

"What has occurred?" he asked curtly.

Grateful for the acknowledgement, Lydia was also irritated. And hurt. Justin's behavior was beyond rude. "A most peculiar thing," she declared sharply.

The tone was not lost on Justin. Annoyed, he set his work aside and directed his attention to his grandmother.

"What has occurred?" he repeated, his voice loaded with forced patience.

"I intended to ask you and Cara to dine with me tonight, but I understand she is not here."

"That's correct."

Lydia waited for him to elaborate. When he didn't, she asked, "Well, where is she?"

"I don't know."

"What do you mean, you don't know?" she retorted, appalled by his indifference.

Justin explained carefully. "I mean she no longer lives here and she left no forwarding address. I assume she has gone to Fairfield."

"What!"

Having no doubt she had heard correctly, Justin didn't bother repeating himself. Instead, he gave his grandmother a bland look.

Lydia was dumbfounded. Something was very wrong. "Justin, what has happened? It isn't like Cara to leave and not tell you where she was going."

Justin struggled with the urge to verbally annihilate his grandmother. Somehow, he summoned forth enough tolerance to endure relating the events of that sickening day. He debated whether or not to tell Lydia the truth. Considering her affection for Cara, a fabrication of some story would be kinder. Unfortunately, he wasn't feeling kind these days.

Turning back to his papers, he ground out, "You have it wrong. Cara did not leave. I threw her out." At Lydia's gasp, he flicked a glance at her shocked features, then continued to scan his documents. "You needn't worry. It was all rather civil, as these things go. But I wasn't about to tolerate having an adulterous wife living under my roof."

Lydia's eyes rounded in shock. "Adulterous? Cara? Surely you are mistaken."

"No, I am not."

"I cannot believe this. Cara would not deceive you in this way. In any way. She loves you, Justin."

Inwardly, Justin flinched, but his face remained as rigid as ever. "The matter of love has always been left open to a great deal of interpretation. In any event, I find cuckolding distasteful in the extreme."

Not knowing what to say, Lydia sat and stared unseeing. She could not, absolutely would not believe Cara had been unfaithful. But obviously, for some reason, Justin did. "Are you certain this isn't just a case of ugly rumors?"

"As certain as a man can be."

Lydia paled. "You . . . you actually saw them together?"

"Precisely."

"In . . . in what capacity?" she whispered.

Rapidly being pushed to his limit, Justin threw his pen aside and leveled a frigid glare on his grandmother. "Out for all the sordid little details, is that it, Lydia?" he sneered, caustically. "Well, here they are. Your precious little Cara didn't even have the sense to be discreet. She let the son of a bitch into the house. Of course neither one of them expected me to come home and find them in the very next room discussing how to keep their secret from me."

What little color remained in Lydia's face disappeared. Cara with another man? No, it wasn't possible. If Lydia had learned one thing in the short time she had come to know Cara, it was that the girl was completely devoted to Justin.

"A mistake has been made," she said in Cara's defense.

"You are right, and I made it the day I married the bitch."

Angered and offended, Lydia shot back, "Don't you speak that way of Cara. She loves you!"

Justin surged to his feet, his face contorted by rage. "Will you stop saying that!"

"Why? It's the truth. I don't care what you think happened. Cara does love you."

"You'd like to think that only because she wormed her way into your good graces and you don't want to admit that she had you fooled."

"No," Lydia exclaimed. "I think that because Cara is too proud to offer you anything less than true, honest emotion."

That was it. Grandmother or not, he was not going to stand there and let her drag him through all the torment he had been striving to control. Stalking to the door, he held it opened in obvious invitation for her to leave. "I won't discuss this further," he bit out.

It was one of the few times Lydia had been genuinely

angry with Justin. Fuming, she marched to the door, but stopped for a parting comment. "You stubborn, arrogant fool. You've let the memory of your mother warp your sense of all that is good and decent. Now, when you've been offered the most worthy gift a man can have, you throw it all away." Despite her best efforts, her eyes filled with sad tears. "You don't deserve to have Cara. I hope you find happiness in your lonely life."

Lydia's words echoed through Justin's mind in the ensuing weeks. The town house, which had always been his private haven, suddenly took on all the properties of a desolate, empty cage, haunted by the images he carried of Cara. He attempted to find peace of mind by traveling to all his estates, except the one in Scotland where he and Cara had spent their honeymoon. He spent hours touring his lands and checking the estate records, working feverishly to keep from remembering. There was a certain degree of satisfaction to be found in his endeavors, but not contentment. That, he reasoned, was never to be his again.

After two months, he had managed to banished Cara to that same remote corner of his consciousness to which he had relegated his mother. She had become a nonentity, despite the fact that she was still his wife. He told himself he didn't care what she did or where she went as long as she stayed out of his way. However, since he had turned her out without a penny, he decided to let her keep the title. For now, he had no use for it. If there ever came a time when he wished to produce an heir, he would pay whatever the amount necessary to divorce her and marry someone else.

Still, he was plagued by that old sense of restlessness. Realizing that only so much diversion could be crammed into each day, he finally looked to the *Wind Dancer* as the source of a remedy. The ship had always provided him with the kind of distraction and challenge he found satisfying. And even though he had no destination in mind, he admitted he looked forward to being at sea again. He returned to London and ordered the ship to be made ready.

The day before he was to set sail, Justin devoted his time to tying up loose ends. As was his routine before the start of every voyage, he scheduled a meeting with his solicitor, Mr. Huggins. Annoyingly, Justin realized when he checked the clock in his study that the normally punctual man was forty minutes late.

With a muttered curse, he was just about to ring for Daniels and have word sent to the lawyer's office, when Daniels quietly entered the study.

"I beg your pardon, my lord, but Mr. Huggins has just arrived."

"It's about time," Justin remarked, irritated with having been kept waiting.

"Shall I show him in?" the butler inquired.

"Yes." And be damn quick about it, he silently amended. Already he was anxious to be on board his ship and gone. He strode to the side table and poured a small amount of bourbon into a glass before coming to stand beside a window. For a brief second he experienced a remembrance of another meeting like this, where he had stood beside this same window, gazing out into the garden. It had been over a year ago, and he had been about to depart for America. It had been the first time he had heard Cara's name.

"I apologize for the delay, my lord," Mr. Huggins declared, entering the study as quickly as his wiry frame would move. "But I have just come across the most extraordinary news."

Jerking away from the window and his memories, Justin strode to his desk and leaned back against the front of the mahogany piece. "Please, Mr. Huggins, if we could get on with our business," he urged. "Let me sign whatever papers need to be signed so I may leave."

Looking decidedly uncomfortable, Mr. Huggins peered over the rim of his glasses. "I am afraid we must attend to a matter of grave importance, my lord," he exclaimed excitedly. "In fact, it is the exact reason for my tardiness this morning."

Taking a sip of his liquor, Justin regarded Mr. Huggins with an appraising eye. Always the epitome of perfect decorum, the thin solicitor was as discomposed as Justin had ever known him to be.

"Then by all means," Justin remarked dryly. Indifferently, he waved a hand toward a nearby seat.

Remarkably, Mr. Huggins ignored the unspoken invitation to sit. "My lord, I admit I do not have a clear picture of how to best proceed with this problem." Nervously, he adjusted the metal rims perched on the bridge of his nose.

Still holding his glass, Justin crossed his arms over his chest, but said nothing. Only one dark brow quirked upward, but that subtle gesture was apparently enough to convince Mr. Huggins to find an expedient way to explain.

"Yes, of course," Mr. Huggins remarked. Immediately, he came to the point. "An hour ago, I was called upon by . . . by Henry Fairchild."

"*What?*" Justin asked, disbelievingly, his eyes narrowing at the shocking revelation.

"I can appreciate your astonishment, my lord. I myself experienced the same exact sentiment when he walked into my office, accompanied by his solicitor, a Mr. Nigel Bennett."

Justin recognized the name. "Go on, Mr. Huggins," he snapped.

"Yes, well, you can imagine my first thoughts. There are all manner of legal dilemmas resulting from this, since you were the man's lawful heir and he is no longer dead."

"Where the hell has he been?" Justin asked.

Looking over his glasses, Mr. Huggins' features took on a bemused cast. "He would not say, other than he had been out of the country and that he would discuss that issue with you personally."

With one last swallow, Justin finished his bourbon. Setting his glass aside, he walked to the other side of his desk and began stacking papers into a neat pile. "I assume he called upon you to make you aware of his return to the living."

"Yes, of course, my lord. However, he is on his way here this very moment. He insisted on meeting with you immediately. However, I convinced him to at least allow me suitable time to break the news to you in a fitting manner."

"How good of you," Justin scoffed. "Did you mention to him that I signed the inheritance over to my wi . . . to the countess?"

"Yes, my lord, I made him aware of that."

"Did you also make him aware of the fact that his daughter is no longer living here?"

Mr. Huggins was well aware of the estrangement between the earl and the countess. "No, my lord, I thought that a matter best imparted by you."

Daniels's knock on the door interrupted the discussion. At Justin's call, the butler entered.

"My lord, there is a Lord Fairchild and a Mr. Nigel Bennett to see you. They said you are expecting them."

Disgusted with the entire mess, Justin ground his teeth. "Very well, Daniels, show them in."

The second the two men entered the study, Justin's heart began a thunderous pounding. He had never laid eyes upon the small, round man, but the taller, older gentleman he recognized instantly. It was the same man he had seen Cara with in her parlor, that day months ago. The man he presumed was her lover.

"My lord," Henry said, extending a hand in greeting. "I am Henry Fairchild. I believe I owe you an explanation."

Chapter Twenty

Alice Bennett heard the rumble of the coach long before she actually saw the vehicle. Reaching for her friend's arm, her steps drew to a halt on the walk outside her house.

"Do you hear that, Miriam?"

Miriam Hedgepeth stopped beside Alice, their afternoon stroll temporarily suspended. Cocking her head, she listened to the approaching low thunder created by a team of horses.

"Yes, I believe I do. And from the sound of things, someone is in a great hurry."

Blatantly curious, the two cronies waited to scrutinize the coach as it passed. When it did, the two turned to each other in amazement.

"Did you see that?" Miriam exclaimed.

"Oh my, the Earl of Ellsworth," Alice whispered. "He's probably come all the way from London."

Miriam craned her neck to catch a last glimpse of the coach. "Do you think he's on his way to Fairfield?"

"Yes, I would imagine so."

Exasperated, Miriam turned back to Alice. "Why didn't you tell me he was going to call on Cara?"

Pressing her hand to her more-than-ample bosom, Alice said, "Because I didn't know."

"How could you not know? Nigel is your husband *and* Cara's solicitor."

"True," Alice agreed, "but Nigel has been very close-mouthed about Cara since she returned. I don't know anything more than you."

Miriam sniffed, starting down the path again. "If you ask me, something is going on."

"I think you're right," Alice concluded, waddling into step beside her friend. "Just yesterday, Nigel was suddenly called away to London to meet with the earl's solicitor."

Miriam's eager eyes lit up. "There, you see? There *is* something going on." She cast a quick glance back over her shoulder to where the coach had passed from sight. "I suppose it is something scandalous."

"Why would you say that?"

"Because everything concerning Cara Fairchild, excuse me, the Countess of Ellsworth, has always been nothing short of shocking. It wasn't enough that she traipsed off to America, of all places, practically thumbing her nose at the earl. But then she returns and marries him." Miriam ticked off each event on her fingers. "Within practically no time at all, workmen of every nature descend on Fairfield, tearing that house apart in an effort to set it to rights. Then, suddenly, all work stops and Cara shows up, without her husband."

Having made her point, Miriam lifted her chin regally.

"It is all rather remarkable." Alice shook her head sadly. "Cara is up there, all alone except for that one maid who insisted on accompanying her."

"Loyalty in servants is so admirable."

"You are right, Miriam. And I'd hate to think how Cara would have gotten along if she hadn't had help. I called on her last week, just to see how she was faring, and the sight nearly broke my heart."

"Not exactly the circumstances you'd expect to find a countess in," Miriam remarked knowingly.

"No, not at all. The renovations were nowhere near complete when work stopped. There are barely two rooms fit to live in."

"How is she managing?"

With a shrug, Alice replied, "She says she is doing fine, but to be quite honest, she does not look well." She lowered her voice, as though the shrubs lining the path might overhear. "I don't think she has any money."

"Did she say as much?" Miriam asked, anxious for proof of a real scandal.

"No, but she didn't have to. She and that maid were sitting down to lunch and there was not much in the way of quantity. Cara did invite me to dine, but I just had to refuse because I felt like I was taking food right out of their mouths."

"She was actually eating with her maid?" Miriam inquired in a shocked voice.

For a moment, Alice contemplated her friend's ability to completely overlook the most significant matters. Then, she mentally shrugged. None of it was any of her concern, and no matter how much she speculated, Cara's affairs would always remain private. Of course, Alice admitted, she was still most curious about what was going on up at Fairfield right then.

"This is the last of the flour, my lady," Molly said quietly, handing a small bowl to Cara.

Cara set aside the chicken she was plucking and wiped her hands on the front of her apron. Frowning, she regarded the meager contents of the bowl. There was barely enough to make one loaf of bread. With a sigh, she mentally added flour to the growing list of foodstuffs they had run out of.

"I suppose it's time to sell another one of my dresses," she concluded pragmatically.

"My lady, not another," Molly protested.

"I'm afraid so."

"But they're so beautiful, and you've already traded off ive."

The young, little maid looked so crestfallen that Cara had o smile. "You have to admit, Molly, I am getting far better ıse of the gowns by selling them for money to buy food han I would by having them hang in a closet."

Molly wanted to debate that, but instead kept silent, her ace scrunched into a perplexed pout. It was all too sad. And bewildering. She didn't understand why the poor count-ss was living in poverty, while the earl was back in his ancy London town house. She had guessed that they had ad some falling-out, but the lady never once told her what ad happened. Well, whatever it was, the earl ought to be shamed of himself, upsetting his wife, making her cry the ay she had when they had first come here. True, there adn't been any tears lately, but rarely a day went by that faraway look didn't come over the countess's face. Molly ould tell she was fighting to keep a terrible hurt inside.

"I know you have to sell your things, my lady, but it n't right."

Cara gave the maid a sidelong glance as she resumed her ork on the hen. There were a great many things that eren't right. But it was either sell her clothes or starve. he would have to contact Nigel Bennett again to see to e matter.

Glancing about Fairfield's kitchen, she considered another oblem she would have to discuss with Nigel. The sale of airfield. It was a painful thought, but one that couldn't be nored any longer. She had only so many dresses and once at source of money was gone, she would be without a nny to her name.

That wasn't quite true, she confessed to herself. Guiltily, e gazed to her left hand, bare of the emerald and diamond ıg Justin had placed on her finger. She had removed it on after she had left London and placed it in a box for fekeeping. The piece was worth a small fortune, but some-w she just couldn't bring herself to sell it. Yet neither could she wear it. The ring was supposed to have been a symbol of their love.

That faraway look that Molly witnessed so often settled on Cara's pale face. She had been such a fool to have ever believed that Justin had truly loved her. She didn't doubt that he had once felt something for her, an affection, desire, lust, but never love. Not as she knew it. If he had, he wouldn't have condemned her so quickly, he would have at least given her a chance to try and explain. He wouldn't have found it so easy to hate her.

Her eyes closed against the thought, but she couldn't block out the memory of that day in his study. He had looked at her with such raging hatred that a part of her had shriveled up and died, leaving her numb inside. She was still numb. She always would be.

The muffled sound of a coach from outside pulled Cara from her thoughts. Thankful for the interruption, sh yanked herself back to the present.

"Who do you suppose that is?" Molly asked.

"I would say Nigel, since he is just about the only perso who ever comes to call. Why don't you run upstairs an let him in."

While Molly went off to do as she was asked, Car washed her hands, then entered the pantry to gather th necessary ingredients to make muffins to go along with th boiled hen.

"Is that you, Nigel?" she called out at the sound footsteps in the kitchen. "You've caught me in the middl of muffins, but I am glad you stopped by. You saved me long walk into town tomorrow." She emerged from th larder. "I needed to talk to you about . . ."

She came to a dead stop, her words choking in her thro at the sight of Justin, his tall, dynamic presence filling th small room. Without warning, everything she was holdi slipped from her suddenly nerveless hands, crashing to th stone floor in a powdery mess.

Justin watched her standing frozen with shock, her fa a mask of tired misery, and he cursed himself to hell a back for having caused her such anguish, for forcing her live in a hovel. Lydia had been right. He didn't deserve Cara, but if she let him, he was going to spend the rest of his life trying to prove his worthiness.

He glanced briefly to the clutter, before meeting her stricken gaze. "I'm not Nigel Bennett, but perhaps you might talk to me instead," he said quietly, remorse tightening every line of his face.

Cara swallowed past the nausea, striving to gain control of her pounding heart. He wanted to talk to her. Now, after two months. It was just like that time in Williamsburg. He had forgotten her for weeks on end, then suddenly walked back into her life. "I have nothing to say to you," she whispered.

Justin acknowledged her words, knowing he deserved her rejection. When he thought of the awful things he had said to her, the deplorable way he had treated her, he couldn't blame her if she never wanted to see him again. He could understand it, but never accept it.

"I would have thought you would have had a great many things you might want to say."

"I did. Once."

"And now?"

"Only good-bye."

"Cara . . ."

"Don't." She closed her eyes against the pain and anger. He had done this to her before, come back only to hurt her. She wouldn't allow him to do that again.

"I'm sorry." His voice was raw with harsh regret, his eyes filled with sorrow.

Biting her lower lip, Cara looked away.

"I met your father," he explained.

Her gaze flew back to his. "And now you're prepared to trust me. Am I supposed to be honored?"

"Hopefully, you'll forgive me."

Again, Cara's eyes shut. Oh, it would be so easy to give in, to accept his apology and go back to being his wife and pretend to be happy. But she wouldn't be. She would always have to live with the doubt and fear that he would discard her again someday.

"It takes more than my forgiveness, Justin," she said gazing straight into his eyes. She paused for a shaky breath. "I've asked this of you before. Please, go away and leave me alone . . ." *Before I shatter into a thousand pieces.*

Justin tried to swallow past the emotion clogging his throat. "I can't," he whispered.

"*Why?*"

"Because . . . I love you."

Cara's eyes rounded, her breath left her in a single gasp.

"I love you, Cara," he repeated, his voice breaking as tears filled his eyes. "God, how I love you."

The words Cara had thought to never hear from him; the words she had thought him incapable of speaking. He was saying them to her like a promise and a declaration and a desperate plea to be loved in return.

Overwhelmed, tears came to her eyes, and her whole body trembled with joy. He had never told anyone, ever, that he loved them. Only her.

"Oh, Justin," she whispered, the numbness within her giving way to sensations of love and forgiveness.

He closed the distance between them in two long strides, taking her in his arms and holding on to her like she was his very lifeline. With a near frantic hunger, his mouth came down on hers as she clung to the hard muscles of his shoulders, kissing him back with all the love radiating from her heart.

"I'll never hurt you again," he vowed, his mouth hovering over hers. "I just want to spend the rest of my life loving you."

Tenderly, she cupped his lean face between her hands. "I love you," she told him with a fierce gentleness.

He turned his head and kissed the inside of her palm, noticing then the absence of her ring. Taking her hand in his, he gently stroked the knuckle of her third finger before raising inquiring, vulnerable eyes to hers.

"I've kept it safe upstairs," she explained gently, answering his unspoken question. "I couldn't wear it without your love."

He raised her hand to his lips. "Will you put it back on?"

With a firm nod, she replied, "Yes, and I'll never take it off again."

Gathering her close, his mouth slanted over hers. When he lifted his head, he smiled down into her glowing face. "You always were the most stubborn woman."

"No," she said, returning his smile. "Just determined."